THE LOST BOOK OF THE GRAIL

ALSO BY CHARLIE LOVETT

The Further Adventures of Ebenezer Scrooge

First Impressions

The Bookman's Tale

THE
LOST BOOK
OF THE
GRAIL

OR, A VISITOR'S GUIDE TO
BARCHESTER CATHEDRAL

CHARLIE LOVETT

VIKING

VIKING
An imprint of Penguin Random House LLC
375 Hudson Street
New York, New York 10014

ISBN: 9780399562518

Printed in the United States of America

Set in Albertina MT Std
Designed by Alissa Rose Theodor

For the TAPS

No age lives entirely alone; every civilization is formed not merely by its own achievements but by what it has inherited from the past. If these things are destroyed, we have lost a part of our past, and we shall be the poorer for it.

—Major Ronald Balfour

To me Barset has been a real county, and its city a real city, and the spires and towers have been before my eyes, and the voices of the people are known to my ears, and the pavement of the city ways are familiar to my footsteps.

—Anthony Trollope

THE LOST BOOK OF THE GRAIL

OR, A VISITOR'S GUIDE TO
BARCHESTER CATHEDRAL

I

THE LADY CHAPEL

The Lady Chapel, at the east end of the cathedral beyond the high altar, once housed the shrine of St. Ewolda, founder of the Saxon monastery on which the cathedral was built. The shrine was pulled down during the Reformation, and for over five hundred years a simple black stone cross in the floor marked its location. Little is known of Ewolda beyond a brief mention by the Venerable Bede: "On the twelfth of October is the feast of the martyr Saint Ewolda, who converted the kingdom of Barsyt and founded a monastery there. With the sacrifice of her life she kept the light of Christ burning in that place."

February 7, 1941, Barchester

Barchester was not equipped with air-raid sirens, being both beyond the range of German bombers and of no strategic value—but bomber squadrons could become lost on nights when fog unexpectedly blanketed the south of England, and while the emergence of a cathedral spire from that fog might confirm to the navigator that he was too far off course to return home safely, to the bombardier it would recall the words of the commanding officer: "Some target is better than no target." And so Edward was woken from his dreams not by sirens but by shouts and the blaring of car horns and a roaring overhead that grew louder every minute.

His brother's bed was empty, and when he had pulled on some

clothes and emerged from his room, he found no one else in the house. A sudden flash of light was followed by an explosion, and in an instant Edward was covered with glass, his ears ringing so loudly that for a moment they drowned out all other sound. Being nine years old hadn't kept him from reading the papers and listening to the wireless—he knew what had been happening in London. His parents had told him Barchester was safe from air raids; obviously, they had been wrong. Edward stumbled to the front door and flung it open. Across the street, the Greshams' house was a blazing pile of rubble. He heard screams and cries from all directions and was just about to add his own to the raucous cacophony when he saw a familiar face and felt a hand on his arm.

"Edward, are you all right? Your parents asked me to look in on you."

"Quite all right, sir," said Edward, for whom the presence of his neighbor and choirmaster was exactly what he needed to steel his nerves and change his outlook from fear to determination. "What can I do to help?"

"Come with me," said Mr. Grantly.

"Where are we going?"

"To the library."

By the time they reached the cathedral precincts, four other members of the choir had joined them—two older boys, and two of the vicars choral, the men who sang the tenor and bass parts. Orange light outlined the spire of the cathedral and as they ran toward the cloister the source became apparent—a raging fire at the east end. Edward could hardly see through the smoke, but it looked as if the Lady Chapel, in which the choir often practiced, was at the center of the blaze.

Mr. Grantly allowed no time for gawking, however, and the musicians quickly made their way through the cloister and up the winding stone stairs to the library, lit only by the flames that flickered outside the windows.

"The fire could reach here any minute," said Mr. Grantly. "We need to save as much as we can. Start with these manuscripts."

Edward had never had occasion to visit the cathedral library, but there was no time to admire the cases of ancient books that glowed in the light of the fire. He reached up and took hold of a vellum-bound manuscript on the shelf in front of him. It was not a huge volume—larger than his schoolbooks, but not as large as the family Bible—yet it felt weighted with mystery. He had just settled the book in his arms and was turning to go when it jerked out of his hands. He reached out to keep it from falling to the floor, only to find the ancient tome floating in midair. It must be a magic book, he thought, watching transfixed as it swayed in front of him, its pages illuminated by the orange light.

Edward loved languages. He had already learned a lot of Latin and a smattering of Old English, but even though he caught only a glimpse of them, the words before him made no sense. The letters were what he expected from Medieval Latin, but the combinations in which they filled the page were meaningless. Each word was the same length, and Edward was just thinking that perhaps all magical incantations came in words of exactly nine letters when a desperate voice rang out next to him.

"How do we get them loose?" asked one of the vicars choral. Edward realized that the volume he had been holding was not hovering in the air through some enchantment but hanging from a chain that connected it to the shelf. Each of the manuscripts in the case before him, he saw, was similarly chained.

"The librarian keeps the key in his lodgings," said the other vicar choral. "But he's gone to Wells to visit his mother." Suddenly there was a crashing sound as one of the high windows burst inward and glass rained down upon a library table.

"There's no time," said Mr. Grantly. "Tear off the covers."

The man next to Edward grabbed the chain of the dangling manuscript in one hand and the book in the other. With a loud grunt, he rent the two apart, leaving the manuscript's front cover hanging by its chain. He thrust the volume at Edward, who clasped it to his chest. As the vicar choral pulled the next manuscript off the shelf, Edward ran for the exit, winding down the stairs until he stumbled into the cloister. He saw that Mr. Grantly, who had dashed down the steps ahead of him, had already begun a pile of books near the yew tree on the far side of the cloister, but the volume Edward held seemed too important to merely cast onto the heap. He crept into the darkest corner of the cloister and laid the book in a niche in the stone wall. He stood breathing heavily for a few seconds, then dashed back to the library.

More and more people crowded the room, and soon a line had formed from the shelves down the stairs and into the cloister. Edward found himself at the top of the stairs, passing volume after volume to a pair of hands that reached out from the shadows. At first the books were like the manuscript he had taken to the cloister—their front covers torn off. Soon the manuscripts were replaced with leather-bound books of every size, boxes of letters and papers, and stacks of documents, some bearing huge wax seals. Edward's arms began to ache as he passed everything that came his way to those mysterious hands. Every few minutes another window broke from the heat of the fire. Edward could feel the room growing hotter.

After more than an hour, he heard Mr. Grantly's voice shouting, "Get out! Get out! The fire's here." Edward looked up to see flames shooting through the windows and licking the tops of the now empty bookcases that lined the far wall. In another second, he felt himself pressed along by the line of people and almost carried down the stairs. He followed the line across the cloister toward the cathedral close.

The mound of books Mr. Grantly had begun in the cloister had been moved far from harm's way by people who had flocked from all over the city to save the cathedral's treasures. Edward stood for a minute gulping in the cool night air. As Mr. Grantly and several others carried the last of the books from the cloister and farther away from the fire, Edward suddenly remembered the manuscript. He ran to the corner of the cloister where he had secreted it, but a man in a strange gray clerical robe was lifting the book from its hiding place. He had seen this man in the library helping to remove a few of the smaller furnishings. Now the man glanced around and, apparently not seeing the choirboy, disappeared around a corner. Edward followed him out of the cloister and beheld a scene of chaos.

Some who had helped empty the library were now passing buckets of water from the river to the fire. Others were busy loading the books and manuscripts, along with other valuables, into a variety of transport. Wagons and carts full of books disappeared into the darkness. In the shadows, Edward saw the man in gray slipping through the crowd toward St. Martin's Lane. He was just about to chase after him, to ask why he had taken the manuscript, when he felt a hand clap on his shoulder.

"A good night's work, Edward," said Mr. Grantly. "But we'd better get you home. Your parents are sure to be worried."

"Won't they need help unloading?"

Mr. Grantly laughed. "You've done enough. We'll unload the wagons in the morning and find safe places for all the books until this"—he waved his hand at the sky in disgust—"until all this is over."

They turned toward Edward's home, and as they walked away from the crowd, the boy glanced back toward the arch that led into St. Martin's Lane, but the strange figure was gone.

The next morning, Edward learned that his father and older brother had helped extinguish the fire, while his mother had worked with the other women of the Flower Guild to remove the plate from the cathedral. Save for some smoke damage, the main body of the cathedral was unharmed. The Lady Chapel had been completely destroyed, and the row of buildings on the east side of the cloister, including the library, had suffered significant damage. Edward read in the newspaper that over eighty medieval manuscripts and almost three thousand books had been saved from the library. Assisting in that rescue was the only part he ever played in the war, but for the rest of his life he was proud of what he had done that night.

April 4, 2016

SECOND MONDAY AFTER EASTER

Arthur Prescott sometimes thought he was born in the wrong generation. It's not that he thought he should be a Knight of the Round Table, but he should at least be living in the 1920s with Jeeves pulling on his morning coat for him, or better yet in the 1880s, discussing the relative merits of Gladstone and Disraeli in a first-class railway carriage. These daydreams generally came to an abrupt end as soon as he thought about things like public sanitation and penicillin. Still, if he was not living in the wrong time, he was at least teaching at the wrong institution—one must grant him that. Arthur was not born for the concrete and glass confines of the modern University of Barchester. Arthur was molded for the ancient stonework of Oxford. Arthur, by all rights, should be climbing a creaking staircase to his top-floor rooms in the great quadrangle of Lazarus College. He should be reading *The Daily Jupiter* in the paneled Senior Common Room and taking his meals in the cavernous hall hung with portraits of scholars past. Instead, he taught at a plate-glass university, which, in a recent ranking of the top fifty universities in the U.K., did not rate a mention, honorable or otherwise.

But Arthur had come to Barchester willingly, not because of the university but in spite of it. For as much as he hated those breeze-block walls that imprisoned him each day, he loved Barchester itself, with its narrow streets, its meandering river, and its ancient cathedral towering over the compact city center. Arthur had taken the job at the university so he could live in his favorite place in the world, the only place he had known happiness as a child. During Arthur's childhood, his father had hopped from job to job and his parents had fought and broken up and gotten back together in an unending cycle. But every summer, Arthur had spent two glorious weeks with his maternal grandfather in Barchester. They had swum in the river and taken long walks in the countryside; they had played chess on rainy days; they had even climbed the tower of the cathedral. Arthur's grandfather was a retired clergyman, and seemed to know every churchman for miles around, from the bishop of Barchester to the verger who kept the keys to every secret part of the cathedral. Arthur's love for his grandfather had expanded into a love for Barchester. He loved how every stone of the old city had a story, how every wall and corner and rooftop dripped with history, and he loved that his grandfather knew all those stories and all that history and shared it all with him. Arthur was eight when he first visited and by the time he was a teenager he had promised himself he would live in Barchester someday. Unfortunately, keeping that promise meant that every morning he rode to the third floor of the humanities building in a lift that somehow managed to seem simultaneously sterile and unsanitary.

The doors opened jerkily to reveal the scowling face of Frederick Slopes, head of the Department of Literature in which Arthur toiled away as a junior lecturer.

"Late again, Prescott," said Slopes.

"And good morning to you, sir," said Arthur.

"You do realize that we had a meeting of the Curriculum Expansion Committee at eight."

"This may be a radical notion, sir, but do you think perhaps the Curriculum Expansion Committee ought to be populated by members of the faculty who actually favor curriculum expansion?"

"Your personal tastes are entirely irrelevant to your committee work, Prescott."

"Now, if you had asked me to serve on the Curriculum Contraction Committee, I would have been here at seven." Arthur turned to walk down the hall, but heard Slopes's steps close behind.

"Prescott, I cannot allow your continued absence from the work of this department to go unpunished."

"Do you know, sir," said Arthur, turning on his heels and facing his tormentor, "that we teach a seminar in this department called 'Anagnorisis in the Existential Hogwarts,' but we do not teach a seminar on Shakespeare?"

"Prescott, you—"

"That's William Shakespeare. He was a playwright. Not bad, actually. Nor do we teach seminars on Charles Dickens or Jane Austen. They wrote books. Cracking good ones."

"They are all covered in the core module. And by the way, Prescott, the Hogwarts course is oversubscribed this term."

"I have no doubt. But that shouldn't mean—"

"This university must move with the times, Prescott. And so must you, or you will be left behind. Do I make myself clear?"

"There was a time," said Arthur, "when universities led the culture rather than followed it."

"There was also a time," barked Slopes, "when the Committee on Curriculum Expansion met. And that time was eight o'clock. Now, if you miss one more meeting, I will have to report you to the Committee on Faculty Disciplinary Affairs."

And no doubt they, thought Arthur as Slopes stomped off, will report my actions to the Committee on Flushing British Culture Down the Loo.

Yes, Arthur would have been happier in an earlier generation. It was a cruel trick of fate that had landed him in a century when universities had "core modules" and taught courses on "anagnorisis" to students who couldn't be bothered to read books they hadn't already read in childhood. The irony was, thought Arthur as he squeezed into his cubicle of an office, that he liked the Harry Potter books. He had read them last summer. But he didn't think they belonged in a university curriculum.

The day that had begun with so little promise continued in that vein for Arthur through two lectures and a tutorial—populated by three students whom he insisted on calling Mr. Crawley, Miss Stanhope, and Miss Robarts, in spite of the fact that they called him "Arthur." The tutorial was part of the dreaded core module and so Arthur had anticipated with pleasure an introductory discussion of Jane Austen. Instead he had to endure a diatribe from Miss Stanhope—meekly supported by Mr. Crawley, who was clearly trying to ingratiate himself with her in the hope of future sexual favors—in which Austen was taken to task for not being "enough of a feminist." Arthur listened for a half hour, doing his best to focus his mind on a P. G. Wodehouse story he had read on the bus that morning, but eventually he could take no more.

"Jane Austen never married," he said in frustration. "She entered the male-dominated field of novel writing and her female heroines are strong, independent characters. Just what do you imagine a feminist in a rural English village in the late eighteenth century looks like?"

"Oh, Arthur," said Miss Stanhope with an exasperated sigh, "you are such a *man*."

"You can't deny the accusation," said Gwyn as she and Arthur took their regular twice-weekly walk around the water meadows the next morning.

"Yes, but she said it with such disdain," said Arthur, stooping to pick up a drool-covered tennis ball that one of the dean's chocolate-colored spaniels had deposited at his feet. Arthur could never tell the two dogs, Mag and Nunc, apart, but he flung the ball as far as he could and they both bounded off after it. He loved these early morning walks with Gwyn. They meant his Tuesdays and Thursdays, at least, could start off on a civilized note.

Gwyneth Bowen had been dean of Barchester Cathedral for almost six years. Arthur had shaken hands with her after Evensong shortly after she was installed, but the two cannot be said to have genuinely met until a few weeks later, when they happened to fall in together while walking in the water meadows outside the cathedral close one foggy morning. They had had a long and heated debate about the nature of faith; Arthur had liked her immediately.

The argument that had engrossed them on their first meeting had gone something like this: The dean did not understand how Arthur could come to services at the cathedral nearly every day yet profess he didn't actually *believe* in the doctrines of the Christian church. Arthur argued that the dean should be pleased to have nonbelievers in her pews—what better place for nonbelievers? Arthur guessed her argument stemmed not so much from the apparent inconsistency of his beliefs and his actions as from her assumption that a nonbeliever in the pews was a rare bird. But Arthur suspected it was not nearly as rare as Gwyn thought, or perhaps wished. He imagined that any number of regular attendees, especially at the main Sunday morning service, if put to the test about their reasons for darkening the doors of the cathedral on a regular basis, might say all sorts of things about music and preaching and architecture and fellowship, but would very carefully skirt around the issue of faith.

Since that first day, they had met twice a week during term time, more often during holidays, immediately after seven o'clock Morning Prayer, for an hour-long walk across the broad expanse of the water meadows, along the riverside path, and back to the cathedral close, where the gardens came down to the river just across from Arthur's cottage. Whatever the weather, when they made the turn at the far end of the meadow, and emerged from a row of trees to catch sight of the cathedral, Arthur always felt as if he were in a Constable painting. On some days they continued the debate that had begun that first morning; more often they engaged on different topics—some found them in agreement; others led to spirited jousting, which Arthur quite enjoyed.

When Gwyn's husband had died a year ago, the walks had continued for a time in a more somber vein, but they had never missed a Tuesday or Thursday that entire term. "I need this," Gwyn had said when Arthur had suggested a hiatus. "I may not be the first woman dean in the Anglican Church, but I believe I am the first who is the single mother of two small children, grieving for her husband, and trying to manage the finances of Britain's poorest cathedral. Sometimes I think our walk is my only hour of sanity in the day." So Arthur listened to her troubles and she listened to his and by the time they reached the river they were more often than not deep into an argument that took them each away from their work on the other side of the water meadows.

"And I don't see why the students have to call the faculty by their first names," said Arthur, continuing his complaint about the previous afternoon's tutorial. "We aren't their mates; we're their instructors. Would it be so awful to be shown a little respect?"

"Come now, Arthur. You don't call me the Very Reverend Bowen."

"That's because we are peers—practically."

"We're nothing of the sort. I'm a dean and you're a layman."

They walked in unusual silence for a few minutes, Arthur again throwing the tennis ball when Mag (or perhaps Nunc) dropped it at his feet. "Something's bothering you," he said at last.

"Some bad news this morning, I'm afraid," said Gwyn.

"Has Daniel been sent down from nursery school?" said Arthur. Daniel was Gwyn's energetic three-year-old.

"No," said Gwyn with a laugh, "but it wouldn't surprise me. He's become overly fond of kissing girls, apparently."

"Ah, to be three and in love!"

"We heard from the Heritage Lottery Fund this morning. Our application was rejected."

"Astounding," said Arthur, shaking his head. "I suppose they think it's more important to build a museum of thread bobbins or a center for the study of Cornish pasties."

"I thought perhaps I could leave a mark as dean," said Gwyn.

"You leave a mark every day," said Arthur.

"But not like this would have been."

For years, Gwyneth had been seeking funding to rebuild the Lady Chapel, destroyed by German bombs in 1941. Under her direction, the chapter and a local firm of architects had spent three years preparing a plan for a chapel that was modern in design—built of local oak, steel, and huge glass panels extending from floor to ceiling on three sides and looking out onto a surrounding garden. Gwyn and the architects had visited several cathedrals as they searched for inspiration, and she had been especially struck by the juxtaposition of the modern cathedral at Coventry with the bombed-out ruins of the medieval building.

"I suppose it's just as well," she said. "Half the community loved the design and the other half hated it."

"I despise modern architecture," said Arthur. "You know with what a searing passion I loathe the so-called campus of my current employer. But I love your chapel. It will be what contemporary architecture ought to be and so seldom is."

"The precentor said it looked like a cheap conservatory on a seaside holiday cottage."

"Yes, well the precentor is a slab of Gorgonzola."

"Thank you, P. G. Wodehouse."

"A pleasure," said Arthur.

"I thought you liked the precentor."

"I never said I liked the man. I just like the style of worship he brings to the cathedral."

"I find all the incense and chanting so . . ." Gwyn trailed off.

"You were going to say Roman, weren't you?" said Arthur.

"Actually I was going to say ancient," said the dean.

"What better place to keep alive ancient practices than Barchester, where Christianity has been practiced for twelve hundred years."

"Has it?" said the dean. "I wouldn't know. You see, the man who is working on the cathedral guidebook has missed his deadline again."

"In a cathedral with twelve centuries of history, what difference could a few months make?"

"How long have you been working on that guide, Arthur? Because it does seem like something approaching a millennium."

"I thought we were talking about the Gorgonzola," said Arthur with disdain.

"Don't you care for Gorgonzola, Mr. Prescott?" said the dean, and they spent the rest of their walk debating the relative merits of English, French, and Italian cheeses.

"I'm truly sorry about the chapel, Gwyn," said Arthur as they stood once again in the close outside the deanery, Mag and Nunc circling round them. "Is there no other way to raise the money?"

"If we do it properly, and follow all the rules about the restoration of ancient monuments—do a full archaeological dig and that sort of thing—we'll need something like two and a half million pounds. So far the generous community of Barchester and our paltry stream of tourists have mustered about a hundred thousand."

"Did they say why the application was refused?"

"They said they would have preferred an application for an educational or multipurpose building. They don't want to fund what they call 'superfluous worship space' in a cathedral that can't fill the pews it has."

"Superfluous!" said Arthur. "Let them come to Compline on a moonlit night in your glass chapel and then talk about 'superfluous.'"

"What would I do without you?" said Gwyn, smiling and squeezing Arthur's hand.

"First of all you might have a new cathedral guide by now," said Arthur. "And second, you might go on naïvely believing that Brie or Romano or chèvre are superior to a good old English Cheddar."

That afternoon, Arthur had a blessed opportunity to leave work early, as the two o'clock meeting of the Campus Sustainability Committee was canceled owing to the fact that all the committee members (excepting Arthur) were going to Manchester for the Conference on Green Technology and Construction. He took the number 42 bus to the city center and walked the short distance to the cathedral, bypassing the path that led to his own cottage for the pleasures of his favorite room in the world.

Arthur had worked in the Bodleian and in most of the Oxford college libraries as an undergraduate. One year he had spent his Easter holidays ensconced in a reading room at the British Library. He had toured the libraries of stately homes and visited fellow book collectors in their own private havens. But nothing compared, in his mind, to what awaited him at the top of the winding stone staircase off the cloister of Barchester Cathedral. The few tourists who strayed far enough from London to visit Barchester rarely noticed the narrow wooden door just past the much larger entry to the chapter house and never suspected what treasures that door hid. Now Arthur turned his key in the lock and stepped inside. He flicked the light on, pulled the door shut, and began to climb.

Slightly breathless from the steep steps, he emerged at the top of the stairs into a long, high-ceilinged room that ran almost the entire length of the east side of the cloister. He stood, by perpetual invitation of the dean, in the library of Barchester Cathedral. The library was overseen by Oscar Dimsdale, a local schoolteacher who volunteered in a variety of capacities around the cathedral. Arthur and Oscar had met in Barchester the summer Arthur was twelve, and had been best friends ever since. Oscar worked odd hours, coming to the library whenever he had the time. He had no training as a librarian, but he kept the books dusted and made arrangements to allow access to any members of the community who wanted to use the collection. Few did. When Arthur had begun working on his guide to Barchester Cathedral some years ago, Oscar, with the permission of the dean, had given him his own key. That Arthur had leave to come to this room whenever he liked seemed a privilege of unparalleled fortune.

Save for a small collection of modern reference books on the shelf behind Oscar's desk, nothing in the room was less than a century old, and many of the books, manuscripts, and furnishings surrounding him were much older. The interior woodwork, from the bookcases to the thick beams overhead, was seventeenth century, having been installed by one of Barchester's only bibliophile bishops, Bishop Atwater, who had also donated a substantial collection of books to the cathedral.

The wall to Arthur's left was covered with oak bookcases, reaching high overhead. Most of these still had their original decorated finials above each section—though those at the far end of the room were badly charred from the wartime fire. On the right wall, several narrow windows looked into the cloister, and paneling bore the scratched initials of long-ago readers. In the center of this wall was a case decorated with elaborate carvings and containing the cathedral's collection of some eighty medieval manuscripts, all, thanks to the events of 1941, lacking their covers.

Down the center of the room was a row of long, wooden trestle tables. One held a few stacks of books Oscar was working with, but most stood empty. In the days when Barchester had been a monastic foundation, long before this space had been constructed, monks would have consulted the cathedral's books for guidance on everything from agriculture to engineering to medicine. For centuries, clergy of the cathedral used the library often, having no place else to look for historical and theological writing. Even into the nineteenth century, young men of Barchester studying for ordination at Oxford or Cambridge made frequent use of the collection when home for the long vacation. In 1890, parts of the collection were opened as a circulating library for the people of the city—an innovation that lasted until the establishment of a public library in Barchester a few years later. Today, however, Barchester was far from the British centers of scholarship, its library held few items that scholars couldn't examine much more easily in Oxford or Cambridge or London, and little on the shelves that surrounded Arthur was of interest to the local population. None of this bothered Arthur; it meant he often had this wonderful space to himself.

He stood a moment with his eyes closed and inhaled the smell of antiquity. He could catch a hint of charred wood and a dash of dried mildew. The library smelled substantial; it smelled of both life and death. The air was stale and still and Arthur felt the atmosphere of the place envelop him. He was home.

Despite the ample space on the tables in the center of the room, Arthur preferred to work at a small table under one of the cloister windows. Though the legs had been made in the nineteenth century, the table top was, according to tradition, the oldest piece of furniture in the cathedral—though no one knew exactly how old. It may have once been a piece of an altar, as the words *Mensa Christi*, or "Table of Christ," were carved into its front edge in Gothic letters. Its surface was uneven and worn, pitted and gouged. It was much too small for spreading out research papers and entirely unsuitable for writing. Arthur loved it.

He started toward his favorite spot, then paused for a moment, listening. Save for the occasional creaking of beams overhead, all was silent—no turning of the door handle far below, no steps upon the staircase. Arthur walked softly to a case at the far end of the room, stood on tiptoe, and removed a plain-looking, squat volume. Its leather binding was badly worn at the joints and corners, and nearly two inches of the lower spine was lacking. It bore no markings, no indications to a casual observer that it was Arthur's favorite book in the library. He loved to take it down from its shelf, to caress its covers, to lose himself in the artwork of the frontispiece, and to read from its pages.

The book was the 1634 William Stansby edition of Malory's *Morte d'Arthur*, or, as the title page called it, *The Most Ancient and Famous History of the Renowned Prince Arthur King of Britaine*. Malory's was the first collection in English of many of the King Arthur tales, some of which had begun as medieval French romances. This wasn't the original printing of Malory—that had been published by England's first printer, William Caxton, in 1485 and survived in only two copies. Four more editions, nearly as rare as the Caxton, followed in the fifteenth and sixteenth centuries. The Stansby 1634 edition was the earliest Arthur was ever likely to hold in his own hands. It was also the first to be updated into what Arthur thought of as Shakespearean English, and the text upon which many future editions were based.

He had first held this book when he was nine years old, the first time his grandfather had brought him to the cathedral library. Even then, before he had any understanding of bibliography or publishing history, before he knew the difference between paper and vellum or calf and morocco, he had felt the history of this place—a deep sense of almost electric connection to the past. Looking back on it, he supposed his first steps into the room, breathless from following his lanky, loping grandfather up the stairs, had been a spiritual experience. He didn't feel God in the library, but he felt something beyond himself.

But his grandfather had not brought him to the library to overwhelm him with history, rather to show him a specific book—the Stansby *Morte d'Arthur.*

"This is a book about your namesake," said his grandfather.

"My namesake?"

"The person you were named after. I suggested the name myself—the name Arthur—because of this book. And since I was to be your godfather, your parents agreed. This book is about a king named Arthur."

"What does he do?" asked Arthur.

"He has adventures," said his grandfather, with a twinkle in his eye.

"Can we check it out and read it?" asked Arthur.

"Not this copy," said his grandfather with a chuckle, as he took the book from the boy. "But I have another edition at home we can read."

Now Arthur opened the book to the title page and turned the volume sideways so he could examine the frontispiece. He had looked at it a thousand times; every detail of the woodcut was burned into his memory, but on days like this, when the modern world exasperated him at every turn, he loved nothing better than returning to this book and this image. The picture showed King Arthur and his knights seated at the

Round Table. Arthur popped up through a circular hole in the center of the table, holding a lance and a sword. He had a large nose and an English mustache—without the extended handlebars. He wore a full suit of plate-mail armor—more Jacobean than Arthurian. On a bench encircling the table and draped with linen sat thirteen of Arthur's knights, similarly mustachioed and armored. There seemed a general air of camaraderie among the knights. Most chatted with one another; one had his hand on another's back. Arthur could almost imagine himself as one of the company. The caption for the woodcut listed thirty knights, with no indication of which of them appeared in the image. Every time Arthur looked at the picture he attributed different names to the figures. Today the knight sitting squarely in the center of the image, the only one with his back completely to the viewer, seemed more Lancelot than Kay. Sir Bors and Sir Gawain were certainly chatting in the bottom right corner. The hardest to put a name to was at the top of the picture, his face almost totally obscured by the feather streaming from Arthur's helmet. Today he was Galahad, achiever of the Grail, sitting in the Siege Perilous.

Arthur turned the soft, worn pages and inhaled the scent of history. The paper was a pale brownish yellow, but the dark type was still as legible as it had been almost four hundred years ago. He had work to do today, so he just read a short passage from a chapter titled "How sir Galahad and his fellowes were fed with the Sancgreall, and how our Lord appeared to them, and of other matters."

> Then King Pelles and his sonne departed. And therewith it beseemed them that there came a man and foure Angels from heaven, clothed in the likenesse of bishops, and had a crosse in his hand, and the foure Angels beare him up in a chaire, and set him downe before the table of silver, whereupon the Sancgreall was.

The Sancgreall—the Holy Grail. Arthur closed his eyes and tried to picture the scene. Malory was not one for detailed descriptions, and he never wrote what the Holy Grail looked like, but to Arthur this meant the Grail could be whatever he needed it to be. Today it was an anchor, a solid link to a past that mattered and that, for Arthur, was as alive as the present—perhaps more alive.

When Arthur returned home that summer after his grandfather had introduced him to the stories of the Round Table, he had run straight to the library and checked out the only volume about King Arthur he could find—a 1911 book called *King Arthur's Knights: The Tales Retold for Boys and Girls*. The title page claimed that the book contained "16 Illustrations in Color by Walter Crane," but some disrespectful former library patron had removed the color plates. Arthur didn't care; he was too busy falling in love with the stories.

King Arthur's Knights had been the first book Arthur had read late at night under the covers with a torch, long after he was supposed to have been asleep. It was the first book that took him completely out of himself, his room, his home, and his hometown to a place that seemed both mythical and real, a place where magic was ordinary and heroes were plenteous. It was, he supposed, thinking back on it, the first book that showed him what reading was really all about.

At first Arthur had been drawn to the adventure in the stories—knights battling other knights, the king holding tournaments at Camelot. Then in his teenage years, the love stories began to be favorites—the great Sir Lancelot's tragic love for Queen Guinevere, Tristram and Isoude drinking a love potion even while he was supposed to be wooing her on behalf of another. But the Grail stories had been a constant source of fascination. In the version of Malory that Arthur read as a boy, the story of the Grail was wonderfully vague, never explicitly stating what the Grail was or why Arthur and his knights were so determined to find it. It was unclear who possessed the Grail or why or what they did with it or even whether it was real or just a vision. Arthur had grown to love the mysterious nature of the Grail, but as a child it had fascinated and frustrated him in equal parts.

"What is the Grail?" Arthur had asked his grandfather the night after his first visit to the cathedral library as his grandfather read to him from an abridged version of Malory.

The popular legend of the Grail, his grandfather told him, was simple—the cup from which Christ served the wine at the Last Supper was taken by Joseph of Arimathea to the island of Britain. Arriving near what is now Glastonbury, Joseph pushed his staff into the ground and it flowered into a bush known as the Glastonbury Thorn. Joseph later buried the Grail under a nearby hill—the Glastonbury Tor—and a torrent of clean, fresh water sprang forth and flows from the spot to this very day. Centuries later, knights of King Arthur's Round Table sought the Grail—a symbol of purity and perfection. In some versions of the tale, the Glastonbury Tor is also the Isle of Avalon, Arthur's mysterious final resting place. In the late twelfth century, monks of Glastonbury claimed to have found the graves of King Arthur and Queen Guinevere, but no one ever found the Grail.

Arthur might have thought the story of the Grail no more than a mysterious legend of a magical cup with healing powers—as fascinating, and as fictional, as Tolkien's One Ring. But the first time his grandfather read him the Grail story from Malory, he laid the book aside and looked Arthur in the eyes.

"King Arthur, and Merlin, and Lancelot, and all the rest—in all likelihood they are only stories. But the Grail, Arthur—the Grail was real. The Grail *is* real. And I'm going to tell you a secret—a secret you must promise to share with no one."

"I promise," said Arthur breathlessly.

"I believe that the Grail is right here in Barchester."

Arthur loved no one in the world more than his grandfather, and that kindly man rarely spoke as seriously as he did now.

"I'm getting too old for adventures," said his grandfather, "but you have your whole life ahead of you. You must be the one to find the Grail. And you must keep it secret."

"But why does it have to be a secret?" said Arthur.

"Do you trust me?" said his grandfather.

"Yes," said the boy.

"Then you must believe. Someday you will understand. You will understand what the Grail is and where it is and why it must be kept a secret, but for now all you have to do is believe in it. Do you, Arthur? Do you believe in the Grail?"

And Arthur's response had been absolutely instinctual. Staring into the deep blue of his grandfather's eyes he had spoken without the slightest shadow of doubt.

"I do."

Arthur opened his eyes and looked back at the page. At the edge of the text block was a bit of marginalia written in browning ink in a seventeenth-century hand.

Libro huic nullus locus melior praeter Baronum Castrum

Baronum Castrum was the name of the Roman settlement that had become Barchester. The marginalia translated, "No better place for this book than Barchester." His grandfather had shown him this mysterious notation on one of their visits to the cathedral library, translating it without comment or explanation. Arthur ran his finger lightly across the inscription, wondering, as he always did when he looked at it, who had written those words and, more importantly, why. Some monk or priest or scholar had thought Barchester the perfect place for a book about King Arthur and had chosen a page about the Holy Grail to note this. How he wished he could see into the past and know the reason.

After another moment, he turned and slipped the book back into its place, carefully aligning the spine with the adjacent volumes so no one would know it had been removed. As much as he wanted to follow his grandfather's exhortation and find a way to seek the Holy Grail in Barchester, that would have to wait for another day. He walked back to his usual table and slid into the worn velvet seat of his Gothic chair—a castoff from the chapter house renovations of the nineteenth century. On the table in front of him lay the Barchester Breviary. It was the only medieval manuscript of Barchester not damaged during the emptying of the library in 1941. Its intact survival was owed to its occasional use, even after the Reformation, as a service book. It had originally been kept in the vestry and so had not been part of the chained library. Occupying, as it did, a place of pride in the library, on a lectern near the entrance, it would have been one of the first books removed on the night of the bombing.

The thirteenth-century manuscript contained the psalms, readings, and prayers for the daily offices—the seven services conducted by monks of the medieval monastery each day. The Barchester Breviary was particularly distinguished for the inclusion of medieval musical settings for several of the psalms and canticles. Many such musical manuscripts had been destroyed at the time of the Civil War by Parliamentarians, who saw chanting as too Roman Catholic. But the breviary had survived and had been an important source for one of the few pieces of scholarship to emerge from the library in the nineteenth century, a book called *Harding's Church Music*, by the then precentor of the cathedral, Septimus Harding.

The breviary also contained prayers and services unique to Barchester. Of these, the one that held the most interest for Arthur was the service for the feast day of St. Ewolda, founder of the monastery that became Barchester Cathedral. He had pored over these four pages of Latin again and again searching for any clue about her life.

The chief sticking point in Arthur's attempts to craft a new guide to Barchester Cathedral was the lack of information about Ewolda. Arthur knew she had been martyred—she was included in the Venerable Bede's *Martyrologium*. But Bede gave no details about either Ewolda's life or her death.

"Our visitors don't care about some seventh-century saint," Gwyn had told him when he explained that he couldn't finish his guide until he knew at least something about Ewolda. "They just want to know when the nave was built, who designed the stained glass windows, and what time the café closes." But Arthur had persisted in the belief that if he stared at those four pages hard enough, they would reveal something of Ewolda's story.

He picked up the manuscript, as he had so many times before, hoping for new insight. The volume had been rebound sometime shortly after the Reformation, and the present binding of brown calf was worn to the softness of suede. There were no markings on the exterior—or at least none that had survived four hundred years of use—but Arthur nonetheless turned the thick volume in his hands, carefully examining the

binding before opening it. Handling this book was, to Arthur, like a li-
turgical rite—there were certain unwritten rubrics he always followed.

The manuscript was about 11 inches high and just over 7 inches wide
and contained 160 vellum leaves, each covered on both sides with closely
spaced Latin text. There was no title page or table of contents. The first
page, to which Arthur now turned, simply began the service of Matins.

Vellum, especially eight-hundred-year-old vellum, felt like nothing
else. Arthur reveled in the texture of the pages as he slowly turned them
over. Each had its own thickness, its own weight, yet each also possessed
those peculiar characteristics of vellum—the sheen; the smooth, almost
slick surface; the supple flexibility; and that underlying strength. When
turning vellum pages, Arthur always took great care, but he also knew
he didn't need to. Unlike paper, vellum was extremely difficult to tear.

Everything about the manuscript transported Arthur back across the
centuries—the faint red lines that had served the scribe as a guide to
keeping his lettering straight; the darkening at the bottom corner of every page, where a thousand, or ten thousand, thumbs had turned the
leaves; and the vellum itself—that calfskin parchment that was so ex-
pensive and difficult to prepare.

Eventually, Arthur arrived at the order for the service of Vespers for
the feast day of St. Ewolda. It differed only slightly from Vespers on other
days, and Arthur had never been able to read anything into the particular selection of psalms and Scripture readings. Only the final prayer
made any direct reference to Ewolda:

> Harken we beseech thee O Lord Christ to our prayers and deign to
> bless with thy grace thy servant Ewolda, whose sacrifice in thy name we
> remember this day and every day. As you made your blessed virgin
> Ewolda come to heaven through the palm frond of martyrdom, grant
> that we by following her example may earn the right to approach you.

As always, the prayer left Arthur with more questions than answers.
Ewolda was a virgin and a martyr—both fairly standard for early female saints. But what was her sacrifice? What was the "palm frond of

martyrdom"? What was her example that those who prayed this prayer sought to follow?

In the margin next to the prayer was a crude sketch, presumably of Ewolda—a blue-robed woman who seemed to hover over the page. While her halo conferred saintly status, the marginalia also displayed the bawdy tradition of some such drawings. From the hem of her robes issued a stream of water that trickled to the bottom of the page. Why some medieval artist would choose to depict St. Ewolda urinating in the margins of her prayer Arthur could not imagine. He looked into her vacant eyes for a long minute, but she offered him no insight.

After reading the prayer one more time without further illumination, Arthur gently closed the manuscript. Perhaps Gwyn was right. Perhaps he should just get on with writing the cathedral guide, pouring into it all the things he *did* know about the history of Barchester. Perhaps he shouldn't worry about the things he *didn't* know. He pulled out his fountain pen; a few sheets of thick, cream-colored paper; and a leather blotter—to provide a smooth writing surface on the ancient table. In an elegant script that he had learned from a nineteenth-century handwriting manual, he wrote: *A Visitor's Guide to Barchester Cathedral.* But what, thought Arthur, comes next?

He stared at the empty page and could think only one thing. If he really wanted to write the guide properly, it wasn't the Holy Grail he needed to find but another missing treasure—the lost Book of Ewolda.

II
THE NAVE

With its massive stone columns, barrel-vaulted ceiling, and heavy Norman arches, the nave is one of the oldest parts of the cathedral. On the walls can be found memorials to various De Courcys, Greshams, and Ullathornes, and in the nave aisle lies the tomb of the Second Duke of Omnium. A much older monument can be found in the floor just inside the main west door. A small gray stone, apparently of Saxon origins, bears a single word—Wigbert. Little is known about this simple memorial. It may mark the resting place of one of the abbots of the Saxon monastery, or Norman builders may have moved it to its present location. In any case, it is likely the oldest, and certainly the most mysterious, monument in Barchester.

A.D. *560, St. Ewolda's Monastery, Baronum Castrum*

Wigbert's chamber was nearly dark. The fire in the middle of the room had burned low, and the corner in which the aged abbot reclined was in such deep shadow that his voice seemed to emanate from nothingness. But Martin had keen eyes, and even by the light of the single taper he was able to transcribe what the abbot dictated.

Although named after Martin of Tours, Martin the scribe had been born in Brittany in 536. As a young man, he had worked as a shepherd, until the day he delivered several of his sheep to a parchment maker. Martin had never heard of parchment, but he returned day after day, watching as the man slaughtered and skinned the sheep, soaked the skin in lime, scraped off the hair, and stretched the thin, translucent material on a frame to dry. Martin had been transfixed, especially when he learned from the man that the parchment would be used by the monks of the nearby monastery of Saint-Brieuc as a writing material.

"The scribes are making a Gospel book," said the man, "and want one hundred hides for the pages."

Just as he had followed his sheep to the parchment maker, Martin followed the parchment to the monastery, taking the monastic vows and soon becoming an apprentice to one of the scribes. He had a remarkable talent for languages and quickly learned the techniques of the scribe, showing great dexterity with a quill and rarely making mistakes in his straight, even lines of text. His fellow scribes said no one understood the variations of the parchment better than the former shepherd. A good scribe appreciated the differences between the outside of the skin, which still had hair follicles, and the inner side; between the hides of sheep and those of goats or calves.

Martin's technique, his work ethic, and his deep familiarity with his materials had him well on his way to becoming chief scribe of Saint-Brieuc when the abbot received a message from an obscure monastery in the kingdom of Barsyt across the water in Britannia. It was a poor house, with no scribes and few brothers who could even read. The services and psalms they committed to memory. The abbot, Wigbert, had sent from his deathbed to Saint-Brieuc for a scribe to record the story of the founding of the monastery. Since Martin was the only scribe who spoke Anglo-Saxon, having learned from a visitor to Saint-Brieuc some years earlier, he had accepted the calling and sailed across rough waters to Britannia, falling on his knees with thanksgiving when the crossing had been safely accomplished. He had traveled on foot to the former Roman settlement of Baronum Castrum and there had found Wigbert, weak in body but strong in mind and ready to tell his story. But it was not Wigbert's story at all. It was the story of his twin sister, Ewolda.

Martin had sat many days listening to Wigbert's tale. Each morning, the old man spent an hour telling Martin a new episode; Martin then questioned him on the details, and in the afternoon the abbot repeated the story slowly, and Martin transcribed his words onto the parchment. But Martin did more than merely transcribe—he embellished, not the facts, but the language—for Wigbert was painfully prosaic. The abbot did not understand the beauty of language, the ways the words themselves could intersect with the story. Wigbert told a tale, but Martin wrote poetry.

"That is enough for today," the abbot said after a long pause. "You may put away your pen and leave me."

"Reverend abbot," said Martin. "May I speak to you freely, with no pen in hand?"

"Indeed, Brother Martin, you may. It soothes me to have company, and though my mind wearies when I reach for the details of times long past, to have your companionship has been a great pleasure in my waning days."

"Tell me, Reverend Abbot—the tales you tell of your sister, are they true or do you . . . do you invent stories to inspire the future brothers and sisters of this house?"

"What is truth?" replied the abbot. "Are the scriptures true?"

"Of course," said Martin.

"Then is our God a god of peace or a god of war?"

"Surely," said Martin, "He is a god of peace—for He sent His Son to bring peace to all the nations."

"Indeed," said Wigbert, "yet the book of Exodus tells us He is a god of war. So which is the truth?"

Martin had not considered this before and found himself vexed by the question. "Truth is not as simple as I supposed," he said at last.

"And so it is with the book that you write for me. It is the best truth I can recall—but what is recollection and what is exaggeration that has merged with recollection over the years? What is my own memory, and what do I trust to the memory of others? How accurate is my mind, and how accurate those of so many who have told these stories? These are questions I cannot answer, any more than you can answer whether God is a god of war or peace. But I believe the stories to contain truth."

"And you believe your sister to be a saint?"

"Of that I have no doubt, for however dim my memories of days long past, miracles still occur at her shrine. Just last year, a woman who could hardly walk from palsy came to pray at the tomb where Ewolda's holy relics lie. The next day she was healed of her infirmities. This I saw with my own eyes and many of my brethren saw it as well. So if the story I tell of my blessed sister's life and death is not perfect in its details, it nonetheless reflects who she truly was and is."

"You are indeed blessed to call such a saint your sister," said Martin.

"I am," said Wigbert softly. "Yet every day I suffer the memory of her death."

"And what was . . ." began Martin. "What was the manner of her death . . . her martyrdom?"

"That, my brother," replied Wigbert, "is a story for tomorrow."

April 6, 2016

SECOND WEDNESDAY AFTER EASTER

The next afternoon Arthur had not been able to leave the university in time to work in the cathedral library, so he walked straight from his bus stop to the cathedral quire, arriving in plenty of time for Evensong. He entered at the west door, and when he passed the precentor rushing through the south transept he nodded politely, doing his best not to imagine the reverend's head as a giant slab of Gorgonzola. In truth he looked more like a freshly caught salmon. His high forehead, made even higher by his receding hairline, glistened with a sheen of sweat and his thin lips hung open in a perfect O. His flustered expression could not completely mask the haughty demeanor etched in his face. It was not fair of Arthur to dislike the precentor, he knew, but the man gave off an air of superiority unbecoming a salmon.

Arthur slipped into a pew opposite where the choristers would stand. The service would not begin for twenty minutes, and he was the only person in the quire. As the minutes slipped by and he felt himself relaxing into the past, a few others drifted in—one or two regulars, a small clutch of visitors, a shopper or two who had finished errands early and decided to stay in the city center an extra half hour to hear the service. Arthur noticed almost none of this, however. As he waited for Evensong he thought of nothing. He knew that others thought of God or Jesus or architecture or music, but to Arthur the miracle of sitting in a quiet cathedral was that it allowed him to empty his mind. The frustrations of his job at the university, the difficulties of his research, even his irrational dislike of the precentor melted away. By the time the precentor began the service, chanting, "O Lord, open thou our lips," Arthur heard only the pure tenor voice, and as the choir responded he fell back into the music.

The beauty of Evensong—the voices of the choir ringing off the ancient stones of the cathedral—did not make Arthur believe in God, but it did make him *want* to believe. The service had been sung in Barchester regularly for half a millennium, and Arthur found that continuity comforting as he slipped into the same seat he occupied in the quire every afternoon.

The Magnificat and the Nunc Dimittis, which were a part of every Evensong, were today sung to especially appropriate music—a Gregorian chant setting taken from the Barchester Breviary. The music, which had been sung in that very space eight hundred years ago, echoed hauntingly through the quire and transported Arthur back to the days before the Reformation, before Evensong, when seven times a day the chants of monks filled this space.

When the service ended, Arthur left by way of the north quire aisle, hoping to avoid the precentor, but as soon as he emerged into the nave, there stood the salmon greeting the few worshippers, and Arthur had no choice but to smile and offer his hand.

"Good afternoon, Arthur," said the precentor. "Always so nice to see you." That tone of voice, thought Arthur, must be what had inspired the invention of the word *disingenuous*. The precentor's hand was cold and damp and Arthur surreptitiously wiped his own hand on his pants as he hurried down the nave.

The precentor had a way of always being where Arthur wanted to be. At receptions, when Arthur crossed the room to speak to the dean, or the choirmaster, or the organist's French wife, the precentor arrived on the scene just in front of him, monopolizing the conversation; at the market, he had an unnerving habit of slipping in front of Arthur just as he was about to join a queue and of buying the last of the Cheddar, or the wholemeal, or the raspberry jam. Arthur had even, on several occasions, arrived in the library to find the precentor sitting in what he thought of as *his* chair at *his* table. While the precentor certainly had a right to sit anywhere in the library he chose, it annoyed Arthur to be relegated to a more modern table while the precentor sat reading, as often as not, a paperback spy novel in Arthur's usual, if not rightful, spot.

So, while Arthur did not exactly seethe at having been delayed, if only for a moment, he was none too pleased as he scurried home to tidy up. He was expecting guests.

Arthur lived at the edge of the cathedral close in one of three cottages that had been fashioned out of a row of almshouses once called Hiram's Hospital. The "hospital" had been endowed and built in 1434 by a wealthy businessman named John Hiram as a home for elderly gentlemen of Barchester. By the mid-twentieth century, the endowment had run dry, and the houses had fallen into disrepair until they had been restored for modern living in the 1990s. Arthur had bought his cottage ten years ago when he came to Barchester, a fitting use of the inheritance his grandfather had left him.

There had been twelve men living in the six almshouses; each of the modern homes was composed of two of those medieval units. Arthur had, on the ground floor, a spacious sitting room, a small kitchen, and a dining area, as well as a small conservatory at the back looking out over the common garden and a bend in the river. Upstairs, in what had once been little more than a garret, were a cozy bedroom, a small bathroom, and Arthur's study, from which he could just glimpse the tower of the cathedral.

He could not imagine a more ideal home. The cottage was close to everything Arthur cared about—not just the cathedral but the shops in the city center (particularly Denning's Bookshop)—and it was blessedly distant from all he loathed, for while Arthur inhabited the world of medieval Barchester, the modern university had been built in a field six miles outside of town. Number Three, Hiram's Cottages, Barchester, was the perfect address for Arthur Prescott.

That evening Arthur would host the weekly meeting of the Barchester Bibliophiles. The bibliophiles consisted of Arthur, Oscar Dimsdale, and David Denning—three confirmed bachelors who shared a love of all things bookish.

Oscar, by trade a maths teacher at the local comprehensive school, lived with his aging mother, and spent much of his time at the cathedral. Not only did he organize the library, he also oversaw the laundering of vestments, stocked supplies in the vestry and sacristy, and helped the vergers in a plethora of ways. He would have liked to be a lay reader—reading the lessons at services—but he was prevented by his peculiar habit of breathing at just the wrong place in a sentence. This impediment made his speech seem both rushed and halting, and while Arthur and David had grown used to it, the precentor had decreed that such a manner of speech disqualified Oscar from reading Scripture. It was the official reason why Oscar, despite his years of service to the cathedral, had never been invited to become a lay canon. Arthur had it on good authority from the dean that the real reason was that the bishop insisted that lay canons be prominent, preferably wealthy, members of the Barchester community, but he would never tell Oscar this. Arthur had always assumed that Oscar was gay, but he fancied himself both too liberal to care and too old-fashioned to ask. Oscar never mentioned his love life.

The same could not be said for David Denning. Oxford educated, though several years younger than Arthur, David had followed a girl to Barchester after university. The romance had lasted just long enough for David to spend his small inheritance on a failing bookshop off Barchester High Street. Since then his relationships with books had been far more enduring than those with women. He had added an antiquarian section to the shop that had previously sold only new bestsellers, started a popular series of author events, and installed a café. However, he also had a bad habit of seducing his shop assistants—who were invariably beautiful young women. Oscar had suggested that perhaps hiring a middle-aged man might bring a little stability to the establishment. Shop assistants at Denning's rarely lasted more than a few months. Once David had cast them aside romantically they had little interest in continuing in his employ. Unlike Oscar, David had few qualms about sharing his sexual exploits with his literary friends—so few, in fact, that Arthur and Oscar had made a rule: No discussing private affairs (in the most obvious sense of the word) at meetings of the Barchester Bibliophiles.

David had wanted to name the group "The Holy Trinity," but Oscar had objected to this as irreverent; Arthur would have none of "The Three Musketeers," saying that they should at least honor English, not French, literature; and David had squashed "The Pickwick Club" on the grounds that there had been four Pickwickians, not three. That left them with the Barchester Bibliophiles (or the BBs for short), which eliminated any reference to the group as a trio, thus leaving open the possibility, remote though it was, of another bachelor book enthusiast one day joining their number.

Arthur would host the bibliophiles in his sitting room, where he carefully displayed his collection of the works of English humorists. He enjoyed sharing this collection with Oscar, David, and anyone else who happened to visit his cottage, but it was not his only collection, or even the collection with which he spent the most time. That collection was shelved upstairs in his study, his sanctum sanctorum, into which neither David, nor Oscar, nor any other visitor had ever been allowed.

The collection in the downstairs of Arthur's cottage covered the years from about 1850 to 1950. On one wall of the sitting room hung five antique prints from *Vanity Fair* magazine—Max Beerbohm, F. C. Burnand, W. S. Gilbert, John Tenniel, and Tom Taylor. Below these a low bookcase ran between the front door and the corner of the room. On the opposite wall, built-in bookcases flanking the fireplace showcased his collection of P. G. Wodehouse.

Arthur's grandfather had given him not only a love for Barchester and Grail lore but also for all books. When Arthur had discovered his collection of P. G. Wodehouse, his grandfather had encouraged the boy's passion, and being able to escape into the world of Jeeves became yet another pleasure associated with those summer visits. Arthur's grandfather had died two weeks after Arthur began his career as an undergraduate at Lazarus, casting a shadow over his Oxford days. But Arthur also inherited the Wodehouse collection, and, as a way of keeping his grandfather's memory alive, he began adding to it, haunting the used bookshops of Oxfordshire. By the time he finished university, Arthur had a growing collection that traced Wodehouse's influences and covered a wide range of English comic writers.

Now books covered the entire fireplace wall of his sitting room, from floor to ceiling. Many of his grandfather's Wodehouse books gleamed in their original dust jackets, carefully preserved in glassine wrappers. Surrounding this core of Jeeves and Blandings Castle and Mr. Mulliner, Arthur had shelved everything from old *Punch* magazines to works by Charles Dickens, Oscar Wilde, Kingsley Amis, and Jerome K. Jerome. In archival boxes he stored comic almanacs illustrated by George Cruikshank and satirical pamphlets by authors as famous as Lewis Carroll and as obscure as Theodore Buckley. He loved the lesser-known humorists, and tonight he would read from a booklet by Buckley.

A reading from a recent acquisition or a beloved old friend was always part of the BB meetings. The bibliophiles met on Wednesday nights, rotating hosts. David convened the group in a cozy room in the back of his bookshop, furnished with comfy leather furniture and lined with the antiquarian stock that was too valuable to display in the main part of the store; Oscar, so as not to disturb his mother, hosted his evenings in a room just off the cathedral library with a small fireplace and cases that held boxes of ancient documents. Arthur was the only one of the trio who welcomed the others into his home.

By seven thirty, drinks had been poured—beer for David, white wine for Oscar, and port for Arthur—and Oscar was showing round his latest acquisition. Oscar had begun as a collector of J. R. R. Tolkien. But as prices for Tolkien skyrocketed after the *Lord of the Rings* movies were released, he changed his focus to Tolkien's influences, from early English poetry to Icelandic epics. The book he proudly displayed tonight was the 1870 first edition of an English translation of the *Völsunga*—a Nordic saga that had also been a source for Richard Wagner, and which featured both a magical golden ring and a broken sword reforged. The translation had been done in part by William Morris, the great designer, poet, and printer of Victorian England. The volume was bound in green cloth, with a stunning floral cover design by Morris's associate Philip Webb.

"The pages are uncut," said Oscar, "which always presents something of a problem." The problem was that a book with uncut pages was considered more valuable—being in its original unread condition—but leaving the pages uncut meant never reading it.

"Cut them," said David, slapping the book with his hand. "A book is to read. Don't tell me you think William Morris wouldn't cut the pages."

"Have nothing in your houses that you do not know to be useful, or believe to be beautiful," said Arthur, repeating his favorite Morris quote.

"Exactly," said David. "No question that book is beautiful, but with uncut pages it's not very useful."

"But I can always read the text somewhere else," said Oscar meekly. "Maybe online?"

"Not the same!" bellowed David. "This is your book. You spent hundreds of hours with miniature cretins and long division to earn it. You should damn well be able to sit in your own chair and read it."

"Hear, hear," said Arthur. "Feel the paper, turn the pages. Neither Tolkien nor Morris would abide reading a book any other way." Arthur passed Oscar a razor-sharp knife that he kept in the drawer of a side table for this very purpose. Oscar took the knife in one hand and gingerly held the book in the other. He laid the book on the coffee table, opened to the first gathering, and slipped the blade between the pages.

"Do it," said David. "William Morris wants you to."

Cringing, Oscar pulled the knife through the paper as the others held their breath. The blade made a muffled hiss. Oscar laid down the knife and opened the now accessible pages to the main body of the text. "This is the same translation Tolkien read as a schoolboy," said Oscar, his voice trembling. The three men sat in silence for a moment as Oscar looked over the first few pages. "Next week," he said. "By next week I'll have cut all the pages and found the perfect passage to read." He closed the book and smiled.

"Well," said Arthur, "I see the glasses are empty, and I think the opening up of pages that haven't seen the light of day since they were printed a hundred and forty-six years ago deserves something special. Champers?"

"I've said it before and I'll say it again," said David. "Hear, hear!"

When the Champagne had been poured, Arthur picked up a small, slim volume from the mantel. He had found this little book several years ago in a bookstall in London's Portobello Road but had not read it all the way through until the previous week. Published in 1848, it contained the sort of long-forgotten wit that Arthur enjoyed sharing with the BBs. He settled into his chair and cleared his throat. "A reading from the book of *The Natural History of Tuft-Hunters and Toadies*," he said solemnly. David did not attend church, but Oscar would understand the allusion. Arthur began to read:

> Everybody has some natural antipathy. There are a great many persons of good sense and taste that entertain a rooted objection to Trafalgar Square, and its fountains, around which the little boys of the metropolis love to congregate, and into which the maid-servant threatens to dip the refractory brat which crieth for the what's-his-name at the top of the great column.
>
> A great many persons dislike Ethiopian Serenaders, the scenery at the Haymarket Theatre, and the farces at the Princess'. Some very good people have a cordial detestation for Joinville ties, halfpenny steampackets, "gents," and amateur performances at the Olympic; and there are equally respectable persons who shun railway speculators, Cheap Clothing Marts, and tariff pine apples. We do not affect singularity, but have our antipathies too, and first and foremost of those antipathies, an unmitigated detestation of, and hostility against all Tuft-hunters whatsoever.

Arthur had chosen this passage because it reminded him of his own "natural antipathy" toward the precentor. He read until the cathedral bells rang a quarter to nine. Then Arthur laid aside his book and, as always, excused himself from the party to go up to the cathedral. He slipped quietly through the west door and walked the entire length of the nave, turning left at the crossing to reach the Epiphany Chapel in the north quire aisle, where he took his usual seat for Compline. He could more easily enter through the north transept door, but Arthur loved the long, sober walk down the empty nave, surrounded by ancient stonework that lurked just out of sight in the dimness. He made a point of wearing hard-soled shoes in the evening, so his footsteps would echo in the vastness.

The precentor had instituted the nightly singing of Compline at Barchester many years earlier, and Arthur loved the service. Unlike Evensong, sung by a full choir, Compline was rarely sung by more than three or four people, but the precentor's rule was strict: Whosoever attends Compline sings Compline. The service was always held in the snug confines of the Epiphany Chapel and lit by only a few candles. The canons took it in turn to lead the service, and some sang better than others. Tonight, the service was led by Canon Howard, who had once been a chorister, so the congregation, of which Arthur constituted one third, stayed on key. Arthur shivered when the canon sang the words:

Be sober, be watchful; your adversary the devil prowls about like a roaring lion, seeking someone to devour. Resist him, firm in your faith.

Arthur's voice trembled slightly as he sang in response, "Thanks be to God."

In the medieval monastery of Barchester, Compline had been the last of the seven daily services, sung just before the monks retired for the night. With its emphasis on endings and its haunting chants, it always put Arthur in a somewhat melancholy mood. The service lasted only a few minutes, and even though he walked home slowly, by nine thirty, he was back in his sitting room, sipping the dregs of the Champagne and listening to David talk about what a coup it was that he had convinced the American author Melanie Stanwick to come to Barchester for a signing. Stanwick was the hottest commodity at the moment in the world of what was politely called "erotic romance."

"What's her latest book called?" asked Arthur, "*Sleazy Passions? Sensual Unpleasantness?*"

"I think it's *The Stultifying Sultriness of a Saucy Suburbanite*," said Oscar.

"Oscar's been reading the OED again," said Arthur.

"It happens to be called *Spring Heat*," said David, "and it's a bestseller."

"And have you read this bestseller?" said Arthur.

"Of course I haven't. It's utter rubbish, but that doesn't mean I won't sell a hundred copies at the signing."

"And it doesn't mean you won't try to reenact some of the scenes from the book with the author," said Arthur.

"Just because a woman writes erotic fiction doesn't mean she sleeps with every bookseller on her tour," said David.

"So you're not going to try to take her to bed?" said Oscar.

"Don't be ridiculous," said David. "Of course I'm going to try to take her to bed—but without prejudice. I'd try just as hard if she were a Nobel Prize winner."

"You're such an egalitarian," said Oscar. The great bell of the cathedral echoed out the first stroke of ten—the accepted sign that the meeting of the BBs was adjourned.

"Well, gentlemen," said Arthur, rising from his seat, "now that we have, as always, broken our solitary rule against the discussion of affairs, and with the unsavory image of David bedding a Nobel laureate ready to haunt my dreams, I bid you good night."

The Champagne had made Arthur feel alert rather than groggy, and so, after the others had left, he repaired to his study and his secret collection—a case of books about King Arthur and his knights, and about the Holy Grail. These were the books that he read again and again, looking for a clue, a hint to help him solve the mystery that had intrigued him since childhood. He turned on a lamp and settled into a wing chair to spend an hour with his books searching for the Grail.

He had kept his promise to his grandfather to keep his search a secret, though he had still not discovered the reason for that secrecy. That promise was why his Grail library was hidden away upstairs. Besides which, he liked having a secret, something that connected him and only him to his grandfather, but he also felt a slight shame and guilt that he kept a part not just of his book collection but of his life from his friends.

Arthur's collection of Arthurian literature was not large and contained few items of great value—this was a working collection. Thomas Malory had worked from several sources, both French and English, and Arthur had modern translations of all the earlier versions of the Grail stories—the works of Chrétien de Troyes and Robert de Boron and Wolfram von Eschenbach. Each of these medieval writers had his own vision of what the Grail really was. He had later works as well—all of Tennyson's volumes of Arthurian poetry, including *The Holy Grail*, in their green cloth bindings, and a number of more recent academic studies on Grail lore and history.

He had bought, and read, many of the twentieth-century adaptations of the Arthur legends—*The Sword in the Stone, The Mists of Avalon*, and so on, but he always preferred Malory. Those later versions, he felt, tried to impose some sort of order into a collection of legends that he loved for their disjointedness, their narrative chaos. It was odd that Arthur, who was himself almost obsessively organized, should be so drawn to such a loosely knit narrative. He supposed it was because of the very medievalness of the legends—reading them in Malory was a constant reminder that these stories were written hundreds of years before the invention of the novel, before the idea that a long narrative could be anything other than a collection of vaguely related short narratives. The one exception to his anti-twentieth-century bias was the film *Monty Python and the Holy Grail*. The cobbling together of comedy sketches that never really told a coherent story seemed to Arthur to fit the idea of the medieval original. And the movie was the perfect union of his two collecting passions—the Arthur legends and British humor. The item in his collection in which he guessed his grandfather would take most delight was a copy of the screenplay signed by every Python.

Tonight he pulled down the second volume of his prized possession— the 1816 edition of Malory's *Morte d'Arthur* edited by Alexander Chalmers.

It was the first edition of Malory published after the Stansby version Arthur had held so recently—a lapse of 182 years in which the Knights of the Round Table were absent from the public consciousness. With the Romantic revival came a surge of interest in all things medieval and King Arthur and the Grail returned. Arthur cringed to think that the legends might have remained buried and obscure—known only to academic medievalists—if the Romantics hadn't dug them up. He read for an hour, words so familiar he could recite many passages from memory, then laid the book on a side table and sighed deeply.

Although he lived quietly, suffering through his job and rarely leaving Barchester, although he had never ridden a horse across a desert, or flown in a plane, or gone on an adventure of any sort, Arthur nonetheless thought of himself as a Grail hunter. Ever since that conversation with his grandfather, he had believed in the Grail. He couldn't help believing in it, the same way he couldn't help *not* believing in God. He believed the Grail was real, he believed it could be found, and, thanks both to his grandfather and to other discoveries he had made over the years, he believed it might well be in or near Barchester. But if it was ever found, it would not be by an action hero, thought Arthur, but by a scholar. And even though the discovery would bring him neither fame nor fortune, because of his promise to his grandfather to keep the Grail a secret, Arthur intended to be that scholar.

This was the life of Arthur Prescott. It was a life of rhythms—rhythms that irritated him, like the cycle of meetings and lectures and tutorials at the university; rhythms that stimulated him, like his walks with Gwyn and his evenings with David and Oscar; rhythms that challenged him, like his perennially exciting yet dependably frustrating work in the cathedral library; rhythms that intrigued him, like his regular rereading of the Grail stories; and the rhythm that soothed him, the daily life of the cathedral: Morning Prayer, Evensong, and Compline repeating like the motion of the planets, eternal and unchanging. Arthur lived by these rhythms; he depended on them; they guaranteed the immutable truths of his life—that work would always be an annoyance, that the cathedral guide would never be completed, that he would remain forever single, that the Grail would always beckon him, and that in spite of all this, he would be reasonably happy, lulled by the ancient rhythms of the cathedral and by the timeless texts and bindings of the books in which he immersed himself, into knowing that his life was only a ripple in rhythms that would drive the world until its end.

In such a mind-set Arthur, so he believed, did not need a stranger to arrive in Barchester; he did not need to be dragged into the twenty-first century; and he certainly did not need to fall in love.

III

THE CHAPTER HOUSE

The chapter house, traditional meeting place of the cathedral canons, is one of the lightest, airiest spaces in the precincts. This octagonal room, supported by a single central pillar, boasts clear windows in the Decorated style that cover every wall from just above the stone seats to the vaulted ceiling and admit sunshine at all times of day. The stained glass in this fourteenth-century structure was destroyed during the Civil War, but the change from the dim meeting room of the Middle Ages to the bright space we see today can hardly be considered for the worse.

A.D. *794, St. Ewolda's Monastery*

The Monastery of St. Cuthbert
Lindisfarne Island

12 June 793

Brethren,

I send tidings of great sadness. Most of my fellow monks at Lindisfarne lie dead—victims of a fierce and savage attack from a pagan race. They came from the sea and attacked like stinging hornets, like ravening wolves; they made raids on all sides, slaying not only

cattle but priests and monks. They came to the Holy
church at Lindisfarne and laid all to waste, trampled
the Holy places with polluted feet, dug down the al-
tars, and bore away the treasures of the church. Some
of the brethren they slew, some they carried away cap-
tive, some they drove out naked after mocking and vex-
ing them. Some they drowned in the sea.

Our waters run with blood, our faces with tears after
this unholy desecration. The cover of our great Gospel
has been rent from the Holy book, but the word of the
Lord remains. Look to your treasures, look to your lives,
look to the sea.

In Christ,
Aelfwic

"And this is what brings you to St. Ewolda's," said Cyneburga, laying the letter on the table. She had been summoned from her private prayers to meet with this stranger and was not well disposed to show him sympathy.

"Yes, Mother Abbess. We received the news at Glastonbury just a few weeks ago," said the monk. He was dressed in a traveling cloak and had arrived on foot at the abbey that morning, along with two heavily laden servants. "Beaduwulf, our father abbot, fears a similar attack could come to Glastonbury and has instructed me to hide certain of the abbey's treasures in foundations that are less likely to . . . interest the infidels."

"So our poverty has attracted you," said the abbess. "Not because you, as one of the wealthiest monasteries in the land, wish to aid us in our need but because you find our destitution convenient."

"Such a small foundation, with so few brothers and sisters, might well avoid the grasp of these monsters," said the monk, ignoring Cyneburga's jab.

"Six," said the abbess.

"Six?"

"We have six brothers and sisters—as devoted to our Lord Christ as any at Glastonbury. The only difference between our foundation and yours is that while we *all* hunger for righteousness, we also hunger."

"I have not come to discuss wealth or poverty," said the monk, throwing off his hood for the first time and rising from his somewhat stooped position to his impressive full height. "I bear relics that are beyond value and Beaduwulf has decreed that one of these shall rest with you for a time. You should show nothing but thanks and humility. You should fall on your knees before this treasure and pray to the God of your salvation, giving thanks for Beaduwulf and his generosity, giving thanks that your suffering has brought the divine into your midst. You have been chosen and yours is not to complain of poverty; yours is to say only 'Let it be according to thy word,' and take the blessed burden you are called to protect."

Cyneburga had passed sixty-two years on the earth. The daughter of a traveling merchant, she had been converted to Christianity by one of the sisters of St. Ewolda's and had entered the monastery at seventeen. She had seen almost fifty years of daily prayer and worship and had risen to the post of abbess in this foundation that, since the death of Wigbert more than two hundred years ago, had always been ruled by women, as a way to honor St. Ewolda. In all her dealings with monks and nuns over those years, in all her interactions with servants and farmers and cooks, in her meetings with priests and bishops—never had anyone spoken to her like this young monk of Glastonbury. She rose out of her chair and was opening her mouth to berate his insolence when she felt a hand on her shoulder. There was no one else in the room, and Cyneburga knew instantly it was the same hand she had felt when she stood outside the monastery as a young woman, trying to decide whether she wished to pass through that gate and commit her life to Christ. Immediately her anger melted away and she fell to her knees.

"Forgive me, brother," she said. "I have allowed my worldly frustrations to cloud my vision of what God calls me to do. What protection we can give through the power of St. Ewolda we shall bestow upon whatever treasures Beaduwulf trusts to our care."

"One treasure only shall rest here in your keeping, good Cyneburga, one most suited to your care, for though it may appear humble and of little worth, it is nonetheless touched by God."

"Show me this treasure," said Cyneburga, "and I will protect it, even with my life."

"Beaduwulf thanks you, Mother Abbess. By taking this charge you are serving God as few will ever have the chance to do."

The monk stepped out of the small hut in which he and the abbess had been speaking and summoned the two servants, who stood waiting in the yard. It took no more than a few minutes to unpack the treasure that had been sent from its home in Glastonbury and set it before the abbess.

"This is not what I expected," said Cyneburga.

"The gifts of God rarely are," replied the monk.

April 12, 2016

THIRD TUESDAY AFTER EASTER

The first time he saw her, he mistook her for a statue. The dean had mentioned the idea of a sculpture show in the chapter house, and when Arthur noticed the door standing open, he glanced in and saw a figure, silhouetted in the afternoon light that streamed down from above. Not the Virgin Mary, he thought, but perhaps Helen—Helen the mother of Constantine and discoverer of the True Cross. Her face was raised to the light, and her eyes seemed fixed on the empty stone panel above the bishop's seat. And then she moved. Arthur felt he should look away, that he had intruded on some moment of intimacy, but something about the way the sun gleamed in her loose blond hair and the puzzled expression on her face as she consulted the worn booklet in her hand held him entranced. Who was she? Not some rare tourist—the chapter house was open to the public only on Sundays. She must be someone with permission from the dean to stand immobile in beams of sunlight. Arthur was just about to back away and head toward the library when she spoke.

"I don't suppose you know where the painting is?" she said calmly, as if she were continuing a conversation already begun rather than turning to confront a man staring at her from the doorway.

"The . . . the painting?" said Arthur, stepping from the shadows of the cloister into the light of the chapter house.

"The portrait of Bishop Gladwyn and the Holy Grail."

Arthur felt the hairs on the back of his neck bristle. How could this stranger know about Gladwyn's portrait?

"It's not the Holy Grail," he said tersely.

"So you *do* know the painting. Churchgirl42 posted a picture of it on Instagram, but the only reason I found it is because I don't just follow the hashtag Holy Grail, but I also follow a bunch of others, and she tagged it with hashtag chalice, but she didn't say where it was except Barchester. So I went to the cathedral Web site to order a guidebook, but apparently they don't have one. I even e-mailed and they said the guy who is writing it keeps missing deadlines, so I got this one on eBay, but it's from the 1890s, so I guess it's a little out of date, but it says that John Collier's portrait of Bishop Gladwyn is supposed to hang in the chapter house, and this is the chapter house, right?"

This speech left Arthur feeling as breathless as he imagined she must be after such a torrent of words.

"I think I understood about a third of what you just said," said Arthur.

"I just wondered if you knew what happened to Bishop Gladwyn's portrait."

"It's moved," he said at last. "It was moved in 1905."

"Excellent—someone who actually knows what I'm talking about," she said, striding forward and extending her hand. "I'm Bethany. Bethany Davis. I'm here to digitize the manuscripts in the library."

She was shaking Arthur's hand vigorously and her words almost did not register on his consciousness. How was he touching the skin—the cool, smooth, utterly relaxed skin—of this living statue? He had managed to escape the university after lunch and was on his way to a peaceful afternoon in the cathedral library and now there was this . . . this American, he guessed from her accent, shaking his hand and looking boldly into his eyes awaiting some sort of response to whatever she had just said.

"You're . . . I'm sorry, you're what?"

"Here for the manuscripts in the library. I'm going to digitize them."

"That sounds perfectly dreadful," said Arthur, extricating his hand from hers and finding the world returning to focus. "What does it even mean?"

"Oh, you must be Mr. Prescott. Gwyn said that would be your reaction. You're exactly who I need to talk to."

"Whom."

"I beg your pardon?" said Bethany.

"I am to whom you need to talk."

"Right."

"But tell me again—what exactly are you doing to our manuscripts?"

"It's part of this worldwide project. It's really exciting. The whole thing is funded by this billionaire in the Midwest who made all his money . . . well, I'm not sure how he made all his money, but anyway. He has this plan to digitize every pre-Reformation Christian manuscript in the world. He's going to put all the images online and make them available to everybody. Can you imagine?"

"And when you say digitize . . ."

"I've got this awesome setup. Most places won't let you do manuscripts automatically, like with books, which I can totally understand. So I have this adjustable stand that holds the volume—cradles it, really—and then this amazing digital camera that works in low light so you don't have to risk damaging pages with flashes and stuff. And then I go over every page in this software program that lets me adjust—well, anything that needs adjusting."

"Sounds revolting."

"You're just like Gwyn said you would be. I knew I was going to like you. How about some tea? Or if it's too early for tea, then lunch. Unless it's too late for lunch. What do you do then? The pub? I don't really drink, but they have Diet Coke at the pub, right? Come on, drinks are on me."

Before Arthur realized what had happened she had linked her arm through his and was dragging him toward the cloister. Given no choice in the matter, he led her out of the cathedral precincts, down Magdalen Street, and through the imposing front door of the Mitre, Barchester's poshest hotel. The bar, where they settled at a small table, had a view across the water meadows to the cathedral, but that was not why Arthur had brought Bethany here. Still not quite sure what he was doing, he allowed her to buy him a pint of bitter.

"So, Gwyn tells me you're a book collector," said Bethany, when she had returned with the drinks.

"Yes, I suppose I'm a species that won't exist once you and your ilk have reduced the world of books to bits and bytes. But for the time being I collect physical copies of the works of the English humorists."

"Anybody I might have heard of?"

"I suppose P. G. Wodehouse is the most famous. I have nearly all his books in first editions." Bethany stared blankly at him as if she were a robot in need of rebooting. "P. G. Wodehouse? He wrote the Jeeves and Wooster stories."

"Oh, right. I've heard of those. I don't read that much fiction these days. I watched one of the shows on YouTube."

"If you don't read fiction, what do you read?"

"Stuff for work, mostly. Lots of blogs on information management and IT, e-magazines. I mean, it's not like I don't read books. I have an e-reader, of course. I just read a great monograph on the postbook library from this guy I heard at ALA."

"I'm sorry, are you speaking English?"

"ALA is the American Library Association."

"But what do you mean by the 'postbook library'?"

"It's amazing. You see, technology is exploding the possibilities for libraries. Now they can exist virtually. Imagine a library that has no building, almost no expenses, and can be used by everyone on the planet."

"A library without books?"

"Yeah, pretty cool, huh?"

"You do know that *library* is derived from the Latin *librarius*, meaning 'concerned with books.' Not computers—books."

"If you want to play the etymology game," said Bethany, "I read in this same article that the word *librarius* is derived from *liber*, meaning 'the inner bark of trees.' Do you really think we need to fill our libraries with the inner bark of trees?"

"Touché," said Arthur, thinking perhaps he had underestimated this young lady.

"The postbook library is a little different from the cathedral library here. Gwyn took me up there this morning just to show me around. Kind of old-fashioned. Can you believe there's no wireless? Honestly, I don't know how you get much work done with no digital technology."

"The only time I employ digital technology," said Arthur, trying his best to sound charming rather than haughty, "is when I use my fingers to turn the pages."

"That's what I mean," said Bethany. "You need to get wired."

Really? thought Arthur. Not a chuckle or a harrumph or even a groan for his little "digital" quip? It might have been a bad joke, but she didn't seem to understand it was a joke at all.

"Why would a library that has served its constituents well for nearly a thousand years need to become, as you say, 'wired'?" He was imagining the priceless books of his beloved library—the objects that soothed and stimulated and educated him, that connected him to scores of generations past and that he believed would connect him to generations yet to come—replaced by blinking lights and metal boxes and flickering screens. It was a horrific vision.

"But who are your constituents?" said Bethany.

"Our constituents have been everyone from monks learning how to raise sheep to priests writing sermons to students studying history—"

"Sure, in the past, but Gwyn said almost nobody uses the library these days."

"I do," said Arthur.

"Is that really an efficient use of resources?" said Bethany. "An entire library for one reader? In the digital world, anybody on the planet could be your constituent. And it works both ways. Let me ask you this—what's keeping you from finishing your guide to the cathedral?"

"To be honest, it's the dearth of information on our founder. She was a Saxon saint called Ewolda. We know she founded a monastery here and we know she was martyred sometime before the early eighth century, but that's about all we—"

"OK, imagine this scenario," said Bethany, interrupting excitedly. "There is a manuscript at, say, the Huntington Library. That's in California. And this manuscript contains information about your St. Ewolda. Now, in the old days you would first have to stumble upon the knowledge that such a manuscript existed and that there was a mention of your saint in it. Then, with no safe or cheap way to copy a medieval manuscript, you would have to fly halfway around the world and examine the manuscript in person. When this project I'm working on is done, you'll type 'Ewolda' into a search engine, in two seconds it will tell you that she is mentioned in a manuscript at the Huntington and you'll click a link and go directly to a high-resolution image of the passage in question. You can't tell me that's not a better way to do research."

Arthur could feel himself being drawn over to the dark side. "I'd love to go to the Huntington," he said at last. "Would I rather go on an exciting journey, visit an amazing museum, work in a beautiful reading room where I might meet other scholars, and get to feel and see and smell the manuscript that holds the key to my research; or would I like to sit alone in my study with a computer screen? It's an easy choice for me."

"Yes, but you're saying research should be elitist. That only people with lots of spare time who can afford to fly around the world deserve to have access to information."

"Point well scored," said Arthur. He was enjoying this.

"You asked why your library should become wired. It's not just so you can access information; it's so you can share information. After all, the purpose of a library is to disseminate information," said Bethany.

"Is it?" said Arthur. "I have always felt that the definition of a library in the *Oxford English Dictionary* was a rather good one. 'A public institution or establishment, charged with the care of a collection of books, and the duty of rendering the books accessible to those who require them.'"

"Yes, but at the moment nobody seems to require the cathedral's books."

"At the moment," said Arthur, "but let me tell you a story. When I was working on my graduate thesis, I needed to consult a copy of a catalog from an exhibit held in Paris in 1875. There was no copy in the Bodleian or the British Library, and when I rang the Bibliothèque National de France, they didn't have a copy either. So I started making the rounds of the college libraries in Oxford, just in case one might turn up, and, to my great delight, I discovered there was a copy where I should have looked first, in my very own college library. Now, Lazarus keeps excellent circulation records, and when I checked the book out, the librarian, who was of course a friend of mine, informed me that I was the first to do so since it was acquired in 1875. I laughed and said to him, 'Who on earth do you suppose they bought it for?' and without pausing a second to think he said, in all seriousness, 'Why, Arthur, they bought it for you.' That's the point of a library. A book that no one wants to read today may be essential for someone in the future. So we save them, we protect them."

"But don't you think," said Bethany, "that libraries should be more proactive in getting the books into the hands of . . . what did you call them, 'those who require them'? A book shouldn't have to wait around a hundred years for a reader to take interest and a reader shouldn't have to stumble around from library to library hoping to find the book he needs. Libraries exist for the active sharing of information."

"Libraries exist to preserve culture," said Arthur.

"But we *are* preserving culture." said Bethany. "By scanning texts, we remove the danger of fire or flood or bugs or careless readers or theft. Books are safe online."

"Let's assume for a moment your statement is true, even though clearly the Internet is much more susceptible to bugs and viruses and power outages than the Barchester Cathedral Library."

"In other words, you're *not* assuming it's true."

"Right. Perhaps I should have said let's set aside that obviously incorrect statement. Would you rather look at a work of art online or in a museum?"

"Does the museum have a good café and a nice gift shop?"

"Say yes, for the sake of argument."

"And you do love a good argument. It's the first thing Gwyn told me about you."

"Guilty," said Arthur.

"Obviously I'd rather look at art in a museum. I'd rather see the original. In that case, there is so much you can't discern in a reproduction—the texture of the paint and the way a sculpture changes in different light. But text is text, no matter where I read it."

"Yes, text is text, but that's not the same as saying books are books whether physical or digital."

"Isn't it?"

"A library is like an art museum where you're allowed to touch the paintings and embrace the sculpture, run your fingers across every brushstroke and chisel mark."

"OK, I admit, I would love that museum."

"In my nondigital world I can feel the smoothness of vellum, the softness of well-worn rag paper, the crispness of a new novel printed on acid-free stock so fresh the pages still stick together at the edges until I wet my thumb to turn the leaf over. What about that thrill of taking a new trade paperback and fanning out the pages—seeing the entire book at once. Can you do that with a digital file? And the smell. Blindfold me and I'll tell you more about a book from its smell than you could ever tell from a computer. How old it is, where it's spent those years, how often it's been read—the smell of a book can tell you more than you think."

This speech left Bethany silent for a change, staring at her empty glass. Arthur hoped she was thinking about what he said, not envisioning some fresh digital hell. Computers smelled so . . . lifeless.

"You make some good points," said Bethany at last. "But still, why not let the two technologies live side by side, each doing what it does best? What happened to make you hate the digital world so much?"

"Why did something have to happen?"

"But something did, didn't it?"

Her insight was annoying, but Arthur saw no reason not to be honest. "When I was a child," he said, "I went to the library every Saturday morning. It was the highlight of my week. Our local city library was in this beautiful nineteenth-century building that used to be the Mechanics Institute. I would push through those oak doors every Saturday and head straight for the card catalog. I loved those little drawers so full of mystery and potential. Most weeks I would just pick a drawer at random and flip through the cards, maybe looking for one that was brand-new or one that had been thumbed ten thousand times. And I always found something amazing. Bookish kids who don't enjoy football or video games don't have a lot of friends, but I always thought of that card catalog as my best friend. Then one Saturday, when I was a teenager, I walked into the central room, with its beamed ceiling and its huge stone fireplace at one end, and the card catalog was gone. There was this great empty space and a little table with two computers on it. They took away my best friend, and the library never felt the same after that. The computer made it easy to find what you were looking for, but I never *knew* what I was looking for. The card catalog had given me serendipity." Arthur paused for a moment, almost misty-eyed as he remembered that awful day. "I suppose that's one thing I like about the cathedral library and its lack of wires. We still have a card catalog."

"Wow," said Bethany. "OK, I understand. That must have sucked." She sat quietly for a moment, her hand next to his on the table. "Can I ask you a question that has nothing to do with books or computers?"

"I suppose."

"This isn't even a proper pub; just a hotel bar. And we passed at least three nice-looking pubs on the way here. The Green Man, right outside the cathedral—which should be perfect given that I saw a green man carving in the cloister; then there was the George and Vulture, which sounds royal and you seem like a royalist to me, being old-fashioned about everything; and then the Swan, next to the river."

"I'm sorry, was there a question buried somewhere in that geography lesson?"

"Yeah. Why did you bring me here? Why the Mitre?"

"And so at last we come full circle. The Mitre is so named because, from about 1570 until after the last war, it was the bishop's palace. The chapter sold it in the 1950s to raise money to repair some of the damage done by German bombers in 1941."

"So this is part of your unpublished guidebook?"

"It might be. But more important, it is the answer to your question."

"Which question?"

"The first one. When I first saw you standing in the chapter house . . ." Arthur paused for a moment. He had been about to say, with your hair glowing in the sun like a halo, but he checked himself. "When I first saw you, you asked me about the portrait of Bishop Gladwyn."

"The one with him holding the Holy Grail."

"The one with him holding a Communion chalice," said Arthur slowly and distinctly. This girl was interesting to debate with, but he didn't want her getting any ideas about the Grail's being connected to Barchester. "After the bishop died, a member of the chapter thought it an inappropriate adornment for the chapter house."

"Because of pagan connections to the Grail?"

"It's not the Grail," he said, trying to temper his anger. "It was moved because of the artist, John Collier, and his second wife."

"Oh, this is sounding better all the time. Do tell."

"You see, in 1879 Collier married Marian Huxley—whose father had argued on the side of science in the great evolution debate with Bishop Samuel Wilberforce in 1860."

"And the canons didn't want that Darwinian bloodline in their chapter house."

"No, it wasn't that. Two years after Marian's death in 1887, Collier decided to marry her younger sister Ethel. Because both the church and English law forbade such a union, the couple married in Norway."

"Wait, why would there be a law against . . . what was the law against?"

"Against marrying your wife's sister. It was considered incest until . . . I would have to check, but I think the law was changed in 1907."

"So the second marriage was . . ."

"In the eyes of the law, it was incestuous."

"Oh, my."

"Apparently one of the Barchester canons didn't care for the scandal, and before Gladwyn was cold in his tomb in the Epiphany Chapel, the portrait was removed from the cathedral precincts."

"How delicious. But what does all that have to do with my question?"

"When they took the portrait out of the chapter house, they hung it at the top of the main stairwell in the bishop's palace."

"And it's still there, isn't it?"

"Would you like to see it?"

"You bet I would."

Arthur pushed back his chair and called out to the barman. "Robert, I'm going to take this young lady to visit Bishop Gladwyn, if you don't mind."

The interior of the bishop's palace had been completely renovated in the eighteenth century, and the main staircase was an elegant affair. Wide steps rose to a spacious landing from which two shorter staircases led to the two wings of the building. On the paneled wall of the landing hung a life-size portrait with a small gold plaque at the bottom of the frame reading "Robert Gladwyn, Bishop of Barchester, 1872–1905."

Arthur led Bethany into the front hallway and then told her to look up. She gasped as she saw the bishop gazing down on them.

"Let's take a closer look, shall we?" said Arthur. "There is a lot to see." He and Bethany mounted the stairs and stopped in front of the portrait. Arthur stood silent for several minutes, letting Bethany take in the richness of the painting's color and its fine details, so that her first impression might not be clouded by his comments.

In front of an altar, a gray-haired clergyman with piercing blue eyes stood holding a golden cup in the air with both hands. Rays of light seemed to emanate from the cup and intersect with other rays streaming in from the stained glass window above. The draping of his vestments was painted in great detail, as were the decorative tiles of the floor. On the altar stood an elaborate gold cross and two flickering candles in gold candlesticks. To the right of the altar, on a small silver table, lay a jewel-encrusted book.

"What do you think?" Arthur asked at last.

"It's beautiful," said Bethany. "The details in the vestments remind me of the tapestry in Waterhouse's painting *The Lady of Shalott*. I've always loved the Pre-Raphaelites—partly because they were so fascinated by the Grail but also for the richness of detail. But I've mostly just seen reproductions in books, not the originals. This is so alive. I guess you like that I appreciate the difference."

"Waterhouse wasn't a Pre-Raphaelite," said Arthur, "and of course *The Lady of Shalott,* though certainly Arthurian in nature, was a nineteenth-century invention of Tennyson."

"Yes, I know that, Arthur," said Bethany. "But in the same way Tennyson was influenced by Malory and that whole crowd, Waterhouse was influenced by the Pre-Raphaelites—that's all I'm trying to say."

"So was Collier," said Arthur.

"You can see every stitch in his vestments," said Bethany, leaning toward the painting until her nose almost touched the canvas.

"Indeed," said Arthur, falling quiet again while Bethany undertook a closer examination.

"OK," she said at last, stepping back. "Now, tell me about all the iconography. I can see you're dying to."

"First of all, we see the bishop is wearing his red Eucharistic vestments—his chasuble but also his stole and his maniple, that's the cloth draped over his arm. The red at that time was for the feasts of martyrs, which is one way we know the painting shows the bishop on the feast day of St. Ewolda. Then there are the four golden images stitched into the vestments."

"They're so small," said Bethany, squinting at the painting. "I can hardly make them out. Is that a woman holding a cup?"

"They each show Ewolda. Nearly all we know about her is contained in those four images."

"No wonder you don't know much."

"The originals are much easier to see," said Arthur.

"The originals?"

"The images on the bishop's vestments are based on four carved ceiling bosses in the cloister of the cathedral. I'll show you sometime, if I can tear you away from your . . . what do you call it—your digitizing."

"Hey, you'll appreciate my digitizing one day. Now tell me about the cup."

Arthur hesitated. She seemed a nice enough young woman, but all that talk of digitizing worried him. Telling her that he had strong reason to believe the cup in the painting *was* meant to be the Holy Grail would not exactly be breaking his promise of secrecy to his grandfather. In Barchester at least, Gladwyn's obsession with medievalism was no great secret. But if this young woman was interested in the Grail, he had no desire to encourage her to pursue that interest on his turf. "Not the Holy Grail, I think," he said. "Simply a Communion cup. I believe the painting is meant to show the moment in the service before the elements are distributed just after the Prayer of Consecration."

"You don't think that's the Grail table?" said Bethany, pointing to the small table in the painting.

"What do you mean?"

"Malory writes about the Grail sitting on a silver table, and that's a silver table."

"I never thought about that," said Arthur, who, to his great consternation, never had. It bothered him that this American knew her *Morte d'Arthur* so well. "A coincidence, I'm sure." But he knew it wasn't. Bethany had pointed out a clue he had completely missed, and that strengthened his own suspicions about the painting.

"Right," she said, "a coincidence. What about that book on the Grail table? What's that?"

"That book is the reason I'm having so much trouble with my cathedral guide."

"How so?"

"That is the lost Book of Ewolda. According to legend, it was a jewel-encrusted manuscript, though that bit is rather unlikely, given Barchester's perennial poverty. It's supposed to contain not just her life story, but also long-lost secrets of the cathedral."

"What happened to it?"

"We've no idea. Probably it was either destroyed by Vikings or destroyed by Normans or destroyed by reformers."

"In other words, there are lots of ways a manuscript could have gone missing in the past thousand years or so."

"Exactly."

"Then why is it in the painting?"

"Gladwyn was a great medievalist. He was fascinated by anything to do with the early history of the cathedral. He wrote that 1890 guidebook you were reading."

"Why didn't he even mention Ewolda?"

"Like me, he knew almost nothing about her," said Arthur, "but I think he believed in the lost manuscript. And he believed one day it would be found."

Arthur felt no guilt about denying to Miss Davis that the cup in the painting of Gladwyn was the Holy Grail. She had been in Barchester a few hours; Arthur had been secretly researching connections between Barchester and the Grail since he was a teenager—and Gladwyn's Grail portrait was one of *his* discoveries. Because the painting was not reproduced in any book, it attracted few visitors, and as far as Arthur knew, no one else had made the specific connection to the Holy Grail that he had made. Even his grandfather had never mentioned Gladwyn's portrait to him. He didn't like the idea of the portrait being on this Instagram, whatever that was, for anyone to see. Barchester and its Grail connections were Arthur's private territory, unknown even to his closest friends. He had no reason to believe that Miss Davis was more than casually interested in the Grail, but if he wasn't going to tell David and Oscar what he knew about Gladwyn's portrait, he certainly wasn't going to tell her. If his grandfather was right and there were ancient secrets lurking in Barchester—secrets about Ewolda or secrets about the Grail—Arthur fully intended to be the one to uncover them.

By the time Arthur and Bethany were back outside, it was nearly time for Evensong. He had meant to get some work done this afternoon, but instead had spent his time . . . doing what? Explaining to a child why books are important? No, that wasn't fair. True, Miss Davis was probably not much older than his students, but she seemed considerably better at mounting a defense against his arguments. Her vision of the future depressed him, but he admired her ability to make her case. If he hadn't gotten to the library today, at least he had engaged in a bit of a battle. As

Bethany wrapped a scarf around her neck against the late afternoon chill, he turned to her and, on a whim, asked, "Why don't you come along with me to Evensong?"

"Oh, I don't think so," said Bethany. "I'm not really a churchgoer. Ironically."

"Why ironically?" asked Arthur, as they walked back toward the cathedral.

"Well, my father is pastor of this megachurch in Florida and ever since I was a kid I was forced to go and I know I'm supposed to be moved to tears by the loud music and the flashing lights and all the preaching and witnessing, but it just never did anything for me, you know. I mean, I don't have a problem with it—whatever works for you, right? It's just not my kind of thing."

"Forgive me for asking, but what exactly is a megachurch?"

"It's a . . . well, the building is more like an auditorium than any church you'd find here in Barchester."

"And the liturgy?"

"There isn't exactly a liturgy. It's mostly a rock band playing and my dad preaching. The original preacher who founded the place—he was amazingly charismatic. Unfortunately, he was so charismatic that he ended up resigning because of what he called 'moral mistakes,' which means he slept with about six church employees. So my dad, who had been an assistant, took over as head pastor. Anyhow, the whole thing left a sour taste in my mouth about churchgoing. I mean, I believe in God, I just don't like to go to church."

"That's funny," said Arthur. "I go to church, but I don't believe in God."

"You don't believe in God?" said Bethany.

"Not in the way that you, or your father, or the Church of England would define him. Anyway, it sounds like we could both use Evensong, and it starts in a few minutes. I'm usually in my seat by now."

"Maybe another time," said Bethany, but Arthur could tell this was her American way of saying no.

"Besides," she said, "I have to stop by my room and pick up an extra USB cable to connect the Wi-Fi hotspot in the library."

"Of course you do," said Arthur, having no idea what she meant.

"I guess we'll be seeing a lot of each other if we're both going to be working up there."

"No doubt," said Arthur coldly. The reintroduction of her purpose in Barchester reminded him of the bibliographical future she claimed to represent.

"Well," said Bethany as they reached the other side of the bridge, "I'm at a little bed-and-breakfast up the road here, so I guess this is where I say good-bye. Thanks for showing me the Holy Grail." Without waiting for a reply, she turned the corner into a narrow lane, and for an instant all Arthur saw of her was her blond hair caught in the wind, flying out behind the head that had already disappeared into the shadows. It was lovely hair, he thought, but why couldn't it be attached to a head that paid attention to what he said. The last thing he wanted in Barchester was some American hunting for the Holy Grail.

IV

THE CLOISTER

The cloister, once used by medieval scribes to pen manuscripts, contains roof bosses dating from the thirteenth century, including four carvings, at the four corners, of St. Ewolda. These bosses still retain flecks of their original paint. The first shows Ewolda in flowing robes, wearing a circlet of gold, indicating royal descent. Next we see her in a nun's habit holding a church, showing that she was in holy orders and was the founder of Barchester's original monastery. In the third carving, she holds two roses, one white and one red, symbols of purity and martyrdom. In the final boss, Ewolda holds a cup overflowing with water.

A.D. 880, St. Ewolda's Monastery

Cenhelm did not like visitors. In the twelve years he had served as abbot of St. Ewolda's, only one visitor had ever come with good news. That had been almost a decade ago, when King Alfred had turned the tide against the Danes at the Battle of Ashdown. For the first time in living memory, the threat of a sacking of the monastery by Vikings had faded. So this morning's visitor was not likely to bring catastrophic news, but still Cenhelm's stomach hardened as he ushered the man into his chamber.

Cenhelm was the first abbot of St. Ewolda's Monastery who oversaw only monks. He had not decided that St. Ewolda's should cease being a dual foundation—it had simply happened. One day, the last of the nuns had died, and no novices had come to the gates since. It had been a peaceful transition, and Cenhelm was happiest when the monastery was peaceful. Sometimes for days, rarely for weeks, once in his memory for nearly three months, he enjoyed a life of quiet contemplation. But inevitably the peace was broken. Two of the brothers would fall into an argument over whose turn it was to tend the monastery's modest flock of sheep. A local merchant would claim he had not been paid for the latest delivery of flour. A fire would break out in the kitchens. Or a visitor would arrive. And a visitor never wanted to speak to a lowly monk; a visitor always wanted the abbot.

"I greet you in the name of Christ, good Cenhelm. Your reputation as a fair and just abbot is known throughout the land." This was an especially unbelievable bit of flattery, as Cenhelm was abbot of possibly the smallest monastery in the British Isles, but he let the visitor continue.

"I am Brother Oswine of the abbey of Glastonbury. I come with greetings from our abbot, Hereferth, who desires me to speak with you on a matter of great importance to our foundation."

"Our kitchens and our place of worship, though surely less grand than what you know at Glastonbury, are open to you, good brother," said Cenhelm, sincerely hoping he could dispense with this monk before the need arose for hospitality.

"If you are able to grant the request of Abbot Hereferth, my stay will be brief and I need not trouble you for food or shelter."

"And what does your abbot request?"

"Nearly a century ago, when word first came of the invasions from the north and the destruction of Lindisfarne, our beloved Abbot Beaduwulf sent to your Abbess Cyneburga one of the great treasures of Glastonbury, that it might be kept safe here from the attacks of the heathens. Now that King Alfred has driven the invaders far from our home, I am sent to retrieve this treasure and restore it to its rightful place at the altar of our monastic church."

"I have no wish to displease your father abbot," said Cenhelm, "but how can you ask of things that happened a century ago? No monk here is older than three score years. How could any remember back through a century?"

"I have no doubt," said Oswine, "that the story of this treasure has been passed down from generation to generation."

"You monks of Glastonbury are wealthy; we are poor. If we had any great treasure we would have sold it long ago."

"No man of God would have sold such a treasure," said Oswine firmly.

Cenhelm feared this visitor would not be as easily dismissed as he had hoped. "I can tell you only this, Brother. I know nothing of any treasure from Glastonbury or anywhere else. You are free to search our church, modest though it is, and any other parts of our meager foundation. You may question any of my brothers and I will instruct them to speak freely and answer you truthfully. But though I offer you hospitality, our means are few. Take no more than three days. Remove any treasure you discover and leave us be."

Oswine agreed to Cenhelm's terms and for the next three days searched every chamber of the monastery, from the kitchens to the cells to the very church itself. Cenhelm was proud of his church. Stone structures were not common in Britain, and part of the foundation's poverty was due to the cost of its construction. He cringed to see the monk pulling stones from the floor to look for hidden treasure.

All sixteen members of the foundation were subjected to Oswine's scowling interrogation. None had any knowledge of a treasure from Glastonbury. Oswine's refusal to reveal what form this treasure took made it difficult for them to cooperate with his search, but, at the instruction of their abbot, they rendered what aid they could.

"It is tragic that such a relic should be lost," said Oswine to Cenhelm at the end of the third day.

"The years in a century are many. I regret that you will never know the fate of what you seek."

"Perhaps," said Oswine icily. "Or perhaps it will yet come to light." By dawn of the following day, he was gone.

Cenhelm waited an entire day after Oswine's departure—followed by a long restless night. Worried the monk might not really be gone, but might instead be spying on St. Ewolda's, he sent several brothers into the surrounding countryside to look for him, but they found no trace. Only then did Cenhelm make his way to the small wattle-and-daub barn that lay some distance outside the precincts. He swept away the hay from the darkest corner of the building to reveal a section of wooden floor. Carefully lifting two of the floorboards, he saw that the box holding the treasure was still in place. He replaced the boards and the hay and was back in his chamber before anyone had noticed his absence. That evening, he sent for the youngest monk in the foundation.

"I serve you, Father," said Leofwine.

"Great service is required of you," said the abbot. "Now that the threat of the northern pagans withdraws, our foundation will not be so isolated. I fear our most recent visitor may be the first of many." He paused for a moment, before adding, almost to himself, "And the power of Glastonbury grows."

"What need we fear from Glastonbury? They serve Christ as we do. We should rejoice in their power. Perhaps now the light of Christ will reach every darkened corner of the land."

"There is a great secret at St. Ewolda's," said the abbot. "A secret I am about to entrust to you."

"I am honored," said the monk.

Cenhelm reached within his robes and withdrew a folded parchment he had kept there since the day he had become Guardian. Its words he had long ago committed to memory, lest anything should happen to the document. Now he held it out to Leofwine.

"This parchment contains all you need to know. You will not sleep this night until its words are deeply etched in your memory. Henceforth you will keep it hidden on yourself at all times. Others may come to St. Ewolda's to seek this parchment and the treasure it describes, but you are to reveal the secrets to no one. Only you will know when the time comes to pass this secret to a new Guardian. Then you must do as I am doing now. But I warn you, the monks of Glastonbury will want to unearth our secret and claim our treasure. Beware of any brother who hails from Somerset."

"But what is this great treasure? And who wrote this document?"

"The document was written by a monk of Glastonbury more than a century ago and has been handed down from one Guardian to the next beginning with holy Cyneburga. The treasure I shall take you to see now. Then you must move with all haste to find a new hiding place. It is dangerous for more than one man to know where such a treasure rests. Mark well how thoroughly our recent visitor searched the monastery, and choose carefully. Now come. The moon is near full, and we shall need no tapers."

Cenhelm led Leofwine into the night and beyond the border of the monastery to the hiding place of the great treasure. He himself had not seen the holy relic since a similar night, more than twenty years ago, shortly after he became Guardian. Then his fear had been attack by Vikings, so he had placed the treasure outside the monastery's precincts. That way, if the heathens came and burned St. Ewolda's to the ground, the treasure would still be safe. Leofwine would have to choose his own hiding place, safe from the new threat of Glastonbury.

The barn was pitch-dark, but Cenhelm had no trouble again uncovering the hidden cavity. This time he removed the box and carried it into the moonlight. He spoke a prayer, and then, with trembling hands, opened the box to reveal the most spectacular treasure in the land.

"I confess," said Leofwine, "I am somewhat disappointed. I expected gold and jewels sparkling in the moonlight."

"There is a saying of Cyneburga that is well known to this day at St. Ewolda's," said Cenhelm. "You have passed but a few months among us, so perhaps you have not yet heard it spoken."

"What is this saying?" said Leofwine.

"The gifts of God are rarely what we expect."

April 19, 2016

FEAST OF ST. ALPHEGE, ARCHBISHOP OF CANTERBURY

"Bethany Davis has gotten her things moved into the library," said the dean with a smile as she hurled a tennis ball across the meadow and watched Mag and Nunc explode after it.

"You know she's doing the devil's work."

"Oh, Arthur, don't be such an old poop. The cathedral is receiving a very tidy sum for allowing the manuscripts to be added to this American database. The chapter thinks we should use the money for technical upgrades: an updated cathedral Web site, a Wi-Fi system. Who knows, maybe we could get you a shiny new computer for the library."

"Why not put the money toward the new Lady Chapel?"

"It's a nice sum, but not that nice a sum," said Gwyn.

"I don't know how I am expected to work in the library with that young woman snapping her camera all day long."

"It will do you some good, Arthur, to be exposed to a member of the general public."

"She's an American."

"A member of the *very* general public."

"And she doesn't breathe when she talks. She just goes on and on and on."

"Then she'll certainly do you some good," said Gwyn. "Someone who can give you a run for your money, conversationally speaking."

"Miss Davis thinks our library isn't fulfilling its purpose because we don't have many users." He had been thinking about what Miss Davis had said and considering how it might be addressed.

"Do we have *any* users other than you, Arthur?"

"A few," said Arthur, "though, I admit, a very few. We don't really have the staff to open the library to the general public."

"The library is an underused resource, certainly."

"I'm not sure computers are the answer, though," said Arthur. "As much as I like spending time alone in the library, I agree that Miss Davis has a point—it shouldn't be just for me. But what makes the library so special is that it's not . . . I don't know, not connected to the modern world. It might be worth thinking about how . . . how other people can experience the same sense of wonder and . . . and sheer joy that I feel when I'm up there. The connection one feels to the past is palpable in that room. If we could help people understand that, we might find ourselves with more of what Miss Davis calls constituents."

"If anyone can figure out a way to do that, Arthur," said the dean, "it's you."

"Might I have a word, Prescott?" said the chairman, poking his head into Arthur's office the next morning.

"I suppose you might," said Arthur, pushing back his chair. Grim as the prospect of a word with Slopes might be, it was still a relief to set aside the grisly essay he had been reading, "Titus Andronicus—Why Shakespeare Condoned Cannibalism."

"You do understand, Prescott, that committee work is one of the requirements of every faculty member."

"Was there a meeting this morning?" asked Arthur. "I assure you I didn't get the memo or the e-mail or whatever other disgusting means of communication is used to summon us to these torture sessions."

"No, there was not a meeting this morning, Prescott, and if you'll calm down, I have a proposal I think you might like."

"You intend to use me for a pilot scheme to see what happens if lecturers are not required to sit on committees?"

"Not precisely. I intend to take you off the Curriculum Expansion Committee."

"Slopes, I could kiss you," said Arthur, leaping up. "May I kiss you?"

"No, you may not," said the chairman, with a stern look. "That is not all I have come to say. I am taking you off the Curriculum Expansion Committee so that I may place you on a committee for which I feel you are eminently more suited."

"The Committee to Eliminate Committees Committee?" said Arthur.

"The Advisory Committee for the Media Center."

"For the what?"

"You like books and libraries and that sort of thing, am I right?"

"I would classify myself as a bibliophile, if that's what you mean," said Arthur. "But what does that have to do with the media center? What is the media center?"

"It's what we used to call the library, you throwback."

"And why do we no longer call it a library?"

"Because we call it a bloody media center!" said the chairman. "Now, do you want to switch committee assignments, or will I see you at the Curriculum Expansion Committee meeting?"

"Is the media center some sort of bookless library?" said Arthur. Was it possible that Miss Davis's vision had already filtered to the silty bottom of the academic world that was Barchester University?

"I see you're already familiar with some of the terminology," said the chairman. "Clearly you'll be a perfect fit. Next meeting is Tuesday at four in Conference Room D."

Slopes turned and marched out of the office, leaving Arthur speechless for a moment, until he thought to shout out, "Where in blazes is Conference Room D?"

"In the media center," came the voice of the chairman from down the hall.

Arthur closed his eyes for a moment, picturing the dark paneling and rows of leather-bound folios in Oxford's Bodleian Library. That was a university library, and for over four hundred years it had preserved printed and manuscript materials, making it an invaluable resource to serious scholars. Arthur cringed to think what Thomas Bodley, who founded the library in 1602, would think if that venerable institution became a "media center." The Bodleian, of course, never had to face the question that had been troubling Arthur since his conversation with Miss Davis. Unlike the cathedral library at Barchester, the Bodleian had a built-in constituency—the students and faculty of one of the great universities of the world. Arthur supposed that when the Barchester collection had begun in the early Middle Ages, those books, though not yet called a library, had a built-in constituency as well. Barchester had been a Benedictine foundation and the Benedictine rule required the monks to spend part of their day reading. Now no such rule existed, and

Barchester's readership had dwindled—but was that a true measure of its importance? The wretched media center had a built-in audience, and no one could argue that that was a more useful institution than the cathedral library. Could they?

The rest of Arthur's day had a distinctly downward trajectory.

"I was thinking for my project I could explore how the epistolary novels of the eighteenth century would have looked as tweets." Miss Stanhope had taken rare advantage of Arthur's office hours to consult about her midterm paper—which everyone now insisted on calling a project, as if, instead of actually writing, they could hand in a sculpture of Charles Dickens made of ice-lolly sticks.

"I'm sorry, you want to do what?"

"Well, tweets today are like letters."

"What in God's name is a tweet?"

"You know, like on Twitter? A tweet."

"Miss Stanhope, this is not an ornithology class."

Twenty minutes later, Miss Stanhope had finally explained that a Web site called Twitter allowed people to exchange messages of up to 140 characters (though why this particular number Miss Stanhope could not say) and that she thought this was the modern equivalent of civilized correspondence. The only satisfaction Arthur had in the conversation was in his own adamant refusal to allow her to rewrite Fanny Burney's *Evelina* as a series of these tweets. He worried, though, what brave new balderdash Miss Stanhope would try next.

As he walked through the cool shadows of the cloister on the way to the library that afternoon, hoping for an hour of peace before Evensong, Arthur could feel the stress and anger of the day seeping away—almost as if the walls of the cathedral could draw the forces of evil from him. Much as he wanted to get to the library, he walked the circuit of the cloister twice, allowing its peace to permeate his mood.

He stopped on the south side and stepped through a stone arch into the open center of the cloister. He stood in the edge of the shadows cast by an ancient yew tree, which spread its gnarled branches over most of that side of the cloister garden. Arthur remembered sitting under that tree as a boy. It had been his favorite place to read in the summer, and it had been the place where he made his own first discovery about Barchester and the Holy Grail. It was the summer after his grandfather had introduced him to Malory, and having spent the year since reading and rereading *King Arthur's Knights,* he had moved on to Tennyson's 1869 collection *The Holy Grail and Other Poems,* borrowed from the Barchester Library. Arthur recalled, as if it had happened last week, reading that book in the cool shadow of the Barchester yew on a warm and hazy summer's day. He remembered the bright green of the textured cloth binding and the sensation of the bumps of words pressed into paper as he ran his fingers across each line. The poem began with Sir Percival, retired to a monastery, recounting his history to a fellow monk. On the second page, Arthur had stopped short at the third line from the top of the page. How funny, he thought, that he could still picture exactly where that line fell on the page.

> *Beneath a world-old yew-tree, darkening half*
> *The cloisters, on a gustful April morn*

Had he been reading those lines anywhere else in Barchester, he might not have thought twice about them, but he read them sitting beneath a "world-old yew-tree, darkening half the cloisters." He had spent months after that day searching through photographs of English cathedrals, looking for a yew tree in a cloister. When he was old enough to travel, he eventually visited every medieval cathedral in England—not one had a yew tree in the cloister. But even before he confirmed that only Barchester matched Tennyson's description, even before he had read another line of poetry on that summer's day, he knew. Sprawled beneath that world-old yew tree he knew that this was no coincidence. His grandfather was right—somehow Barchester and the Grail were inexorably linked. When he showed the passage to his grandfather that evening and told him what he thought it meant, the old man only smiled mysteriously.

Arthur turned from that familiar spot back into the shelter of the cloister walk. By the time he reached the library there was a spring in his step—a spring that immediately fell flat when he saw the morass of wires, computers, tripods, and cameras that took up the entire far end of the room. The cathedral library had found a new constituent, thought Arthur, and he wasn't at all convinced that was a good thing.

"Good afternoon, Mr. Prescott. Nice day at work?" Bethany had her hair pulled back and was wearing a worn pair of jeans and a crisp new T-shirt bearing the crest, such as it was, of Barchester University. The ponytail did little to restrain the wisps of hair around her forehead. "Took me all morning to finish setting up, but I'm really getting down to it now."

Arthur sighed wearily. Not only would he not have the peaceful dimness of the library to himself, he would be subjected to the clicking of Bethany's camera as an incessant reminder that the world of the book was being eroded in his very presence.

"How long are you going to be here?" he said with an audible sigh.

"Wow, way to sound welcoming."

"I'm not trying to be unwelcoming; I'm just seeking a piece of information."

"Judging from the number of pages I've gotten done this afternoon, because like I said I spent the whole morning setting up and then went to the refectory—is that what you call it, or is it just the café? Anyway, I had this ploughman's lunch thing with, I have to tell you, *the* best cheese I have ever put in my mouth. And my grandmother lives in Wisconsin."

"I'm sorry," said Arthur, interrupting when she seemed about to take a breath, "but does this have anything to do with my question?"

"How long am I going to be here, right. I think I can probably digitize an average of about two manuscripts per day, and there are eighty-two manuscripts so I guess that's forty-one days."

"There are eighty-three manuscripts," said Arthur firmly.

"No, there are eighty-two manuscripts. The first thing I did when I got here was count them."

"I have been working at Barchester Cathedral Library since before you were born," said Arthur harshly, exaggerating his point. "I have examined the collection in detail and I keep a copy of Bishop Gladwyn's inventory of 1894 in my desk at home. There are eighty-three manuscripts."

"You want to count them?" said Bethany, as if she were challenging him to arm-wrestle. "I have the Barchester Breviary on the stand in front of my camera, and eighty-one volumes were in the chained library."

"Fine," said Arthur, dropping his satchel on one of the few tables not cluttered with coils of wire and empty canvas equipment bags. He crossed to the manuscript case, where the chains that had once attached to the books still hung from the underside of each shelf. His mood completely ruined and all hope of either work or relaxation before Evensong lost, he began to count.

"No," said Bethany, who had somehow moved directly behind him without his noticing. "Aloud, so I know you're not cheating."

"Why on earth would I be cheating?" said Arthur.

"Because you like to win arguments," said Bethany.

Arthur could not, in good conscience, dispute this assertion, so he started over. It was unnerving to stand here counting aloud like a schoolboy while she hovered over him. She seemed taller than when they had met and he could feel her breath on the back of his neck.

"Is it necessary that you stand quite so close?" said Arthur.

"I need to see what you're doing, don't I?" said Bethany. "You were at the end of the first shelf and you had reached twenty-eight."

Arthur shifted his weight so that he was an inch or two farther away from Bethany, but it did no good. Now she was breathing on the side of his head—practically right into his ear. It was all he could do to remember what number came after twenty-eight.

"Shall I help you?" said Bethany, giving Arthur a gentle shove, which was all it took for him to stumble to the side and allow her to step forward. "I believe the number you're looking for is twenty-nine." She continued to count the manuscripts, slowly and distinctly, as if she were teaching numbers to a toddler. Arthur would have liked to leave her there—simply walk out with his bag and head home, where he might do a little work in peace—but he didn't want to give her the satisfaction. In his mind, this was now a battle for control of the library, so he stayed where he was, growing more exasperated with each crisply enunciated number.

"I have peripheral vision, you know," said Bethany. "Just because I am accurately counting eighty-two manuscripts, doesn't mean I didn't see you roll your eyes just then."

"You were on number sixty-five," said Arthur, crossing his arms against his chest.

"Plus the Breviary means sixteen to go," said Bethany cheerfully.

"Seventeen to go."

But she was right. When the total reached eighty-two and there were no more manuscripts left to count, Arthur dropped his arms from his chest in puzzlement. He wasn't even bothered by the smug look on her face, the almost taunting sparkle in her eyes. This was no longer a contest; this was a mystery.

"There's one missing," said Arthur softly.

"I didn't take it."

"No," said Arthur, "I know you didn't. It's just . . . it's odd. I'm sure Bishop Gladwyn listed eighty-three. I have a copy of his inventory at home. I'll bring it in tomorrow."

"If you had a digital image of it on your phone, we wouldn't have to wait until tomorrow," said Bethany.

"Yes, well, my phone is . . ."

"Anyway, we should go get it. We have to figure out what's missing."

"Do we?" said Arthur.

"Come, come, Mr. Prescott, it's a mystery. Don't you enjoy a mystery? When I was a kid I read those *Petunia and Priscilla* mysteries. Did you ever read those? Probably not, because you were a boy. I loved those books. That's when I first knew I wanted to go to England. Petunia and Priscilla lived next door to each other in two thatched cottages in this little village and they solved . . ."

"Miss Davis." Arthur had meant to say her name sharply, but somehow it came out softly.

"I was doing it again, wasn't I?" said Bethany.

"Digressing," said Arthur.

"Sorry. But you really should read *Petunia and Priscilla*—after we solve the mystery."

"We?"

"You obviously need help if you can't even count on your own," she said.

"I shall consult Bishop Gladwyn's list when I get home this evening," he said. "Now, as you have wasted the precious hour I had reserved for work in the library, I will excuse myself and go to Evensong."

"We didn't waste anything like an hour," said Bethany. "And besides, you like talking to me. It allows you to be righteously indignant and that's your favorite state of being."

"It is most certainly not my . . ."

"You see," interrupted Bethany. "There you go again."

"I really must go, Miss Davis," said Arthur. This young woman was most infuriating. Thank goodness she was no longer pestering him about the Grail. Perhaps her mind flitted from topic to topic as rapidly as her conversation, and her interest in the Grail was long forgotten. And at least she was . . . no—push all such thoughts from the mind. She is a nuisance and nothing more. But as he hoisted his bag over his shoulder, Arthur couldn't help stealing a look back at Miss Davis, who had returned to her work. She was leaning over a manuscript and brushed a stray strand of hair from her face. A beautiful nuisance, he thought, and he shook his head and turned away.

"I suppose you're still not interested in joining me for Evensong," said Arthur, pausing in the doorway, but not daring to look back at her.

"Not exactly the first date I had in mind," she said. He waited for her to add a laugh to this comment—or anything to indicate she was being facetious—but all was silence behind him.

Arthur felt an unfamiliar hot glow creeping up his neck to his cheeks and muttered, "Another time, then," before rushing down the stairs.

He had nearly regained his composure sitting in the quiet of the quire waiting for Evensong to begin when he looked up to see Miss Davis, whispering to one of the vergers as if they were old friends. Arthur closed his eyes and tried to banish all thought of her by playing in his mind the music of William Byrd he would be hearing the choir sing in a few minutes. Arthur had been particularly looking forward to this evening, as the Byrd second service was one of his favorites. During breakfast that morning he had listened to his CD of the Lazarus College Choir singing it. But even those Renaissance tones could not distract him from the conversation taking place a few feet away. He opened his eyes, the music stopped, and the verger was leading Miss Davis to the far end of Arthur's pew. She looked at Arthur and gave a slight nod, then slipped into the pew and took a seat. Arthur could not see her without leaning forward and looking down the row of worshippers, which he was not about to do, and he certainly couldn't speak to her from that distance with the service about to start. But why had she come? Why, when he had issued her a perfectly civil invitation, had she refused him and then come on her own? She had annoyed him before, but this was the first time she had seemed actively rude.

The service was ruined. Distracted by Miss Davis's presence, Arthur could not keep his mind on the Byrd. By the time he could extricate himself from the middle of the pew, she had disappeared. Never mind, he thought. He had a meeting with the BBs that night and would be in civilized company once again.

Arthur's mood brightened considerably when he got home and saw that the post contained a parcel from Christie's. He did not often buy books at auction, but he had had some modest success lately, and although he knew what the package contained, unwrapping it brought him the sort of excitement he once felt on Christmas morning. Inside was a small book bound in green cloth. The condition was far from fine, but Arthur liked how the well-worn cover felt smooth to his touch. The spine was faded from sunlight, and the words *Idylls of the King* were just visible. This was the 1859 first edition of Alfred Lord Tennyson's earliest collection of Arthurian poetry.

Arthur had a later edition of the book already on his shelf upstairs, but this copy was special not only because it was a first but because it had been owned by Robert Gladwyn. If anyone knew more about Barchester, its medieval history, and its possible connections to King Arthur and the Holy Grail than Arthur Prescott, it had certainly been Bishop Gladwyn. Several months ago Arthur had, for a mere two hundred pounds, bought at a small provincial auction house a pair of worn notebooks in which Bishop Gladwyn had kept notes on a wide variety of topics, including the history of the cathedral. Arthur had hoped, when he placed his bid, that the notebooks might contain Gladwyn's thoughts on the Grail, and he had not been entirely disappointed. Although he had read through much of Gladwyn's official correspondence in the cathedral archives, holding those notebooks, and knowing the bishop had owned them, had made Arthur feel more connected to Gladwyn than ever before.

He carefully removed the rest of the brown paper wrapping from the Tennyson volume, opened it to the half title, and gazed at the simple inscription in the familiar hand: "Robert Gladwyn, July 11, 1859." The auction catalog had stated only "with the ownership signature of Robert Gladwyn, later Bishop of Barchester," and Arthur was thrilled to see the addition of the date. July 11 was publication day for *Idylls of the King*; Gladwyn had bought his copy on the first day it was available. Once again, Arthur felt a surge of connection to the long-departed bishop, who had not even been a bishop when he inscribed this book. How often had Gladwyn reached for this volume and reread the words of the poet laureate? Although Arthur preferred Tennyson's *The Holy Grail and Other Poems*, he knew that the *Idylls* had been a big part of the resurgence of interest in Arthurian legend in the nineteenth century, and in writing it Tennyson had certainly referred to the same 1816 edition of *Morte d'Arthur* that Arthur owned.

Arthur opened the book to "Elaine," and read the familiar first lines:

Elaine the fair, Elaine the loveable,
Elaine, the lily maid of Astolat,
High in her chamber up a tower to the east
Guarded the sacred shield of Lancelot;

Which first she placed where morning's earliest ray
Might strike it, and awaken her with the gleam.

"High in her chamber"—like me in my library, Arthur thought. He loved the old-fashioned style of Tennyson's poetry, and he trembled to think that Gladwyn may have lain in his bed at the bishop's palace on a cold night and read these very words; the unique combination of ink and paper that now caused him to murmur verses aloud may have done the same for the good bishop. With a shiver, Arthur closed the book and took it upstairs to give it a place of honor in his study. One day, he thought, he would donate both Gladwyn's notebooks and his copy of the *Idylls* to the cathedral library. The library had, after all, been largely built on donations—from benefactors who commissioned manuscripts to bishops, deans, and canons who, over the centuries, had generously filled the shelves. Arthur would be proud to be part of that tradition.

Just before he left for the cathedral, where Oscar would be hosting the BBs in the library anteroom, Arthur slipped his photocopy of Bishop Gladwyn's inventory of the cathedral manuscripts into his jacket pocket. Oscar should know, he thought, that a manuscript was missing. Tonight was not the time for a formal inventory, but it might be worth looking over Gladwyn's list with Oscar to see if either of them saw a title he did not recognize from the collection.

A few minutes before seven, Arthur arrived at the library and stepped into the anteroom, where Oscar had already set out two bottles of wine and lit a fire. Except in the hottest days of summer, there was always a chill in this windowless room with its thick stone walls, and the fire made the place feel more like a cozy study and less like a dank dungeon. The host was not in evidence, so Arthur poured himself some Pinot Noir and settled into one of the Gothic armchairs in front of the fireplace.

Since he was early, Arthur decided he would read through Bishop Gladwyn's inventory to see if anything stood out—anything that might be missing. He had read about halfway down the first page and found nothing but familiar titles when he heard the door open behind him.

"Our host is in pursuit of crisps," boomed David as he stepped into the room. "I passed him as I was coming down the High Street." He picked up the bottle of Pinot, examined the label, and poured himself a glass. "Though it is beyond my understanding how anyone could eat crisps with a wine this fine."

"We all have our peculiarities," said Arthur, rising to greet his friend. "I like crisps; you like women."

"And I suppose you think we consume them at the same rate?"

"Something like that."

"Ah, gentlemen, I see you've started already. Excellent." Oscar bounced into the room with a bag full of crisp packets. Though only Arthur ever ate crisps and he always ate Salt & Vinegar, Oscar laid out an array of flavors on the table next to the wine.

"Roast Chicken?" said Arthur. "Prawn Cocktail? Is it a special occasion?"

"You might say that. Now let me catch up with you gents on the wine front and you can tell me about your latest bibliographical adventures. Arthur, how are you getting on with our new tenant?"

"You mean the blasted woman who is digitizing all the manuscripts in my library . . . *our* library. She is becoming increasingly annoying by the hour. I couldn't get a bit of work done this afternoon. She picked a fight with me and then she made me count the manuscripts."

"She picked a fight?" said David.

"I think we all know which one of you is more likely to have started a fight," said Oscar.

"So you've met her," said Arthur.

"The dean was nervous about giving her a set of keys—"

"Too right!" interrupted Arthur. "I would be, too."

"So I let her in every morning before I go to school. She starts early. Sweet girl."

"She may be sweet in the morning," said Arthur, "but by the afternoon she's soured. She insisted that there were only eighty-two manuscripts when I know Bishop Gladwyn's inventory lists eighty-three, so she made me count them—out loud!"

"She made you?" said David.

"Yes. And she stood right next to me the whole time—breathing on my back, shoving me in the side—the gall of that American. She was, what do they call it in the faculty manual, 'invading my personal space and engaging in unwanted contact.'"

"Methinks," said David.

"Methinks, too," said Oscar.

"You thinks what?" said Arthur, abandoning for once his usual grammatical precision.

"We thinks the gentleman doth protest too much," said David.

"What are you saying? That I like her?"

"More than like, I'd say," said Oscar, "judging by the color of your face at the moment."

"There is a difference between the blush of anger and the blush of affection," said Arthur.

"There is indeed," said David, "and I, more than anyone, am attuned to that difference. I suppose no man in Barchester has made more women both affectionate and angry than myself."

"And what is your diagnosis?" said Oscar.

David looked closely at Arthur's increasingly reddening face.

"Affection," he said emphatically. "Though he may be angry at himself for feeling it."

"Oh, you two are insufferable," said Arthur. "I have no more affection for her than I have for . . . for . . . bookless libraries. Besides, it's against the rules to discuss our personal lives."

"So you admit that your relationship with Bethany is part of your personal life?" said David.

"I admit nothing of the sort. For God's sake, I'm old enough to be her father."

"Hardly," said Oscar. "She's twenty-six and you're forty."

"How do you know she's twenty-six?" asked Arthur, who found himself oddly disturbed that Oscar should possess a piece of personal information about Miss Davis that he did not have.

"She filled out the form to borrow books from the library," said Oscar.

"She's borrowing books from the library? Real, actual, printed-on-paper and bound-in-covers books?"

"She is."

"I thought only cathedral clergy could borrow books from the library."

"You're not cathedral clergy," said Oscar.

"Yes," said Arthur, "but I'm hardly the general public."

"First of all, she's not the general public either, she's a visiting scholar." Arthur snorted at the word *scholar*, but Oscar went on. "And second, I asked the dean and she's not aware of any specific policy one way or another. There seems to be no reason why we shouldn't circulate volumes that aren't rare or valuable, particularly if they're not available at the city library or at the university." Arthur was glad Oscar did not add the words *media center*, as these would have undoubtedly elicited another snort. He wondered if circulating some of the less valuable books might be one way to make more people aware of the cathedral library.

"What's she checked out?" asked Arthur.

"Can't tell you," said Oscar with a smile. "Client confidentiality."

"There's no such thing."

"Oh, but there is. Bethany told me all about it. Government snooping and all that. They had a whole session at the American Library Association, apparently."

"If you really want to know what she's reading, why don't you just ask her," said David.

"The last thing I want to do," said Arthur, "is get into another conversation with that woman."

"Well, that's awkward," said Oscar, "because she's going to be here any minute."

"She's going to . . . I'm sorry, she's what?"

"I invited her," said Oscar. "It's the first time in years I've met anyone who loves books enough to deserve to join us."

"Loves books!" spewed Arthur.

"Suppose we change the subject," said Oscar gently.

"I absolutely insist that we do nothing of the sort until Arthur has answered one more question," said David.

"I am not answering any questions about my feelings, or nonfeelings, toward that woman."

"That's not what I was going to ask," said David. "I merely wanted to know how many manuscripts you counted."

"Eighty-two," said a cheerful voice behind them.

"Ah, Miss Davis," said Oscar. "Welcome to our little soirée." Oscar gave Bethany a peck on the cheek and accepted a bottle of wine she had brought. David introduced himself and made a production out of kissing Bethany on the hand and lingering just longer than propriety dictated. Arthur stood by the fire and took a long drink of wine, willing his face to return to its usual color. When he looked up from his glass, Bethany was eyeing him from across the room.

"Good evening, Mr. Prescott, it's nice to see you," she said.

"Good evening," he replied. "It's nice to see you as well." And Arthur was surprised to discover that it was. He hadn't realized just how dark and dour the room had seemed until Miss Davis had brightened it with her presence.

"Oh, please," said David, "call him Arthur. Even his students don't call him Mr. Prescott."

"And you must all call me Bethany," she said. "Even you, Arthur."

"So," said Oscar when he had settled in his chair, "is this true?"

For a moment Arthur thought he was asking if Arthur were really pleased to see Bethany, but then he remembered the question Bethany had answered on her entrance.

"Yes," he said. "Gladwyn's inventory lists eight-three manuscripts, but Miss Davis . . . Bethany and I counted only eighty-two."

"I counted them again after you left for Evensong, just to be sure," said Bethany.

"And then you came to Evensong. You said you weren't coming."

"I said nothing of the sort. I said it wasn't the first date I had in mind. You left before I had a chance to say anything else. You should learn to listen, Arthur."

"All right, you two," said David, "we didn't come here to bicker, as much as Arthur enjoys that. We came to read, and Bethany, as our guest, has the privilege."

"Who decided that?" said Arthur.

"The guest always reads," said Oscar.

"But we've never had a guest," said Arthur.

"So we've never had a chance to enforce the rule," said David. "Now, Bethany, as soon as Arthur settles in his chair, we'll be ready for you to begin."

Arthur couldn't help but feel he was being set up by the other three—for what he wasn't sure—but he reluctantly took his seat.

"I couldn't find quite what I wanted in the cathedral library," began Bethany, as she pulled a bruised and battered leather-bound volume from her purse. "I discovered this in the basement room of the Barchester Public Library—last checked out on October 21, 1926. It's one of those three-volume novels. Arthur thought I should read fiction for a change, so I'm giving it a try. It's all about poverty in East London, and how these two young heirs, Angela and Harry, decide they are going to do something about it and they create this sort of community college kind of institution, and apparently the book inspired the founding of something called the People's Palace—you know, life imitating art. So this is the first volume, which—I think this is really cool—is inscribed on the endpaper to somebody named Angela."

Arthur smiled as he observed David and Oscar experience the digressive powers of Bethany's monologues.

"Will you be reading from the beginning?" said David, apparently sensing an opening and a chance to get Bethany back on course.

"Almost," said Bethany. "It's a scene in the prologue where Angela and her friend Constance have just finished their studies at Cambridge—women's colleges were a novelty in 1882, but I guess you know that. That's when the book was published, 1882. Oh, and it's by Walter Besant and it's called *All Sorts and Conditions of Men*—I thought Arthur and Oscar at least would appreciate that the title comes from your prayer book. And I love the subtitle: *An Impossible Story*."

"And will you . . ." ventured Oscar.

"Yes, I'll read," said Bethany. "I just needed to ramble breathlessly on for a minute so Arthur would know it was really me." With this comment, Bethany winked at Arthur, who could not suppress a smile, and then she read.

> *The two women were talking about themselves and their own lives, and what they were to do each with that one life which happened, by the mere accident of birth, to belong to herself. It must be a curious subject for reflection in extreme old age, when everything has happened that is going to happen, including rheumatism, that, but for this accident, one's life might have been so very different.*
>
> *'Because, Angela,' said the one who wore spectacles, 'we have but this one life before us, and if we make mistakes with it, or throw it away, or waste it, or lose our chances, it is such a dreadful pity. Oh, to think of those girls who drift and let every chance go by, and get nothing out of their lives at all—except babies' (she spoke of babies with great contempt). 'Oh! it seems as if every moment were precious: oh! It is a sin to waste an hour of it. Yes, my dear, all my life, short or long, shall be given to science. I will have no love in it, or marriage, or—or—anything of that kind at all.'*
>
> *'Nor will I,' said the other stoutly, yet with apparent effort. 'Marriage spoils a woman's career; we must live our life to its utmost, Constance.'*

Arthur did not hear much after this—or at least he did not comprehend much after this. He heard Bethany's voice—a different voice from what he had heard before. As she read she seemed less . . . well, less American, and less sure of being right. Her voice sounded more musical and less abrasive—like the difference between a perfectly rehearsed choir and an egotistical soloist. Arthur briefly considered the question posed by the beginning of the passage—did marriage ruin a woman's career?—but decided it had been answered in the negative long ago. And so he allowed his mind to empty and his body to relax, lulled by Bethany's reading.

When Arthur excused himself to go to Compline, David, Oscar, and Bethany were still talking about Bethany's digitization project. Arthur had remained largely silent through the evening—his distaste for what

Bethany was doing in the library prevented his speaking politely on the topic, and as he seemed to be outnumbered, for Oscar and David showed nothing but enthusiasm for Bethany's work, he decided it best to hold his peace. With a sense of resignation, he slid into his usual seat in the Epiphany Chapel. The precentor was leading Compline that evening, and he gave a perfunctory nod to Arthur as he entered the chapel. Always punctual, the precentor began the service as the last nine o'clock bell was still reverberating. Arthur was the only other soul present.

"The Lord Almighty grant us a peaceful night and a perfect end," chanted the precentor.

Arthur replied, with more feeling than usual, "Amen." As the short service progressed, he thought how much easier life would be if worship at the cathedral were more than just a comforting rhythm, more than lovely music and sonorous words. If only he believed in the underlying foundation of it all. And then the precentor reached that familiar and colorful phrase—*your adversary the devil prowls about like a roaring lion*—and Arthur thought, yes. There is something I can believe. The devil may not be prowling around this cathedral like a roaring lion, but Bethany Davis certainly is.

V

THE TOWER

The central tower of the cathedral is of late Norman con-struction, but the graceful spire that sits atop that solid base is considerably later. Originally, a wooden spire topped the tower, but this was destroyed by fire sometime early in the fourteenth century. The tower sat without adornment for nearly fifty years, before a stone-clad spire was constructed. Most of the sculptures that once adorned the tower were pulled down at the Reformation or in the years that followed.

A.D. 950, St. Ewolda's Monastery

Eadweard knelt before the altar of the monastic church, his face illuminated by a beam of moonlight that shone through one of the narrow windows overhead. He felt the task before him should be done in the most holy place possible—on the altar of the church. At this hour of night, he was safe from the prying eyes of the other monks. He prayed that he might perform his work with skill and accuracy.

He had spent thirty years as Guardian. Soon after Leofwine had passed the responsibility to him, his fellow monk had died peacefully in his sleep. The early years of his guardianship had been quiet ones, with no threats coming from Glastonbury or anywhere else. Eadweard had eventually risen to the post of abbot, and his daily responsibilities had almost made him forget his job as Guardian.

But then the enthusiastic new abbot of Glastonbury, Dunstan, began rebuilding the abbey church in that place and soon emissaries arrived at Barchester asking about a treasure from Glastonbury hidden at St. Ewolda's in the years of the Viking invasions. Three times Eadweard had moved the treasure, and three times had he denied its existence. Most recently, Dunstan himself had come, ostensibly to talk with Eadweard about establishing the Benedictine rule at Barchester as Dunstan had done in Glastonbury. Even the great abbot had asked about the lost treasure, and when Eadweard had disavowed any knowledge of it, Dunstan had departed and promised that Glastonbury would pester Barchester no more. Eadweard felt confident that Dunstan believed the treasure was nothing but a myth and, for now at least, the secret would remain safe.

Tonight, Eadweard turned his attention to another problem. He had worried for many years about the condition of the document with which Leofwine had entrusted him so long ago. Even then it had been difficult to read without the help of bright sunlight, and the corners of the folds had created holes in the parchment. Eadweard feared that the next Guardian might not be able to read every word. He had memorized the text within hours of first reading it, which made his task tonight easier.

As abbot, he had control over the paltry resources of the monastery, and it had been a simple matter for him to obtain a fresh piece of parchment. He had insisted on a well-prepared sheet—thin, gleaming white, and well scraped of hairs. Eadweard had spent a lifetime handling the few books that belonged to the impoverished monastery—the founder's book, the service book, a Psalter, and the Gospels. Just that morning he had read from the pages of a newly transcribed Gospel of John—a treasure created by one of his own monks, but financed by a local landowner who wished to make penance for some unnamed sin. As he had turned those fresh parchment pages, and as he ran his hand across the blank sheet before him now, Eadweard marveled that the sheep and cattle and goats in the fields surrounding the monastery could be transformed into such a beautiful and durable writing surface. St. Ewolda's had small enough need for parchment that none of the brothers were trained in the technique of cleaning, curing, and scraping the animal hides, but when an animal was slaughtered, the monks often sold the skin to the merchant who had provided Eadweard with the piece of vellum now on the altar. Beside it lay the faded, worn document that Eadweard had kept hidden for so many years.

Finishing his prayers, Eadweard rose and stood at the altar. His script was far from beautiful, but he could write legibly. The text he must copy tonight was not long and he had at least four hours before the disappearance of the moon would signal that brothers would soon arrive to prepare the altar for Prime. He lit a taper, placed it on the altar, and, in the mixture of the warm candlelight and the cold moonlight, began to write.

Well before dawn, his work was done. Being sure that the ink was fully dry, he folded the new parchment and slipped it within his robes. The original document he placed in a chalice he had set on the altar for this purpose. He held the flame of the candle to its corner and watched as the glow slowly spread to the vellum. The flames leaped up and the fire flared and then died as the precious words were consumed. When he was sure nothing remained but ash, he carefully transferred the contents of the chalice to a small phial. This he set in a niche in the wall next to the altar. For the day that dawned was Ash Wednesday. In a few hours, Eadweard would strew these ashes on the heads of the monks in his charge, repeating the words that reminded them of their mortality: "Remember, man, that thou art dust, and unto dust thou shalt return."

Eadweard would remain at St. Ewolda's for his Lenten fast, and on Easter Sunday, after proclaiming the glorious Resurrection of Christ the Savior, he would appoint a new Guardian. With the mantle of responsibility lifted, he would leave St. Ewolda's. He thought he might walk to the sea. He had never seen the sea, and he would like to do so before he died.

April 21, 2016

FEAST OF ST. ANSELM, ARCHBISHOP OF CANTERBURY

Mist rose from the water meadows in wisps and fog clung to the river-
bank, glowing in the morning sun. Arthur's dark thoughts of the night
before seemed silly in this lovely morning light. Bethany was no minion
of the devil; she was here to save books, not destroy them. And she saw
things Arthur had never noticed.

"Miss Davis and I made a rather interesting discovery yesterday," said
Arthur as he and Gwyn slogged through the mud toward the river.

"Bethany, you mean?"

"Yes, Bethany. We discovered there is a manuscript missing from the
library."

"Do you think we have a thief in our midst?"

"Not likely," said Arthur. "I imagine it's been missing at least since the
war. Bishop Gladwyn's inventory of the manuscripts lists eighty-three
and Miss Davis . . . that is, Bethany, astutely pointed out to me that the
library contains only eighty-two."

"Well, I certainly hope you'll find it for us, Arthur, since you don't
have anything else to do, like finish a guidebook."

"We'll check the inventory to see what it is—probably nothing interesting. But one does wonder."

"You think it's the lost Book of Ewolda?"

"I doubt it's a jewel-encrusted treasure, if that's what you mean. More
likely some dull treatise on medieval medicine."

"If a medieval manuscript is dull to you, Arthur, that would be saying
something."

"I just don't want to get my hopes up."

"So you intend to go looking for it?"

"I think it's more that Bethany intends to go looking for it and she intends to drag me along."

"Arthur, you can pretend you're not excited about searching for a lost
manuscript, and you can pretend you're not . . . perhaps aroused is not
quite the right word, but pleased, certainly, by the prospect of Bethany

Davis joining you on the quest—but unfortunately, my friend, you're not that good an actor."

"I'll admit, the prospect of returning a missing manuscript to the library is intriguing."

"And the prospect of Bethany Davis?"

But before Arthur could express any opinion on Bethany, Mag (or perhaps Nunc) came bounding out of the weeds and leaped up onto Arthur's chest, licking him in the face and leaving muddy paw prints all over his shirt.

"Oh, Arthur, I am sorry," said Gwyn, suppressing giggles.

"Not sorry enough to keep from laughing," said Arthur with a wry smile. The dogs never jumped on him in dry weather, only when they had been romping in the mud. "I wasn't going to wear this to work anyway."

The dean was by now doubled over with laughter, for the other dog had attacked, and Arthur found himself drenched in mud and drool. "So pleased I can provide for your amusement," he said. In truth, he found the situation fairly amusing himself. "You do have them well trained."

"Here, take my scarf," said Gwyn, catching her breath. "You might want to wipe your face."

"I've no intention of wiping away anything that causes you such pleasure," said Arthur.

"Thank you, Arthur," said Gwyn, smiling. "It's a true friend who sacrifices his dignity for the amusement of his walking companion. I think I've gone the past forty-five seconds without sparing a thought for this morning's chapter meeting."

"Planning to vote on my excommunication?"

"I'm not sure how we could excommunicate someone who never communes," said Gwyn, "but no, it's worse than that, I'm afraid."

"Money," said Arthur grimly.

"Money," repeated Gwyn. "It saddens me that my job, which I thought was supposed to be about religion, is so often about money. The coffers are getting close to empty, and there is a movement afoot in the chapter to begin cutting costs and increasing income."

"How?" asked Arthur.

"On the cost-cutting side one of the canons has suggested fewer vergers, fewer altar flowers, even curtailing the music program."

"Curtailing . . . you mean no more choir?" Arthur felt a sudden knot in the pit of his stomach at the thought of no more music at cathedral services.

"Not that drastic, perhaps, but fewer choral scholarships, fewer sung services, maybe even making the organist part-time."

Arthur shook his head at this sad prospect. "And on the increasing-income side?"

"You won't like it," said Gwyn, quickening her pace and looking straight ahead to where the dogs waited, panting at the gate to the close.

"Won't like what?" asked Arthur, taking hold of Gwyn's wrist and pulling her to a halt.

"There are at least four canons ready to vote today to sell off the manuscripts in the library."

"Sell off . . ." Arthur could not even process this information. He found himself gasping for breath. "How could they . . ."

"Trust me Arthur, I don't want it, and I still think we have the votes to defeat any such proposal, but the canons see a cathedral that can't pay its bills and a collection of perhaps millions of pounds' worth of manuscripts. They say we are a church, not a museum."

"Is that why Bethany . . ." Arthur could not quite form the thought.

"There were rumblings before she came, but I do think they added one vote to their side with the knowledge that the manuscripts would be digitized—that we would still have access to their contents."

Arthur tried to swallow his anger. This was the sort of disaster that happened when you let meddlesome digitizers into a medieval library. "Do they know what they're throwing away?" he said between clenched teeth.

"They're not throwing anything away," said Gwyn. "If anything they're considering selling the manuscripts to people and institutions who are better suited to care for them than we are."

"We have a Gospel of John," said Arthur. "A handwritten Gospel of John that has been used in services at Barchester for over a thousand years. A thousand years! Can you even conceive of how much history, how much faith is connected to that one book? And that's just one. What about the Barchester Breviary—that has musical settings we've been using for eight hundred years. We have a manuscript of medical cures that was used during the plague. We have a book on agriculture that helped the monks six hundred years ago raise the sheep that gave them the hides on which they wrote the very books that stand next to that one on the shelf. And these manuscripts have survived wars and invasion and plundering and bombing and fire—all so we can sell them when we're a little strapped for cash. This is our history, Gwyn. Every one of those manuscripts is a part of Barchester, just like every organ in your body is a part of you."

"Arthur, I'm on your side, I promise. But if the body can't survive, then the organs aren't much good."

"You can't let this happen," said Arthur, gripping Gwyn's wrist tighter. "You can't."

"I don't want to," said Gwyn. "But if the financial situation doesn't change, it might not be my choice anymore."

Arthur sat in his office hoping that no one would take advantage of his presence during posted "consultation hours" to actually consult with him. On his desk lay the first book his grandfather had ever given him—a thick blue volume called *The Romance of King Arthur*. He could still remember unwrapping that book on Christmas morning when he was ten, peeling back the gaudy paper to reveal the luxurious blue cloth stamped in gold with the image of a feather-capped herald astride a richly adorned steed. The book was published in 1917, and Arthur couldn't believe he could actually own such an old volume. Unlike *King Arthur's Knights*, this volume was not missing its illustrations, and what entrancing images they were— lush plates with swirls of color and chapter headings in the style of medieval woodcuts, all created by the remarkable Arthur Rackham.

"I thought it was high time you had a copy of your own," his grandfather had said. "And not only does this have all the stories about King Arthur, but it has pictures by a man named Arthur as well, so it's doubly appropriate for you."

Before he even read this slightly more grown-up version of the stories, Arthur flipped through the book, stopping at every illustration. His favorite image had been the one he found most mysterious: a color plate of a woman in a white robe standing in profile on a cushion of fire. Her robe and hair glowed orange with flames and in her hands she held an ornate golden cup similarly engulfed, from which radiated beams of light. Her head was bowed as if in prayer and the room in which she stood was far plainer than the background of Rackham's other pictures—a row of crosshatched windows above brown paneling and a brown tiled floor. The artist clearly wanted Arthur's eye to be drawn to the cup and now, thirty years after he had first gazed upon this illustration, it still was. On the tissue guard in front of the glossy color plate was the caption, printed in red ink: "How at the Castle of Corbin a maiden bare in the Sangreal and foretold the achievements of Galahad." Arthur wondered what Bethany would think if she saw the picture. Surely she would notice Rackham's Holy Grail was exactly the same as the cup held by Bishop Gladwyn in the portrait by John Collier.

Collier's portrait, Arthur had discovered, had been displayed in London at the Royal Academy exhibit of 1888, when a young Arthur Rackham was just beginning art school. Rackham must have seen the portrait and tracked it down in Barchester decades later to copy the cup when he was working on his Arthurian illustrations. Arthur wondered what it was about Gladwyn's cup that made Rackham want to copy it.

It was a question that had intrigued him since he had first seen Gladwyn's portrait. He had read about the painting in Gladwyn's guide to the cathedral—the first book he had read before beginning work on his own guide and the same guide that had led Bethany to the chapter house. It had taken him a month to track down the painting—no one at the cathedral knew where it had gone, but when he finally found it in the former bishop's palace he immediately recognized the Grail and suddenly flashed back to that Christmas Day when he first looked at Rackham's illustration. Did his grandfather know about the painting? In giving him that thick blue book was he leading Arthur to discover the connection between Gladwyn's portrait and Rackham's picture?

Ever since childhood, remembering what his grandfather had told him, Arthur had worked to ferret out connections between Barchester and the Grail. At university he studied as much about the Arthurian legends as he could, secretly searching for anything that would connect the stories to Barchester. When the time came to choose a topic for his master's thesis, he decided to make a comparative inventory of all the pre-1500 manuscripts of King Arthur and Grail stories. His work took him to libraries across Europe, and allowed him to hold books like the Winchester Manuscript—the only medieval manuscript version of Malory's *Morte d'Arthur*. The fifteenth-century manuscript had been discovered in 1934, sitting on the library shelves at Winchester College. No one knew how long it had been there or where it had come from, but even the library of a boys' boarding school had done what libraries were supposed to do—it had preserved the volume until such time as its importance was recognized. Although his census did not require extensive examination of the Winchester manuscript, Arthur had spent days in the British Library poring over the text. He loved the fact that nearly every proper noun had been rendered in red ink—ink that had, in over five hundred years, not faded at all. And when he reached the section about the Grail, he stared for several minutes at a spot near the middle of the page where the word *Sangreall* was written in that same red ink. The Holy Grail, written in blood, thought Arthur.

Arthur's thesis had given him the opportunity to examine a wide variety of medieval manuscripts in person, but it had not uncovered any clues that might connect the Arthur stories, or the Grail, to Barchester. After university, he had spent several years going from one teaching job to another, always hoping to return to Barchester. When the chance came to teach at the University of Barchester, Arthur seized it. No matter how uninspiring the campus, it was in the city that he loved. Arthur had put his quest aside during his peripatetic years, but when he saw the Grail image from his childhood in Collier's portrait, his passion was reawakened and he became an active Grail seeker once more. He began to add to his small collection of books on King Arthur and the Grail, and he began to scour the cathedral library for clues. He wasn't even surprised when he found one.

In the Barchester Breviary, Arthur discovered a curious notation in the margins next to the Prayer of Consecration—the prayer during which, according to the medieval Roman Catholic beliefs of Barchester, the bread and wine are transformed into the body and blood of Christ. The note was in Old English, not Latin, and read, as Arthur had translated: "Here I remember the great treasure of Barsyt." The word for "treasure" in the note was "déorwyrðnes," which indicated something worthy of veneration.

But Barchester didn't have a great treasure. It was one of the reasons the cathedral had always been relatively poor. There had been a small cult of Ewolda, a few miracles attributed to her relics, and a trickle of pilgrims hoping to be healed. But even in legend, Barchester had never housed a fragment of the True Cross or the bones of some great king or archbishop. True, the lost Book of Ewolda was rumored to have been covered in jewels, but it was in no way connected to the Prayer of Consecration. But what if, Arthur wondered, the treasure was a secret? And what if Bishop Gladwyn, the great historian of Barchester, had discovered that secret and left a hint about it in his portrait? If Barchester really was the resting place of the Holy Grail, what better place in the service to remember the Cup of Christ than during the prayer that commemorates his first passing that cup to his disciples?

Arthur kept a notebook of all his findings, carefully detailing all the evidence that Barchester was connected to the Holy Grail and legends of King Arthur from the curious marginalia in the breviary and in Stansby's edition of *Morte d'Arthur* to the yew tree in the cloisters. He also recorded his memory of one of the last days he ever spent with his grandfather. They had, with permission, climbed to the top of the central tower of the cathedral, emerging onto a tiny parapet just below the spire. It was a crisp, clear, early summer day and the views in every direction were magnificent. Arthur's grandfather pointed out villages fifteen and twenty miles away, identifiable by their church towers. Just before they headed back down, Arthur noticed a pair of sculptures, worn by centuries of rain, sitting just behind the parapet, where they could never be seen from below—two lions looking west toward the cathedral's main door. Arthur instantly recalled a passage in *The Romance of King Arthur*, describing the castle in which Launcelot saw the Holy Grail:

"There was a postern opened toward the sea, and was open without any keeping, save two lions kept the entry." He excitedly recited the passage to his grandfather, pointing out the lion statues, but his grandfather only smiled, winked, and ducked back through the low doorway that led into the darkness inside the tower.

Arthur meticulously recorded all this evidence, without a thought of sharing his findings. He had promised his grandfather to keep the Grail and his search for it a secret. To Arthur, the mystery was deeply private, and deeply connected to his memories of those happy summer days with his grandfather.

Now, looking back over his notes about Collier and Rackham, Arthur added a sentence about the Grail table, which Bethany had noticed—the table on which the lost Book of Ewolda lay. What he hadn't considered before was that *two* treasures featured prominently in Gladwyn's portrait—the Holy Grail and the lost Book of Ewolda—and that the silver table connected the two. If something in the Book of Ewolda allowed Arthur to prove conclusively that Barchester was associated with the Grail, it might be time to break his promise to his grandfather and share the secret. That sort of discovery could mean grants and lottery funding and museums and a national outcry against selling off the manuscripts of the great Barchester Cathedral Library.

With an hour remaining in his consultation period, Arthur decided to call it a day. If he left now he could be back at the cathedral by three o'clock and have time to compare Bishop Gladwyn's inventory to the eighty-two manuscripts on the library shelves.

As he was locking his office door he heard footsteps behind him. "Arthur, I'm glad I caught you," said Miss Stanhope. "Don't your office hours last until three thirty?"

"Miss Stanhope," said Arthur, "what a delight." It was anything but.

"I just wanted to discuss the last section of *Mansfield Park* for a few minutes." Miss Stanhope waved not a book but a flat silver tablet in the air.

"And how are we to discuss *Mansfield Park*," said Arthur, "if you have not brought *Mansfield Park* with you?"

"Oh, don't be such an old grouch," said Miss Stanhope. "I downloaded the text file from Project Gutenberg and I'm reading it on my iPad."

Students didn't even read books anymore, thought Arthur. They dispensed with design and layout and cover art and illustrations and reduced reading to nothing but a stream of text in whatever font and size they chose. Reading without books, thought Arthur, was like playing cricket without dressing in white. It could be done, but why?

"Miss Stanhope," said Arthur, "may I ask you a question?"

"Sure, Arthur."

"Do you ever go to the media center?"

"Sure, I go there all the time."

"And what do you do when you are there?"

"Well, they have very comfortable chairs, and the coffee is good, and the Wi-Fi is superfast."

Was that it? wondered Arthur. Were libraries now just places with good coffee and fast Internet connections? Was there no way to get students to actually interact with books even in a building once devoted to those very objects? Arthur wasn't sure he yet understood what the media center's purpose was in this digital age, but he hoped he might find a way to make it more than the provision of hot beverages and comfy chairs.

"I'm sorry, Miss Stanhope," said Arthur, shoving his keys in his pocket. "I won't be able to meet with you this afternoon. Family emergency."

He scurried off down the hall before Miss Stanhope could reply.

Thirty minutes later, Arthur was walking across the close on a stunningly bright spring day. The spire of the cathedral was silhouetted against a deep blue sky lightly dusted with wisps of cloud. He stood for a moment, gazing up at the spire—that remarkable structure that had towered over Barchester for six centuries. It had no doubt been a beacon to those few pilgrims who sought out the shrine of Ewolda; sadly it had also been a beacon to Nazi bombers. But the spire had survived, and the survival of such a fragile structure gave Arthur hope that the rest of the cathedral, and the treasures it contained, would survive as well.

Arthur crept into the library, hoping perhaps Bethany would not notice him, but he needn't have bothered. She was nowhere to be seen. He carefully withdrew from his bag his photocopy of Bishop Gladwyn's inventory, pulled a pencil from his pocket, and stood in front of the shelves of medieval manuscripts.

Arthur loved the ancient feel of that case, with its iron chains, though no longer attached to the manuscripts, still hanging above each shelf. But he also loved that, as old as the chained library felt, for some of these manuscripts it had been a *new* form of storage. The oldest book in the library was the tenth-century Gospel of John, transcribed at least six centuries before this case had been built. It, and other manuscripts, would originally have been stored flat on their sides. As the collection grew and books were piled on top of each other, access became difficult. No records existed of where the books were kept in the following centuries, but Arthur suspected that some, at least, were stacked in wide niches in the wall in the cloisters, close to where the scribes worked. Eventually they may have been placed in wooden chests with iron locks for protection, but not until this chained case had been built, in about 1600, were any of these books ever stored upright. Even then, the manuscripts were kept with their spines inward, to leave room for the chains that were attached to the outer edge of the front covers. This was why most had titles written on their fore edges. But because the front covers had been torn off when the library was reassembled after the war, the manuscripts had been shelved spine out, in the modern fashion, hiding the titles. There had been talk in the 1970s, Arthur had heard, about putting new covers on the manuscripts, but the debate between those who said this would be historically inappropriate and those who claimed it would help protect the books' contents had been settled by a distinct lack of money.

Arthur was now confronted with three shelves of blank spines. To inventory the manuscripts, he would have to take each volume off the shelf. Most had shelf numbers penciled in the top right corner of the first page—not surprisingly in the handwriting of Bishop Gladwyn—so Arthur could fairly quickly go through Gladwyn's list, which was arranged by shelf number, to determine what was missing. He had made his way through most of the first shelf and was beginning to think he could succeed in completing this task in peace when Bethany bounded through the door.

"Arthur! Hi," she said. "Oh, I just photographed the most beautiful Gospel. I could have looked at every page for hours. Had to pop to the washroom after. I wash my hands freshly every ten pages or so. Are you checking Gladwyn's inventory? That was fun last night. It was sweet of Oscar to invite me."

For an instant, Arthur thought about ignoring her, but he couldn't. He shelved manuscript A-22 and turned to see her standing a few feet away, that ever-present wisp of hair dangling in front of her eyes and a warm smile on her face.

"Oscar is the kindest man I know," said Arthur.

"You were awfully quiet," said Bethany.

"Lost in thought, I'm afraid," said Arthur. He was on the verge of adding a comment about the irony of a digital warrior in the encampment of bibliophiles, but something about Bethany's smile made him want to keep their conversation civil. Then again, Gwyn had told him that morning that Bethany's project had convinced at least one canon to vote to sell off the cathedral manuscripts. Perhaps that smile *was* the grin of a roaring lion seeking someone to devour.

"You know there's an easier way to do that," said Bethany, peering over his shoulder at Gladwyn's inventory.

"I beg your pardon?"

"The manuscripts are still arranged by their original shelf numbers. A-1, A-2, and so on. One letter for each shelf. All you have to do is—"

"Is count the number of volumes on each shelf . . ."

"And see which total doesn't match the highest number on Gladwyn's list. It's shelf B, by the way."

"How do you know that?"

"A head for numbers, believe it or not. Ever since I first counted the manuscripts I can tell you exactly how many are on each shelf, and there are twenty-seven on shelf B."

Arthur looked at Gladwyn's list and saw that there was an entry for B-28.

"I'll bet it's the last one that's missing," said Bethany. "If there was one missing in sequence you would have noticed."

"But if B-28 is missing," said Arthur excitedly as he pulled out the volume at the far right of the shelf, "I would have assumed there were only twenty-seven volumes on shelf B." He turned to the first page of the manuscript and saw Bishop Gladwyn's light pencil marking on the upper corner: B-27.

"So what was B-28?" said Bethany.

Arthur looked back down at the inventory. "Looks rather dull, I'm afraid. It just says 'Psalter, no illuminations, early sixteenth century.' Looks like the missing manuscript is utterly ordinary."

"You really have no imagination, do you, Arthur?" said Bethany. "We're a strange pair, you and I. I'm obsessed with technology and the modern world, yet to me every book in this library, every stone in this cathedral is pulsing with mystery and intrigue. You live in the past, in a world of manuscripts and illuminations, but to you a five-hundred-year-old Psalter can be 'utterly ordinary.'"

"You're really intrigued by the library?" said Arthur, feeling a new respect for Bethany.

"For God's sake, Arthur, look around you. Who wouldn't be? You may take all this for granted, because you have the privilege of coming up here all the time, but to most people being in a room like this would be a once-in-a-lifetime experience. It's a shame so few people get to see it. But just because I'm somewhat mesmerized by all this . . . this history, doesn't mean I take things at face value. I don't believe for a minute that the one manuscript that's gone missing is the most boring one in the collection."

Arthur thought about telling her that any intrigue involving the Barchester manuscripts might soon be put to an end, as they might all be heading to the auction block, and that her presence in the library was not exactly helping their cause, but when he looked up and saw the excitement in her eyes he couldn't bear to squelch it. "So you think that B-28 is something more than an unillustrated Psalter?"

"Wouldn't it make a better mystery if it were?" she said.

Arthur wanted to believe she was right. He wanted to believe that B-28 was the lost Book of Ewolda, that it would answer all his questions about the cathedral's founder, even that it would finally cement the connection between Barchester and the Holy Grail. But he found the same part of him that precluded his belief in God kept him from sharing her excitement. Arthur believed what he saw, and what he saw was an entry that said "Psalter, no illuminations, early sixteenth century."

"It would make a better mystery," said Arthur. "But perhaps it's not a mystery, after all."

"Oh, Arthur, you're no fun. What do you say we have a cup of tea?"

"I really ought to get some work done," said Arthur.

"Yes, but it's three thirty. Isn't that teatime? Plus, my back is killing me from leaning over manuscripts. I could use a few laps around the cloister with a friend."

The devil, said Arthur to himself. The devil is tempting you away from your work with a pretty girl. But even as he formed the thought he knew he could not believe it any more than he could believe that the teacher Jesus was the son of a divine being. Bethany was not evil; she was just doing her job. And was her job really that horrible? Arthur had a sudden vision of a student in some remote western part of the United States, sitting at a computer, examining the pages of the Barchester Breviary, learning about medieval music from a book that few people would ever have the thrill of holding in their hands. Arthur decided to try a new approach with Bethany. He decided to try being exactly what she had called him—a friend.

"So," said Bethany when they had settled in the café with a pot of tea for two, "how are we going to start searching for the missing manuscript?"

"*Are* we going to start searching for the missing manuscript?" said Arthur. "It seems we both have more important work to do." Arthur instantly realized this had sounded sharp, that he was already failing in his vow to be friendly. And if she really wanted to look for this manuscript, why not? What better way to be a friend than to help her have a little adventure? "Sorry," he said. "I didn't mean to be short. It's been . . ." Again he hesitated to tell her about the plan to sell the manuscripts. "It's been a stressful day."

"What's this," said Bethany, "a kinder, gentler Arthur? I'm not sure I like that, but we'll see. Now, the first question we have to answer is when did the manuscript disappear. Gladwyn made his list in, what, 1894? That's more than a hundred years ago. Kind of hard to know when the theft took place—like in those crime dramas when they're always so focused on time of death. We need to figure out the time of death."

"I know," said Arthur, wanting to respond to Bethany's monologue with as few syllables as possible.

"You know? How could you possibly know?" said Bethany. "It's been a hundred and twenty years."

"In 1894, just after he prepared the inventory, Bishop Gladwyn designated one of the canons as canon librarian, and that post remained until the 1930s. For all that time, the only person with a key to the library was that canon. Since the war, the manuscripts have been equally secure, though there wasn't an appointed librarian."

"But how do you know that one of those librarians didn't—"

"They didn't," said Arthur. "They were trustworthy men. I can tell you all their names and all about them. They cared for the manuscripts with a passion. And remember, before the war the manuscripts were still chained to the shelves. It would have been extremely difficult to remove one without anyone knowing."

"So when did it happen?"

"On the one night when it would have been extremely *easy* to remove a manuscript without anyone knowing. February 7, 1941."

"That's quite specific."

"It's the night the Nazis bombed Barchester. The Lady Chapel was destroyed and for a few hours it looked as if the entire cathedral might burn. So volunteers took all the valuables out and moved them away for safekeeping for the remainder of the war."

"All the valuables? Including the manuscripts?"

"Including the manuscripts."

"Well," said Bethany, "we need to find out more about that night."

"That's exactly what I was thinking," said Arthur. "We could go next Thursday to the county archives. They're only open one day a week, but they have a file of all the area newspapers and . . . are you even listening to what I'm saying?"

Bethany had pulled out her phone and was tapping away on it. "Of course I'm listening, Arthur," she said as her fingers moved in a blur. "I just don't feel like waiting until next Thursday. Here we are." She handed the phone to Arthur.

"What's this?"

"The British Newspaper Archive—fully digitized and searchable. I'm surprised you haven't used it."

Arthur pulled on his reading glasses and squinted at the phone. "What am I looking at exactly?"

"The *Barsetshire Chronicle* for February 8, 1941, old man," said Bethany.

"You mean you just typed in . . ." Arthur was amazed. True, what he was looking at was not the original paper, only an image on a screen. But still, she had found in seconds what it would have taken him nearly a week to find. And what else might she find in an archive of . . . "How big is the archive?"

"Over ten million pages," said Bethany.

"And you can search it?"

"Sure. Just type in what you want to know, and every newspaper article for two hundred years shows up."

"The print is awfully small," said Arthur.

"So you zoom in," said Bethany. "But why don't I just read it to you." She took the phone back and read, in the same soft voice that had lulled Arthur on the previous evening.

> An unexpected and barbaric raid took place on the city of Barchester last night. Although Nazi bombs fell for only a short time, the incendiaries led to many fires and indiscriminate destruction. More than forty people are believed dead. Barchester's medieval cathedral narrowly escaped a direct hit, but the Lady Chapel at the building's east end was completely destroyed. While firemen doused the flames, bravely preserving the rest of the much-loved structure, others raced to remove treasures from the cathedral in preparation for the worst. Even choirboys were enlisted to help empty the cathedral library of more than eighty medieval manuscripts and nearly three thousand books, which were transported to safety. The dean this morning said he feared that efforts to extinguish the fire in the Lady Chapel would lead to the flooding of the main cathedral, but this did not come to pass. The people of Barchester have borne

their ordeal with bravery, and this morning cathedral services went on as
usual even while the remains of the Lady Chapel smoldered.

"It's not much to go on," said Arthur. "Papers were pretty slim during the war."

"But at least it gives us a lead," said Bethany.

"It does?"

"Arthur, for a researcher you're not very observant. 'Even choirboys were enlisted to help empty the cathedral library.' Maybe some of those choirboys are still alive."

Bethany went up to London for the weekend and Arthur spent Saturday afternoon digging through the cathedral records trying to find lists of choirboys, but without success. His schedule at the university the following week was so hectic that he did not make it back to the library until Thursday afternoon. That morning Gwyn had informed him that the manuscripts had received a temporary stay of execution in the latest chapter meeting.

"One of the canons pointed out that the manuscripts are worth considerably less with their covers ripped off," said Gwyn. "So Canon Dale suggested that we have the covers repaired and I said that nobody knows where the covers are, and we ended up tabling the whole issue. *Do* we know where the covers are?"

"I certainly don't," said Arthur. "And Oscar has no idea. If it keeps the manuscripts here, I say the covers can stay lost forever."

He had been looking forward all day to some time in the library, and he was surprised to find as he mounted the stairs that he had really been looking forward to seeing Bethany. Since she had found the newspaper story so easily he thought she might have an idea about how to track down old choirboys. But when he arrived in the library the atmosphere seemed lifeless. Bethany's equipment stood silent at the far end of the room, and she was nowhere to be seen.

Arthur sat at his usual table, feeling somewhat deflated, and had just been about to try, for the hundredth time, to write a section in his cathedral guide about the central tower when he heard a voice behind him.

"Arthur," said Oscar, "escaped the Barchester prison, I see."

"An insufferably busy week," said Arthur, pushing back his chair. "I think the chairman invents committees to infuriate me."

"Well, good to see you here. I was just catching up on some library correspondence. Don't want to disturb you."

"I say, Oscar, is Beth . . . I mean, is Miss Davis working today?"

"Gone out for tea, I think," said Oscar. "Apparently she's a regular down in the café these days. Did you need her for something?"

"No," said Arthur. "Just wondered how long I'll be able to work in peace." Oscar suppressed a smile as he took a seat at his desk by the door. Arthur chose not to notice and turned back to his work. He had read his first and only sentence over about ten times, until the words swirled before him as meaningless strings of characters, when he thought to ask Oscar something else. "Do you know where the records of choir membership are kept?"

"Moved them to the choral office a few years ago," said Oscar, "along with some other music-related materials. The choir rolls are in a bound book and the choirmaster got tired of coming up here every year to make the new entries."

Ten minutes later, Arthur was in the music office, copying out the names of the sixteen 1941 choirboys onto the back of an old service bulletin. He was about to rush back upstairs when he remembered what else was kept in that office.

"Do you have the original copy of *Harding's Church Music?*" he asked the choirmaster.

"Certainly, I keep it in this cabinet," said the choirmaster, pulling a small key out of his pocket. In a moment the two men were poring over a sumptuous vellum volume produced in the mid-nineteenth century by Barchester's own Septimus Harding. Harding had done much of his research for this book about early church music in Britain in the cathedral library, and made frequent reference to the Barchester Breviary, reproducing many of the musical settings from that book. As they turned the broad pages and admired the fine printing, Arthur thought that this book came from a time when the library was a much busier place, when it sent its knowledge and treasures out into the world not as electronic impulses but as new works of scholarship. The trade edition of *Harding's Church Music* was still occasionally reprinted and was a standard reference for choir directors and music teachers around the world. If the Barchester Cathedral Library could produce something that beautiful and useful, perhaps it still had more to contribute. Maybe the library could once again be part of a network of scholars and researchers who wrote new works to share with the world.

"He produced a beautiful book," said the choirmaster.

"He certainly did," said Arthur.

"Where've you been all my life, Arthur Prescott?" said Bethany as Arthur entered the library. Oscar had left, and Bethany was just pulling a manuscript off shelf C. Arthur found himself hoping that she was not scanning the volumes in order, that she had not already made so much progress.

"You're the one who went traipsing off to London," said Arthur. "I was here all day on Saturday. And I've been working on our little mystery while you've been out guzzling tea."

"You can't blame me for the tea, Arthur. That's *your* culture. Help me with this, will you?" The manuscript she was struggling to remove from the case was an unusually thick and heavy one, and the rending of its cover had left a loose bit of linen tape hanging from the spine. This had gotten caught under the adjacent volume. Arthur helped Bethany extract the book. When they had placed the manuscript on Bethany's stand, she said, "There, now you've done at least one useful thing today."

"I've done two useful things," said Arthur. "I've got a list of the choirboys from 1941."

"You don't!"

"I do. Why else would I have said so?"

"It's a figure of speech, Arthur," said Bethany. "So, are any of them alive and well and living in Barchester?"

"I've no idea," said Arthur, "I only just . . ."

"I thought you said you'd done something useful," said Bethany.

"You're not too bad at coming up with primary source material, Arthur, but you're rubbish at interpreting it."

"I'm rubbish?"

"See, I'm picking up the English idiom. Another couple of weeks and I'll be just like you. Now show me your list."

Arthur handed her the bulletin on which he had scrawled the names of the choirboys and she immediately disappeared behind her laptop.

"Not much to go on, I realize," said Arthur. "But I can ask some of the vergers if any of the names are familiar. Some of those men have been around for fifty years or more. They might remember . . ."

"This one's dead," said Bethany. "Herbert Foster died in 1982."

"How do you . . ."

"The Internet is a wonderful thing, Arthur, if only you know how to use it. It's good for a lot more than buying old books and looking at dirty pictures."

"I beg your pardon, but I have never—"

"And James Lindsay—he's dead as well. He was a schoolteacher." Within thirty minutes, Bethany had found evidence that seven of the sixteen choirboys had died. "Some of these names are pretty common," she said, "so I'm only counting the ones that seem to have some sort of connection to Barchester." She showed Arthur how she was searching not just the local newspaper in the British Newspaper Archive, but various genealogy sites and even social media. Before Evensong, she had tracked down two survivors of the 1941 choir—one living in London and one still in Barchester at the River View Elder Care home.

"Are you a believer yet, Arthur?" said Bethany.

"Not yet," said Arthur, "but I'm going to Evensong nonetheless. It's the Tallis Mag and Nunc tonight."

"Not that sort of believer," said Bethany. "I mean are you a believer in the wonders of the digital world?"

"I can see how such wonders might be useful under certain circumstances," said Arthur. "But I still prefer paper and ink."

"The Internet will have to use you as a celebrity spokesman with a ringing endorsement like that. Wait up, I just need to get my purse."

"Wait up?" said Arthur.

"I'm coming with you. To Evensong. You don't mind, do you?"

"I thought you didn't like going to church."

"People can change, Arthur—you should try it sometime. So I'm coming to Evensong and I'm asking if I can sit next to you."

"Yes," said Arthur softly, "that would be lovely."

VI

THE REGIMENTAL CHAPEL

Located in the south transept, this chapel pays tribute to all those of the Royal Barsetshire Regiment who have lost their lives in wars of the last two centuries. Of special interest is a monument, installed by Bishop Gladwyn, to the fallen of those parishes in the gift of the cathedral chapter—St. Cuthbert's and Plumstead Episcopi. This beautiful tile memorial was designed and built by the ceramicist William De Morgan, and includes images of these churches.

1068, near Barcaster

Brother Harold looked out across the green fields and tried to imagine what would flourish there. Not crops or livestock but prayers and praise. He stood two miles upstream from St. Ewolda's, or what had been St. Ewolda's until the arrival of the Normans two years ago. They were a strange sort of invader. They shed no blood at the monastery or in the small town of Barcaster that had grown up around its gates. They brought with them wealth and learning and the ability to raise buildings beyond Harold's imagination. It was, one of the brothers had said, as if the Romans had returned. But they were not altruistic. They did not kill, but they took what they desired. In the case of Barcaster, what they desired was the small rise of land above the River Esk. Situated on a sweeping bend of the river and in the lee of a larger hill, this spot provided views for nearly a mile up and downstream. It was, said the Norman commander who arrived at the gate of St. Ewolda's one morning, of strategic importance. Already a stone castle was under construction at one end of this rise. At the other end stood the soon-to-be-abandoned monastery of St. Ewolda's. For more than four hundred years, the monks of St. Ewolda's had worshipped peacefully on the spot where their founder was martyred. But now they were to move to a new home, in fields that the monastery owned upstream.

"We come in the name of Christ" had been the first words of the commander to Harold. And in His name the Normans had been busy. Even before the castle construction began, they had started making plans for a grand cathedral on the site of St. Ewolda's—the seat of a newly formed diocese of Barsytshire.

"The doors alone will dwarf any building you have ever seen," said one of the builders to Harold. "The arches will soar overhead, and the very ceiling will be lost in darkness on all but the brightest days, so far toward heaven will it be." And Harold could stay and watch it happen, for the new cathedral would be a monastic foundation. But the bishop and the abbot would be French-speaking Normans. The bishop had visited once already, to view the plans for the cathedral, and he had told Harold that the monks of St. Ewolda's could be absorbed into the new foundation, which he thought of dedicating to St. Martin of Tours.

But St. Ewolda's was a Saxon foundation in honor of a Saxon saint, and Harold had no desire for Norman grandeur. He wanted simply to live out his days in the peace that St. Ewolda's had always known.

And then there was the matter of his guardianship. As Guardian, he could not allow the relic to fall into the hands of the Normans. And so he had asked the bishop to approve a different plan.

"What if, My Lord, we were to reestablish the foundation of St. Ewolda's on a plot of land already owned by the monastery, some two miles hence. With us we would take our few belongings—a small collection of books and furnishings, and of course the relics of our blessed St. Ewolda, who lies entombed below the altar of our church. You could then build your cathedral on this spot, which has been blessed with worship for four centuries."

But the wily bishop was not so easily fooled. "I accept your proposal with two caveats," he said to Harold as the two stood before the altar of what the Norman visitor must surely have thought of as a crude chapel. "We must not disturb the rest of your blessed St. Ewolda. To remove her from her shrine would be a sacrilege of the highest order. She shall rest in peace where she is."

Harold knew, of course, that the bishop's desire to keep the mortal remains of St. Ewolda had nothing to do with sacrilege. Already a cult of pilgrimage was growing up around the shrines of saints, and the bishop surely hoped that Ewolda's shrine would mean pilgrims and offerings even in a place as remote as Barcaster. Insisting on leaving Ewolda undisturbed was all about finance.

"And the second caveat?" asked Harold, wondering if he dare leave behind the bones of his patron in order to save a relic he wasn't even sure he believed in.

"That you allow our builders to erect your new monastic church. It need not be so grand as my cathedral, but a foundation of four hundred years deserves something more than . . . ," the bishop looked around and sniffed with condescension, ". . . than a barn."

Harold could see no other way. If they stayed where they were, the monks of St. Ewolda's would be subsumed into a new monastery with a new patron and the relic he had sworn to guard would almost certainly, within a generation, fall into the hands of these invaders. If they moved, they would lose the shrine of their founder but would be able to continue the traditions of her monastery in a modern building and with the relic properly secured, possibly for hundreds of years to come.

Eventually he had prevailed upon his brothers to see the wisdom of the move. They knew nothing of the relic, of course, and so did not understand the situation as clearly as he, but he subtly played on their feelings toward the Normans, which ranged from quiet resentment to outright hostility, and presented his plan as one that would take advantage of the invaders' expertise and wealth while, at the same time, preserving their own autonomy.

And so he stood at the edge of the field, and imagined a church growing there. It might take a generation or more to complete, and Harold would almost certainly not live to worship under its roof, but smaller buildings could house them for now. They had made do with simple structures since the founding of the monastery; they could continue to do so. Within a few months, there would be enough of a settlement in this empty field that he would be able to move the relic from Barcaster to safety at the new St. Ewolda's. He hoped the Normans would not discover it, or at least, not knowing its true nature, would release it to his care. Fearing the worst, and feeling that some record, at least, of the treasure that had been handed down for so many centuries should survive, Harold had taken the great risk of writing a marginal note in the monastic service book. Beside the Prayer of Consecration he had written, "Here I remember the great treasure of Barsyt." He prayed that, when the Norman takeover was complete, these words would not be the final record of that treasure.

April 30, 2016

FIFTH SATURDAY AFTER EASTER

The River View Elder Care facility smelled faintly of ammonia and less faintly of overcooked Brussels sprouts, but the view from the south-facing rooms was as advertised in the name, and Edward Alford lived in one such room. Arthur and Bethany had taken advantage of their open schedules early Saturday evening to seek out Mr. Alford, and they found him sleeping in a chair, an open copy of *Bleak House* on his lap and an open window in front of him, the fresh air washing away the odors of the place. He opened his eyes before they had spoken and gave a deep sigh.

"Never tire of that view," he said, gazing out across the water mead-ows to where the curve of the river still glimmered in the sun. On the far side of the stream, beyond where a lone willow drooped over the water, the ground rose steeply and sheep dotted the hillside.

"Mr. Alford?" said Bethany gently. "Are you Mr. Edward Alford?"

"Been him all my life," Edward responded. "And look—it's finally earned me a visit from a pretty girl."

"I'm sure I'm not the first," said Bethany. "May we sit down?"

"You sit here by me," said Edward, motioning to a second chair positioned to take in the view. "My competition can sit over there." He waved his hand vaguely in the direction of a couch in front of a small television.

"Oh, I'm not your competition," said Arthur. "We're not . . . that is . . ."

"Can I get you a cup of tea?" said Edward to Bethany, ignoring Arthur's stumbling speech.

"That would be lovely," said Bethany.

Edward leaned forward and whispered to her. "What's his name?"

"Arthur," she whispered back.

"Arthur," he bellowed, "get this lovely young lady a cup of tea. How do you take it?"

"Two sugars, no milk," said Bethany.

"Two sugars, no milk," Edward repeated for Arthur's benefit. "Everything's in the kitchen."

The kitchen was no more than a narrow counter with an electric kettle, a sink, and a small refrigerator. Arthur put the kettle on and wondered how he had so quickly become a third wheel.

"Now," said Edward, "you know my name, but I don't know yours. All I know is how you take your tea and that you're an American."

"Bethany," she said, extending a hand. "Bethany Davis."

"I'm very pleased to meet you, Bethany Davis," said Edward. He turned her hand in his and held it for a moment, then lifted it to his lips and gave it a surprisingly soft kiss. "And to what do I owe the pleasure of your visit?"

"You were a choirboy at the cathedral during the war," said Bethany.

"Oh, dear, if you want me to sing for you, I'm afraid you're about forty years too late. I could recite some poetry, though. Do you prefer Tennyson or Browning?"

"Tennyson. But I actually wanted to talk to you about the night of the bombing."

Edward sat silently for nearly a minute as the smile gradually faded from his face. "That was a long time ago," he said.

"Do you remember that night?"

"Bethany," said Edward, reaching for her hand, "there's a good chance that tomorrow I won't remember you—which is a sin, because you are such a vision." He turned and looked her in the eyes for the first time and squeezed her hand tightly. "But I remember that night like it was yesterday, and I shall until the day I die."

"Can you tell us about what happened?" asked Arthur.

"How's the tea coming?" said Edward.

"Nearly ready," said Arthur.

"Should I send him out for biscuits?" said Edward, leaning conspiratorially toward Bethany but speaking loudly enough that Arthur could hear him.

"I think it's all right if he stays," said Bethany. "We probably should have a chaperone."

"Right you are, my dear. It's quite dangerous for you to be around so much charm."

Bethany returned the squeeze to Edward's hand, which she continued to hold as she settled back in her chair and stared out at the view. The sun was lowering and the shadows of the sheep striped the green of the hillside. "Was it terrible?" she said.

"It was the proudest moment of my life," said Edward. "And no one ever asked me about it."

Bethany turned to see a tear trickling down his cheek. She reached up with her free hand and brushed it away gently. "I'm asking," she said. "Tell me everything."

For the next hour, Edward sat holding hands with Bethany and recounting the events of seventy-five years earlier in almost cinematic detail, as the tea grew cold. While he listened to the story, Arthur marveled at Bethany's transformation. This was not the combative, overly talkative, digital Bethany; this Bethany was pure analogue—gentle, soothing, and as comfortable with this old man as Arthur was with an old book. He felt a hint of jealousy that Bethany could be so at ease with someone she'd only just met.

Edward told the whole story, from the moment the noise had awoken him, to the strange uniform words of the manuscript he carried into the cloister, to the frantic hour of passing books out of the library, to the moment he was standing breathless outside the cathedral cloister watching as the volumes were carted away. Then, after a long pause, he turned to Bethany and said, "And that was the last time I saw him."

"Saw who?" said Bethany.

Arthur resisted the urge to correct her grammar.

"The man in the gray robe. I had seen him in the cloister with my manuscript, the magical manuscript, and then I saw him again walking toward the arch that leads into St. Martin's Lane—the one with the stone steps next to it." Edward paused and turned from Bethany to look once again out the window, where the setting sun had turned the meadow a riot of colors from eggplant to flame red.

"The steps to St. Cuthbert's," said Arthur.

"I didn't know that at the time, but yes. He was still holding the manuscript," said Edward, his gaze fixed on the hillside. He paused again and they all watched as the sun dipped below the hill and the colors disappeared as suddenly as if someone had turned off a light switch. The sheep now huddled in the dusky shelter of a horse chestnut tree. Edward squeezed Bethany's hand, let out a small sigh, and turned his attention back to her.

"There were lots of manuscripts being rescued that night," said Edward. "I don't know why he should have taken that particular one. He had both his arms wrapped around it, and he seemed to look right at me and then . . . then he turned and faded into the shadows."

They sat quietly for a few moments before Edward spoke again. "I suppose now that you've heard the story of that night you won't be coming back to visit me."

"Of course I will," said Bethany. "I'm sure there are other nights you could tell me about."

"None quite like that," he said, smiling.

"One night like that is enough for a lifetime," said Bethany. She leaned across and kissed him gently on the cheek. Edward let go of her hand,

and Arthur could see the regret in his eyes as he did so. There would not be time, he thought, for Edward to tell Bethany about all the nights.

"Thank you for the tea," said Arthur.

"Are you still here, Arthur?" said Edward with a smile. "Perhaps you'd be so kind as to walk this young lady back to her lodgings?"

"I'd be happy to," said Arthur. As they crossed to the door, he stopped and turned back. "Could I ask you a question, Mr. Alford?"

"I won't forbid it."

"Have you ever been back to the library?"

Edward was silent for a moment before answering. "I used to go back every year on the anniversary."

"And were there people there? People working?"

"Sometimes. Mostly theology students in the years after the war, and some of the older cathedral clergy. But fewer as the years went by. I haven't been back in a long time now."

"I'll take you," said Bethany. "Someday soon."

"Good night, Miss Davis," Edward called out as they left his room.

"How did you do that?" asked Arthur when he and Bethany were back out in the street.

"What do you mean?"

"You were so good with him."

"He's not a wild animal, Arthur."

"Yes, but you were . . . different."

"You know I reserve my evil side just for you. Sorry he didn't tell us anything useful."

"You're kidding, right?"

"No, Arthur, I'm not kidding. Don't you know you have to be over eighty for me to kid with you?"

"But he told us something tremendously useful."

"The man in the gray robe?" said Bethany.

"The man in the gray robe."

"OK, lecture me."

"Consider the evidence carefully," said Arthur, warming to his analysis. He had hardly spoken a word since they'd arrived in Edward's room and was ready to pontificate. "Edward said the manuscript he carried to the cloister was in some language he didn't understand and that all the words were the same length. That sounds like a cipher to me, and it makes perfect sense that the monastery's biggest secrets would have been kept in code. And there are no coded manuscripts in the collection now, so that *has* to be our missing manuscript."

"So you admit it's not a boring old Psalter," said Bethany.

"Yes," said Arthur, giving her a slight bow, "I admit that you were right and I was wrong." Bethany smiled.

"Now," said Arthur, "consider the two clues about the man who took the manuscript: he was wearing a gray robe and he disappeared in the direction of St. Cuthbert's Church. The gray robe is the traditional vestment of an order of Franciscan monks—that's why they became known in England as the Greyfriars. In the thirteenth century, a small Franciscan house called Greyfriars was founded just outside the cathedral close in what is now St. Martin's Lane. When Henry VIII dissolved that monastery, most of it was destroyed, but one of the monastic chapels was absorbed into the cathedral precincts and reconsecrated as the parish church of St. Cuthbert. Since then, it's been traditional for the vicar of St. Cuthbert's to wear the Greyfriars' robes."

"You do love to give lectures, don't you?"

Arthur considered this question thoughtfully, for Bethany had asked it not with a tone of judgment but with true curiosity. He considered all the interactions he had with students and staff at the university—the meetings, the tutorials, the office hours—and he had to admit that giving lectures was just about the only part of his job that he enjoyed.

"Yes," he said, "I really do."

"And you think the man in gray was the vicar of St. Cuthbert's?"

"I do. And for some reason he wanted to take personal charge of the coded manuscript."

"So who was the vicar of St. Cuthbert's in 1941?"

"Easy enough to find out," said Arthur. "The diocesan records are in the county archive."

"And the archive is only open on Thursdays."

"You remember that, do you? As it happens I have to attend a meeting of the Media Some-Damn-Thing Committee on Thursday afternoon, but I can get you a pass so you can go and request the parish records."

"Arthur," said Bethany, "sometimes you overthink things."

"What do you mean?"

"What's through this archway?"

"I beg your pardon?" Arthur had not paid attention to the direction they had been walking since leaving River View, and he realized now that Bethany had been guiding their path. "The cathedral close, but why—"

"And what is *above* this archway?" said Bethany.

"The Church of St. Cuthbert," said Arthur with a sigh.

"The Church of St. Cuthbert. You see, I know a little something about the cathedral precincts myself," said Bethany, striding through the great stone arch and turning to mount a narrow flight of stone steps. "It was unlocked when I peeked in last week. Are you coming?"

Arthur hurried up the steps just in time to see Bethany pull open a heavy oak door. In another moment, they stood in St. Cuthbert's. The small space was lit only by the candle of the sanctuary lamp burning at the east end and the street light that filtered through the single stained glass window above the altar. Only half a dozen pews separated Arthur and Bethany from the Communion rail. The only other furnishings were the simple altar table and an old carved pulpit.

"I love this place," said Bethany softly. "I was just wandering around the close and happened to discover it last week and I must have sat in here for an hour. It's so peaceful and dim. It's the exact opposite of my father's church. I like the cathedral, but this is . . . intimate."

"I haven't been up here in years," said Arthur.

"So, anyway," said Bethany, taking Arthur by the hand, "I remember seeing something the other day." She pulled him down the aisle and through a low curtained doorway to the left of the altar and into the sacristy, little more than a closet. Arthur tried not to think what it felt like to be holding hands with Bethany, and instead to wonder what she wanted to show him, but he felt a pang of disappointment when she dropped his hand.

"What is it?" said Arthur. "Why are we in here?"

"That," said Bethany, pointing to the wall above Arthur's head.

He turned to see a painted wooden board. At the top it read: Rectors of St. Cuthbert's. "There," said Bethany, pointing toward the bottom of the board, "just above Charles Edward Harding. That's our man: Henry Albert Naylor, 1937–1946. That must be the man in the gray robe. The question is, where did Mr. Naylor hide the book?"

But Arthur didn't hear her. While Bethany stood waiting for his response, brushing her hair out of her face, Arthur stared at the board on the wall and the name just below Henry Albert Naylor. Charles Edward Harding had been rector of St. Cuthbert's from 1946 to 1980. Charles Edward Harding was Arthur's grandfather. The man who had told Arthur that Barchester was the resting place of the Holy Grail had succeeded Henry Albert Naylor, the last man seen with the missing manuscript. Arthur had known, as a child, that his grandfather was a retired clergyman, but he had never asked for, nor had his grandfather ever offered, details of his service. But now it seemed the Holy Grail might be linked to the Book of Ewolda; the Book of Ewolda was linked to Henry Albert Naylor; and Henry Albert Naylor was linked to Arthur's grandfather. Had his grandfather seen the missing manuscript? Did he know what secrets it contained? And did those secrets lead him to believe the Grail was in Barchester and to send his grandson looking for it?

"Arthur! Ground control to Major Prescott. Can you hear me?"

"Yes, sorry," said Arthur. "My mind wandered for a moment."

"Wandered," said Bethany. "It took a hike."

Arthur thought for an instant about telling Bethany that his grandfather's name was on the board, but even though they were cohorts in the search for the Book of Ewolda, he still didn't want her knowing his suspicions about the Grail. For now, he would, as his grandfather had asked, keep the Grail and anything not directly pertaining to the search for the manuscript secret.

"Sorry, what were you asking?" said Arthur.

"I was asking where Mr. Naylor hid your precious manuscript."

"That," said Arthur, "is a very good question."

"I'm afraid I've some . . . difficult news, Arthur," said Gwyn sternly as the two were just passing into the water meadows the following Tuesday morning.

"The cathedral is to be turned into flats," said Arthur. "And the manuscript collection used for wallpaper."

"It's not quite to that point yet," said the dean. "This is more to do with you personally. One of the canons has insisted that we get the new guidebook to the designers by the end of the month. He seems to think we are missing out on tourist dollars by not having an up-to-date guide. So that means I really must insist that you deliver the text to me by the end of next week."

"It's the precentor, isn't it?"

"It doesn't matter who it is," said Gwyn, "I agree. It must get done."

"Very well," said Arthur. "I may well be on the way to discovering the story of our founder, but if you insist on a half-written guide I shall endeavor to provide it."

"Arthur, you are always on the verge of discovering the story of our founder. And you had better do more than endeavor. The chapter are insistent that if the manuscript is not delivered they will pass the assignment to someone else and demand the advance back."

"Who else could do it?" said Arthur. "No one else could do it."

"I'm sure Oscar could be persuaded to step in," said Gwyn.

"Oscar would never do that to me."

"He wouldn't be doing anything to you, but he might do something for me."

"Oh, my Lord in heaven."

"Please don't take the Lord's name in vain, Arthur."

"I didn't take his name in vain—only his address."

"Nothing!" said Bethany as Arthur stepped into the library.

"Good afternoon to you, too," said Arthur. Bethany's equipment stood idle, there was no manuscript on her stand awaiting digitization, and if her unkempt hair was any sign, as Arthur had come to suspect that it was, she was extremely frustrated. Arthur could not judge her mood by her eyes, as these remained hidden behind the screen of her laptop.

"I took a break from work to see if I could find out anything about Henry Albert Naylor. I've been searching for two hours and I've got nothing. No obituary, no publications. It's like this guy was intentionally trying to avoid having a digital footprint."

"Yes, a lot of people did that in 1946," said Arthur.

"Oh, ha-ha-ha," said Bethany. "You've no idea how frustrating it is when you can't find what you're looking for."

Arthur could not prevent himself from laughing out loud. "I've no idea? Really? I've been trying for years to find out something about St. Ewolda, and you've given up after two hours? Never was a generation so addicted to instant gratification."

"My generation is not that removed from yours, Arthur," said Bethany, closing her laptop and leaning back in her chair. "Just because you *act* like you're from the same generation as Henry Albert Naylor doesn't make it true. And yes, I understand that research is usually fruitless and that sometimes you never find what you're looking for. I'm not an idiot and I'm not a brat, I'm just, at this moment, annoyed because I wanted to impress you and now I can't."

"I keep doing that, don't I?" said Arthur.

"What, being an ass?"

"Something like that. I'm sorry. And I certainly understand the frustration of the researcher, but I think this is one case in which I can help you out." He walked across the library to Oscar's desk and ran his finger along a group of thick volumes, bound in black cloth, that filled two shelves behind Oscar's chair. He pulled out one of these tomes and opened it on the desk. As soon as the pages fell open a musty smell filled the air. Arthur usually paused to savor this smell, slightly different for every book, but today he flipped quickly through the pages until he found what he was looking for. "Here you are," he said. "Henry Albert Naylor. I guess today books win."

"You like that, don't you?" said Bethany crossing the room to see the book that Arthur now turned around for her. "Lecturing and winning, the two favorite occupations of Mr. Arthur Prescott. So what is this?"

"*Crockford's Clerical Directory* for 1941," said Arthur. "It's a list of all the clergymen in the U.K. with short biographies."

"Why 1941?" asked Bethany, pulling up a chair to the other side of Oscar's desk.

"Last edition published before Naylor died in 1946. Died or stopped being the vicar of St. Cuthbert's. Because of the war, I suppose; it didn't come out again until 1947."

"A book, eh?" said Bethany.

"Who would have thought?" said Arthur.

Bethany leaned over the open volume and read:

> **NAYLOR, Henry Albert,** Hogglestock, Barsetshire.—*St. Laz. Ox. B.A. (2nd cl. Lit. Hum.) 1924, M.A. 1926; Deac. 1927, Pr. 1928. C. of Uffley Dio. Bst. 1929, R. St. Cuthbert's, Dio. Bst. 1937, Canon Bchr. Cathedral 1938, R. Plumstead Episcopi 1938.*

"Does this mean anything to you, Arthur?"

"With thousands of listings, *Crockford's* does use a few abbreviations." Arthur spun the book back around. "Let's see what we can make of this. Henry Albert Naylor, born in Hogglestock, Barsetshire. That's just a few miles out past the university. Went to St. Lazarus College, Oxford, where he earned a second class in Classics, so he's competent but no genius. Got his bachelor's degree in 1924, his master's in 1926. That would put him in one of the first classes after the Great War. He was too young to fight, lucky boy. Curate of Uffley in the Diocese of Barsetshire. That's south-west of here not more than fifteen miles or so. Then in 1937 he becomes rector of St. Cuthbert's, we knew that, but look at this. In 1938 he becomes a canon of Barchester Cathedral and rector of Plumstead Episcopi."

"Sounds like he was a busy man."

"Not necessarily," said Arthur. "St. Cuthbert's is a tiny parish, and even in those days not many people lived in that part of the city. And Plumstead Episcopi—let's just say Plumstead Episcopi would be a good place to hide a manuscript."

"What is Plumstead Episcopi?" said Bethany. "Is that a church?"

"It's a rural parish," said Arthur, turning back to the shelves behind Oscar's desk. "With a lovely little parish church. I wouldn't want to bore you with a lecture, so I'll just show you this." Arthur took a slim booklet off the shelf and handed it to Bethany.

"A *History of Plumstead Episcopi* by Arthur Prescott," said Bethany. "OK, Mister Church Historian, suppose you save me the trouble of reading what I'm sure is a scintillating narrative and just tell me why Plumstead Episcopi would make such a good hiding place."

"It had a rather lovely rectory," said Arthur. "Georgian construction. But the parish itself was sparsely populated. The first two rectors of the last century chose to live in town rather than in the isolated surroundings of Plumstead, and during the Great War the rectory was used to billet soldiers who, I'm afraid, did not treat the place well. It was pulled down in the 1920s and the parish subsumed into the neighboring parish of Ullathorne, but since the living had always been in the hands of the cathedral chapter, there has been a tradition since then that a member of the chapter is made rector of Plumstead Episcopi. The only real duties that come with the title are seeing that the church doesn't fall down and holding a service there once a year—usually it's a sort of summer festival. Most people who go just want to see the inside of the church—it was restored by George Gilbert Scott in the Victorian Gothic style."

"And since the church is only unlocked one day a year, you think it wouldn't be a bad place to stash a mysterious manuscript."

"Certainly if I were Henry Albert Naylor on the night of February 7, 1941, and I were looking for a place where a manuscript would be safe from both prying eyes and Nazi bombs, I might have whisked it off to a church to which only I had the keys and which was nearly always closed. Naylor died in 1946, but the books and manuscripts weren't returned to the cathedral library until after the repairs were completed in the early fifties. Maybe he hadn't told anybody about the manuscript."

"But did he die in 1946 or did he just stop being rector of St. Cuthbert's?"

"Looks like he died," said Arthur, who had pulled another volume of *Crockford's* off the shelf. "He's not listed in the 1947 volume."

"So how do we get into the church at Plumstead Episcopi? I'm not waiting until some summer festival. Who's the rector now? Couldn't we just ask him for the keys? You can tell him I'm some sort of Victorian Gothic fanatic and that I'm only here for a few more weeks and I'm dying to see the church."

"Is it really just a few more weeks?" said Arthur.

"Arthur, focus. We are hatching a diabolical plot here and you're asking about insignificant details. Who is the rector of Plumstead?"

"We're not getting the keys from the rector," said Arthur.

"Why not? Is it someone you know?"

"Someone I have tried, without success, to avoid whenever possible. The current rector of Plumstead Episcopi is the precentor."

Arthur lay awake that night thinking. He had gone back to the library after dinner and looked in a copy of *Crockford's Clerical Directory* from just before his grandfather's death in 1992. There was the biography:

> **HARDING, Charles Edward,** Barchester, Barsetshire.—Ch.
> Ch. Ox. B.A. (1st cl. Lit. Hum.) 1933, M.A. 1935; Deac. 1936, Pr.
> 1938. Chap. RAF 1938–1945, R. St. Cuthbert's, Dio. Bst. 1946, Canon
> Bchr. Cathedral 1958, R. Plumstead Episcopi, Dio. Bst, 1964. Ret. 1980.

Arthur's grandfather had served as a chaplain in the Royal Air Force during the war and then become rector of St. Cuthbert's, eventually adding the same posts (canon of Barchester Cathedral and rector of Plumstead) that Henry Albert Naylor had held. Had Naylor passed the manuscript on to his grandfather? And if so, why hadn't his grandfather told Arthur anything about it? He considered dismissing the similarities in the two men's careers as coincidence, but the summer before his grandfather had died, Arthur had again mentioned his discovery about the similar yew trees in Barchester and Tennyson.

"Of course it could be a coincidence," said Arthur, trying to prod his grandfather into telling him more about the Grail.

But the old man only answered with his typical enigmatic smile,

"There are no coincidences." Was he trying to tell Arthur something? Did he know that one day Arthur would learn about the manuscript and Naylor's connection to it? That he would discover that Naylor and his grandfather had shared not just the post at St. Cuthbert's, but the one at Plumstead Episcopi—a position now held by the precentor?

Arthur wondered what it was about the precentor that bothered him so much. True, there was plenty to dislike—from his clammy handshake to his air of superiority to the way he had mistreated Oscar. But there had always been something else. The day he had met the man, Arthur had felt instantly averse. He had no doubt it was the precentor who was agitating to sell the library's manuscripts, the precentor who suddenly demanded Arthur turn in the text for the guidebook, the precentor who was responsible for all that was wrong with the cathedral. Arthur knew this was a completely unfair assessment—after all, over the years the precentor had brought ritual back to cathedral worship, he had revitalized the choir program, and he had supported the dean in many of her efforts, even, in spite of his disdain for the design, in the attempt to rebuild the Lady Chapel. But whether Arthur's assessment was fair or not, he took what he knew was unjustified pleasure in making it. At the root of the problem, he decided, was that the precentor always seemed to be saying one thing and meaning another. "Good afternoon, Arthur" meant "I'm sitting in your usual spot because I am better than you, now get some work done on that damned guidebook." "Good evening, Arthur" meant "You have no place in this cathedral if you stubbornly refuse to believe in God." And "It's a lovely day" invariably meant "There is something about this day that I know and that you do not and that I will not be telling you." Yes, the precentor, Arthur felt sure, was a man who kept secrets. And what better secret than the lost manuscript of Ewolda—perhaps the manuscript that had convinced Gladwyn, and Arthur's grandfather, that Barchester was the resting place of the Holy Grail. But if the precentor had discovered such a secret in the locked church of Plumstead Episcopi, he would hardly take kindly to a request by the lazy, ignorant, pagan Arthur Prescott to provide the key. What's more, if anyone, and especially Arthur, with his interest in the history of the cathedral, asked for the Plumstead key, the precentor would immediately smell a rat, and would no doubt move the manuscript to a . . . what did the Americans call it . . . a secure location.

Just as Arthur was drifting off to sleep, it occurred to him that all his musings about the precentor and his grandfather and the lost manuscript and the Grail were irrelevant. He could not go gallivanting about the countryside looking for ancient secrets. He had to produce a text for the new guidebook in less than ten days. There was no question of allowing someone else to do it. The cathedral had advanced Arthur five hundred pounds for the work, and that money was long ago spent on books. Arthur couldn't afford to pay back the advance, and besides, after all the work he had done, he desperately wanted to be the one to write the guidebook. So he would have to set aside all thought of adventures with Bethany and produce a manuscript of his own.

VII

THE QUIRE

The quire was built in the Decorated style in the second half of the thirteenth century. Bishop Samuel Giffard, who began the rebuilding of the original Norman structure, is buried in the quire aisle. Although some of the woodwork was damaged or destroyed during the Civil War, many of the carvings, and particularly the misericords, date from the late thirteenth century and are thought to be the work of a single craftsman.

1280, Barchester

Adam Lyngwode stepped back from the wood to admire his work. The face of the woman was beginning to emerge from the oak—not as close a likeness as he wanted but recognizable. Certainly the hair that streamed from the side of the head could belong to no one but Clarice. It had been a cold winter in Barchester, and though a fire burned nearby, the stonemasons seemed constantly to surround it, warming their hands. Adam felt cold to his core, yet somehow his fingers could still carve. Over the years, they had memorized the motions needed to peel back the layers of wood and reveal the figures within.

Adam had come to Barchester almost ten years ago, when Bishop Giffard had decided to pull down the old Norman quire and replace it with a new, higher, lighter structure in the latest style. The bishop had given Adam a test—build and decorate an oaken chest to hold the cathedral's growing collection of manuscripts. The result had been both practical and beautiful—a solid locking chest, inscribed around the top with the opening verses of the Gospel of John. The bishop had been impressed, and Adam had moved to Barchester, where he joined masons, glaziers, carpenters, and others. For the past decade, they had worked to achieve the bishop's vision for the new quire. For some time now, Adam had been working on the carvings for the quire stalls. He had created arches over the canons' seats that echoed the design of the clerestory windows, carved biblical scenes for the pew ends, and fashioned elaborate figures to separate each canon's stall from the next. For the last few months, he had been engaged in his favorite part of the entire process—carving figures for the misericords. Because these images would rarely be seen, he was allowed considerable leeway in crafting them. Today he was, with the special permission of the dean, working on a portrait of his wife.

Although Adam was a lowly craftsman, becoming friends with the new dean, who had been installed two years ago, had proved simple. He had observed how, whenever the bishop was on the work site, he and the dean argued incessantly. Adam rarely followed the argument, but he had no doubt that the dean loathed the bishop. A few months ago, he had asked the dean to come look at his latest misericord carving. The dean had seemed exasperated at this request, but had complied nonetheless. Adam had pulled back the cloth that covered the carving to reveal the figure of a scowling man with batlike wings and ears. In one hand he held a book, but his other hand was raised as if in command. In place of a human hand he had the claw of a raptor.

"Is that . . ." The dean leaned over to inspect the carving more closely. "Is that the face of the bishop?"

"Is it?" said Adam. "Must be a coincidence. I can change it if you like."

The dean turned to Adam with a wide grin. "No need to change it at all," he said. "Nor is there any need to show this to His Lordship." From that day forward, Adam and the dean were fast friends.

At least once a week the dean would stop by to inspect Adam's latest carvings. On one such day, three months ago, he found Adam in tears, still working but unable to hide his emotions.

"What troubles you, my friend?" said the dean.

"My wife, Clarice, is taken ill," said Adam. "Her fever will not abate and she grows weaker by the hour. She is with child and I fear by the time I return home this evening I shall have lost two whom I love."

"Have you prayed at the shrine of Ewolda?" asked the dean. One reason for the reconstruction of the quire was to provide a grander entrance to the shrine of the cathedral's founder. Many miracles of healing had been attributed to Ewolda's shrine, and she seemed to smile especially on women.

"Every day for three days," said Adam. "But blessed Ewolda hears me not. The fever only worsens."

"It grieves me to see you in such distress," said the dean. "There is perhaps something I can do to help. I shall return anon."

A few minutes later, the dean returned, carrying what looked like an ancient cup of wood. The cup was brimming with fresh, clear water. "Show me to your wife," he said.

Adam laid aside his tools, removed his apron, and led the way through the muddy streets of Barchester to a small cottage on the edge of town. He did not remove his boots or think to apologize to the dean for the meagerness of his hospitality, so great was his urgency to avail himself of whatever help his friend might provide. In an instant, the dean was kneeling at Clarice's bedside. Her face seemed almost translucent and her shallow breaths came at irregular intervals. She raised her eyes to Adam in question but did not speak.

"Drink of this," said the dean, holding the cup to her lips. Adam watched as Clarice sipped from the cup. She swallowed and drank more. Soon the cup was empty and directly Clarice fell into a slumber. "Stay with her," said the dean. "Your work will wait a day."

The following day Adam found the dean in the Lady Chapel. "I owe you all that I have, sir," he said. "For my precious Clarice has been brought back from the very brink of death. Her fever has broken and color returns to her cheeks."

"I am pleased," said the dean.

Adam desired more than anything to ask the dean about the miraculous cup of healing. Whence had it come? Was it some relic of Ewolda known only to the dean? He dared not ask, but the dean must have seen the curiosity in Adam's eyes.

"There are secrets at Barchester," said the dean, "that must remain secret."

"I understand, Father," said Adam, though he did not.

Two months later, Adam's first son was born, joining two healthy daughters. He had brought the good news to the dean and had, on that day, asked permission to carve two misericords—one a portrait of his wife, and the other a simple cup. "I shall not carve it as it truly appears," said Adam. "No one will know it is aught other than a Communion chalice."

The dean had given his consent, and Adam had already completed the carving of the cup. He wanted to give thanks for the miracle of his wife's salvation—a thanks that someone might one day understand. So he did not place a cross on the cup, as would have been usual for a Communion chalice. That small omission, he thought, might at least hint to some future monk that a woodcarver was grateful for the miracle of the cup of Barchester.

Now he turned his attention to his wife's portrait and began to search within the wood for her beautiful eyes.

Dean Henry de Beaumont stood in the cloister waiting for the head stonemason to climb down from his scaffolding. He had been happy to grant Adam Lyngwode permission to carve an image of his wife on a misericord—after all, no one ever saw a misericord. The roof bosses in the cloister were another matter, however. Since the roof here was only twice the height of a man, the bosses would be among the most visible carved images in the monastic complex, seen by the brothers every day. The dean had an idea about what the four most prominent bosses should depict.

Over the past two years, Henry had become close friends with

Peter of Amesbury, prior of the nearby Priory of St. Ewolda. Henry and Peter understood the close links between Barchester Cathedral and St. Ewolda's, and each year, on the feast day of that saint, they held a joint service at the cathedral, during which Peter recounted the story of Ewolda's life. Henry's idea about the cloister bosses had been inspired by a monk's reaction to hearing the Ewolda story. Without permission, this monk had drawn a picture of Ewolda in the priory's service book, next to the service used on her feast day. Peter had been displeased at the defacement, but it made Henry wonder if Ewolda's story might be recorded in some way in the cathedral. He had gone to Peter with his idea, and the prior had approved.

So Henry de Beaumont instructed his stonemason to create four roof bosses in the four corners of the cloister depicting the life of St. Ewolda. Henry did not live to see the bosses completed, but almost eight hundred years later, they would still be there, silently paying tribute to the life of the founder.

May 4, 2016

FEAST OF THE ENGLISH SAINTS AND MARTYRS OF THE REFORMATION ERA

"Is it true," said Miss Stanhope as they were settling down for Wednesday afternoon's tutorial, "that one of Jesse Johnson's minions is working at the cathedral?"

"I'm sorry, Miss Stanhope," said Arthur, "but as usual I have no idea what you are talking about."

"Jesse Johnson? The American industrialist? He's been doing all the chat shows. How have you not seen him?"

"Reading your papers, Miss Stanhope, takes up the time I have normally reserved for chat shows."

"I hear he has, like, a billion dollars from some sort of computer chip," said Mr. Crawley.

"And how exactly does this relate to today's discussion of religion in early-nineteenth-century fiction?" asked Arthur.

"The guy is a religious fanatic," chimed in Miss Robarts. "I mean real crackpot stuff. He believes everything in the Bible and I mean *everything*—two aardvarks on Noah's ark, plagues of locusts in Egypt, the snake feeding Eve an apple."

"It's called fundamentalism, and that concept is actually not a bad place to begin our discussion. Now if—"

"Yeah, but this guy doesn't just believe it," said Mr. Crawley. "He wants to take his billion dollars and *prove* it."

"He's building this huge museum in America," said Miss Stanhope. "And he has people all over the world looking for biblical artifacts he can put into it. Like if people don't believe the Bible they're going to be convinced by an old rock."

"He's after more than rocks," said Mr. Crawley. "He has oceanographers doing sonar mapping of the Red Sea looking for Pharaoh's chariots that got washed away by Moses. He's got archaeologists looking for pieces of Noah's ark. The whole thing is very Indiana Jones."

"I saw him on Graham Norton," said Miss Robarts, "and he's a showman, that's what he is. He's like one of those American TV preachers. And don't kid yourself—he's not building this museum to convince people to believe. He's building it so that people who already do believe can feel even more self-righteous. If he tells people they're looking at the apple core from the Garden of Eden, they'll buy it."

"Yeah," said Miss Stanhope, "but if they'll believe whatever he says, why spend all that money actually looking for real artifacts? Why not just plop an apple core in a glass case and start charging admission?"

"He's a showman, yes," said Mr. Crawley, "but I think this guy genuinely believes he's going to find authentic biblical artifacts. And not all of what he's doing is crazy."

"What's he doing that's not crazy?" asked Miss Robarts, crossing her arms in front of her chest in the way she always did when she was ready to pick a fight with Mr. Crawley.

"Well, the manuscripts, for one thing," said Mr. Crawley.

Arthur had been letting the conversation sail past him, and vaguely considering whether it was worth his trouble to try to steer his students back into the waters of English literature, but at the mention of manuscripts he suddenly began to listen.

"That's why he has representatives in Barchester and Winchester and Salisbury and everywhere else," said Mr. Crawley. "He wants to digitize every pre-Reformation religious manuscript. And he's not even that particular, I hear. Apparently wherever he sends his . . ."

"His minions," said Miss Stanhope.

"Wherever they go," said Mr. Crawley, "they're digitizing *all* the manuscripts, no matter what the subject. And he's going to put it all on the Web for free. Can you imagine what a resource that will be for scholars?"

"Yes," said Miss Robarts, "it's true that even the looniest lunatic might do something worthwhile once in a while. But do you know *why* he's digitizing all those manuscripts? And do you know why he's starting in England?" The others looked at her blankly. "Because he's looking for the Holy Grail."

"I beg your pardon," said Arthur, now fully attentive to the conversation.

"I read it in the *Daily Mail*," said Miss Robarts. "They said one of the artifacts he's looking for is the Holy Grail. He doesn't just believe the Bible. He believes the whole King Arthur story, too—Joseph of Arimathea bringing the Grail to England, Galahad gallivanting around looking for it. And Jesse Johnson thinks that even though no one has succeeded in finding it in two thousand years, he's going to uncover it with his billion dollars."

"The Holy Grail?" said Miss Stanhope sarcastically. "I suppose next he'll be looking for Cinderella's glass slipper."

"I'm sorry," said Arthur, shoving his chair back from the table. "Something has come up and I have to . . . I have to go."

"Are you all right, Arthur?" asked Miss Stanhope. "You look ill."

"Miss Robarts, perhaps you could lead the discussion," said Arthur, shoving his papers into his bag. "The topic, as I'm sure you will recall, was religion in early-nineteenth-century fiction. You seem to be off to a good start. I'll see you next week."

Arthur rushed from the room on not completely false pretenses. He did feel ill. The idea that Bethany had been lying to him all this time made his stomach churn. He could picture it: how she carefully staged their first meeting in the chapter house so she could find out everything he knew about Bishop Gladwyn's portrait and its association with the Grail. She probably already believed the Grail was hidden in Barchester. Somehow Bethany and this sleazy-sounding billionaire coming into Arthur's town, looking for his dream so that they could take it back to America, made the Grail that much more real to Arthur. And it made Bethany, with whom he had been trying so hard to be friends, exactly what he had feared all along: the devil prowling about like a roaring lion seeking someone to devour. It was up to Arthur to resist her.

Arthur made his way straight to the library, ready to confront Bethany, only to discover the room locked and empty. After letting himself in and locking the door behind him, he set his bag by his usual table and crept over to Bethany's digitization station. The table was covered with cords and metal boxes. Her purse was gone, along with her laptop, but on the floor, leaning against one of the table legs, was a canvas carrier bag with the words "American Library Association" printed on the side. Without touching the bag, Arthur peeked in. A couple of books, a few magazines, a thick sheaf of papers bound with plastic rings, and a small notebook— hard to tell much without . . . was he really going to do this? Was Arthur going to rummage through Bethany's things looking for evidence that she was . . . What? A liar? A spy? The devil prowling about? The door to the cloister was locked, he thought, and although he felt considerably worse about going through Bethany's things without her permission than about the possibility of being caught, the security of the room pushed him over the edge. He picked up the canvas bag and dumped its contents onto an empty table.

Arthur was not given to dramatic gasps, and the sound of air sucking into his mouth as he looked at what fell onto the table made him even more shocked than he already was. Lying in front of him was a rather tatty copy of the same book of Arthurian legends he had loved as a child—only the color of the binding was different. As Arthur well knew, the American edition had been published in green cloth, not blue. In it, he knew, was Arthur Rackham's illustration of the Sangreal, an illustration Bethany must have seen. But did she see it before or after he had shown her the Collier portrait of Bishop Gladwyn—the portrait from which Rackham had copied his vision of the Grail? Arthur gently opened the olive-green cover. In the upper right corner of the endpaper, in a childish hand, were written the words, "Bethany's Book," and below that, in the center of the page, in a more practiced hand, "To Bethany, from Aunt Caroline, Merry Christmas 1999." She had known about the Rackham connection all along, and yet she had stood there in front of the portrait with Arthur not saying a word.

The presence of the Rackham book among Bethany's things should not be, Arthur thought, enough to condemn her, but it did seem sufficient cause for further investigation. He picked up a small black notebook and began slowly flipping through its pages. He could feel his pulse quicken and beads of sweat break out on his forehead as he saw the words *Arthur, Malory, Collier,* and, over and over, *Grail.* Bethany had a Grail notebook, a notebook she had clearly been adding to for many years, to judge from the wear to the cover, the multiple colors of ink, and the curl of the pages. Arthur slowed his flipping, then stopped when he saw an even more familiar pair of words: *Arthur Prescott.*

At the top of the page, Bethany had written, "Gifford's Auction House, Lot #157—two manuscript notebooks of Robert Gladwyn, Bsp. Barchester, estimated £50–£75. Possible notes on Grail or Collier painting?" The next line read, "bid £175." Arthur, of course, had been the successful bidder on Bishop Gladwyn's notebooks, and somehow Bethany had found that out, for just below her own bid she had written, "Purchased £200 Arthur Prescott, #3 Hiram's Cottages, Barchester. Take Jesse Johnson job and request Barchester?"

Arthur's stomach dropped. Bethany had been stalking him. She was a Grail hunter working for a Grail hunter and she had insinuated herself into his life at Barchester for one reason—to find out what he knew. She had no interest in being his friend; she was using him to get to the Grail.

Arthur picked up the bound pile of papers from Bethany's things, turned it over, and read the familiar words on the cover page, words he knew by heart, although he had not read them in many years: *A Comparative Survey of Pre-Reformation Grail Manuscripts: A Thesis Submitted in Partial Fulfillment of the Requirements of a Master's Degree* by Arthur Prescott. Arthur's thesis had never been published; it had never been posted online, and yet here it was with Bethany's things. How long had she been researching him? Surely longer than she had been working for Jesse Johnson. Did that mean she wasn't trying to find the Grail for Johnson or that he had hired her because of what she already knew about Arthur?

He had never felt so angry. His eyes watered and he could hardly see the other items on the table as he sifted through them. Magazines with articles about the Grail, loose pages of notes, and . . . could that be the Stansby *Morte d'Arthur?* Surely Oscar wouldn't let her check that out. He felt his fingers trembling and his ears rang so loudly he didn't hear the footsteps on the stairs, or even the voice of Bethany when she first spoke to him. Only when she raised her voice and said, "Arthur! What are you doing?" did he realize she was standing in the doorway, looking as angry as he felt.

"Why are you going through my things?" she demanded, marching across the room until she stood across the table from him.

"How did you . . . the door was locked," sputtered Arthur.

"Some people trust me—but not you obviously. What the hell do you think you're doing?"

"You didn't just happen to meet me," said Arthur. "You came here looking for me. You were stalking me. You lay in wait for me like a . . . a . . . like a spider."

"Oh, grow up. I would have told you everything eventually."

"You stalked me," said Arthur again, still not quite able to believe it.

"Yeah, well, you went poking around in my private things," said Bethany, raising her voice.

"You lied to me," said Arthur, matching her volume.

"I never lied to you. I didn't tell you everything about myself the first day we met, but I never lied to you. You, on the other hand, did lie to me. The very first thing you told me was a lie."

"I . . ."

"You told me the cup in Gladwyn's painting wasn't the Grail when

you knew it was. Don't tell me you didn't know about the Rackham connection."

"But why even ask me if you already knew?"

"I didn't *ask* you if it was the Grail, Arthur. I just asked you where the
painting was. You took it on yourself to start lying to me then and there.
I know you never liked me, but you really never gave me much of a
chance."

"You came here . . . why? To find the Holy Grail and take it back to
your . . . your . . . crazy boss."

"I have a job to do, OK? I am here to help scholars around the world
have access to those manuscripts. You may think that's evil, but I happen
to think it's noble. And yes, the guy who's paying the bills is overreach-
ing a bit, but it doesn't mean good things can't come out of it."

"But why all the Grail materials? And why . . . why me?"

"Because yes, I happen to be a fan of Grail lore. And when I saw the
painting of Gladwyn online and recognized the Holy Grail from my
Rackham book—my favorite book in the world, by the way, not that you
would ever bother to ask me that since you seem to think I hate books—
well, when I saw that painting I got interested in Gladwyn, too. And I
thought it would be cool to own his notebooks, because, you know, he
was obviously into the Grail. So when you outbid me, I called the auction house and told them I wanted to be sure they had the shipping information right, and they gave me your name and address. And yes, I
suppose that was kind of a sneaky, deceptive thing to do, but I thought,
how cool would it be to meet someone else who was interested in Gladwyn and probably interested in the Grail, too. And then I found you on
the Oxford University alumni site and I tracked down your thesis in
your college library and ordered a copy. It was . . . it is amazing—all
those details about medieval manuscripts that mentioned the Grail. I'd
never seen anything quite like it before. So when I got to choose where I
wanted to work, I chose Barchester because I wanted to meet you, Arthur. Not spy on you or steal your work, just to meet you and, you know,
hang out with somebody who shared one of my passions, who had actually held all those medieval Grail manuscripts in his hands. Maybe we
could be friends, I thought. And then I met you and you lied to me and

you fought with me and now you're violating my privacy and I'm wondering what the hell I'm doing here and why I even cared about Gladwyn or the Grail or stupid Arthur Prescott in the first place."

Arthur had been ready for this argument when Bethany had come into the room. He had been filled with righteous fury. The possibility that he might be wrong never even entered his mind. Now Bethany stood in front of him, choking back sobs as she shoved her books and papers back into the canvas bag, and the lump in his gut turned from anger to guilt. He had, in fact, treated her pretty badly.

"I'm sorry," he said softly.

"Sorry doesn't cut it, Arthur. Let's just agree to live at opposite ends of the room, shall we."

"No," said Arthur. "I don't agree. And the fact is, I know it doesn't seem like it, but I do."

"You do what?" said Bethany, wiping her eyes on her sleeve and looking at him in exasperation.

"I do like you," he said.

They stood staring at each other in silence, Bethany's half-filled bag still sitting on the table and Arthur trying to compose what he wanted to say next.

"I liked you from the moment I saw you," he said. "I like that you can put me in my place and win arguments with me. I like how hard you work and how much you care and I like the way that wisp of hair always falls down in front of your face." It was there now, and Bethany quickly swept it away. "And I really wanted to be friends; I was trying, I was. And that's why it hurt so much when I thought you were . . . were deceiving me."

Bethany crossed her arms over her chest and kept staring at Arthur but did not speak.

"And I'm sorry I went through your things. And you're right—I do like the Grail and its . . . its lore. But if we have this in common, this fascination with the Grail, then yes, maybe we *can* talk about that; maybe we *can* share that . . . that passion. It's the kind of thing that friends do, isn't it?"

"God, you're an ass, Arthur," said Bethany, her arms still crossed. Arthur felt the rock in his gut harden. He hadn't expected to feel this way.

Of course she would stay mad, but why was her anger making him feel so sick? He had tried to apologize. Shouldn't that be enough?

"It's one of the things I like about you," said Bethany, dropping her arms and returning to the work of packing up her carrier bag. "So, as long as we can agree that I was right and you were wrong, I suppose we can be Grail buddies."

"What if we agree," said Arthur, "that we were both wrong but that I was more wrong than you?"

"Seriously?"

"That I was *much* more wrong than you?" said Arthur hopefully.

"OK, fine," said Bethany.

Arthur hadn't realized that his entire body had been tense until he felt his muscles relax. The wretched tightness in his belly began to dissolve. "So we can be friends?"

"I'm willing to give it a shot," said Bethany. "But let's *both* be honest, OK?"

"Fair enough," said Arthur, smiling. "We can start on Monday."

"Monday! What the hell!"

"Oh, it's nothing to do with you—it's me and the dean and the chapter. They've given me an ultimatum."

"An ultimatum?"

"I didn't tell you yesterday because we . . . I got distracted researching Henry Albert Naylor. It's about the cathedral guide. Either I hand in the completed text next week or they ask for the advance back and assign someone else to the job."

"And I'm guessing you don't have the advance."

"Not unless I sell you Gladwyn's notebooks at a tidy profit," said Arthur. "So, I shall be sitting right here all weekend working on the bloody guide and trying to make it sound good even though there is still so much I don't know. In fact, I think I shall take the next two days off work and write from now until Monday morning and hope I can come up with something the chapter will approve. So I shan't have much time for friendship or Grail stories or chasing after missing manuscripts."

"I'll help you."

"How could you possibly help me?" said Arthur. "You've been at

Barchester for, what, three weeks? I've been studying the history of the cathedral for years."

"I'm not going to write it, you idiot," said Bethany, striding across to the ancient table where Arthur worked and picking up a sheaf of papers. "But I don't think they'll want you to hand in *this*. You, my nineteenth-century friend, have lovely handwriting, but I imagine your printer will want digital files. I'll be your typist."

"My typist?"

"Yes, Arthur. There is this wonderful new invention called a type-writer. And someday they might even add electricity to it and put a screen on it and—"

"OK, OK, I accept. That's very kind of you really. Sadly, I don't have much of anything to type at the moment."

"I thought you had been working on this thing for years."

"True, but I've mostly just done research and taken notes. I don't actu-ally have any finished text. And I spent so long wanting to start out with the story of St. Ewolda that now I don't know where to start."

"Start with the nave," said Bethany.

"I beg your pardon?"

"Start with the nave. It's the oldest part of the church."

"How do you know that?"

"From Bishop Gladwyn's guide—the one I'm forced to use because you are taking so long to write yours. He started with the nave. Start with the nave and when you have a few pages done bring them to me and I'll type them."

"I suppose it's as good a place as any," said Arthur.

"By the way," said Bethany, "how will you get out of work at the uni-versity?"

"The classic," said Arthur. "I'll call in sick. I just hope my chairman doesn't make one of his infrequent visits to Evensong."

"Why don't you just skip Evensong?" said Bethany.

"I don't think I could," said Arthur, "especially with the work I have to do over the next four days. It will . . . it will center me."

"You don't believe in God, but you can't make it through a day with-out going to church. You're an odd duck, Arthur Prescott."

By Friday night, Arthur had come to the conclusion that he did not work well under pressure. His table had become an increasingly cluttered morass of notes, discarded efforts, and false starts. He had most of the information he needed, but wrestling that information into a guidebook, reducing the history of a thousand-year-old building into ten thousand words, required an entirely different skill set from researching and note-taking. Arthur's first attempt at the nave section had weighed in at over four thousand words. When he tried to rewrite it more succinctly he kept remembering things he had left out and ended up with five thousand. He knew because before he had given up and gone to bed on Thursday night, he had counted every one.

With nothing to type, Bethany had taken Friday off to meet up with an old college friend who was visiting Salisbury. Arthur envied her. He had not been to Salisbury in years and on such a clear day the view from the tower toward Old Sarum would be magnificent. Arthur's view was of piles of papers, heaps of notebooks, and a blank page. He had worked all day except for brief breaks for Evensong and Compline. Now, as the cathedral clock struck ten, he was starting to make a list of the books he would have to sell to raise the £500 he would soon owe the cathedral, when Bethany bounded up the stairs into the library.

"God, Arthur, turn some lights on. It's not the twelfth century." The small lamp on his table was the only light in the library. Bethany flicked a switch by the doorway and bright light filled the room. Arthur was blinded for an instant, but he could still hear Bethany's voice.

"Making progress? I brought you the guidebook from Salisbury. It was beautiful. Have you seen the new baptismal font? I mean new for an eight-hundred-year-old building. It sits right in the middle of the nave aisle and the surface of the water is like a mirror—you can see the vaulted ceiling reflected in it. But then it drains at the corners, cascades right down and through the floor, so the water is always moving, too. It's super modern but it really works in the medieval context, I think. Oh, and I went to Evensong—they have it earlier there. They sang a contemporary setting; I think the composer was Armenian. I brought you the service leaflet. The choir was good, but I think I like Byrd and Tallis and all those old English guys better than the modern Europeans, don't you?"

Arthur fell into the breathlessness of Bethany's voice and for a moment forgot about the task that lay before him. When she stopped for air he gazed at her across the room.

"Oh, God, I was rambling again, wasn't I?"

"Not at all," said Arthur, pushing back his chair. "In fact, I should like to hear all about your day."

"But you have work to do. And you must have pages and pages for me to type by now."

Arthur sat in silence. He was suddenly back in school, sitting at his desk with an incomplete assignment, his teacher about to discover that instead of writing an essay on the Peloponnesian War, he had spent the previous afternoon reading *A Connecticut Yankee in King Arthur's Court*. He had forgotten that day, but Bethany's youth and her expectant smile brought it all back.

"Arthur? Are you OK? What have you got for me?"

"Nothing," said Arthur timidly.

"Nothing? It's been two days."

"I don't think I was cut out to write guidebooks. I can't seem to boil things down to their essence. I want to include everything I know and I know far too much."

"Read me something," said Bethany.

"I beg your pardon?"

"Just read me something. Read me a section of your guidebook. Read me whatever's on the first page you pick up."

"All right, all right, if you insist."

"I do."

"Here's a bit about the altar screen."

"What's that?"

"The altar screen. It's the screen behind the altar. Well, not behind, more above, I suppose. It had all these carvings of saints in little niches. It's not a screen exactly, although I suppose it does screen the ambulatory from the chancel, but it's not like a rood screen—you know, not screening the service from the congregation."

"You do such a good job of explaining. I can see why they picked you to write the guidebook."

"Oh, stop it."

"Read." Bethany pulled a chair up next to Arthur, plopped down, and kicked off her shoes.

Arthur began: "The great altar screen of this cathedral church was erected in the course of the fifteenth century, primarily under the aegis of Bishop Maywood. It contained sculptures of over one hundred and twenty saints and martyrs, including such English saints as Alban, Paulinus, and Hilda. In the year 1538, at the hands of King Henry VIII's commissioners, it was grievously mutilated and despoiled of the figures that had adorned it. In succeeding ages, it was subjected to various tasteless alterations until its original beauty was almost entirely effaced."

"God, Arthur—who would read this?"

"Someone interested in the cathedral?"

"Someone with insomnia, maybe."

"I adapted the wording from a memorial in the nave."

"I thought you were a fan of P. G. Wodehouse. Couldn't you put a little . . . I don't know, a little humor in the thing?"

"You think I should write the cathedral guide in the style of P. G. Wodehouse."

"Perfect idea, Arthur. Couldn't have put it any better myself. Think of it as a writing exercise."

"A writing—"

"Only don't write it, just tell me."

"Very well," said Arthur, leaning back in his chair. How would Wodehouse describe the altar screen? he thought. How would Gussie Fink-Nottle describe it? He closed his eyes and gave it a go.

"Sometime longer ago than I care to think, a certain bishop what's-his-name took into his head the idea that the wall behind the altar should be chockablock with his betters and by Jove the next thing you knew the place was filled to the ceiling with blokes who had gotten themselves so deep into the mulligatawny with the whole religion thing that they ended up losing their heads or being roasted alive or other various bally good ways of shuffling off the old mortal coil. The next thing you know the whole country was Reformation mad, and old King Henry, when not working his way through wives like Galahad Threepwood through dry martinis, had taken something of a dislike to saintly types, and so in 1538, his cronies depopulated the screen—leaving the dean, if not actually disgruntled, far from being gruntled."

Arthur had expected some reaction from Bethany and was surprised at the silence that met this recitation. He turned and saw that her face was unusually red, her eyes seemed to be watering, and she was having some sort of small spasm, as if she were gasping for breath and trying to stay quiet all at once.

"Are you quite well?" asked Arthur, but he did not question her health for long, for she fell back in her chair and put an end to her silence with an explosion of laughter. Bethany had a sense of humor after all.

When she quieted a few moments later, she managed to say, between shallow breaths, "Ever so much better, Arthur."

"Can you imagine the look on the dean's face if I handed *that* in?" said Arthur.

"Oh, the dean would love it. It's the precentor's face I'd like to see. The old codfish would blow smoke out of his gills."

"How do you know the precentor?"

"Gwyn threw a little dinner party for me to meet the chapter last week. You don't get invited to everything, you know, Arthur."

"I always thought he looked more like a salmon."

"No, definitely a codfish."

"Anyhow, I can't write it like this."

"OK, so don't be Wodehouse, but loosen up a bit. I mean you did all that—made me laugh so hard I nearly peed myself—without putting pen to paper. You were just talking to me. So talk to me if you need to. Tell me a story. You're good at telling stories, Arthur. Tell me the story of the nave."

And so he did. He told her the story of the nave and then the story of the west front and then the story of the cloister. Each time she asked questions and suggested which bits were uninteresting enough to be cut from the next version and then Arthur told her the story again and again, and eventually they hit on a version that seemed worth preserving.

Then Arthur would tell her that version one more time and Bethany would record his voice on her computer. After each recording, Bethany sent Arthur back to his notes to prepare for the next section while she typed up what he had just dictated.

"OK," said Arthur, after he had finished another story, "read that bit back to me."

"Are you sure?" said Bethany.

"Even if it's wasted time, I'd still like to hear it." And so Bethany read.

> It begins with a field of sheep, tended carefully from the time they are lambs, shorn of their wool and slaughtered not just to provide meat for the village, but to make a great book. A hundred sheep hides are soaked in lime to soften the skin and loosen the hair, scraped clean, and dried on frames. Cut into rectangles, what was once a sheep is now parchment— soft and flexible, durable for centuries, and easily bound. But not yet. Now the scribe takes over. He has labored for years copying manuscripts in the light of the cloister, perhaps saving works that might otherwise have been lost to time. He "pounces" the parchment, rubbing it with a small stone to achieve the right texture for the adhering of the ink. Then he carefully rules faint lines in red ink to guide him in writing evenly. A young monk has brought swan feathers gathered at the nearby river, and the scribe cuts one of these to make his pen. He has mixed his own ink, using a combination of charcoal and gum arabic. It is an ancient recipe, one he understands better than the iron gall ink used by the younger scribes. He dips the pen in the ink and begins his task—he is copying a Gospel of John. The quill scratching on the vellum and the birds in the yew tree are the only sounds that disturb the silence of the cloister. Days, weeks, and months pass and the scribe scratches away, as many hours a day as the sunlight allows. At other, wealthier monasteries he might pass the pages to an illuminator, who would decorate capital letters and add illustrations using colored ink and even gold. But Barchester can afford no such luxuries. And so the manuscript is at last delivered to the binder, who cleans any stray smudges from the parchment, sews the gatherings of pages onto bands of fabric, and then into wooden covers wrapped in parchment. The new Gospel of John is complete, and at the

next day's service a priest will read from the pristine pages, "In principio erat Verbum et Verbum erat apud Deum et Deus erat Verbum."

"What do you think?" said Arthur.

"I think it's beautiful," said Bethany, "but you can't put it in the guide-book. The library isn't even open to tourists."

"Maybe it should be," said Arthur.

Bethany stood up to stretch and glanced at the clock on her computer. "Arthur, it's almost three A.M.," she said. "You should get some sleep."

"I can't sleep," said Arthur, "I'm . . . what do you Americans call it? I'm on a roll. But I need to check something."

"OK, what book can I bring you?"

"Not in a book, in the cathedral."

"I am not going into the cathedral by myself at three o'clock in the morning," said Bethany.

"I know," said Arthur. "We're going together."

Arthur took a key from the top drawer of Oscar's desk and led Bethany down the winding library stairs and into the cloister. A pale moon shone overhead, giving just enough light for them to find their way to the south transept door, where Arthur fiddled with the keys in the darkness for a moment before he heard a click in the lock. He pushed and the door creaked open. They peered into blackness, feeling a slight flow of air from the cathedral. The bell tolled three times. When the final hour had died in the night, Bethany took a small step forward.

"It's pitch-dark in there," she said. "I have a flashlight on my phone."

"That's hardly the thing for wandering round a cathedral in the dead of night," said Arthur. "Luckily the key isn't the only thing I borrowed from Oscar's desk." He withdrew a partially burned altar candle from his pocket along with a packet of matches from the Indian restaurant in the High Street. In a moment a warm yellow light illuminated the doorway.

"Oscar keeps candles in his desk?"

"We've been known to have a power cut now and then," said Arthur. They stepped into the transept and Arthur shut the door behind them. The darkness above and around them seemed to suck the light from the candle. After only a few steps they could see neither walls nor ceiling, which made the cathedral feel even more cavernous than it was.

"This is spooky," said Bethany, slipping her hand into the crook of Arthur's arm.

"It's lovely, isn't it?" said Arthur, leading her toward the quire. "I've never been in here quite this deep into the night, but it's . . . mystical." It was just the word Arthur was searching for. He always felt moved when he entered the cathedral—such a space, with its soaring vaults and ancient arches, could never seem commonplace to him. But he usually felt the *history* of the building—from the Saxons to the Normans, from one bishop to the next, from the Reformation to the Civil War—the wonder of Barchester Cathedral to Arthur was the way it connected him to a thousand years of the past. Tonight's feeling was different. Tonight the cathedral felt mysterious and laden with . . . well, Arthur supposed, laden with religion. In his unbelief, he thought much more about the political and artistic history of the cathedral than about the fact that for more than a millennium, people of faith had poured forth that faith on this spot. Tonight, Arthur felt as if he were swimming in a pool of that ancient belief.

In the quire, the huge stained glass window above the denuded altar screen admitted the merest hint of moonlight. Arthur walked away from the high altar toward the rood screen, stopping just before they passed under the organ to step up into a short pew that faced the altar.

"What are we looking for?" said Bethany. Around them the candlelight provided glimpses of grotesque carvings—griffins and trees with "green man" faces peeking from the foliage, mermaids and batwinged men.

Arthur stopped in front of a pair of misericords. These "mercy seats" were ledges carved so that monks, required to stand for hours of services each day, could lean against them for some relief. They were hinged to create regular seats when lowered. Under each ledge was a decorative carving. Arthur held his candle low so they could see the figures. On the left was a woman with flowing, almost Pre-Raphaelite hair that extended out on either side of her head to support the misericord. It was an elaborate carving, especially considering that at the time it was carved, it was intended to stay hidden. By comparison, the image on the right was plain—a simple chalice with no markings.

"These were carved in the thirteenth century," said Arthur.

"Is that the Grail?" said Bethany, leaning to take a closer look at the carving of the chalice."

"It's probably just a Communion vessel," said Arthur.

"Wouldn't a Communion vessel have a cross on it?"

"Usually."

"And this is what you came to see?"

"No, I needed to copy down the wording on a memorial in the Epiphany Chapel."

"Then why did you bring me here?"

Arthur reached down and lowered each misericord to create two seats. "It seemed like a good place to have a chat."

"That's the precentor's seat," said Bethany, pointing to the painted title above the seat that hid the chalice carving.

"He's not here to complain, is he? Besides, it's the perfect seat for you to sit in to tell me your story."

"What story is that?" asked Bethany, lowering herself onto the hard wooden seat.

"The story of you and the Grail," said Arthur, sitting beside her and placing the candle in a holder in front of them.

"The story of me and the Holy Grail," repeated Bethany quietly.

"Call it penance," said Arthur. "For stalking me."

"Fair enough," said Bethany. "We'll decide your penance later on."

They sat in silence for a minute or two—a silence that seemed to weigh on Arthur's shoulders. It was as if all the prayers ever spoken in that holy place were sitting on top of him—prayers he still believed, in his core, had been offered in vain to a God who did not exist. He found the weight both peaceful and horrifying, much the way he found the idea of faith itself. Bethany shifted slightly in her seat, and the very figures carved in the wood above them seemed to lean forward to listen for her words. Softly, she began.

"My great-aunt gave me the Arthur Rackham book for Christmas when I was nine. It was one of the few books my father would let me read. That and the Bible, of course. He said he liked it because all the characters were Christian and the men were in charge. Dad said that's the way things were supposed to be. At first I wouldn't read it—just because Dad said it was OK. I was kind of rebellious. It's not the easiest thing to have your father be second-in-command at a church of two thousand people, to listen to him practicing sermons that will bring people to tears but that just sound to you like a criticism of everything you do. But eventually I started looking at the pictures. I loved the one of Tristram and Isoude right after they drank the love potion. I knew just enough about sex to find it suggestive and to suspect that there might be some things in this book my father wouldn't approve of. So I read it.

"At first I wasn't that impressed. I was never particularly interested in knights and sword fighting, and frankly the fact that the damsels were always in distress kind of pissed me off. . . . Oh, I'm sorry. I forgot we were in church. I shouldn't have said that."

"Don't worry," said Arthur, "the Bible is full of stories about God getting pissed off. I'm sure he'll understand."

"But then I got to the part about the Holy Grail," said Bethany, "and I was just enthralled. It was the first time I'd ever read anything that I wanted to go right back and read again. And again. Now the damsels weren't in distress; the women seemed to be in charge of the Grail. I liked that. And I liked that the Grail story mentioned Joseph of Arimathea— this minor little character from the Crucifixion narrative. That made it seem real to me, made it seem like the Grail could really exist. It also sent me back to the Bible and got me thinking—what about all those other people who have one little mention in the scriptures? What did they do then? I guess my father would have been happy, because in the end the Grail story made me think more deeply about the Bible. But it also seemed like a pretty good mystery. And then I was at a sleepover at a friend's house a year or so later, and we saw the Indiana Jones movie where he finds the Holy Grail, and I loved the thought that maybe it was really out there."

"So you believed in the Grail?" said Arthur.

"Not quite," said Bethany. "Not yet. A couple of years later I was visiting my grandmother, my mom's mother, in Alabama. She lived in this big white house outside of this little two-stoplight town. I always loved going to visit her because her house was full of stuff. Everything—collector plates with pictures of national parks, boxes of scraps for decoupage projects that never happened, jars of buttons and heaps of empty wooden spools, drawers full of rubber bands and paper clips and folded-up bits of wrapping paper. And magazines. Grammy never had any books that I saw, except for a Bible on her nightstand, but she had magazines in heaps all over the house and since I liked to read—"

"Wait a minute," said Arthur. "You liked to read? You, the digital evangelist who scoffs at fiction and talks about bookless libraries, liked to read?"

"Yes, Mr. Smarty-pants, I liked to read. Oh, my God, right now I'm reading an edition of Malory printed in 1634 from the cathedral library. It's amazing. I mean, can you imagine? 1634."

"I know it well," said Arthur, smiling. "But you were telling a story."

"Right, my story. Anyhow, my aunt had been buying magazines for a long time. We're talking *Life*, the *Saturday Evening Post*, but my favorite was *Ladies' Home Journal*. On the cover it said 'The Magazine Women Believe In,' and since the only thing my family every talked about believing in was God and Jesus and all that, I thought it must be interesting. It had articles about celebrities and fashion and homemaking, but it had other stuff, too. Travel articles and short stories, and one day I found a copy in the basement with an article called 'My Search for the Holy Grail.'"

"In a magazine called . . . what did you say it was called?"

"*Ladies' Home Journal.*"

"There was an article about the Holy Grail?"

"Yes, Mister Antiquarian-Book, Illuminated-Manuscript Snob—the *Ladies' Home Journal* had an article about the Grail. I must have read that article a hundred times. The man who wrote it had heard a story about a priest named Father Wharton, who had been cured of rheumatism when he drank water from this wooden cup. This was in 1958. And he wasn't the only one. The house where the priest had found the cup had records of lots of cases of healing, going back over a hundred years. So the guy who wrote the article set out to find this cup, this scrap of wood that had healed so many people. Supposedly it was moved from Glastonbury when Henry VIII was about to dissolve the monastery there. The magazine story was written in 1971 and the man who wrote it interviewed the rector of Glastonbury. The rector said he had requested twice that the cup be returned—so *he* obviously believed there was something to the story."

"And Glastonbury is one of the legendary resting places of the Grail," said Arthur.

"I know that, of course," said Bethany. "Anyhow, when the writer got to the house where Father Wharton had found the cup, it was gone. The family who had supposedly guarded the cup for centuries had sold the house and the current guardian, if that's what you want to call her, had moved to a secret address."

Arthur sat quietly listening to Bethany's story, trying his best not to react in any way, but apparently his efforts were not completely successful.

"Stop smiling like that, Arthur," she said. "It's a true story and he wrote it much better than I'm telling it and if you had been a twelve-year-old obsessed with Grail stories and were sitting up late at night in a creaking old house reading this article . . . well, just stop smiling and let me finish."

Arthur stopped smiling, not without effort.

"So he ends up finding this old lady, who was a servant to the last member of the family to live at the house, and she tells him all about the cup. People would send handkerchiefs to be dipped in the water of the cup and people would come to the house to drink. She said the lady who owned it valued the cup more than her own life. So this ex-servant referred him to another former servant, and he gave directions to the secret home of the cup. So he goes there, and there it is, in the top drawer of a hallway bureau—the Holy Grail. I thought it was so cool that the Grail would just be in a drawer at somebody's house instead of in some shrine or museum. And I loved how hard it was for him to find and how . . . how insignificant it seemed. It was just a gnarled piece of old wood, hardly in the shape of a cup anymore. That seemed right to me— that the Grail should be something so humble. And whether or not it was the Grail, there were all these stories of miraculous healings

associated with it. People believed in the Grail and somehow that made miracles happen. Mrs. Mirylees, the lady who owned it then, said she didn't want to submit it for scientific analysis and I'll never forget her reason. She said history would be served but faith would be destroyed. She never had any doubt about which was more important. And that's when I started believing in the Grail."

The candle had burned low, but neither Bethany nor Arthur seemed inclined to move. Arthur had never read the article that had so affected Bethany, but he knew the story of that broken and worn wooden cup. He wondered if Bethany knew the whole truth and he almost hoped she didn't. He certainly didn't want to be the one to challenge her faith with history.

"The Nanteos Cup," he whispered at last.

"Yes," said Bethany. "The Nanteos Cup. The King Arthur stories were so obviously just that—stories. But this was real. This wasn't some made-up adventure from a thousand years ago; this had just happened."

"And you didn't go straight to the Internet and look it up?"

"I didn't want to. I wanted to believe. It was the first time I ever realized that belief is more important than reality."

"What do you mean?"

"I mean, Arthur, that maybe it's more important that you believe in God than that he actually exists. So I didn't look it up online or read anything else about it for probably five years after I read that article. I didn't want to know."

"And now?"

"Now I know, Arthur. You don't have to worry."

Arthur, whose work at the cathedral had been so much about discovering the truth of the past, as separate from myth and legend and even faith, sighed with disappointment. Somehow he felt that being in the presence of someone who believed completely not only in the idea of the Grail but in a specific relic would be like standing in the light of a candle in a cathedral of darkness. The Nanteos Cup was a medieval wooden bowl, probably no more than six or seven hundred years old. It was not associated in any way with legends of the Grail until the early twentieth century.

"But even though I finally read the truth about the cup, I had believed in the Grail for years by then and it's not as easy to kill faith as Mrs. Mirylees thought." Bethany leaned forward in her seat. "I still believe in the Grail, Arthur. I still think it's out there somewhere. So when I got the opportunity to come to England and digitize ancient manuscripts, the first thing I thought was maybe one of those old manuscripts will tell me something about the Grail. And the second thing I thought was maybe they'll let me go to Barchester and I can meet Arthur Prescott—because yes, I had sort of been stalking you since you bought those notebooks."

"So you didn't come here to find the Holy Grail for your employer and his museum?"

"I'm sure if Jesse Johnson thought he could get hold of the Holy Grail he would do everything in his considerable power to do so, but I hardly think he'd start looking in Barchester. This place has nothing to do with Grail legend, you know that."

"You haven't asked to hear my story," said Arthur.

"It was part of my plan," said Bethany. "Follow you into a dark cathedral in the dead of night and tell you about an old magazine just so I could get you to spill all your secrets." She stared into the unwavering flame of the candle for a moment. "But seriously, will you tell me your story?"

"That was part of *my* plan," said Arthur. He leaned back into his seat so that the woodwork completely hid Bethany from view. He wasn't sure how to start.

"Have you left us again, Arthur?" said Bethany at last. "The candle isn't going to last forever, you know."

Arthur swallowed hard. He had kept his belief in the Grail a secret since childhood; not talking about it would be a hard habit to break, but if he didn't break it he might lose . . . well, something more important than a childhood connection to his grandfather.

"This is a big deal for me," said Arthur.

"You don't think that was a big deal for me," said Bethany. "I'm sitting in an empty cathedral spilling all my darkest Grail secrets."

"Fair enough," said Arthur. "I have some secrets, too."

"How old were you?" said Bethany. "I mean, when you first found out about the Grail."

"I was nine," said Arthur, "just like you. My grandfather showed me the Stansby *Morte d'Arthur*, the copy you've been reading. And then he took me home and he read to me from his edition of Malory and then I asked him."

"About the Grail?"

"I didn't know what that word meant, so I asked and he told me. And he told me what he believed about the Grail and made me promise to keep it a secret." Arthur sat in silence for a moment, measuring the night with the slow intake and exhaling of breath. Bethany matched his breathing but said nothing.

"He told me that the Grail was real."

"And you believed him?"

"I did," said Arthur.

"But that's not all he told you," said Bethany.

"No," said Arthur. "He told me three other things. He told me that I could be the person to find the Grail; he told me I had to keep the Grail and everything I learned about it a secret; and he told me that the Grail is here in Barchester."

"Wow," said Bethany. "No wonder you were so worried about me."

"When I heard about Jesse Johnson and then I found all those Grail materials in your bag—my thesis and notes about me and everything— I thought he had sent you here to look for the Grail, especially after what happened to the Nanteos Cup."

"What happened to it?"

"It was stolen," said Arthur. "A couple of years ago. It had been borrowed by a family member who was ill and while she was in hospital someone stole it from her house."

"And you figured Jesse Johnson . . ."

"When I heard he was looking for the Grail, the thought did cross my mind."

"Did they ever find it?"

"It was returned last summer by what the police called an anonymous intermediary."

"Thank goodness," said Bethany. "But listen, you've got to believe that I am not here looking for the Grail; I'm just here to digitize manuscripts.

And if I did find the Grail . . . if *we* found the Grail, the last person I'd tell about it would be Jesse Johnson. You do believe me, don't you?"

"It's rather strange," said Arthur, "what I do and don't believe. I'm surrounded by a five-hundred-year-old monument to God, and I don't believe in Him, but I believe in a cup that most people think is a myth or a legend. And I'm sitting here with someone who was a total stranger less than a month ago and with whom I was furious quite recently, but I believe her. I trust her. I trust you."

"Thank you, Arthur," said Bethany. "That means a lot to me. And do you know what else would mean a lot to me?"

"What?"

"Getting out of here before that candle burns out. So where is that memorial you need to transcribe?"

When they returned to the library, Arthur told Bethany all about his search for the Grail—how he had discovered the lions on the tower and the yew tree in the cloister. He shared his suspicion that the lost Book of Ewolda was somehow connected to the Grail. He showed her the marginalia in the medieval service book that spoke of a great treasure of Barchester and the note in the Stansby *Morte d'Arthur* about Barchester being the perfect place for that book.

"I should have noticed that," said Bethany, "but I was only on chapter twenty-six."

"What's your favorite part?" said Arthur. "I mean apart from the Grail."

"Merlin," said Bethany. "I love his mysticism. He always felt very Old Testament to me, but like somebody from the Old Testament you'd actually want to sit down and talk to. They're not all that way. I think I liked that he could be wise and kind and frightening all at once. My dad is a little like that, but he lacks the . . . I don't know, the mystery. My dad is an open book and Merlin was anything but. And of course I love the idea that he transcended time. This idea that he might still be asleep in a cave somewhere—it's very Christian in a way, but in a weird way that my dad would call heresy. Did you ever read C. S. Lewis's space trilogy? He brings Merlin back in the third book."

"I've read just about everything by Lewis," said Arthur. "He was a nonbeliever who became a believer. I wanted to see if I thought I might follow in his path. A lot of my college friends scoffed at the space trilogy—I mean it is a bit muddled. But I liked parts of it, and I loved that Merlin was part of the story."

"Who was your favorite?"

"My favorite C. S. Lewis character?"

"No, silly, your favorite in the Arthur stories."

"I suppose it should be one of the ones who achieved the Grail. . . ."

"So, Percival, Bors, or Galahad?" said Bethany.

"It's none of them," said Arthur. "Oddly enough, my favorite was always Lancelot. I could never really relate to purity—the near perfection of the knights who saw the Grail. But Lancelot was anything but pure; Lancelot had faults but he was still a great knight. That seemed a lot more achievable to me."

"So you wanted to be a knight?"

"Not as such," said Arthur, "but I wanted to see that people with weaknesses could still have success. I think it was part of my whole struggle with belief. I went to a Church of England school and that's when I started to love church without believing in God. As a child I thought that meant something was wrong with me—so I related to Lancelot. He defied the biggest rule in chivalry but he was still Arthur's best friend and most talented knight."

"Until the bit where his affair with Queen Guinevere brings the whole kingdom crashing down."

"Well, there is that. But I still liked him." They sat in silence for a moment, until they heard the sound of a bird in the cloister. Arthur wondered if it was a nightingale or a lark.

"Listen, as long as we're telling secrets," he said, "there's one more thing you need to know. I'm not sure if it has anything to do with the Grail or the Book of Ewolda, and I might never have even found out if it hadn't been for you."

"What do you mean?"

"One of the names in the list of rectors of St. Cuthbert's—the one that came right after Henry Albert Naylor—was my grandfather."

"The same grandfather who told you to go Grail hunting but keep it a secret?"

"The same one. And eventually he was rector of Plumstead Episcopi, too."

"The same posts that Naylor held. Arthur, your grandfather must be a part of this story, somehow."

"It could just be a coincidence."

"There are no coincidences," said Bethany.

"That's what he always said," said Arthur.

VIII

THE HIGH ALTAR

In ancient religions the first altars were tombs; they later developed into places of sacrifice. At Barchester, the high altar is both. It serves as a tomb just once a year, when, after the Maundy Thursday service, the Communion elements, signifying the body and blood of Christ, are "entombed" in a chamber in the side of the altar as Christ's death and burial are commemorated. From this "Easter sepulchre" the elements are retrieved when Christ's Resurrection is proclaimed at the Great Vigil of Easter. As a place of sacrifice, the altar serves at least once a week, as the sacrificial service of the Eucharist is performed here.

1285, Priory of St. Ewolda

Walter de Bingham knelt at the high altar of the monastic church of the Priory of St. Ewolda, just outside Barchester. The morning sun streamed through the east window, dappling his face with blues and greens. Around him, the massive columns and heavy curved vaults of the church rose toward heaven—though not as far toward heaven as the nearby Barchester Cathedral. The Norman architecture of the priory church was, in fact, a bit out of fashion. The thick walls, rounded arches, and small windows meant the church was often dark and cold. Walter had heard one monk say, after the fifth service of the day, that the place felt more like hell than heaven, but that young man had soon left the priory for a posting at one of the new cathedrals, with their soaring pointed arches, vast windows, and ribbed vaulting. But Walter liked St. Ewolda's, old-fashioned though it might be. He liked dimness and damp and mystery, and every morning after Terce, when the other brothers had left the church and returned to their work or their studies or their private devotions in their cells, he took a few minutes to pray, and he always prayed to that saint whom he saw as his own private protector—St. Ewolda.

The brothers knew that the monastery had been founded by a saint named Ewolda; but they knew her in name only. Walter alone knew the details of her life, for Walter was, and had been for nearly thirty years, the keeper of the Book of Ewolda. When this responsibility had first been passed to him he had been a young monk, freshly arrived from Cluny to a foundation that was both ancient and new. St. Ewolda had founded the monastery hundreds of years ago, early in the first great age of English monasticism. Unlike so many of its contemporary foundations, it had survived through the centuries—probably, thought Walter, because St. Ewolda's always managed to have barely enough wealth to feed its monks but never enough to invite sacking, whether by Vikings or by someone else. After the Norman invasion, the monastery had been refounded on a new site, and twenty years later became a Cluniac house—part of the new order of monasticism based in Cluny. But Walter thought of the priory as a Saxon foundation with a Saxon patron.

Often, following his prayers to this patron, Walter would sit in the small chapel of St. Martin—a chapel that would not hold more than two or three—and read from the book of St. Ewolda. He remembered well the day that one of the oldest monks, Brother Simon, had called Walter into his cell.

"There is a secret with which I must entrust you," Simon had said. "And you must be the bearer of this secret for the next generation."

"I am at your service, Brother," said Walter. "What is this secret?"

"You will know in time," said Simon, "but first you must learn a strange and unfamiliar language."

Walter had come to Simon's cell every day for an hour after Terce and had proved a quick study. Within a few months, he could read the Saxon language, and Simon showed him, for the first time, the Book of Ewolda.

"The book was copied from an ancient manuscript in the last days before the coming of the Normans," said Simon, "so that Ewolda's story might be kept alive." Walter read to Simon from the book every day, translating each sentence as he read. Simon gently corrected him when his translation was not perfect. And thus Walter learned the full story of Ewolda, founder of the priory.

"But why should this story be a secret?" asked Walter one day after Simon had closed the book and placed it in its hiding place under his bed.

"When the priory joined the order of Cluny," said Simon, "the new prior allowed us to keep the name of St. Ewolda and to celebrate her feast day. But he felt that any further allegiance to a Saxon founder was allegiance that ought properly to be paid to Cluny or to our Lady. So knowledge of Ewolda was forced underground, and the book was hidden by a monk named Harold, who had once been the abbot of the original St. Ewolda's Monastery. He decreed that the book should always have a single protector, so that the story of St. Ewolda might be kept alive. But Harold was also the custodian of another secret—a deeper, more holy secret—that the keeper of Ewolda's book must protect."

"And what is this secret?" asked Walter, leaning forward, trembling with wonder.

"You have mastered the language," said Simon, "so only you among the monks of the priory will be able to read Ewolda's book, and only you will be able to read this." From within his robes, Simon pulled out a single sheet of parchment, twice folded. "Take it with you. Read it only in the privacy of your cell. Guard it with the greatest care, and choose your successor wisely, for none but the Guardian must ever know."

That night, by the light of a single taper, Walter read the

document. The words had faded in places, but some Guardian, perhaps Simon, had traced the originals with fresh ink, so the text was
legible. Yet the secret it revealed was nearly incomprehensible.
How could such a secret have remained hidden at Barchester for so
many centuries? When he went to see Simon in his cell the next
morning, eager to discuss this monumental intelligence, the old
monk was gone. Walter never saw Simon again. The message had
been clear—there is only ever one Guardian. And Walter knew
what he had to guard.

Now Walter read again from the story of St. Ewolda's life. As priceless treasures go, the Book of Ewolda was unassuming. It was small
enough to slip into a pouch that Walter had sewn inside his robe. The
vellum covers were worn at the edges and scratched. They were
blotched with smears and smudges, spots that could be wine or ink or
blood. The interior boasted no illuminations or decorative capitals.
The pages themselves often lacked a corner or a bit of fore edge.
Walter was proud to think, though, that the book was in no worse
condition than when he had taken over the guardianship thirty years
ago. The same could not be said, however, for the document that Walter also kept in his pocket. He had folded and unfolded the parchment so many times—even though he had committed the text to
memory decades ago—that the words on the folds were illegible. He
knew old age was stalking him and that the time was near when he
must appoint a new Guardian. That brother must be able to read the
words that had so amazed Walter all those years ago.

It seemed foolish to Walter that the document should be separate from the book. A single parchment could so easily be lost or
destroyed, but a book, even an ancient and tattered book, was a
thing of value. A book was easier to protect. He turned to the last
pages of the volume. Because of the small format, the original
sheets of parchment had been folded twice to create the pages—
eight pages from each sheet. But the text of Ewolda's history extended across only five of the last eight pages. In any other book,
this valuable space would have been filled with prayers or Scripture
verses or illuminations, but in Ewolda's book, the pages remained

blank. There was just enough room on those three pages, thought Walter, to copy the text of the document—to bring together into a single volume all the great secrets of St. Ewolda's.

Walter felt he was well suited to copy the document. After all, he had worked as a scribe for more then twenty years. He had copied some of the most important books at St. Ewolda's—including the breviary from which many of the services were taken. The old breviary book had been used for centuries and was so worn it was in danger of becoming illegible. Walter had copied the prayers and services with great care, adding musical notations to some of the psalms and canticles to assist the monks with their chanting. He had even copied a small bit of marginalia that only he understood—for only he could read the language in which it was written. "Here I remember the great treasure of Barsyt," Walter had written, keeping the words in the Saxon tongue that was foreign to his fellow monks. After such a task as creating the breviary, copying out a document of a few paragraphs would be a simple matter.

And so Walter became the last Guardian to copy the Saxon text of the document. He worked slowly over the next several days to fill the empty pages with his careful script, knowing he must finish his work by midnight on the twelfth of October—the feast day of St. Ewolda. He completed the task early that morning, and after Compline, when the rest of the priory had retired, Walter returned to the high altar. He spoke a long prayer to Ewolda and placed the document in a pottery basin he had borrowed from the kitchen earlier in the day. He held his candle to the edge of the parchment, then watched as the flame licked the document and smoked curled into the darkness.

When the monks assembled at midnight for Matins, only Walter noticed the faint smell of smoke in the air, not knowing that he wasn't the first monk in St. Ewolda's history to perform this peculiar rite.

May 8, 2016

FEAST OF DAME JULIAN OF NORWICH

By Saturday afternoon, Arthur had a rough draft of the entire guide-book. In the end, writing ten thousand words wasn't that difficult, especially with Bethany keeping him on course. Whenever he tried to dive into some digression, she would repeat, "Just tell the story, Arthur." He found this ironic, since Bethany herself was the master of the conversational digression, but he nonetheless appreciated her guidance. Arthur knew just about all there was to know about Barchester Cathedral—or all that one could know given the surviving sources. Condensing that knowledge into a story had only required the one thing he never had during his solitary years of research—a listener. Of course he had told David and Oscar and Gwyn about various discoveries he had made in his studies of the cathedral's history, but he hadn't tried to tell the entire story of the cathedral as just that—a story.

Now, as the sound of the choir rehearsing the psalm one last time before the main Sunday morning service drifted up from below, Arthur sat at his usual table. Gone were the piles of notes and stacks of books with slips of paper marking relevant passages. Gone was his fountain pen and his ream of fresh writing paper. In front of him lay a neat stack of computer-printed pages and a red felt-tip pen—a gift from Bethany.

They had worked through Friday night, and just before Evensong on Saturday Bethany had pushed "print" on her computer. Arthur had agreed not to look at the manuscript until he got a good night's sleep. Even standing up he had almost dozed off during the Magnificat, an early-seventeenth-century setting by Thomas Weelkes that had soothed him to the edge of sleep until Bethany dug an elbow into his side and brought him back just in time for the Gloria Patri. After the service, he had gone home and slept. It was the first time he had missed Compline in months.

On Sunday, he had attended Morning Prayer at seven and had been tempted to head to the library and begin proofreading right away, but he wasn't used to missing a night's sleep, and even after almost twelve hours of slumber, he felt caffeine was required. He had sat and chatted with

David over a mug of coffee at the bookshop—mostly listening to the story of how David had failed to seduce a poet who had given a reading at the university the night before. It was exactly the sort of mindless narrative Arthur needed to ease back into reality.

Now, as the bells called the worshippers of Barchester to Sunday morning Eucharist, Arthur sat comfortably in the peace of the library. He picked up Bethany's printout, leaned back in his chair, and began to read.

> *The early history of Barchester Cathedral is shrouded in mystery, but we do know there was a religious foundation dedicated to St. Ewolda on this site from at least the early eighth century, making it one of the oldest Christian monasteries in southern Britain. Of the founder, St. Ewolda, little is known.*

It wasn't exactly the opening he had hoped for, but it wasn't bad. He was just finishing the first page without any cause to reach for the red pen, when he heard feet on the stairs and the slightly breathless voice of Oscar.

"Ah, Arthur, I thought I might find you here. I was on my way to services and I thought I'd drop off those keys you wanted."

"What keys?" said Arthur.

"Bethany rang last night and said you wanted to take her out to Plumstead Episcopi to see the interior." He laid down a pair of keys on the table in front of Arthur. "This is the key to the outside door, and this, I think, is to the sacristy, not that there's anything to see there."

"I'm sorry, did you say Bethany rang you?"

"Yes. You did want to go out there, didn't you?"

"Absolutely," said Arthur. "I just wondered how you have the keys. And for that matter how Bethany knew you had the keys."

"Oh, she didn't. She just rang to check on Mother. She's been in hospital again, you know." Arthur didn't know, and he felt both guilty and jealous that Bethany was doing a better job of keeping up with Oscar than he was. "And we were chatting and she mentioned wanting to go to Plumstead and I said I could get you the keys."

"But I thought the precentor . . ."

"The precentor is the rector, technically. But it's just an honorary position. The chapel belongs to the cathedral chapter and the keys to all the cathedral properties are kept in the vestry."

"And you, of course, have access to the vestry."

"I don't think anyone will mind your peeking into Plumstead. You might find a few cobwebs; it hasn't been swept out since last summer's festival, but hopefully everything is in good order. You'll let me know if there are any problems?"

"Yes, of course," said Arthur.

"Well, bells are ringing so I'd best be off. Don't suppose I can convince you to come along?"

"You know Sunday morning at eleven o'clock is the one time I have no interest in going to church."

"You don't have to take Communion."

"Good-bye, Oscar. Enjoy the sermon."

"Someday, my friend, someday," said Oscar, and disappeared down the stairs.

There was much about the eleven o'clock service that kept Arthur away. First and foremost was the crowd—he felt more connected to the cathedral and its history with three people at Compline than he ever could with five hundred. The larger service also meant it was held in the nave, with a modern altar in the crossing. Arthur preferred either the high altar, used for services in the quire, or the peacefulness of one of the side chapels, used for Morning Prayer and Compline. Oscar, of course, would have been quick to point out that the nine o'clock Eucharist on Sundays was celebrated at the high altar. But Arthur carefully avoided services that featured either a sermon or Communion. The first he simply did not care to hear. If the dean had anything interesting to say, she would say it to Arthur on one of their morning walks; if someone else was preaching, particularly the precentor, Arthur could certainly do without. As for Communion—it was the only rite that made Arthur self-conscious about his unbelief. He could not, in good conscience, partake, but not to do so seemed a much too public declaration of his lack of faith. So, as the sermon droned on (it was the precentor this morning) and as the congregants waited their turn at the Communion rail, Arthur read the rest of his manuscript, making occasional marks with the red pen, keenly aware of those two keys staring up at him from his table.

"OK, put that thing away," said Bethany, bursting into the library with an energy Arthur could only attribute to youth and a good night's sleep. "We're going to go searching for a lost medieval manuscript full of Grail secrets. I see Oscar brought you the keys."

"How was the sermon?"

"Good, actually. I think I'm adapting to the notion that a sermon isn't thirty minutes of screaming and arm waving. There were no roars from the crowd like my dad gets sometimes, but he made some valid points. The precentor is a very thoughtful preacher."

"He's good at telling other people what to do, you mean."

"Now, now, Arthur. If you're not going to come to the service, you can't criticize the preacher."

"I can criticize him; I just can't criticize his preaching."

"Come on, we can argue in the car. I want to get going."

"I don't have a car."

"Neither do I. David is loaning us his." She dangled a set of car keys in front of Arthur as if he were the type to be lured by shiny objects.

"I thought we might walk," he said. "It's a lovely day."

"It's five miles, Arthur. And then we'd have to walk back. I may seem chipper but I'm still exhausted because someone made me pull an all-nighter on Friday."

"Fine," said Arthur, pushing back from the table. "Since you got the keys from Oscar and a car from David, I'm not sure why you even need me to come."

"I have to have someone around to tell me I'm doing everything wrong," said Bethany.

"In that case, I'm your man."

Once Arthur had extricated David's car from the narrow alley behind the bookshop, the drive to Plumstead Episcopi took about fifteen minutes, but that was long enough for Bethany to read aloud from her latest purchase.

"What is that?" said Arthur as she drew a small green book out of her handbag.

"*Black's Picturesque Guide to Barsetshire,*" said Bethany. "Second edition, 1870. I bought it from David last week—since there seems to be a dearth of *new* guidebooks about this place. It has a section on Plumstead Episcopi."

"What about *my* history of Plumstead?" said Arthur.

"Oh, don't be so self-centered, Arthur. You of all people know how much fun it is to read from an old book. Here's what it says:

> *Few parish churches in England are in better repair, or better worth keeping so, than that at Plumstead Episcopi; and yet it is built in a faulty style: the body of the church is low—so low, that the nearly flat leaden roof would be visible from the churchyard, were it not for the carved parapet with which it is surrounded. It is cruciform, though the transepts are irregular, one being larger than the other; and the tower is much too high in proportion to the church. But the stonework is beautiful; the mullions of the windows and the thick tracery of the Gothic workmanship is as rich as fancy can desire.*

"When did you say your guidebook was published?" said Arthur.

"In 1870."

"Two years before the interior of the church was done over by George Gilbert Scott. Do you like High Gothic décor?"

"I'm not sure I've ever seen High Gothic décor," said Bethany. "I'm pretty sure we don't have it at Jubilee Christian Fellowship Church."

"Do I detect a hint of cynicism about your home church?"

"Everybody has to find God in her own way," said Bethany. "I'm just realizing that he speaks to me more in Evensong and choral music and soaring arches than in theater seats and projection screens and rock bands. It doesn't make me right and it doesn't make the two thousand people who come to hear my father preach every week wrong. I just think maybe we're . . . different."

Arthur turned off the paved road onto a narrow gravel lane that wound for a half mile or so through thick woods before emerging into a small clearing. Before them stood St. Nicholas, the parish church of Plumstead Episcopi. The churchyard was surrounded by a low stone wall, and grass and weeds grew wildly around the gravestones, many of which leaned at alarming angles.

"They usually tidy up before the summer festival," said Arthur as he pushed the lych-gate through the tangle of flora. He stomped down the grass as he made his way to the south door, hoping to smooth a path for Bethany, who was still wearing a cheerful-looking church dress and a pair of shoes not suited for country walking.

Arthur turned the key in the lock, pushed open the door, and they stepped inside.

"Wow!" said Bethany.

There was almost no stained glass, and sunshine streamed through the windows. On the walls above and to the side of the chancel arch was a triptych of frescoes depicting the Last Supper, the Crucifixion, and the Resurrection. The precise detail in the flowing hair and garments of Christ and the apostles gave the paintings a Pre-Raphaelite air. The floor of the aisle and chancel were tiled in terra-cotta, black, ivory, dull yellow, and pale blue in elaborate geometric patterns. Every surface dripped with color—the paintings, mosaics of the apostles set into the wall behind the altar, even the organ pipes, vividly decorated with fleurs-de-lis of gold against a rust-red background.

"It seems kind of . . . not that I know that much about it, but it seems Catholic," said Bethany, after she had stood in silence for a moment or two.

"Anglo-Catholic. There were a number of church leaders in Barsetshire in the nineteenth century who were keen followers of the Oxford Movement. They wanted to bring ritual and beauty back into the church. The precentor would have fit right in with them. He's a true High Churchman."

"Hey look," said Bethany, walking up to the stone altar. "This looks just like the one at the cathedral."

"George Gilbert Scott did some work at Barchester three years after he redecorated Plumstead. Apparently Bishop Gladwyn admired the Plumstead altar and asked Scott to do one just like it at the cathedral. The only difference is that the cathedral altar is exactly three times the size."

"It's so beautiful," said Bethany, running her fingers across the bas-relief on the front of the altar.

"It could easily distract you from . . . searching for a lost manuscript, for example."

"We will," said Bethany, standing and looking around her. "Just give me a few minutes to take it in."

Arthur smiled as he slipped into a pew near the front of the nave. He had hoped Bethany would enjoy this place. He had rarely been here when the church wasn't crowded for the annual service and summer festival. To sit in such a stunning space, the quiet broken only by Bethany's footsteps as she explored the corners of the church, was a treat for Arthur. He found his mind relaxing for the first time in days. He took a deep breath through his nose and behind the must and staleness of the air, he detected just a hint of incense. It had been burned so many times here it was part of the atmosphere—embedded, no doubt, in the very woodwork. He wondered if some of that incense had been lit by his grandfather.

Two hours later, Arthur, sweaty and dusty, collapsed back into a pew. "I think we can say with as much authority as anyone alive that there is no hidden manuscript in this church," he said. They had crawled on the floor peering under pews; looked under, behind, and within the few furnishings; tapped on walls searching for secret compartments; and scoured every cabinet in the tiny sacristy, where they found nothing but a few candle stubs and some old hymnbooks. They had even looked inside the Easter sepulchre in the side of the altar. It would have been a perfect place to hide a book. But the sepulchre was empty.

"It's a shame," said Bethany. "It would have been exciting to find your lost Book of Ewolda."

"I am inclined to look on the bright side," said Arthur, who felt a little disappointed that their search had been fruitless.

"What is the bright side?" said Bethany, plopping down in the pew just in front of the pulpit. A sheen of sweat glistened on her forehead, and a smudge of dust outlined her left cheekbone. Instead of a single wisp of hair falling in front of her face, there were at least a half dozen.

"The bright side is that if we had found the lost Book of Ewolda, we would have had to start the guidebook all over again."

"We? It's not my guidebook, Arthur; it's yours. And my job is to digitize manuscripts, so as far as I'm concerned, the more lost ones we dig up the better."

"In that case, I suppose the bright side is that we spent a Sunday afternoon in a beautiful church, enjoying the best the Victorians had to offer."

"It is beautiful," said Bethany. "I might be distracted by all this amazing art if I actually went to a service here, but to sit here and just soak it up . . ."

"We'd better get going," said Arthur, glancing at his watch. "They're singing a Rutter anthem at Evensong and I'd hate to miss it."

"You are a creature of habit, Arthur, aren't you?"

"I am," said Arthur as they walked down the aisle together. But he thought, as she passed through the door in front of him and into the late afternoon light, At least I was until I met you.

The morning sun sparkled on the dew in the water meadows, the birds sang with unusual gusto, and Arthur leaned against the gate waiting for Gwyn and reading a Penguin paperback of *Right Ho, Jeeves*. He hadn't been so relaxed in . . . well, in years. He hadn't realized what a weight the unfinished guidebook had been until he finished it. Add to that a lovely Sunday afternoon spent with Bethany and the fact that he was reading not for research or work but for sheer enjoyment, and Arthur felt as much a part of the joy of this morning as the birds and the sunshine. He had nearly sprinted out of Morning Prayer to the gate where he usually met Gwyn, precisely so he could have this moment. And what could be better—the medieval grandeur of the cathedral towering behind him, the fresh air with just a hint of dampness blowing through his hair, the view across the water meadows to a section of the winding river lined with beech trees, and an old friend to read. He hadn't visited Jeeves in far too long, but he still couldn't resist raising his eyes to the morning at every turn of the page. He hardly flinched when the gate opened, Mag and Nunc burst through, and one of them stopped to shake off the dew all over Arthur's trousers.

"You're positively beaming," said Gwyn. "I'm glad someone is having a good morning."

"I am having a good morning," said Arthur enthusiastically. "And what about you? Trouble in the chapter?"

"No more than usual. But Daniel is sick and the nanny is sick and the back-up nanny is up in London visiting her aunt."

"You don't have to chaperone me around the field if you need to get back and look after Daniel. I'm quite capable of finding the way on my own."

"Oh, Arthur, we both know your morning wouldn't be complete without a good dousing from Mag and Nunc," said Gwyn. "Besides, I need the escape. The precentor's better half is sitting with Daniel for the morning and then I'll take my work home after lunch." Gwyn closed the gate and they headed out across the field where the dogs were already romping in the grass.

"The precentor has a wife?" said Arthur.

"Oh, God, no," said Gwyn. "He has a twin sister. She's as confirmed in her spinsterhood as he is in his bachelorhood. She spends the winters in what I gather is little more than a boardinghouse in Kent and the summers in a rented cottage in Scotland and every spring and autumn she stops off in Barchester for a couple of weeks when she's on her migration."

"The precentor has a twin," said Arthur. "It's nice to know, I suppose. He always seems so . . . alone in the world."

"I suppose he is, in many ways," said Gwyn. "I've never spoken to him much about his private life, but I gather he had his heart broken when he was a young man and he never quite got over the girl."

"I'm sure it's very unchristian of me to say it," said Arthur, "but I find it hard to imagine anyone being in love with the precentor."

"Confidentially, so do I. But his sister is a very kind woman, and infinitely patient when she's in Barchester."

"I've no doubt," said Arthur.

"So, what has that smile plastered to your face this morning? Have you won the lottery, or are you just in love?"

In the cool of the morning air, Arthur could feel the blush rise to his cheek, but nothing could bother him today. "Actually," he said, "you shall have a nice little surprise when you get to your office. I e-mailed you the final draft of the text for the guidebook this morning."

"You . . . you what? You e-mailed it? Do you even know what e-mail is, Arthur?"

"I do," said Arthur cheerily. "And yesterday I learned how to include an attachment. So you'll have a nice digital file waiting for you."

"Arthur, put aside my absolute glee at your having miraculously finished this project. How is it that you just used the word *digital* in a sentence without rolling your eyes?"

"I am not saying I believe in all this nonsense about a world without books," said Arthur, "but I did save myself the climb up to your office to shove the manuscript under the door and I saved you, or your long-suffering assistant, from having to retype the whole thing."

"Arthur Prescott, I could hug you right here in front of God and the world."

"You're certainly welcome to," said Arthur.

"Not in front of the dogs," said Gwyn, smiling and linking her arm through his. "So tell me, Mr. Prescott, what brought on this transformation from a grumpy man who could not imagine finishing his manuscript, to a smiling fellow who's handed in his homework?"

"I did have some help. You know Bethany Davis, who's digitizing the manuscripts in the library."

"Your friend and nemesis, yes, I know her well. We have lunch together a couple of days a week. She speaks very highly of you, Arthur."

"Does she? And did she call me a friend and nemesis?"

"No, I sussed that bit out myself," said Gwyn.

"Well, nemesis or not, she helped me get the damned thing finished. She convinced me that I just needed to tell the story of the cathedral, so I told it and she typed it up."

"Aha! So you sent me the file, but you didn't actually create the file."

"No, but I did load it onto my computer at the office with something called a flash drive."

"I'm pleased to hear that Bethany is dragging you into the twentieth century, even though the rest of us are getting well on with the twenty-first. I rather like that girl, and I gather you do, too."

"I have done my best to be her friend," said Arthur, "in spite of our . . . differences."

"I'm proud of you, Arthur. Making friends with an American digitizer. That's a real accomplishment for you. I'm sure the fact that she's charming, intelligent, and beautiful makes it even harder to like her." Gwyn jabbed Arthur in the side with her elbow.

"We are friends," said Arthur, a bit more stiffly than he had intended. "That's all."

"I'm glad she makes you happy," said Gwyn.

Arthur didn't want to argue this point further, so he proceeded to a question that had been bothering him lately. "What would you think about opening the library to tourists?"

"Are you serious? Arthur Prescott wants to descend from his ivory tower and share his books with the sullied masses?"

"Something Bethany said the other day made me think of it," said Arthur. "And I do think the library has been far too empty for far too long."

"It's a nice idea," said Gwyn, "but we haven't anyone to staff it or any funds for security and who knows what it would mean for insurance. But I do need to ask you a favor."

"You want me to adopt your dogs?"

"Worse, I'm afraid. I need you to show the cathedral's manuscript collection to a gentleman from Sotheby's who's coming down from London to assess the possibility of a sale."

"You do realize that what I wrote was only the *story* of Barchester Cathedral's history. Those manuscripts *are* the history. They are as important a part of this church as the south transept or the cloister. But I suppose those will be up for sale soon."

"You're not far from the truth, Arthur. Our annual visit from the structural engineer turned up some weaknesses in the north transept.

We'll try a fund-raising campaign of course—'Save the Cathedral' and all that. But if we don't get some funding, and quickly, we could very well be looking at major damage to the cathedral."

"God, Gwyn, I'm so sorry. I had no idea. How much will you have to raise?"

"Ideally the chapter would like about ten million," said Gwyn. "That would pay for the repairs with enough left over for the Lady Chapel. I hate to be in this position, but if I have to choose between the collapse of the north transept and the sale of the manuscript collection, I have to choose the building."

"Of course you do," said Arthur. "And of course I will assist the devil in his prowling around the library seeking something to devour."

"And there's one more thing, Arthur."

"What's that?"

"We just have to find those missing covers—the ones that were ripped off the manuscripts the night of the bombing. I've asked Oscar to look into it, but if you have any ideas—"

"Because if you find the covers you're much more likely to be able to sell the manuscripts."

"Sotheby's have offered to pay the cost of repairs if we sell through them."

"My dear Gwyn, nothing would pain me more than to be the one who smoothed the way to the dissolution of the Barchester Cathedral Library, but as you are my dear Gwyn, if I do have any ideas about the covers, you will be the first to know." The fact of the matter was that Arthur had no clue where to look for the missing covers. Gwyn had been right to ask Oscar— he was the one who knew where things were kept in the cathedral.

"Thank you, Arthur," said Gwyn, lifting her head and giving him a quick, dry kiss on the cheek. "I know it's difficult for you. I just don't see any other way."

On the bus to work later that morning, Arthur pondered Gwyn's words: "I just don't see any other way." For her, Arthur would help the appraiser from Sotheby's, but perhaps, somehow, he might also work to find just what she had said—another way.

For the first time in his life Arthur found himself, later that day, looking forward to a committee meeting. True, his first foray into the Advisory Committee for the Media Center had been as dull as every other committee meeting he had ever attended—and, he felt, rife with misunderstanding about the purpose of a university library. Several of the members of the committee seemed to think the media center existed primarily to provide the students with DVDs of movies to watch in their spare time. But finishing his guidebook had emboldened Arthur, and after his conversation with his department head, Mr. Slopes, that morning, he had been counting the seconds until four o'clock. Now he looked around the table of Conference Room D at the faces of the Advisory Committee for the Media Center and smiled. This would be a bloody good meeting.

"I believe we're all here," said Arthur, "so I'd like to call the meeting to order. If you checked your e-mail today you will have seen that I have accepted Mr. Slopes's invitation to chair this committee following the nervous breakdown of Mr. Radclyffe."

"It wasn't a nervous breakdown," said Slopes. "He merely requested—"

"The chairman has the floor," said Arthur. "And he intends to run this committee with order and decorum, so there can be no interruptions."

Slopes stared wide-eyed at this and was apparently so shocked by Arthur's assertion of authority that he found himself unable to defend poor Radclyffe.

"First of all," said Arthur, "I would like to thank Miss Stanhope for joining us on such short notice. Mr. Slopes informed me this morning that the university has adopted the policy, idiotic though it is, of placing students who spend only a short time in our midst on committees that decide our distant future. I was pleased, Miss Stanhope, that you were able to accept my last-minute invitation. Inappropriate though your presence may be, we welcome you."

No one tried to interrupt him this time, not even Miss Stanhope, and Arthur thought his little speech was going rather well.

"Now," he said, "it has recently come to my attention that the main reasons students come to the media center are threefold: it has a nice coffee shop, it has comfortable chairs, and it has speedy Internet connections. Now, to be sure, these are laudable achievements, but I feel we are missing an opportunity to have our charges interact with knowledge in a more meaningful way. There are, if you look hard enough for them, books in this building, though our students could be forgiven for not knowing that. A student crossing our threshold encounters no evidence that knowledge has ever been bound in covers, but only a blank wall. Passing by this empty expanse, our student might spend hours in the media center without ever encountering such a thing as a book—for to see one of that breed requires the determination to go past upholstery and caffeine and into that long-forgotten area known as the stacks. Now, I believe that those neglected books represent the heart and soul of this institution, and I put it to you that, as things stand, our beloved media center is rather deep in the anti-intellectual mulligatawny. We are the metaphorical ship without a rudder; we are Hansel and Gretel sans bread crumbs; in short, we are without direction and we require both rudder and bag of crumbs, and I fancy I know just where we can get both of those and a packet of crisps."

"And where is that?" said Slopes, who had apparently recovered himself enough to insert this short query into the proceedings.

"Ah, I am glad you asked that, Mr. Slopes. The question that prods me on with my oration is precisely the sort of contribution I expect from you on this committee, and you have done your job well. What this committee needs, what this media center needs, is a good dose of Jeeves."

"I'm sorry," said Mr. Peabody, a mathematics lecturer who hunched at the far end of the table taking the minutes. "How do you spell that?"

"Is it possible," said Arthur, raising both his shoulders and his voice, "that we are working in a university where lecturers are not aware of the identity of one Reginald Jeeves, the gentleman's personal gentleman and the personal gentleman's gentleman? What has happened to cultural literacy, my fellow members of the Advisory Committee for the Media Center? This sort of ignorance is exactly what needs addressing. What I mean, Mr. Peabody, when I say that we need a dose of Jeeves, is that we need quiet and reasoned wisdom that leads to prompt and directed action."

"And do I gather that you are to be the source of this wisdom?" asked Mr. Slopes.

"Well done, again, Mr. Slopes," said Arthur. "You have sussed out the essence of this meeting. Keep this up and we may make you chairman one day. Now, I should like to put before this committee four proposals for immediate approval. First, that, in order to impress upon our community the importance of the books that are cared for on its premises, the name of the building in which we now meet be changed from the "Media Center" to the "Library." I would suggest the Francis Slopes Memorial Library, but Mr. Slopes's mortal coil is as yet unshuffled, so for now the word *Library* will suffice solo. Second, is the matter of that empty wall that greets our eager students when they enter this sacred space. Certainly the symbolism is clear—like the minds of those who approach it, the wall is a perfect and absolute blank. But symbolism, in my opinion, is overrated. So I propose we cover that wall with bookcases and that we fill those bookcases with books—actual printed-on-paper and bound-in-covers books of the type that were once so popular on university campuses. These books should be drawn from every field, and I would suggest that we appoint Mr. Peabody to choose those mathematical treatises that will grace this wall of knowledge. In the center of that wall, I propose we erect a glass display case to be filled with the sorts of books that may open new avenues of thought to our constituents—a display of rare materials loaned from local collectors, perhaps even from the cathedral library, which, like our own media center, is a much underused resource. Third, that we invite the American expert on digital media, Miss Bethany Davis, to serve this committee in an advisory capacity. While I believe that the primary purpose of a library should be to house and disseminate books, I am prepared to concede to other members of this committee the point that digital media has its place, and I believe this committee, and in particular its chair, could benefit from Miss Davis's counsel. And finally, that the library provide, posthaste, a copy of *The Code of the Woosters* to Mr. Peabody for his personal edification. Now, I have a bus to catch, so I suggest that we dispense with discussion and proceed directly to a vote."

"But," said Mr. Slopes.

"Ah, you have not quite mastered it, Mr. Slopes," said Arthur. "That was not the time for an interruption. All in favor of my proposals?"

Arthur was quite pleased, if a little surprised, to see five hands rise. "Now, five of you plus me makes six out of eight, so that's a majority. Motions are approved and this meeting of the Advisory Committee for the *Library* stands adjourned." Before Slopes or anyone else whose hand was not raised could react, Arthur swept up his bag and marched out of the room, breaking into a run as soon as he was in the hall. He felt jubilant.

He had no idea if Bethany would agree to consult with him on university matters, or if what she would say would be of any use, but he had seen the looks on the faces of the committee members when he had proposed input from a digital media expert—they thought that Arthur was *not* stuck in the Dark Ages and they thought he knew what he was talking about. And as a result he had, in the course of a ten-minute meeting, done some real good for the university. And for Mr. Peabody.

IX

THE LIBRARY

Above the rooms on the east side of the cloister is the cathedral library. The collections here comprise over eighty medieval manuscripts, more than three thousand books, and a wide variety of documents relating to the cathedral's history. The earliest pieces in the collection are pre-Norman manuscripts that came to Barchester when the cathedral's collections were merged with those of the nearby Priory of St. Ewolda at the time of the Reformation.

October 28, 1539, Priory of St. Ewolda

It was the tradition of the monks of St. Ewolda's to observe silence between the hours of Prime and Sext, save for words spoken or chanted at the service of Terce—one of the seven services held in the abbey church each day. In this silence, Brother Thomas was working in the scriptorium in the cloister, carefully copying the words of Psalm LIX onto a sheet of parchment that would eventually be bound with other such sheets to serve as a Psalter for a nearby parish church. The sunlight streaming into the cloister from the garden illuminated his work but would do so for only a few hours that day, now that Michaelmas was nearly a month past. He had just dipped his swan-feather quill into the inkwell in order to copy the second verse, "Libera me ab operariis iniquitatis et a viris sanguinum salva me," when the door from the south transept was flung open and a voice rent the peace.

"They are coming. The king's commissioners are coming. The day we feared is at hand."

"Brother James, calm yourself. We are not to speak until Sext."

"You do not understand, Brother. They will be here by nightfall. They bear an indictment for the prior for treason and will no doubt plunder what few treasures we have before the day is out."

Thomas could not confess himself surprised. King Henry had been dissolving the monasteries for years now; only a few remained. Just last month news had come of the fall of Glastonbury, and that should have been enough to reveal the truth to Robert Ward, the stubborn prior of St. Ewolda's. But Ward had clung to his belief that the king's plan was to leave a few uncorrupt monasteries standing. He had posited to Thomas just a few days ago that St. Ewolda's was neither so poor as to have been dissolved when the smaller houses were swept away nor so wealthy as to attract the greedy eyes of the king and his regent Thomas Cromwell, with whom the prior had refused to negotiate. But now the commissioners would soon be at the door.

"What are we to do?" said Thomas. "If we secret the plate and other treasures we will be tried for treason."

"The plate is lost, there can be no doubt, but I come to speak to you of the books."

"Surely they will be plundered, too," said Thomas, who had heard stories of manuscripts from other monasteries being toted away to Oxford or Cambridge or even to the private collections of the commissioners and their friends.

"Perhaps," said James. "But we may be able to save some of them."

"But to what end?" asked Thomas. "The monastery will be torn apart, if we are to believe the reports from other houses."

"But the cathedral will remain," said James. "True, the shrine of St. Ewolda will be plundered, but some, at least, of our books might remain safe. I come to ask your aid. How quickly could you prepare an inventory of those manuscripts kept in the book chest in the treasury?"

"They number fewer than fifty," said Thomas. "It would be the work of an hour or two if done with haste."

"You must undertake the work at once," said James.

"But I have no parchment prepared for such a list," said Thomas.

"What is that you write?" asked James, nodding toward the un-completed psalm on Thomas's desk.

"The Psalter for St. Savior's. This sheet begins Psalm Fifty-nine."

"And have you written on both sides?"

"All I have inscribed is what you see," said Thomas.

"Then you must use this very parchment."

"But to write such a list on a Psalter page would be a sacrilege," said Thomas.

"My brother, before this day is out we shall see acts of sacrilege such as St. Ewolda's has never known. Now let me explain exactly how you are to prepare the inventory, and then you must make haste, for our time is short."

James shuddered to think of the responsibility that had now be-fallen him as Guardian. He had served in that post for almost forty years, since the day when a brother named Peter had passed the title to him. Peter had spoken of threats, but James knew he had never imagined the disastrous fate that now faced England's mon-asteries. The greatest threat Peter had faced had been a curious knight, Sir Thomas Malory, who was thinking of writing a book.

"He came here early in my guardianship," Peter had told James, "claiming to have heard rumors of an ancient treasure at Barches-ter. How such rumors are started one never knows." James sus-pected that Peter himself had started the rumor—the old man had a penchant for drink, and his lips could be dangerously loose when he was under its influence.

"He pestered me for two days to tell him stories, to show him treasures. When I refused, he partook of our wine and our bread and read to the brothers from a book of history by someone called William of Monmouth—a book about the ancient kings of England and about one king who particularly interested him. Though this visitor had the credentials of a knight, the curiosity of a scholar, and the language of a poet, he seemed more like a rogue than anything else to me. I feared he would uncover the relic of which you are about to become Guardian," Peter had said to James. "But in the end he departed. Many years later, I saw his book. We could not afford such things as printed volumes here in those days, but another visitor showed me a copy. Although the visiting knight had told me his proposed title, *King Arthur and His Noble Knights of the Round Table*, William Caxton, the publisher, called it simply *Le Morte d'Arthur*. I looked through the book for evidence of our secret and was relieved to find none."

A single visitor curious about an old secret who drank wine and told stories—if only the present threat to the priory's treasures were so petty.

Two miles away, at Barchester Cathedral, two monks stood blinking in the sunlight. Brother Humphrey and Brother Samuel had just emerged from the darkness where they had been working to secure the secrets of the monastic foundation before the arrival of the king's commissioners. The abbot of Barchester had been far less recalcitrant than the prior of St. Ewolda's, having reached an agreement already with Thomas Cromwell that while the monastery would be dissolved, the cathedral would remain and most of the monks would continue on as members of the chapter. Humphrey and his brothers were not so foolish, however, as to believe that the commissioners would not despoil Barchester of its visible treasures. Certainly they would pull down the shrine of St. Ewolda—which had become a modest source of income over the years as word of its healing power spread throughout the region and pilgrims came to seek miracles and leave offerings. But, with the abbot and Cromwell on speaking, if not friendly, terms, Barchester might avoid such excesses as had been seen in Glastonbury, where the abbot had been drawn and quartered atop the Glastonbury Tor.

"The work is done," said Samuel, emerging into the light of the cloister to stand next to Humphrey. "The commissioners may pull down Ewolda's shrine, they may loot the treasury, but some secrets shall remain hidden."

"Are you and I the only brothers who know this secret?" said Humphrey. "Does not even the abbot know, and might he not tell Cromwell?"

"He knows not," said Samuel. "But there is no surprise there. The abbot knows little except how to feast and how to squander money. There is one other who knows—a brother at St. Ewolda's named James. He suggested that we undertake the work we have now completed. He also believes that the books at St. Ewolda's should be removed here, for that place will certainly be fully sacked, and the prior will be lucky to escape with his life. Here some of the books may escape the hands of the commissioners."

"But surely the commissioners will be there within hours. Is it not too late to remove the books to Barchester?"

"That is a question," said Samuel, "we shall be able to answer soon."

May 11, 2016

SEVENTH WEDNESDAY AFTER EASTER

The next afternoon, Arthur bounded up the stairs to the cathedral library with a lightness in his step he hadn't felt in ages. With the guidebook finished, he had no particular agenda; he just wanted to spend a couple of hours in his favorite place. He might pull out a manuscript of medieval prayers and try to brush up on his Latin or he might read through some of Bishop Gladwyn's correspondence in the archive files. Perhaps he would return to one of the nineteenth-century books about life in Barchester, such as *The Almshouse* or *Barchester Towers*, or maybe he would choose *Lives of Twelve Christian Men*, a two-volume collection of short biographies of nineteenth-century churchmen that included the only biography of Bishop Gladwyn. Arthur had read those thirty pages over many times, but he had never read about any of the other eleven men.

After depositing his satchel on the floor by his now empty usual table, Arthur crossed the room and stood beside the wall of books. For a long minute he just gazed at their beauty. In this room, he thought, he would never lack for something to read. He saw gleaming leather bindings of the eighteenth and nineteenth centuries with spines decorated in gilt floral patterns and overlaid with leather labels in contrasting colors. Side by side with these beauties were books like *Barchester Towers*—volumes bound in brown or green or red cloth frayed at the spine from a thousand fingers pulling them off the shelves. Then there were the books of greatest value, unassuming bindings of mottled leather or smudged vellum with no markings on the spines—books on science and medicine, agriculture and art, theology and history, all dating from before the eighteenth century. Taking down one of these books was always an adventure for Arthur. Until he gently opened to the engraved title page he had no idea what the volume would hold. But he had had enough adventure lately. What he needed, he decided as he basked in the atmosphere of thousands of books, was an old friend.

He scanned the shelf of biographies where he expected to find *Lives of Twelve Christian Men*, but there was a gap where the two volumes ought to be. Because he spent so much time there alone, Arthur sometimes thought of the cathedral library as his private collection, and he was always a little taken aback to discover that other people used it, too. No matter, though. As he looked at the empty spot on the shelf he began to think that minibiographies of nineteenth-century churchmen were not, perhaps, the perfect reading for this afternoon.

He slipped his hand in his jacket pocket and felt what he had placed there that morning. In spite of all the wisdom that stood arrayed in cloth and leather and vellum before him, on this afternoon this was what he wanted to read—his Penguin paperback copy of *Right Ho, Jeeves*. Penguins were a marvel of publishing design, he thought. They nestled perfectly in your hand or your pocket, their pages turned like thick cream pouring from a pitcher, and, while most old paperbacks eventually fell apart, Penguins mellowed. They accumulated brown blotches of foxing on their covers and pages and they absorbed a subtle odor that spoke of pipes and damp and long walks in the countryside. Arthur opened to his bookmark, pressed his nose into the book, and inhaled deeply. Yes, he thought, as he settled into his chair and began to read, this was going to be a wonderful afternoon.

But Arthur had finished only a paragraph or two when it occurred to him Bethany was not clicking away at the far end of the room. Her equipment stood silent like some abandoned ruin. Arthur loved a quiet library, so why did he have so much trouble concentrating without the incessant click of her camera and tapping of her keyboard? He hadn't seen her since they had returned from their unsuccessful expedition to Plumstead Episcopi. Perhaps she had gone into London for a few days to hobnob with some of her fellow digitizers, but wouldn't she have told him? Maybe she was having a late lunch, or taking a walk to clear her head, or taking the three o'clock tour of Barchester Castle, but wherever she was, Arthur found that her absence made concentration impossible. He couldn't spend more than a page with Jeeves and Wooster before stopping to listen for her footsteps. He had just reached the point in the narrative where Bertie was spiking Gussie Fink-Nottle's orange juice when, at last, he heard feet on the stairs.

"I've been wondering where you've been," said Arthur as the footsteps entered the library.

"At school like I am every day."

Arthur turned to see Oscar, and found himself surprisingly disappointed. "Sorry," he said, "I thought you were Bethany."

"Yes, people often mistake us," said Oscar. "I think it's my girlish figure."

"When did you become such a wit?"

"A coping mechanism, I suppose."

"I find," said Arthur, holding up his book, "I have become so used to the sound of Miss Davis's equipment, that I can't seem to concentrate on Jeeves without it. I can't imagine why she's not at work this afternoon."

"Actually, she's with Mother," said Oscar. "I asked Bethany to look in on her and she's just rung a few minutes ago to say she's going to stay a bit longer until I can get over there. I just stopped by here to pick up a book to read to her. Mum likes to hear me read in spite of . . . you know, my voice."

"Oh, God, Oscar, I'm so sorry. You told me she was back in hospital. Here I am nattering on about silly noises and reading Wodehouse, and you've got genuine problems to deal with. How is she getting on?"

"Not well, I'm afraid. They had thought she'd be ready to go home by yesterday, but now they think she might have developed pneumonia, so they want her to stay for a few more days at least."

"Is there anything I can do?"

"Would you mind acting as host tonight?"

"Lord, I almost forgot it was Wednesday, and your week to host the BBs as well. Certainly I can take care of it. I'll ring David. Will you still be able to come?"

"She's usually asleep by six," said Oscar. "I'll tell Bethany about the change of venue."

Bethany had become a regular at the BB meetings and although Arthur had resented her presence that first week, he had come to enjoy sparring with her over matters of digital media and watching David fail to seduce her.

"Does she spend a lot of time with your mother? Bethany, I mean."

"She does," said Oscar, smiling. "She's been a real friend these past couple of weeks. Don't know what I would have done without her. Bethany is . . . she's a breath of fresh air, I guess you would say. I thank God for her every day."

"I'd say maybe you're the one with a bit of a crush."

"No need to get jealous," said Oscar. "I'm not moving in on your girl."

"She's not my girl," said Arthur, rather more forcefully than he intended. "I have come to tolerate her, yes, and at times enjoy her company, but I'm no more interested in her romantically than you are."

"That seems unlikely," said Oscar with a wry smile. He turned and picked up a book from his desk. "Thanks for helping out tonight. I'll get there as soon as I can."

"Give my best to your mother," said Arthur as Oscar disappeared through the doorway. He felt a stab of guilt that he had not given his best to Mrs. Dimsdale personally. She had been in hospital for several days, and Arthur had been so caught up in his own concerns that he hadn't even thought of going to visit her. On several occasions over the years, Mrs. Dimsdale had invited the BBs to dinner. David had flirted with her shamelessly, bringing a blush to her cheeks, and Arthur had eaten her heavenly trifle and done his best to be solicitous, but even though he had known her since childhood, he had never felt particularly close to her. That was no excuse, he knew, to avoid visiting her in hospital. He would go tomorrow afternoon, he vowed, as he slipped his book back in his jacket pocket. For now he would go home and tidy up in preparation for the BBs meeting, but tomorrow he would visit Mrs. Dimsdale. Maybe Bethany would go with him.

Arthur had just pulled a tray of scones out of the oven when David and Oscar arrived on his doorstep simultaneously.

"Thank you for doing this," said Oscar.

"Don't be foolish," bellowed David, striding into the sitting room swinging a bottle of wine. "He's always happiest when he's hosting. That way he doesn't have to leave his little nest. Now, corkscrew, please."

"I've just made some scones," said Arthur.

"Fine," said David. "You enjoy teatime, but I am ready for some proper liquid refreshment." David plopped down into his usual chair and Arthur ducked into the kitchen, appearing a moment later with a corkscrew, three wineglasses, and a plate of scones.

"Four glasses, Arthur," said David, grabbing the corkscrew and setting to work on the bottle. "Bethany is coming, right?"

"I thought she didn't drink," said Arthur, remembering the Diet Coke Bethany had ordered when they first met.

"Don't be ridiculous," said David. "Of course she drinks. I had a drink with her last night."

Arthur took a moment to digest this piece of intelligence. He realized that he had come to think of Bethany as something like his own private acquaintance. Outside of her interactions with him, he had imagined, she did nothing but digitize manuscripts, eat, and sleep. But, in fact,

Arthur was just one of her many friends in Barchester. She was sitting with Mrs. Dimsdale, and drinking with David, and dining with Gwyn, and who knew what else.

"How's Mum, Oscar?" said David, once he had poured himself a glass of wine and attacked it with some ferocity.

"Better this evening, they say. Some chance she might be able to go home in a day or two."

"I was thinking of going to visit her tomorrow," said Arthur, determined to follow through on his resolution.

"I'm sure she'd appreciate that. She loves to be read to. She'll listen to absolutely anything. Today, Bethany was reading to her from something called *Lives of Twelve Christian Men*."

"Bethany has that book?" said Arthur.

"Yes," said Oscar.

"I was looking for it in the library this afternoon."

"Of course I can't tell you what books Miss Davis checked out because of confidentiality rules, but I can tell you she was reading to my mother about Bishop Gladwyn this afternoon."

"Seems an odd choice."

"I don't know about that," said David. "From what she told me, she spent the weekend transcribing your stories about the history of the cathedral. In fact, I gather that, thanks to Bethany, you have now completed the grand task of your professional life and that a toast is in order." David stood and raised his glass.

"Of course," said Oscar. "With all the worry about Mother, I'd nearly forgotten. Bethany said you've finished the guidebook at long last."

"To Arthur," said David, "who may be the slowest writer in the history of English tourism, who may require the coaxing of an American assistant to finally give birth to what is undoubtedly a masterpiece, but who knows whereof he writes and who, furthermore, has impeccable taste in women."

"To Arthur," said Oscar, and as they lifted their glasses to drink, there was a knock on the door.

"I'm glad you could join us," said Arthur to Bethany when he had shown her in. He would have liked a moment to take issue with some of the points in David's toast, but he was nonetheless touched by his friends' congratulations, in which Bethany now joined.

"Gwyn told me you e-mailed her the manuscript," she said. "She says she really likes it."

"Does she? I haven't heard the first word from her."

"I went to talk to her after Communion this morning."

"You went to morning Communion?" said Arthur.

"I've been going every morning. It's in St. Dunstan's Chapel, which thanks to you, I know was originally a fifteenth-century chantry chapel dedicated to Bishop Draper. It's tiny—it only fits about five of us, but it's so beautiful with the fan-vaulted ceiling. It's like a miniature cathedral. Anyway, they have Morning Prayer in the Epiphany Chapel on one side of the quire and Communion right after in St. Dunstan's Chapel on the other side. So Arthur can go to Morning Prayer without ever knowing that I'm quietly praying just a few yards away before the Communion service starts."

"I had no idea," said Arthur.

"My point exactly," said Bethany.

"The things about which Arthur has no idea are without number," said David.

"Anyway, the dean was celebrating this morning and afterward I had a nice long chat with her over coffee and we happened to touch on the subject of your manuscript."

"And she liked it?"

"She said there might be a few revisions and possibly a bit of trimming, but that could wait until the photos are selected. I gather the precentor has been put in charge of that."

"Of course he has," said Arthur, rolling his eyes.

"Apparently," said Bethany, "Teresa has a friend who's a professional photographer and she invited her down from London for the party on Friday and this woman has agreed to bring all her equipment and spend a few days shooting the cathedral. I suppose we'll all meet her on Friday."

"I'm sorry," said Arthur, "but how will we meet her on Friday?"

"At Teresa's party," said Oscar.

"I've no idea what you're talking about," said Arthur.

"And my point is proven," said David.

"She told me she invited you," said Oscar.

"Have you stopped checking your e-mail again, Arthur?" asked Bethany. "He never checks his e-mail."

"Who in God's name is Teresa?"

"The precentor's sister," said Oscar.

"Why does everyone know people but me?"

"Because," said David, "you're antisocial and stay hidden away in the library all the time."

"Oh, thank God you said that, David," said Bethany. "I was afraid I was going to have to be the one to tell him."

This comment brought a roar of laughter from David and even a chuckle from Oscar, but Arthur felt chastened. Was he really so far removed from the world?

"Now," said David, "I propose we move forward with the reading. I believe Bethany has volunteered to fill in for Oscar, who was to have been our host."

"Thank you, David," said Bethany, taking a seat and pulling a book out of her handbag. "I've brought a little something that I think you'll find interesting. This is from a book called *Lives of Twelve Christian Men*. You see, Arthur has convinced me that actual books can sometimes be worth reading. And on rare occasions they might even include information unavailable on my laptop."

"I think you misunderstand the purpose of our readings," said Arthur. "They are meant to amuse, or at the very least to entertain."

"Come now," said David. "You don't think *Lives of Twelve Christian Men* will be entertaining?"

"You said you were looking for it yourself this afternoon," said Oscar.

"Not for entertainment exactly."

"I'm sure I shall find it greatly entertaining," said David, "especially if it annoys Arthur."

"If you gentlemen would care to stop bickering, I can explain why I chose this particular volume. You, Arthur, may find it pleasant to rest on your laurels after completing the soon to be best-selling *Visitor's Guide to Barchester Cathedral*, but as far as I'm concerned, we still have a mystery to solve involving a certain missing manuscript—a manuscript, I might add, that could very well force you to rewrite your entire opening section when it tells you the story of St. Ewolda. And Bishop Gladwyn's biography holds some tantalizing clues about that manuscript."

Arthur had been afraid for a moment that Bethany would mention the Grail, but she kept his confidence.

"I've read Gladwyn's biography a dozen times," said Arthur. "There's nothing in there about a lost manuscript."

"How did he ever become a researcher?" said Bethany to David.

"Search me."

"You have to read between the lines, Arthur. We know there is a manuscript missing from the library. You guessed that it went missing on the night of the Nazi bombing, and maybe it did. But who is the last person we *know* saw the manuscript? Bishop Gladwyn, who included it in his inventory. So what does the biography tell us about Bishop Gladwyn? Some very interesting things, as it turns out." Bethany picked up the volume of *Twelve Christian Men*. The section on Gladwyn bristled with sticky notes.

"You've been busy," said Arthur, nodding toward the pink and yellow place markers.

"Evelyn fell asleep this afternoon and I had an hour or two. The biography's only thirty pages long."

"Evelyn?"

"My mother," said Oscar.

Arthur felt admonished again. He had been friends with Oscar for decades and hadn't even remembered his mother's Christian name.

"So," said Bethany, "I'm going to skip around, because I've marked the important bits—or at least the important bits for solving this little mystery."

"More than a *little* mystery, I'd say," said Oscar. "Arthur if you and Bethany can recover the lost Book of Ewolda, that would be something."

"OK, a little background to start with. Gladwyn was the son of a country rector in rural Barsetshire, someplace called Uffley, but he apparently came to the cathedral often as a boy. He went off to Oxford, took his degree at Lazarus College, and then came back and served as curate for his father until the old man died in 1863. Then he became rector himself, but his eyes seemed to always be on the cathedral. In 1865, he became examining chaplain to Bishop Bridewell and the next year he became a canon of the cathedral. He hired a curate for Uffley and moved to Barchester. Then, in 1870, he picked up another job—I love the way these Victorian clergymen would hold all these different livings, rake in the money, and then pay curates a pittance to do all the work."

"Actually," said Arthur, "that practice was dying out by the 1870s. It was the eighteenth century that—"

"Hush, Arthur," said David.

Arthur hushed.

"Anyway, guess what living he was given. I'll give you a hint—tiny, almost no money associated with it, but also almost no responsibilities. Plus, tremendously important to our little mystery."

"St. Ewolda's of the Missing Manuscript?" said David.

"Practically. He was made rector of St. Cuthbert's."

"Why should that make any difference?" said Oscar.

"Because Arthur and I think another rector of St. Cuthbert's, Henry Albert Naylor, took the manuscript on the night of the bombing. Don't you think it's a pretty big coincidence that the last two people who saw that manuscript were both rectors of St. Cuthbert's?"

"I'd completely forgotten that Gladwyn held the St. Cuthbert's living," said Arthur, shaking his head. There seemed no end to what Bethany could discover that had escaped his notice. And of course his grandfather had also been rector of St. Cuthbert's. Arthur wondered if he, too, had been somehow connected to the manuscript.

"But that's not all," said Bethany. "In 1872, Gladwyn became bishop and eventually he rebuilt the residences in the precincts that were damaged in the Civil War and then get this, he moved out of the bishop's palace so it could be renovated and into the 'modest cottage,' as the book describes it, at Number Four, St. Martin's Close. And he settled in. He never moved back because he liked being so close to the cathedral. And then listen to this. It's from a letter written after his death by one of his fellow canons.

Robert Gladwyn, in addition to his many good works, was a gracious host, a renowned wit, and a man of keen intellect. He could converse on almost any topic and outspar his opponent in any controversy. His knowledge of Barchester, its cathedral, and the outlying parishes of Barsetshire was encyclopaedic and his visitor's guide to the cathedral will no doubt be read for generations to come. He was a regular fixture in the cathedral library, where he was known to read for hours on end at a worn and gouged table that he preferred to more modern furnishings.

"That's my table," said Arthur. "That bit is one of the things that made me feel connected to Gladwyn." Bethany continued.

But the true source of his erudition was said to come from his personal library of some thousand volumes, which he kept in his own lodgings and which he generously shared with those of the cathedral community who wished to borrow books. Many of these volumes he left to the cathedral at the time of his death, but some remained in his lodgings, where he established a library for future residents.

Bethany stopped reading and set the book on the table.

"Am I missing something?" said Arthur.

"Usually," said David.

"Tell him the rest, Oscar," said Bethany.

"Ah, so you and Oscar have been working the problem without me."

"Oh, don't get your knickers in a twist. Oscar knew where to find the records of the choirboys, so I figured he'd know where to find the records of who else lived at Number Four, St. Martin's Close."

"And who else lived at Number Four, St. Martin's Close?" asked Arthur.

"Henry Albert Naylor," said Oscar.

Arthur gave a low whistle.

"Naylor," said Bethany, "who may have stolen the manuscript on the night of the bombing, lived in a house with a private library established by Gladwyn, the last man we know examined the manuscript. What better place to squirrel away a book?"

"We should look," said Arthur excitedly. "Who lives there now?"

"Once again the rector of St. Cuthbert's," said Oscar.

"And who is the rector of St. Cuthbert's?" said David.

"The precentor," said Oscar.

"The precentor," said Arthur, expelling a breath.

"The precentor," said Bethany. "And I have an idea how we can swim into the salmon's library."

The BBs broke up early because Oscar wanted to get back to the hospital and check on his mother. Arthur announced his intention to go to Compline, and was pleased when Bethany took his arm and walked with him to the cathedral. They composed two-thirds of the worshippers, the other being Canon Dale, whose best singing days were some decades behind him. Bethany had never been to Compline, but she read music well and Arthur was surprised to find her the best singer of the three of them by some margin.

"That's a lovely service," she said after Canon Dale had slipped away to his lodgings and she and Arthur sat alone in the chapel in the light of the dying candles. "I understand why you want to end your days like this."

"I find it very comforting," said Arthur.

"Even though you believe all those beautiful prayers fall on deaf ears?"

"Just because I don't believe in God doesn't mean that I don't want to. And it doesn't mean I can't find comfort in routine and in connecting myself through those words and this space to a hundred generations who have come before me here."

"That's a nice thought," said Bethany. They sat in silence for several minutes, until one of the candles flickered out. "Will you walk me home?"

"Gladly," said Arthur. He blew out the remaining candles, and they made their way through the dimness of the cathedral out into a cool night. The spire stood in silhouette against the rising moon and only a few lights glowed in the windows of the houses in the close.

"I didn't tell David and Oscar about the Grail," said Bethany as they walked under the archway that led them into the High Street. "That's just between you and me."

"I appreciate that. I don't know why my grandfather wanted me to keep the Grail search a secret, but I'd like to respect that wish as much as I can—at least for now."

"I was looking at the marginalia in the Barchester Breviary today," said Bethany. "If Barchester has a secret treasure, like the Holy Grail, for instance, it makes sense for it to be described in a coded manuscript, and it makes sense for that manuscript to be hidden by someone in authority."

"I just hope the missing book really is a coded manuscript and not just a Psalter."

"Have faith, Arthur," said Bethany. They walked on in silence for a few minutes.

"Do you think I'm an antisocial recluse?" asked Arthur as they turned the corner into the lane leading to Bethany's lodgings.

"I think you live in a world of books more than in a world of people. But that doesn't have to be a bad thing. And we still love you."

"We?"

"Your friends, Arthur. And yes, I count myself in that number."

"Bethany, would you . . . that is, I wonder if you might . . ."

"Spit it out, Arthur, before I change my mind about just how socially awkward you are."

"I was thinking of visiting Mrs. Dimsdale tomorrow afternoon, and I wondered if you would go with me."

"I thought you were busy tomorrow afternoon."

"Whatever gave you that idea?"

"Gwyn said this morning that a man was coming up from Sotheby's to look at the manuscripts tomorrow afternoon and that you were going to show him around."

"Blast!" said Arthur. "I completely forgot. What a lovely prospect, showing the manuscripts to the man who will eviscerate the Barchester Cathedral Library."

"Do you really think they'll sell them?"

"I don't know."

"Did Gwyn tell you about the north transept?"

"Yes," said Arthur.

"I suppose the history of English cathedrals is full of stories of bits that almost fell down."

"It's also full of stories about bits that *did* fall down. I'm thinking of a new opening for the guidebook. 'Widely considered, by those who bother to consider it at all, to be the most neglected cathedral in Britain, Barchester attracts little in the way of tourists, little in the way of historical or architectural study, and little in the way of funding—so little, in fact, that parts of it may well have collapsed into rubble by the time this guidebook is published.'"

"Would selling the manuscripts raise enough for the repairs?"

"I've no idea. But tomorrow afternoon I shall bite my tongue and smile and show Mr. Sotheby or whatever his name is around the library and just hope he doesn't see too many things that appeal to him."

"I'm not sure you have it in you to talk trash about rare books, Arthur."

"Well, then," said Arthur, thinking of the resolution he had made after talking with Gwyn. "I'll just have to find another way."

"Another way to do what?"

"To raise the money the cathedral needs to repair the north transept and maybe even build the Lady Chapel."

"How much would that take?"

"Gwyn thinks about ten million pounds."

"What's that, fifteen or twenty million dollars?"

"Why, are you planning to write a check?"

"I'm not, but to Jesse Johnson twenty million dollars is chump change."

"Are you saying that your boss, the evangelical nutcase who is dredging the Red Sea for Pharaoh's chariots, would give obscure, forgotten Barchester Cathedral twenty million dollars?"

"I highly doubt it, especially if you keep referring to him as a nutcase just because his religious views are different from yours. But if we find the Holy Grail, or even something that *could be* the Holy Grail—he'd pay millions for that. Lots of people would."

"And that fact may be exactly why my grandfather wanted me to keep the Grail a secret. But you bring up an interesting point."

"And what is that?"

"That Jesse Johnson could easily afford to save Barchester Cathedral."

"Do you want me to hit him up for a donation?"

"It couldn't hurt."

"I can do that," said Bethany. "I'll drop him an e-mail and tell him about the transept and the danger of the manuscripts being sold off. You never know—apparently he is very generous to causes that interest him."

"Thank you," said Arthur. "It may lead to nothing, but it seems worth a try." They had reached the door to Bethany's lodgings and she fumbled to retrieve her key from her handbag.

"Shall I make myself scarce tomorrow while you're talking to the appraiser or whatever he is?" said Bethany. "I could go visit Evelyn. Tell her I'm bringing your good wishes."

"That's very kind, and probably just as well that we have a little peace and quiet."

"Yes, I am such a loud and obnoxious American—how do you ever put up with me?"

"That's not what I meant," said Arthur. "I only meant—"

"It was a joke, Arthur. Thank you for taking me to Compline. And thank you for walking me home." She stood on her toes and gave Arthur a light kiss on the cheek, then disappeared inside and closed the door. She had kissed David and Oscar good-bye when they had left Arthur's cottage earlier that evening, so there was nothing unusual about her doing the same with him, but as he walked home, Arthur could not decide just how he felt about this new form of saying good night.

X

ST. DUNSTAN'S CHAPEL

*This beautiful chapel in the Perpendicular style was one of
the last pieces of new construction in the cathedral prior to
the Reformation. It was built in 1450 as a chantry chapel
for the late Bishop Draper. A chantry was an endowment
left by wealthy donors to pay for Masses to be said for their
souls every day in perpetuity. For Bishop Draper, perpetuity turned out to be about ninety years. At the Reformation,
the chantry's endowment was confiscated by the king, and
the chapel stripped of its finery and rededicated to St. Dunstan, a tenth-century abbot of Glastonbury.*

October 28, 1539, Priory of St. Ewolda

"The inventory is complete," said Thomas, "and prepared as you
requested."

"Excellent," said James. The two men stood in the treasury,
over the open chest that held the monastery's books. "Where is the
volume of mathematical studies?"

"Is this the time to be reading about mathematics?"

"This is *not* the time to ask questions," said James sharply. "Find
the volume." As Thomas sorted through the books, James took a
quill and quietly added a column of numbers, memorized long ago,
to the list of manuscripts.

"Here is the book," said Thomas, passing the volume to James.

James inserted the inventory into the manuscript and returned the book to the chest. Then from within his robes he withdrew another volume.

"I have one more book to add to our collection," he said. "It is a volume I have toiled many months to prepare."

"What book is this?" said Thomas.

"There is but little time for me to acquaint you with its contents," said James. "For now I must entrust you with the most important task of your life. You must enlist the aid of Brother Anthony to help carry the books to the cathedral, where they might find at least some protection from the commissioners. But there is another object you must take with you, and of this great treasure and its history, with which I shall burden you, you must tell no one."

"What is this treasure?" asked Thomas, who could not believe that anything of great import could reside at St. Ewolda's.

"The most sacred relic of St. Ewolda's or of any monastery, and today you shall return it to its home in Barchester, whence our Saxon brothers removed it nearly five hundred years ago—for you, my brother, are now the Guardian."

An hour later, James watched as Thomas and Anthony made their way across the field outside the monastic precincts and toward the city of Barchester, carrying the book chest. Only Thomas and James knew the truth about the rest of their burden. James had prepared in every way he could for this day, even marking the treasure itself with a clue as to its true nature. He felt he had chosen the new Guardian well, that Thomas would do everything in his power to protect the treasure—he only hoped, in this time of great uncertainty, it would be enough.

Brother James now turned his attention to the task he had dreaded since he first heard the king had begun taking over the monasteries. With tears in his eyes, he made his way furtively through the lengthening shadows to the monastic kitchen. Several servants were already busy preparing dinner, and James stood watching them for a moment. As far as they knew, this was an ordinary day, no different from any other day of their lives. They had risen at four to prepare breakfast and would work in the kitchen until the evening bell tolled eight. Then, as required, they would sit in the nave, behind the screen, and listen to the murmured sounds of Vespers before returning to their lodgings. They were fed, sheltered, and clothed, which was more than many men of the realm could claim. And the monks of St. Ewolda's prayed for them each day. Now James was about to destroy all that. He wiped the tears away with his sleeve, drew a deep breath, and stepped forward from the shadows.

"Servants!" he called. "The monastery is under attack. You are dismissed. Fly or face the consequences."

"Pardon, sir, but where are we to fly?" asked a young man holding an onion in one hand and a knife in the other. "This monastery is our home."

"There is no home for you here anymore," said James. "The king's commissioners are upon us."

"But mustn't they eat?" asked the man.

"Fly, I tell you. Do you not understand that I bring instructions from the prior himself? No one who remains within the precincts of the monastery is safe for another hour." James knew he was exaggerating the threat to mere servants of the monastery. Only the prior was likely in any real bodily danger. Still, he needed the kitchen to himself, and it was true that within a few days the monastery's coffers would be emptied and there would be no money to pay the servants. "Now go!" he roared.

The servants needed no further encouragement. While they may have had little understanding of theology or politics, they did understand that if one of the monks spoke to them in such an authoritative voice, it was best to do as he asked. In another moment, James had the kitchen to himself.

From beneath his robe, he withdrew a cracked and soiled volume, a book that he had kept on his person for more than twenty years. More than anything, he wanted to sit in the quiet warmth of the kitchen and read this book one last time. Though he knew every word, every wonder of it by heart, he still loved to run his eyes over those mysterious Saxon words he had mastered so long ago. Now the new manuscript he had prepared and explained to Thomas would keep Ewolda's secrets safe. Never again would there be need for a monk of St. Ewolda's to learn ancient Saxon. Never again, he thought with renewed tears, would there *be* monks of St. Ewolda's.

Laying the book on the table, amid potato parings and mutton grease, James stepped toward the fire and threw several fresh pieces of wood on the embers. Sparks flew up and in a few seconds the fire leaped forth hungrily. James picked up the book and stood staring into the flames. As much as he longed to read the words within, words to which he had dedicated his life, he could not risk being too late. The book and its secrets could not fall into the hands of the invaders. He threw the book into the fire.

Sparks scattered into the room, and James stepped aside to avoid lighting his robe on fire. Yet perhaps fire was what he deserved. Perhaps he should plunge headfirst into the flames to either retrieve the book before it was destroyed or to follow it into nothingness, but he had not the courage for either. He watched as the flames consumed the volume, the pages of vellum peeling back one at a time, blackening, and then dissolving into ash. From outside he heard the shouts of his brothers, as word spread that the commissioners were at the gates.

James had loved his life at St. Ewolda's—the rhythm of daily prayer and worship, his work with Brother Thomas copying out manuscripts, the quiet fraternity of his fellow monks. But now, he thought, as he watched the last ashes of the manuscript flutter above the fire, his life was over. With his final act, he had done the best and the worst that he could. No pain could be greater than what he now felt, he thought, as he picked up the knife from the table.

A few minutes later, when a commissioner of King Henry VIII entered the kitchen, he saw only a dying fire and the body of Brother James lying on the floor.

May 12, 2016

SEVENTH THURSDAY AFTER EASTER

Once a week, on Thursday mornings, Arthur treated himself to a full English breakfast at the Old Mill Restaurant in the High Street. He didn't have to be on campus until ten o'clock, so he had plenty of time to go to Morning Prayer, take his walk with Gwyn, and still enjoy breakfast before his bus arrived. He always sat at the same table in the front window, so he would have a view of the bus stop. When he pushed open the door of the restaurant the next morning, he saw a familiar figure seated at his table.

"How did you know I would be here?" said Arthur, sliding into the chair opposite Bethany.

"Barchester's a small town, Arthur, and, as previously established, you are a creature of habit. And since I've yet to try the cholesterol fest that your people call breakfast and I needed to talk, I thought I'd join you."

Arthur was still settling in his seat when the waiter deposited two fry-ups on the table.

"Morning, Mr. Prescott," he said. "First time I've ever seen you with a date."

"Not a date, John. Just showing this young American one of the best parts of British culture."

"Sounds like a date to me," said the waiter as he walked away.

"So what was it you needed to tell me?" said Arthur, tucking into his meal.

"I found something yesterday," said Bethany. "Maybe you know about it already. You probably do, which is why I didn't mention it last night. And if you do know, then I have no reason to be eating this . . . is this, what do you call it, black pudding? It's made of blood, right? I think I'll stick to the sausage. So, anyway, I was photographing a manuscript of excerpts from different mathematicians, do you know the one? And I was in the section by Fibonacci—I looked him up and he's the reason we use Arabic numerals. Can you imagine long division with Roman numerals? And he discovered the Fibonacci sequence. I don't know if *discovered* is the right word, but . . ."

"Bethany," said Arthur gently between bites of egg. "My bus will be here in fifteen minutes."

"Oh, God, I'm sorry. I thought I'd stopped doing that. Maybe it's the coffee. Anyway, I found a parchment inserted into the book, just a single sheet. On one side is a fragment of Psalm Fifty-nine in Latin, but on the other is what looks like an inventory of manuscripts, headed St. Ewolda's Priory and dated October 28, 1539."

"The day the king's commissioners arrived and dissolved the monastery," said Arthur excitedly.

"So you know about it?"

"No, I've never seen it—but it makes sense to make a list of what you have just before it's about to be plundered. And even if the king's commissioners didn't take any books home with them, which is unlikely, that was when the collection of St. Ewolda's merged with that of Barchester Cathedral."

"My Latin's not great, but as far as I could tell there's no reference to any manuscript about Ewolda."

"What about the mystery manuscript?" said Arthur. "The missing Psalter?"

"There are three Psalters listed. I think two of them are still in the library; the other one could be the same as the one on Bishop Gladwyn's list, but it's hard to tell. The descriptions are pretty basic. There are thirty-five titles on the list. It looks to me like nineteen of those correspond with manuscripts that are still in the library."

"The rest of them were hauled off by the commissioners," said Arthur. "The libraries of Oxford and Cambridge are filled with manuscripts stolen from monasteries during the Reformation. If we have a list of the St. Ewolda's collection prior to the dissolution, we might be able to identify some of those missing manuscripts. Bethany, this is a brilliant find."

Bethany beamed as Arthur took a bite of toast, but he had a thought as he swallowed. "Of course," he said, "if the descriptions are, as you say, pretty basic, it may be difficult to tie them to specific manuscripts."

"That's the best part," said Bethany. "There are two columns of

Roman numerals on the inventory. One, to the right of the titles, I haven't figured out yet. But the numbers to the left are each followed by a single word. I started comparing manuscripts in the library to the list. I thought at first these might be page numbers, but it turns out they're leaf numbers. I go to the leaf that corresponds to the left-hand number and see if the first word on that leaf matches the word next to the number. And it works. That's how I found out we still have nineteen of the manuscripts. And it should make it easy to identify the St. Ewolda manuscripts in other collections."

"Where did you come from?" said Arthur in amazement.

"Pretty cool, huh?"

"Pretty cool? Bethany, knowing what was in the St. Ewolda's collection before it was broken up—that's tremendous. I can't believe I never found that inventory."

"Be honest, Arthur," said Bethany, "have you ever been even slightly interested in mathematics?"

"Point well taken. Ah, here comes my bus."

"I'll put the inventory on your table," said Bethany as Arthur rose to go.

"This business with the missing Psalter and thinking we're on the trail of the lost Book of Ewolda, or even the Holy Grail—" said Arthur, "sometimes I'm afraid that's all just chasing shadows. But an inventory of the St. Ewolda library—that's a brilliant discovery. It could give us a much clearer view of life and scholarship at the priory. Well done, Bethany."

He stood awkwardly for a moment as the bus eased into its stop. He wondered if he ought to lean down and kiss her on the cheek. Was that now the . . . what was the expression . . . the new normal for good-byes? But he couldn't bring himself to do it. He simply nodded, smiled, and left her prodding her blood pudding with a fork.

"Put Miss Davis's breakfast on my tab," he said to the waiter as he headed for the door.

Arthur's afternoon with Stephen Mangum from Sotheby's turned out to be quite pleasant. How could it be otherwise? thought Arthur afterward. Sifting through a collection of medieval manuscripts with a fellow booklover was Arthur's idea of the perfect way to spend a few hours. From the moment they met in the cloister, the two men connected over their mutual love of books. When Stephen stepped into the library, he gasped audibly—the only proper reaction, as far as Arthur was concerned. Soon Arthur was pulling one manuscript after another off the shelves to show Stephen.

"How is the library used?" asked Stephen as Arthur was setting a manuscript onto one of the wide oak tables.

"Sadly, it's not used much," said Arthur. "I've been thinking about that a lot lately—how this resource can become important again. I'll be honest, I'd like it to become important enough to render your job superfluous."

"There must be ways to bring researchers and students here," said Stephen, "even in a place as remote as Barchester. There's a stately home near where my family lives in Gloucestershire that works with schools and even the local university to do programs for students. I think the university teaches a course on the history of the book in the library."

"That's a rather brilliant idea," said Arthur. "I had thought about seeing if the library could loan some things to the university—set up a display to get students interested in books. But why not bring Muhammad to the mountain?"

"Do you know anyone at the university?" said Stephen.

"I have a few connections," said Arthur, smiling.

It was impossible to closely examine eighty-two manuscripts in three hours, so Arthur had concentrated on what he saw as the greatest treasures of Barchester. Stephen's job that day was simply to write a short description of the collection and come up with estimated prices for a dozen or so of the most valuable pieces. Arthur could have shown off only the least interesting of the Barchester manuscripts—late medieval works of theology with no illuminations. But Bethany had been right; he did not have it in him to disparage the collection. In the excitement of sharing the manuscripts with a fellow bibliophile, he soon forgot the underlying purpose of the afternoon and simply reveled in exploring treasures with Stephen.

"This is our oldest manuscript," said Arthur, setting a small, browning volume on the table. Like most of the manuscripts, it lacked its front cover and the text began on the first page. There were almost no margins, many of the leaves were chipped, and the ink was faded to illegibility in places. "A Latin Gospel of John. Not much to look at," he said with a smile.

"Fantastic," whispered Stephen reverently. "What do you reckon? Late tenth century?"

"We think so," said Arthur.

Stephen gently ran a finger across the first few lines of text. "Feeling that vellum and touching those words that have been there for a thousand years—that never gets old."

"Sometimes I pull it out and read a page or two and I feel like it just . . . pulls me back through time," said Arthur.

"You read medieval Latin?"

"Reasonably well," said Arthur. "I learned it because of this book, because I couldn't resist the desire to read these words." He picked up the manuscript and read the first verse of John's Gospel, words that priests and monks had read from its pages a millennium ago: *In principio erat Verbum et Verbum erat apud Deum et Deus erat Verbum.*"

The words hung in the air for a moment as the two men stood gazing at the ancient manuscript. "You know my job is to secure pieces for auction," said Stephen as Arthur returned the Gospel to its place on the shelf. "But I have to admit, it would be a shame for a manuscript like that, that's been at Barchester for a thousand years, to wind up in some private collection."

"I had a feeling we were going to be friends," said Arthur.

"Still, I have to do my job."

"I understand," said Arthur, and over the next two hours he showed him another twenty or so of the finest manuscripts. Stephen was especially taken with the Barchester Breviary.

"This is extraordinarily fine musical notation. Quite rare in an English manuscript this early."

"We had a scribe in Barchester in the thirteenth century who seemed to specialize in musical notation. His work appears in three of our manuscripts, but most of it is here in the breviary. We never had great illuminators here—the monastery was perennially poor—but we're very proud of our nameless musical scribe. His work is really marvelous."

"And would fetch a marvelous price," said Stephen. "And I notice that, unlike the rest of the manuscripts, this breviary still has its front cover attached."

"And how much of a problem is that? That the covers are missing?"

"It depends on the book. Certainly they would be more valuable to collectors with the covers intact, but the rarest and most valuable will still sell at quite high prices. For many of the others, though, finding the covers might make the difference between a strong estimate and a rather more cautious one."

Arthur showed Stephen works on medicine, history, and theology, and was just about to pull out a manuscript that he had never examined closely, a collection of excerpts from mathematical treatises, when he remembered what Bethany had found within its pages the day before. Not even sure what he was hiding, he pushed the volume back onto the shelf. "It's getting late," he said. "I generally go to Evensong before dinner. Would you care to join me before catching your train?"

"I think I have enough information to advise the dean on the next step," said Stephen. "And Evensong sounds lovely."

Arthur crossed over to his usual table and swept a few papers into his satchel, taking care that the piece of parchment that Bethany had left there was among them. He had been dying to look at it since he arrived at the library, but part of him wanted to keep it hidden from Stephen. He would have to wait. "Right, well, the service starts in ten minutes, so we'd best be going."

Bethany was not at Evensong, which was too bad, thought Arthur. He would have liked introducing her to Stephen and she would, he thought, have liked the Orlando Gibbons setting the choir sang. After the service, he walked Stephen to the station and bid him farewell, afraid to ask the question that had nagged at him all the way through the service: What was the "next step"?

When Bethany stepped out of St. Dunstan's Chapel after Communion the next morning, Arthur was waiting for her. He had sat in the nave after

Morning Prayer, just close enough to St. Dunstan's that he could hear the rise and fall of the service—the softness of the prayers spoken by the celebrant (this morning, Canon Dale) and the marginally louder responses of the three-person congregation. Even though he avoided Communion services, he knew, from reading the Book of Common Prayer, the pattern of the service, and he made his way to the chapel just as it ended.

"Can you spare a moment?" Arthur said, smiling at Bethany.

"For you, of course," said Bethany, winking at him.

"Since you are one of the few people who have read both Bishop Gladwyn's guidebook and my own, I wanted to show you something that we both left out. I didn't include it on purpose, so it would stay my little secret; I've no idea why he didn't mention it. I didn't tell you about it the other night because . . . well, it's a visual."

"What is it?" asked Bethany. "I can't dawdle around all day looking for the Holy Grail, you know. I've got work to do."

"Well," said Arthur, "since you told me you go to Communion in St. Dunstan's Chapel every day, I thought you might have noticed yourself. It's rather curious." Arthur led Bethany back into the small confines of the chapel. "See anything unusual?"

"I grew up in a Florida megachurch," said Bethany. "It's all unusual."

"Take a look at the carvings above the altar."

Bethany stepped toward the altar and leaned forward to examine four rows of small carvings—each barely bigger than a child's toy. The first row of figures was a series of animals attacking men—a lion, a dragon, a serpent, and an eagle. Above those, four men were killing four beasts—another dragon, a wolf, a bear, and some sort of sea monster. The third row might well have been a lineup of King Arthur's knights: four men in armor, the central two astride mighty steeds. At the top of the frieze hovered four angels.

"What do you think?" said Arthur when Bethany had had time to examine all the figures.

"Not exactly sacred," she said, "other than the angels at the top, and I suppose that could be St. George slaying the dragon. But why does it seem familiar to me?"

Arthur spoke gently:

> *For all the sacred mount of Camelot . . .*
>
> *Climbs to the mighty hall that Merlin built.*
> *And four great zones of sculpture, set betwixt*
> *With many a mystic symbol, gird the hall:*
> *And in the lowest beasts are slaying men,*
> *And in the second men are slaying beasts,*
> *And on the third are warriors, perfect men,*
> *And on the fourth are men with growing wings.*

"Tennyson," said Bethany excitedly. "It's his description of Camelot from 'The Holy Grail.'"

"You know your Grail literature."

"But what does Camelot have to do with Bishop Draper's chantry chapel?"

"I've absolutely no idea," said Arthur. "But Tennyson must have seen these carvings. It's too big a coincidence; and I've not seen others like them anywhere else. It's just one more curious link between Barchester and the Arthur legends."

"Do you think Malory could have seen these carvings?" asked Bethany, once again leaning to inspect the figures.

"Who knows?" said Arthur. "The chapel was built just before the time when Malory was most likely writing *Morte d'Arthur*. If he ever visited Barchester, this would have been the newest work in the cathedral."

"But he never described the sculptures of Camelot."

"No," said Arthur, "he didn't."

"Why, Arthur Prescott," said Gwyn, striding toward Arthur on Friday night, drink in hand, "I don't believe I've ever seen you at a party before."

Arthur fidgeted nervously, not so much because he was unused to parties—he was perfectly adept at making small talk when the occasion called for it—but because of his purpose at this particular party. He had had a meeting with Oscar, David, and Bethany in the library after Evensong and they had all agreed on the plan for the evening—a plan that, if all went well, would end with their being guilty of having stolen a medieval manuscript out of the private residence of a cathedral official. Arthur's nervousness as he chatted with Gwyn had nothing to do with the party. It was just that he had never been part of a heist.

Arthur, David, Oscar, and Bethany had all read enough Agatha Christie and Ngaio Marsh and Sherlock Holmes that they had no trouble concocting an unnecessarily complicated plan to steal the manuscript from the precentor. The plot depended on knowing the exact size of the missing manuscript, but Bishop Gladwyn's inventory described it only as "8vo." That meant octavo, which meant the book was roughly the size of an ordinary hardback novel but roughly wasn't good enough for tonight. They needed the exact measurements. This need led to Arthur's first contribution—a rather masterful piece of detective work, he thought. The shelves of the former chained library on which the manuscripts sat were constructed specifically to hold these manuscripts, Arthur guessed. And he knew from experience that each shelf was about six inches too long—inches that would have been taken up by the width of the manuscripts' covers if they had not been torn off. But the second shelf had almost eight inches of extra space. That meant, reasoned Arthur, that the missing manuscript had been about two inches thick.

"But what about the height?" said David.

"When the manuscripts were returned after the war," said Arthur, "they were returned to the shelf in their original order. The same order given on Bishop Gladwyn's inventory. And we know that manuscript B-28 was the last volume on the right of the second shelf."

"What good does it do for us to know that?" asked David, but Arthur was already at the bookcase.

"The chains are still here," said Arthur. "They are all pushed to the end of the iron rod, behind the molding at the edge of the bookcase, but they're still attached."

"So?" said David.

"The chains were originally attached to the top corners of the manuscripts, and each chain was just long enough to allow its manuscript to rest on the reading ledge."

"That means if we compare the length of the chain for the missing manuscript to the chain for a manuscript that's still here . . . ," said Bethany.

"We can get a pretty close estimate of the height of the missing Psalter," said Arthur. It took longer for someone to find a tape measure than to do the actual measuring and math.

"So," said David, "the manuscript is two inches thick and nine inches tall."

"And even though there is some variation in handmade manuscripts, we can guess that if it's nine inches tall it will be about six inches wide."

"Arthur, you're a genius," said Bethany, and she flung her arms around him.

"I always did think he was rather clever," said David, smiling.

But Arthur only heard Bethany whispering into his ear, "Well done." Even that he almost didn't hear, for he was suddenly not thinking of manuscripts and chains but trying to recall the last time he had felt a woman's embrace. He honestly could not remember. It felt nice, he thought. And as Bethany let her arms fall away from him and stepped back, he was a bit surprised to find that he was not blushing. Not only had it felt nice, it had felt natural.

"Here we are," said Oscar, entering the library from the anteroom. "George Gilbert Scott's plans for St. Martin's Close. It's a funny thing, I've seen it referred to as the most beautiful residential development in Britain and as the most hideous."

"All depends on whether you like Victorian Gothic domestic architecture," said David. "I myself find it appalling."

"And I find it breathtaking," said Arthur.

"But the real question," said Bethany, "is where the precentor's study is."

"Right there," said Oscar, pointing to an architectural drawing. "And," he added, pulling another sheet to the top of the pile, "according to these renovation plans from the 1920s, the downstairs loo is right next to it."

"Right," said David, "I think that means we have a manuscript to steal."

"So," said Gwyn, once she had gotten Arthur a glass of wine, "I gather you had an excellent session with Mr. Mangum yesterday. I really appreciate your doing that. I realize you're not on our staff, but you know more about those manuscripts than anyone."

"It was my pleasure," said Arthur, glancing around to see if Bethany had arrived yet. "We actually had a lovely afternoon, in spite of the black cloud that hung over the occasion."

"Black cloud?"

"The possibility that Barchester's history will be sold to the highest bidder."

"Thankfully we're not quite there yet."

"And what did Mr. Mangum suggest as a next step?"

"He feels we should hire an appraiser to evaluate the manuscripts in more detail. But I'm sure you'll be pleased to know that he also suggested very strongly that we hold back a few of the items most important to the cathedral's history. He was particularly firm in warning me not to sell the Barchester Breviary or the early Gospel of John."

"I think Mr. Mangum's sense of business is surpassed by his sense of history," said Arthur with a smile.

The precentor, Arthur had discovered when he finally got around to checking his e-mail, was holding a party on Friday night. His sister Teresa acted as hostess, and Arthur suspected, as she greeted him at the door, that the party was more hers than her brother's, but the precentor seemed perfectly capable of playing the role of host. He even managed to look less like a salmon than usual.

To most of the partygoers that night—canons and their spouses, friends of the cathedral, parents of the choirboys—the gathering seemed no different from any other year. Crowded rooms, flowing drink, heaps of food, and the deafening din of conversation that all but drowned out the choral music playing in the background. Not unusually, there had been a small disturbance by a guest who had overindulged in the liquid refreshment, but he had been politely sent on his way and would no doubt arrive at Sunday morning's service contrite and sober. One of the other guests had come to the aid of the precentor when the drunken man had knocked over a pitcher of Pimm's, but considering the loud altercation Arthur Prescott had with the precentor earlier in the evening on the subject of selling off the cathedral manuscripts, the spilling of a little Pimm's was not even the most dramatic thing that happened at the party. For most, it was an enjoyable night.

But had there been a careful observer at the party, he might have seen something altogether different. He might have seen that the drunken man, local bookstore owner David Denning, had arrived quite sober, and never actually drank anything. True, he acted more and more tipsy as the evening wore on, but the source of this intoxication remained a mystery. Next, he might have seen a schoolteacher named Oscar Dimsdale make his way down a short hallway to the downstairs loo almost immediately upon arrival. And had this careful observer had need of the loo himself thereafter, he would not have found two neatly folded hand towels by the sink but only one. He then would have watched the arrival of an American researcher named Bethany, who carried a large handbag and spent several minutes flirting shamelessly with the precentor. And from there things would have gotten even more interesting.

Arthur checked his watch. Nine forty-five. He sipped his wine as Gwyn spoke about the manuscripts, but his eyes were focused on the host. Bethany laid a hand on the precentor's forearm and tossed her hair back, letting out a loud laugh. Arthur didn't know what she was saying, but he knew it was working. The precentor would not forget talking with Bethany tonight. As soon as she patted him on the cheek and moved on, Arthur nodded to David and made his own move.

"So kind of you to include me, sir," he said, holding his hand out as he approached the precentor.

"Of course, my good man, of course," said the precentor, and then turning to his sister, he added, "This is Arthur Prescott. He's just completed the text for our new cathedral guidebook. It's a bang-up job, Arthur. I've not had the chance to tell you, but I truly enjoyed it."

"Thank you, sir," said Arthur. "It's a shame it will be the only piece of the cathedral's history left."

"Why whatever can you mean?" said Teresa.

"Only that your brother has decided that the cathedral should sell off its history to the highest bidder," said Arthur, slowly raising his voice.

"Arthur, I don't—" said the precentor, but Arthur let him get no further.

"Our host," he said waving his arm and turning to the nearest clump of partygoers, "thinks that Barchester should sell its very soul to a bunch of Americans who will no doubt put it on display in some place like . . . like Chicago and charge thirty dollars' admission." Chicago was the first American city Arthur could think of, and he spat the word at the precentor and drew the attention of a dozen or so guests with his little speech. He wasn't sure exactly how much thirty dollars was, but it sounded an unholy amount.

"Mr. Prescott," said the precentor calmly, "in the first place, I was not the one who proposed the sale of the manuscripts. In the second place, as you well know, their contents are being fully digitized and will be available to anyone free of charge, and lastly, if we do not raise some funds and quickly, there will be no cathedral. The north transept is in serious danger of collapse."

"The cathedral is a house of God," said Arthur as he watched Bethany disappear unnoticed down the hall, past the loo, and through the door into the precentor's study. "Better that it should lose an arm than lose its very soul." Bethany closed the door behind her. Now came the tricky part. Arthur had no idea how long Bethany would spend in the study. If she found the manuscript, she would replace it with a manuscript on the history of the kings of England—a manuscript that happened to be two inches thick, nine inches tall, and six inches wide and that had entered the party in her voluminous handbag. But Arthur had to continue being a distraction until Bethany was back among the guests. If she ended up having to do a thorough search of the study, that could take quite a while. It was, he thought, the flaw in the plan. But Bethany had insisted she could search the room quickly and that Arthur was as good at arguing as anyone in Britain.

"I would contend," said the precentor, "that the soul of the cathedral lies in its very stones. Think of the lives of the men who raised that glorious structure. How many were killed in the process? For that matter, how many are entombed below the aisles and in the walls? The cathedral is sacred space and sacred ground and we owe it to the generations that have come before us and to those that will come after us to preserve it."

Arthur completely agreed with this assertion, but his job tonight was not to agree but to contest. "But at what cost? Would you sell your heart to preserve your . . . your . . ."

"Worship is the heart of the cathedral," said the precentor as Arthur fumbled for a metaphor. "It has been for a thousand years and, God willing, it will be for a thousand more. Worship. Not a pile of dusty old manuscripts."

Arthur was discovering that, as talented as he was at disputation, the task was much more difficult when one agreed with one's opponent. Luckily, Bethany slipped out of the study at that very moment, and he could tell by her smile that she had found something.

"I bow to your argument," said Arthur, backing away from the precentor. His part was finished now. "Sell the manuscripts, sell the books, and let us all enjoy the smell and the feel and the history of glowing computer screens."

"Wash all dis den?" said David, staggering past Arthur to take up his part in the drama. He poked the precentor in the chest as he spoke. "Are you selling the cathedral?" Arthur hoped he wasn't overdoing it.

"You've had a bit too much," said Arthur." "Suppose we get you home."

David timed the flail of his arms perfectly. Teresa had just stepped up with a pitcher of Pimm's and with one swoop he knocked it from her arms and sloshed half of it down the front of the precentor. It couldn't have worked any better if Teresa had been in on the plot. David was supposed to have thrown a drink at the precentor, but this was even better. While everyone's attention turned to the precentor, Arthur looked down the hall. Oscar had retrieved David's coat and stood next to Bethany. Her arm hidden by the drapes of the coat, she slipped something from her handbag into the voluminous inner pocket. Oscar passed her a hand towel and she came striding forward from the hallway that led to the loo.

"Oh my goodness, let me help get you cleaned up," she said, approaching the precentor.

"Sorry about that," said David. "Praps a bit too much . . ."

Now Oscar stepped forward, holding out the coat. "Come on. Let's get you home," he said, slipping the coat over David's shoulders.

In the meantime, Bethany was wiping up the precentor with the hand towel. "I know I have some wet wipes in my bag somewhere," she said, opening the bag wide and holding it where the precentor could easily look in. She began pulling items out and setting them on the coffee table—a wallet, lipstick, keys, hairbrush. Finally she turned the bag upside down and the last few items tumbled onto the table, including a packet of wet wipes. By the time she had finished wiping up the precentor's face, he was beet red with embarrassment, but he, and everyone else, had seen the entire contents of Bethany's bag.

"I'm so sorry about this," said Bethany. "I'm afraid he came with me and he ordered a whole bottle of wine with dinner and then I hardly drank anything because I've been a little under the weather lately and . . . well, I suppose I should help you walk him home, Oscar."

A minute later the party was back in full swing and the four conspirators were hurrying across the close toward the cloister. No one spoke until they were all safely in the library. Oscar flicked on a light and they stood in a circle looking at one another in silence for a moment.

"Well," said David, "that was fun." Suddenly the tension was broken and all four burst out laughing.

"Did you see the look on his face when you spilled the Pimm's?" said Arthur.

"What about when you told him to cut off the cathedral's arm?" said Oscar.

"Uhm, gentlemen," said Bethany, when the laughter had subsided, "don't you want to know what I found?"

"Yes, yes," said David. "Out with it."

"It's in your pocket," said Bethany.

"Christ, I forgot," said David. "I am sober, I promise."

"Only a sober man could act that drunk," said Oscar.

David reached into his coat pocket and withdrew a volume with no front cover. He laid it on the nearest table and for a moment the four just gazed at it.

"Have you looked inside?" said Arthur.

"No time," said Bethany. "I found it pretty quickly, just in among the books on the shelf behind his desk. I made the switch and got out of there. I didn't want to leave Arthur hanging."

"You do the honors, Arthur," said Oscar.

Arthur pulled out a chair, sat down and slid the volume closer. Gingerly he turned over the first leaf. In a script that he guessed was late fifteenth-century the text began:

> *Beatus vir qui non abiit in consilio impiorum et in via peccatorum*
> *non stetit in cathedra derisorum non sedit*

"Psalm one, verse one," said Oscar, running his fingers along the text.

"Damn," said David.

"So it is the missing manuscript," said Arthur, "but it's not an encrypted book of ancient history. It's just what Gladwyn's inventory called it—an ordinary Psalter. No illuminations, no—"

"You're very trusting, aren't you, Arthur?" said Bethany.

"I beg your pardon?"

"And you believe your first impressions. Have you noticed that? It was true with me, wasn't it? You saw me in the chapter house and you thought I was beautiful and then we met and you thought I was annoying and that's been me ever since, as far as you're concerned—beautiful and annoying."

"How did you know I thought—"

"And it's the same thing here. You look at the first page and you assume Psalter."

"I'm sorry," said Arthur, "do you have a point?"

"My point is you have to look further than your first impressions,

Arthur. It's possible that I am *more* than beautiful and annoying, and it's possible that this manuscript is *more* than a Psalter." Bethany sat down next to Arthur and took the manuscript from him, slowly turning its pages.

"Wanting there to be a mystery won't make it so," said Arthur.

"Yes," said Bethany, "but ignoring a mystery won't make it go away. See." She had turned about a third of the pages in the Psalter and she laid the book in front of Arthur. On the left side of the spread was the text, in Latin, of Psalm XXX. On the right page, Psalm XXXI began, but after the beginning of the third verse the Latin changed to incomprehensible groups of letters, each group nine letters long.

"Look at that," said Oscar.

"Be my strong rock, a castle to keep me safe," said Arthur quietly, looking at the unfinished verse.

"Your Latin is impressive," said Bethany.

"It's from Compline," said Arthur. "We sing that verse every night."

"I think we found your coded manuscript," said Bethany.

"Damn," said David again, in an entirely different tone. "I thought this was all just a lark, but . . ."

"But the precentor really was hiding something," said Oscar.

"We should return it," said Bethany.

"Are you crazy?" said Arthur, pulling the manuscript back from her and staring at the mysterious groups of letters. His pulse rate soared as he considered what this might be—no one would take the trouble to encode psalms. A code meant a secret and a secret meant something worth keeping secret. Something like the Holy Grail. "There is no way in hell we're giving this back."

"If it's as important as you want it to be," said Bethany, "then it won't take the precentor long to discover it's missing, no matter how good a job we did tonight."

"So before we even have a go at cracking the code we just hand it back?" said Arthur.

"Of course not, you nincompoop," said Bethany, swatting Arthur on the back of the head. "This is the twenty-first century, Arthur. There are"—Bethany flipped through the manuscript until the nonsense syllables returned to the Latin of the Psalms—"thirty-two pages of coded manuscript. I can have those photographed in an hour with a little help. The party will still be going on. I only need ten seconds in the study this time, because I know where the manuscript belongs. Oscar will come with me—you two can't go back without looking suspicious. Now, Oscar, give me a hand and we can knock out these images in no time."

Bethany picked up the manuscript and headed across the room to her equipment.

"Was this part of the original plan?" said Arthur to David.

"No idea," said David, shedding his coat and sliding into Oscar's desk chair. "But the girl's got pluck."

"It wasn't part of the plan, Arthur," said Bethany, who was busy flicking switches and focusing lenses, "because we didn't know the thing was only thirty-two pages. And by the way, just because you're across the room doesn't mean I can't hear you."

"You see," said David, propping his feet up on Oscar's desk. "Pluck!"

XI

THE WEST FAÇADE

The eighty-nine niches on the façade of the cathedral facing the broad green once held statues of saints, including the apostles, St. Mary, and many early martyrs. The number eighty-nine is not a coincidence—this is the number of chapters in the four canonical Gospels. The saints' statues were pulled down and destroyed at the Reformation, but in the twentieth century, four new statues were erected commemorating martyrs of Barchester: Ewolda, the Saxon founder; Robert Ward, the last prior of St. Ewolda's Priory; Bishop Babbington; and a fourth figure representing the unnamed clergy who lost their lives during the Reformation and Counter-Reformation.

November 25, 1558, Barchester Cathedral

Edmund Lufton knew that many of his fellow clergymen criticized him for his failure to take a stand. Edmund, they said, didn't believe in anything. Edmund simply blew with the wind. But the wind had been blowing in many directions of late, and Edmund had greater worries than the opinions of his colleagues. Immediately upon completing his degree at Oxford he had come to Barsetshire as curate of Puddingdale and risen quickly through the ranks to become a canon of Barchester Cathedral. He had welcomed a new group of clergy into the cathedral when the nearby monastery of St. Ewolda's had been dissolved and had watched as the king's commissioners had desecrated Barchester—pulling down statues and destroying Ewolda's shrine. But Edmund had managed to hold on to his job, and when Edward VI had risen to the throne a few years later, Edmund, like many of his fellow clergymen, had embraced Protestantism. They had seen it coming, and most of those who could not abide it had long ago left for France.

One of those who left, a priest named Thomas Piers, had, before his departure, entrusted Edmund with a great responsibility. It was this burden, and not his lack of any loyalty, that had kept him at Barchester in the years since. For Edward VI had died in 1553, and his Catholic sister Mary had risen to the throne. Mary had reinstated the Catholic Church and it was the Protestants who feared for their lives. Edmund had quietly returned to practicing the Catholic rites, but many had fled Barchester, and Bishop Babbington, who had refused to either leave or recant his Protestant beliefs, had been burned at the stake on the green in front of the cathedral's west end. It had been a horrible sight—Edmund had known the bishop, had celebrated the Eucharist with him, had even dined with him on occasion. He and the rest of the newly Catholic clergy had been forced to watch the bishop's grisly death—as a warning, he supposed, to those who might still harbor secret Protestant tendencies.

But Edmund guarded a secret that outweighed the particulars of how he worshipped his God. As long as he could remain at the cathedral, and remain alive, he could do the job God and Father Piers had chosen him to do. And now, only three years after Parliament had made Protestantism a capital crime, Mary was dead and her sister, Elizabeth, queen. The wind seemed to be blowing again, for Elizabeth gave every indication of being a Protestant, and Edmund imagined he would soon be reading once again from the Anglican Book of Common Prayer rather than from the Catholic missal.

He sat in his bedroom in the canons' lodgings long after and considered all that had happened since he had become Guardian— changes of monarch, changes of worship, and purges of anyone who disagreed with those in power. It had been a dangerous time, and he doubted the danger was past. He had seen fellow canons flee in the night or be pulled from their rooms and murdered in cold blood, all because of the book from which they chose to read their evening prayers. He had seen Catholics burn books deemed "too Protestant" and Protestants burn books deemed "too Catholic." He counted himself lucky that he had navigated the treacherous waters of the past few years, but what if a future Guardian did not have such fortune? What if a Guardian were to be killed, or even to die of a sudden illness, before passing on the secret of Barchester and its priceless treasure? He knew other Guardians had had the same concern, for one of them had placed a mark on the treasure itself—not giving away its true nature, but providing a hint.

Only the manuscript could tell the whole story, and as it stood, the manuscript could not be completely decoded, even by one who knew the secret of its enciphering. Edmund knew its contents, for Father Piers had taught him, and he would teach them to the next Guardian—if he had the time. But after the turmoil of the past few years, Edmund feared that some Guardian would *not* have the time. The manuscript, like the treasure, needed to bear a sign, some hint as to its contents and importance. He could not tell the secret outright, but he could leave a clue.

At university, Edmund had landed himself in trouble for defacing the books in the Lazarus College library—not the illuminated manuscripts in the Bodleian or even the illustrated books on natural history or medicine in the college collection; those books he loved just as they were. Edmund's mind thought in pictures more than in words, so he gravitated toward illustrated volumes. But far too often his studies led him to books with no pictures—theological treatises, histories, and biographical studies. These he often could not resist illustrating himself, and so, when the master of Lazarus discovered in the blank space at the end of each section of an edition of Livy's *History of Rome*, miniature portraits that Edmund had foolishly signed, he called him into his study for a severe reprimand. Edmund had promised not to deface any books in the future, but the time had come, he thought, to break that promise.

He trimmed the wick on his candle, opened the manuscript, and began to draw.

May 21, 2016

EVE OF PENTECOST

Arthur went straight to the library after Morning Prayer the following day. While he ought to be spending his weekend reading student essays, he much preferred the prospect of cracking a centuries-old code and reading the secrets contained in the manuscript that now nestled securely back in the precentor's study. Both the photography and the return of the book had gone off without a hitch, and Bethany had promised a high-resolution printout of the coded pages would be waiting on Arthur's table Saturday morning.

This turned out not to be the case, for Oscar was studying the printout at his desk, as he had been, he told Arthur, since dawn.

"Well, you're the maths teacher," said Arthur. "Have you cracked it yet?"

"When do we reckon this was written?" asked Oscar, pushing his chair back and taking off his reading glasses.

"Judging from the script in the Psalter I would have said early sixteenth century—almost certainly at the time of the Reformation. For a medieval manuscript, it's young."

"But for a complex cipher, it's old," said Oscar. "Most medieval ciphers are what's called simple alphabetic substitutions. Each letter of the alphabet is substituted by another letter of the alphabet—so A becomes X, for example, or B becomes W. On the surface, that's what this looks like, so it should be pretty easy to crack."

"How do you do it?" said Arthur, settling into a chair across from Oscar.

"Frequency analysis," said Oscar. "You look for the most frequently recurring letters and try substituting the most common letters in the language that's been enciphered. In English that would be E, T, A, and O.

On the other end, you look for rarely occurring characters and those are likely to represent Q, X, and Z. I'm assuming this text is Latin, but I can't get anywhere with frequency analysis."

"Could it be something older than Latin? Saxon?"

"Possibly," said Oscar, "but that would present a whole different set of cryptographic challenges—this is written in the Roman alphabet; I'm not sure how you would encrypt the Saxon alphabet into Roman. For that you'd need a linguist; I just do maths. But if it's fifteenth or sixteenth century, it's almost certainly Latin. Nobody was reading and writing Saxon by then."

"True," said Arthur.

"Well," said Oscar, pushing the pages across the desk to Arthur, "I leave you to it. I have a student to tutor at ten and then it's back to the hospital to see Mum. There's a chance they might let her go home later today."

"I'm afraid I'll be rubbish at this," said Arthur. "Maths was never my strong suit."

"Take this," said Oscar, handing Arthur a slim paperback. "This isn't the Enigma code. Anything encoded in the fifteenth century we should be able to break, even if it turns out to be polyalphabetic—but that seems unlikely for Britain."

"Polyalphabetic?" said Arthur, feeling more confused by the moment.

"It's all in the book," said Oscar. "It's a basic guide to simple ciphers and cryptanalysis. You'll be an expert by this afternoon."

"I doubt that," said Arthur, picking up the book.

"*Bonam fortunam!*" said Oscar, and he was off.

Three hours later Arthur was bleary-eyed with confusion. He had read all about simple substitution ciphers without learning much more than Oscar had already told him. He had pored over the section on polyalphabetic substitution—which worked the same way as simple substitution but used multiple alphabets. This did not come into use in Europe until the sixteenth century, shortly before the time Arthur believed the Barchester manuscript was encoded. He had tried to understand transposition ciphers, which had to do with shifting the positions of the letters according to some regular pattern; none of the patterns suggested by the book yielded any results when applied to the pages of the manuscript. Annoyingly, in the description of each of these types of ciphers, Arthur found phrases such as "quite easy to crack" or "trivial to break." Arthur was not fond of feeling stupid. He had before him the instructions for decrypting virtually any medieval cipher, and though he was no skilled mathematician, he could certainly follow instructions. But these instructions had produced a total of precisely nil. Once in a while a group of letters would transform itself into a word, but if he tried to apply the rule that had led to that metamorphosis to another group, it yielded gibberish. He had been excited at first by the idea of frequency analysis, because the letters U, Q, and D appeared much more often than any others, but no matter what substitutions he made, the results were always nonsense. Besides, most of the rest of the alphabet seemed pretty evenly distributed, except that letters at the end of the alphabet appeared quite rarely. But this whisper of a pattern didn't lead him to any results.

He had just slammed the book on ciphers down on the table—not for the first time—when Bethany swept into the room. She wore a bright floral print dress that seemed to waft sunshine into the library.

"Good morning, my fellow conspirator," she said. "That was an adventure last night, wasn't it?"

"More of an adventure than I'm used to," said Arthur. It had taken him hours to get to sleep—he assumed because adrenaline was still coursing through him.

"It's good for you, old man," said Bethany. "So how was your morning? Because my morning was amazing. First of all, I decided I'm going to have to start getting more exercise than one gets in manuscript heists if I'm going to eat any more full English breakfasts, and I have to say, I'm a fan. So I took a long walk this morning. Did you know that if you go straight up St. George Street out of town you get to the top of this hill in a mile or so with an amazing view of the whole city? The cathedral looks like a little toy church and the river was a ribbon of sunshine cutting through the meadows. Have you ever been up there?"

"I thought you wanted to know how my morning was," said Arthur.

"I do," said Bethany, "but we're doing mine first."

"In that case, yes, I've been there often. It's lovely."

"What are those ruins up the river outside of town?"

"That's the Priory of St. Ewolda," said Arthur.

"Of course," said Bethany.

"I'll take you there sometime," said Arthur, pushing the manuscript away and turning his chair around to face Bethany, who had ceased puttering around the room and was now seated. How was it that she could smile like that? he wondered. He hadn't thought about it before, but she almost always smiled. And it was the sort of smile one couldn't ignore. He had seen it with the old man in the rest home, and with Oscar and David—Bethany had a way of making other people happy just by her presence. It was remarkable that, with a centuries-old mystery on the table and thousands of rare books and manuscripts surrounding him, what he wanted to do more than anything else at this moment was listen to Bethany natter on about the meaningless minutiae of her morning.

"Anyway, that view was just the first cool thing to happen this morning. I had breakfast with Gwyn, and guess what? She has actually seen the Nanteos Cup."

Arthur sat up in his seat. "You're kidding. I can't believe she never told me, knowing how much I like . . . old things."

"She didn't tell you because she knew you wouldn't believe," said Bethany. "Remember the story of Mrs. Mirylees, who owned the cup? She didn't want to have it scientifically tested because she thought people's belief in the cup was more important that anything tests would prove. The Grail is about faith, Arthur. Anyway, Gwyn grew up in Wales and when she was eight she was riding her bicycle through the village and was hit by a car. She was in a coma for two weeks and apparently her mother knew the woman who owned the cup and she asked if she could have some water from the cup for her daughter. Ten minutes after the water touched Gwyn's lips, she woke up."

"Oh, my God," said Arthur.

"And Gwyn didn't know anything about the cup. Anyway, when she got out of the hospital, her mother took her to visit the owner—Gwyn wouldn't say where—so she could say thank you, and she got to hold the cup, just for a minute. She said she had never felt such power. That's the moment she knew she was going to be a priest. They didn't even have female priests in the Church of England at the time, but she knew she was going to be one."

Arthur stared at Bethany slack-jawed. Could the legends about the Nanteos Cup be true? It was easy to dismiss tales from the nineteenth century; it was much harder to ignore a story from a trusted friend, even if it was a story Gwyn had never shared. Then again, thought Arthur, he had never asked her what inspired her to become a priest.

"Arthur Prescott," said Bethany, grinning even wider than usual, "is it possible that I have rendered you speechless?"

"Rather," said Arthur.

"Well, then tell me about your morning."

"My morning has done little more than provide proof that as a code breaker my career is likely to be short and fruitless."

"Nothing?" said Bethany.

"Nothing," said Arthur.

"Why don't you take a break and come back tomorrow with fresh eyes," said Bethany. "That's what I do with crossword puzzles."

"You solve crossword puzzles?" said Arthur.

"*New York Times*, every day on my iPad," said Bethany. "The Friday and Saturday puzzles are the tough ones. But usually if I get stuck and come back to it the next day I can finish right up. It's a funny thing."

"Perhaps I will set it aside for a while. Do you fancy grabbing some lunch?"

"Kind of you to ask, Arthur, but first of all, a full English breakfast is enough to keep me going until dinnertime, and second, I am taking the train up to Wells for the weekend. I just popped up here to tell you about my morning. I'm meeting a fellow digitizer and we're going to Glastonbury to hike up the Tor and see King Arthur's tomb and the burial spot of the Holy Grail and before you roll your eyes at me and ask me how there can be two Holy Grails and tell me that King Arthur's tomb was conveniently 'discovered' when the monastery was in need of money, I am going to waltz off to the station. So have a lovely weekend, Arthur, and I will see you on Monday."

"I'll probably be sitting here as frustrated as ever," said Arthur.

"I doubt that," said Bethany. "You'll have broken it by then." And with that she was off, leaving Arthur to return to his attempts at deciphering the manuscript. As he leaned over the pages, a cloud passed in front of the sun and the room dimmed. Appropriate, thought Arthur, and he set to work.

Five hours later, with no progress made, he decided to give Bethany's strategy of walking away from the problem a try. He pushed back his chair and thought of her, in the brightness of that spring afternoon, adding her own sunshine to the ancient sites. Arthur could remember the excitement of his own first pilgrimage to Glastonbury. He had been sixteen, and it had been his first trip away from home by himself. Glastonbury was steeped in Arthurian lore and Arthur had explored every inch of it. He had climbed the great rolling green hill at the edge of town where Joseph of Arimathea was said to have placed his staff in the ground, where it rooted into the Glastonbury Thorn. At the time, a descendant of the original thorn still grew there, but in 2010 some ruffian had cut it down. He had walked the path to the top of the Glastonbury Tor, the strange-looking hill that some claimed was the legendary Isle of Avalon. He had soaked his feet in the frigid waters of Chalice Well, the spring that gushed forth from the spot where the Holy Grail was supposedly buried. And he had stood in the ruins of what had once been one of England's largest and wealthiest monasteries. Although he moved among other tourists, with whom he presumably shared his fascination with the Grail, Arthur kept to himself, for he had, he believed, a secret. But to all those around him who snapped pictures of the tor and the thorn and the ruins and the marker indicating the supposed gravesite of Arthur and Guinevere, and especially to those who sought the Grail at Chalice Well, he did not speak the words, "It isn't here; it's in Barchester."

Sunday proved no more beneficial for Arthur's future as a code breaker than Saturday had been. He worked away at the manuscript for a few hours in the afternoon but made no headway, and finally gave up and went downstairs to read Wodehouse under the yew tree in the cloister. On such a sunny, blue-sky day with the heights of Barchester Cathedral towering above him and his favorite author in hand, not even clever medieval monks could dampen Arthur's spirits.

"I say, Peabody, do you know much about ciphers?"

It was the first time Arthur had ever been in the maths building at Barchester University and he was impressed that it was even uglier and more sterile than the humanities building. Arthur knew Peabody only from the Advisory Committee for the Library, but on the basis of this meager acquaintance, he thought he might solicit a little help with the coded manuscript.

"Prescott, is it? From the library committee? I quite liked that Jeeves book."

"Did you?" said Arthur. "I'm pleased to hear it."

"What can I do for you?"

"Well," said Arthur, stepping into Peabody's cluttered office, "I'm trying to decipher a coded passage from a late medieval British manuscript."

"Shouldn't be too hard," said Peabody. "Anything from that period in Britain is probably a simple substitution cipher—quite easy to decrypt."

"Yes, well I've used frequency analysis and gotten nowhere and I don't think it's a polyalphabetic cipher or a transposition cipher."

"My, my," said Peabody, pushing back his chair and propping his feet on a mass of papers that obscured his desktop. "You know a little something about ciphers yourself, I see."

"Only what can be learned in a couple of days," said Arthur.

"My great-aunt was at Bletchley during the war, you know," said Peabody. "She never talked about it. Official Secrets Act meant they all had to stay mum for fifty years and she died after forty-six."

"So you've no other suggestions for breaking a medieval cipher?" said Arthur.

"Enigma—that was a cipher," said Peabody, lost in his thoughts. "In a way, it was a simple polyalphabetic substitution cipher—each letter substituted by another letter. But it was as if the key word and the order of the alphabet changed with every character entered into the machine. Positively brilliant."

"Indeed," said Arthur. "But back to the subject of medieval ciphers."

"I'm afraid if you've tried frequency analysis and checked for transposition you've reached the end of my knowledge. But I'm sure it's got to be either simple substitution or transposition. Unless you've got the date wrong. It could be polyalphabetic, but even a late medieval version of that is fairly easy to break. I could take a look at it, but I doubt I'll see anything you haven't."

"If it keeps giving me trouble, perhaps I'll bring it by," said Arthur, but he was already worried that consulting Peabody had been a bad idea. The last thing he wanted was for word to spread around town that he was trying to break a medieval cipher. The precentor knew everyone in Barchester, it seemed, and Arthur had no wish to arouse the salmon's suspicion. "I'd appreciate it if you'd keep this confidential," he said.

"I'll have forgotten all about it by the time you're halfway down the hall," said Peabody, and Arthur suspected this was true.

Arthur sat in his usual pew waiting for Evensong to begin, still troubled by the cipher. Bethany's attendance at Evensong had been fairly regular over the past few weeks, and he missed her presence beside him. He supposed she had spent an extra day in Wells. He never spoke to her before the service, but afterward they always sat together listening to the organ postlude. Sometimes she rushed off without so much as a "See you later, Arthur," but often they sat for a few minutes after the quire had emptied and talked about the music or the weather or nothing in particular. But today he sat alone and almost didn't notice the service, so cluttered was his mind with alphabets and substitutions and transpositions. He stood for the Magnificat and the Nunc Dimittis only because his body was programmed to do so.

Something Peabody had said kept running through his head—that Enigma was like a substitution cipher in which the key word and the order of the alphabet changed with every character. Arthur understood just enough about substitution ciphers to know what he meant. In the case of a simple substitution cipher, all one needed to decode a passage was the key word. But what if the key word was constantly changing? Then frequency analysis wouldn't work, because every time the key word changed, the frequency of each letter would change. But if Arthur couldn't figure out one key word, how could he figure out scores or even hundreds of them?

He had no idea how long he had been sitting in the pew after the postlude, trying to think what he was missing. The slamming of a door in the north transept finally brought him back to reality, and when he stood to go, the service bulletin fluttered to the floor. Arthur stooped to pick it up and read, at the bottom of the page, the words "Psalms XXII–XXIII." He was sorry he hadn't paid attention—he had always liked the Twenty-third psalm. "The Lord is my shepherd," he repeated softly, "therefore can I lack nothing."

And he solved it.

Arthur took the steps to the library two at a time and arrived breathless on the landing to see the door ajar. Bethany stood at the far end of the library. She was not busily moving books from the real world into the digital world; she was simply standing.

"Good weekend?" Arthur called out when he had caught his breath, but she only stood there, arms slack at her side, a cell phone cradled in one palm. Only when Arthur had covered more than half the distance between them did he realize she was sobbing. Not gently tearing up like someone who has read a particularly moving passage of Dickens or watched an advertisement for greeting cards, but honest to God, eyes red, cheeks wet, nose dripping, shoulders shaking sobbing, like someone who had lost a spouse.

"Bethany, what is it?" said Arthur. He knew almost nothing of her home life, he suddenly realized, but he couldn't imagine anything less than the death of her mother could bring on such a reaction.

"I was just talking to her yesterday," said Bethany in between gasps for air. "She was fine. She was home. Oh, Arthur," and without warning she ran to him and threw her arms around him and began sobbing even harder, if such a thing was possible, on his shoulder. Arthur hadn't the slightest idea how to react. He tried patting her on the back, but she only squeezed him tighter, so finally he put his arms around her and squeezed back. They stood that way for what seemed an awkward eternity to Arthur. He felt his foot go numb, but thought it impolite to shift his weight—as if this might betray his impatience—so he stood as still as he could until at last he felt Bethany's shaking abate and her sobs turn to sniffles. Only then did she slacken her grip and slowly step back from the embrace. In the space of a few seconds she looked at him with agony, then puzzlement, then sympathy.

"Oh, Arthur, you haven't heard, have you?"

"Heard what?" he said. Was it Gwyn? Had something happened to Gwyn?

"Evelyn."

"Evelyn?" Arthur racked his mind for any mutual acquaintance named Evelyn.

"Oscar's mother, Mrs. Dimsdale, Evelyn. She . . . she died."

"Oscar's mother died?" Arthur's first reaction was a spasm of guilt—he had promised to go visit Mrs. Dimsdale and he hadn't done it, and now it was too late. And of course he was sorry for Oscar. But Mrs. Dimsdale had been in her eighties and Bethany could hardly have known her well. Arthur couldn't imagine the reason for such an emotional outburst.

"I didn't see her today. I could have gone to see her but she was out of the hospital and Oscar said she was doing fine, so I said I'd stop by tomorrow afternoon. I never thought . . ."

"What . . . what happened?" said Arthur.

"Heart attack maybe," said Bethany. "My train was late and I was going to sneak in for the end of Evensong and then Oscar called and said . . . said she took a nap this afternoon and just didn't . . . didn't wake up."

"How's Oscar?" said Arthur.

"Oh, you know Oscar," said Bethany. And Arthur suddenly realized that he didn't. He knew Oscar's taste in books and what Oscar did for the cathedral, but he had no idea how Oscar would react to his mother's death.

"He's putting on a brave face," Bethany continued. "But he's crushed. He lived with her almost his whole life. I just hate to think—"

"We'd better go . . . I don't know, go be with him," said Arthur. What did one do for a friend whose mother had died, he wondered. Some sort of action was required, but what? He had no idea, but he felt certain Bethany would know.

"Right," said Bethany, drawing a sleeve over her eyes and taking in a deep breath. "I suppose you boys will all put on a British stiff upper lip or whatever, so I'll do my best, too, for Oscar's sake. He'll need help with . . . well, probably with everything. You're right, the first thing is just to go be with him."

The next few days passed in a blur as David, Arthur, and Bethany, along with Gwyn when she could spare the time, helped Oscar deal with everything from solicitors to funeral arrangements. Bethany was right, Oscar was both stoic and devastated. His mother, Arthur discovered he was the last to know, had been a lover of church music, just like Arthur. She had been mostly a Sunday morning churchgoer in her later years, which was why Arthur had so rarely seen her at the cathedral, but she had a huge collection of LPs of choral and organ music. It was an interest Arthur could have shared if he had bothered to get to know her. Now he could only help transport boxes of records and the turntable that would play them to the choir room at the cathedral. Evelyn had made arrangements long ago with the precentor and the choirmaster to donate her collection to the music program.

She had also left instructions for her funeral that kept both the precentor and the choirmaster busy. She wanted a full Funeral Mass, with the settings for the service music taken from John Rutter's *Requiem*. The precentor, who liked nothing more than services full of high ceremony and beautiful music, was in his element and, Arthur noticed, wonderfully solicitous of Oscar. He didn't seem fishy at all.

On Saturday afternoon, Arthur marveled to see the cavernous nave of the cathedral nearly half full of mourners. If he had not really known Evelyn Dimsdale, hundreds of people in Barchester apparently had. The altar used for Sunday morning worship had been set up in the crossing, and the instrumentalists were already seated on either side when Arthur and Bethany walked with Oscar down the aisle and slipped into the front, reserved pew. David was waiting for them there. Oscar had no siblings, and though two of his cousins sat in the pew behind them, he was adamant that he wanted his closest Barchester friends sitting with him. Apparently, thought Arthur in amazement, that included Bethany.

The choir filed in quietly and took their place behind the altar. The soft sounds of the congregation, the whispers and the shuffling of service bulletins, faded to naught and for a moment Arthur experienced the almost mystical feeling of being a part of a group of five hundred people sitting in absolute silence. And then the "Requiem Aeternam" began, its low, growling opening notes building to the soft, birdlike *lux perpetua* and then fading away into almost nothing before blooming into the beautifully melodic theme of the composition. Arthur had heard this piece scores of times, both in concert and in recordings, but it had never held such power, such reality, as it did now. This was more than just music, he thought, this was the full realization of the composition: This was a requiem. And, he thought, if this is what it sounds like to be welcomed into heaven, it might be a rather nice place.

When the time came, late in the service, to take Communion, Arthur was torn. He did not think it right, as a nonbeliever, to partake of the elements, but he did not wish to offend Oscar by sitting alone in the pew while the others made the walk up to the altar rail. He knew he could go to the rail and simply receive a blessing—and that wouldn't be so bad, he supposed. So he stood and made his way to the altar, with Oscar in front of him and Bethany and David behind him. As he knelt next to his friend, Arthur felt a surge of sympathy. He rarely talked to his own parents—they had finally divorced when he was at university and each was remarried to someone whom Arthur quietly despised. The rift between himself and his parents had been gradual, but it seemed, as he crossed his hands over his chest, that he would never kneel at an altar rail in silent grief for either of them. He realized, as the precentor stopped in front of him and whispered a blessing, that his sympathy for Oscar's loss was tinged with jealousy for what his friend had had. As they walked back toward their pew, Arthur laid a hand on Oscar's shoulder. Oscar turned to him and wrapped him in a tight embrace that lasted several seconds. Other members of the congregation waited politely in the aisle as Oscar clung to Arthur and Arthur wondered if he was simply the closest person to a grieving man, or if Oscar felt something . . . something for him that he did not feel for anyone else. Finally Oscar let go, giving Arthur one last squeeze on the shoulder and a grim smile that seemed to say, "Life has ended, and life goes on."

As soon as Oscar was seated in the pew, the choir began the "Pie Jesu." It was Arthur's favorite piece in the *Requiem*, sung for the most part by a single soprano choirboy—a pure and innocent tone that put Arthur in mind of Wordsworth's idea that children should be seen as fresh from the hands of God. The music shifted from major to minor for a few bars and then back to major as the soprano struck and held a high A-flat, a note of such soaring splendor it did not seem human. Arthur couldn't help but smile, and he turned to look at Bethany and saw that she was crying—not with grief, he thought from the look on her face, but from the sheer beauty of the music.

He held out his hand toward her, not sure what he should do to comfort her—certainly not a pat on the knee, perhaps a squeeze on the arm. As his hand wavered in the space between them she grasped it with a grip of iron and turned toward him for just an instant. She looked into his eyes, her own rimmed with tears, and then turned back toward the music, not relaxing the grip on his hand the slightest bit—and in that instant Arthur had a stunning revelation. He loved Bethany, was in love with Bethany. Arthur Prescott was fully, neck deep in the mulligatawny in love with Bethany Davis—with much too young for him, much too American for him, much too digital and combative and beautiful and good for him Bethany Davis. As the choir gently underscored the soloist, he realized there were only two possible paths stretching before him—that he would spend the rest of his life listening to her maddening conversational digressions and arguing with her over everything, or that he would spend the rest of his life without her. Both seemed unbearable.

He felt in that moment that he would do anything she asked. If she leaned over and said, "Arthur, we're going to find the Holy Grail," then by God he would go and find the damn thing. And if she said they needed to digitize it to render the original superfluous, he would hold it still while she did the deed.

The soprano sang the final high A with an exquisiteness that seemed impossible, and the note hung in the air long after the choirmaster had given his cutoff. Bethany wasn't crying anymore. But she was smiling, and she was still holding his hand. I, thought Arthur, am in serious trouble.

XII

THE PRIORY OF ST. EWOLDA

*Though strictly speaking not a part of the cathedral, the
ruins of St. Ewolda's Priory, two miles away, are an inte-
gral part of Barchester Cathedral's history. The monastery
founded at Barchester in Saxon times moved to this new
site after the Norman invasion. During the Reformation,
St. Ewolda's was suppressed, its few treasures plundered
by Henry VIII. Some of the books and furnishings found
their way back to Barchester, where they can still be seen
in the cathedral, but St. Ewolda's was soon stripped of its
valuable lead roofs and the stonework became a quarry for
local builders. Now only a few ruins mark the site where
the monastery stood for nearly five hundred years.*

1601, Barchester Cathedral Library

Bishop Atwater examined the mechanism that held the chains in
place. Each chain was hooked at one end onto an iron bar. This bar
passed through iron loops affixed to either end of the shelf. At one
end the bar was shaped like a *T* to prevent its sliding through the
loop. At the other end the bar was held in place with a lock—a lock
to which only the bishop held the key.

"And all the manuscripts will fit in this case?" asked the bishop.

"They will fit perfectly," said the blacksmith, "with just enough
room left for the one additional volume you showed me."

Bishop Atwater had seen a chained library a few months ago and had decided it could be part of his solution to a growing problem. Often canons knew the cathedral possessed certain books, but they were nearly as often uncertain about where those books might be. Bishop Atwater planned to bring together all the books belonging to the cathedral—some sitting on lecterns, some stored in wooden chests, some piled up in chapels, and some, no doubt, at the lodgings of canons or vergers. They would be gathered into a single room, a library that the bishop had had constructed on the east side of the cloister.

With the Reformation finally over, it was time to build a solid Protestant library—not just for theological reading by the cathedral clergy and those working toward ordination but for all types of study. The church had always been, as far as Bishop Atwater was concerned, an institution of teaching, and with this new renaissance of learning and publishing that was sweeping through England, the time was right to take a haphazard collection of old books strewn around the cathedral precincts and mold it into a true library. Once the volumes had been gathered together, the bishop would donate his own books to the library and begin to build the collection from his substantial private fortune. It was, he felt, the best possible mark he could leave on the cathedral.

To secure the most valuable items, those handwritten manuscripts from before the Reformation, he would use the method of chaining volumes to the shelves. The cathedral employed talented blacksmiths and carpenters, and the bishop was impressed with the case that now stood perpendicular to the west wall of the new library. It was over six feet high and had three shelves, each divided into three sections. From the lowest shelf protruded a slanted surface on which priests or scholars could study any book while the volume remained safely chained to the case.

"How will the chains attach to the books?" asked the bishop.

"The last link on each chain is a small circle," said the blacksmith. "That will pass through a strap of iron that I will bend together and press through the binding where the front cover protrudes past the pages."

"Then the books can be shelved standing up?" asked the bishop. The books at Barchester were traditionally stored lying on their sides.

"Yes, My Lord. It's an ingenious plan. It means each book can be accessed without moving any other book."

"Perfect," said the bishop.

Bishop Atwater loved books. He had consulted manuscripts during his days at Oxford and had always felt a connection to the scribes and artists who had created them. Now, of course, a new type of book had swept the world—books printed on printing presses. Unlike the manuscripts he loved so much, each of which was unique, these printed books were made in hundreds or even thousands of identical copies. Already the collection at Barchester had hundreds of printed books—some purchased by previous deans and bishops, others donated by local benefactors. Reading a printed book never felt quite the same to Bishop Atwater. When he picked up a manuscript, he knew he was the only person in the world reading that particular book at that specific moment. When he read a printed book, as he seemed to do more and more often, anyone else might be reading the same book at the same time. He knew there was no point in fighting it—printed books were cheaper by far and some said the even type was easy on the eye, though the bishop had never found this so. And with the availability of inexpensive printed books, the bishop could take what had always been a rather meager collection, in comparison with many other cathedrals, and expand it into a substantial library. Still, he believed in the value of the old manuscripts; he believed that in their art and craftsmanship they told stories that could never be reproduced in a printed volume. He relished the idea that he would, in the coming days, watch as every manuscript owned by the cathedral was chained into place, so that future users of the Bishop Atwater Library would always be able to have that experience he loved so much of opening up a manuscript and falling into the past.

After a thorough search of the cathedral and its precincts, the bishop had gathered eighty-two such volumes. This did not include the book he now held—a volume whose secret he had been charged with keeping. If he placed this book in the chained library, it would be much safer from theft than it had been for the past twelve years of his guardianship, when it stayed in his bedroom in the bishop's palace. On the other hand, the volume would be available to any member of the clergy with access to the library. But why build a chained library if not to protect the most valuable volumes in his care—and no volume was more valuable than this. Besides, the code within was unbreakable—only the Guardian knew the true content of the manuscript and only he could pass on that meaning to the next Guardian. Chained in the new cathedral library, the manuscript would be as safe as it had ever been. Safer.

May 24, 2016

COMMEMORATION OF JOHN AND CHARLES WESLEY

The only way Arthur could avoid Bethany was to avoid the library, and he knew he wouldn't be able to do that for long, but he could last a day or two, and perhaps by then he would be over his foolishness. On Sunday, she hadn't come to Evensong, so she missed a bit of unexpected drama. Halfway through the Magnificat there was a snapping sound from somewhere high above and all the electric lights flickered out. The choir continued singing in the diminished light, even as the organ, which used an electric blower to fill its bellows, wheezed into silence. When Arthur returned for Compline, there were several electricians' vans parked outside the west door.

On Monday, Arthur arrived at Evensong at the last possible minute and took a seat on the opposite side of the quire from his usual spot and as far away from where Bethany sat as he could. Power had been restored, so the organist was able to play a postlude, during which Arthur slipped out, though not before glancing over to see her looking at him with a quizzical expression. He was half afraid to take his usual Tuesday morning walk with Gwyn. Bethany was now apparently friends with everyone in Barchester—what if she showed up as well?

Gwyn was a few minutes late, but she arrived at the gate to the water meadows alone, save for the marauding Mag and Nunc, and they set out on their usual circuit. Arthur was so anxious to keep secret his feelings for Bethany that he decided to distract himself by at least hinting to Gwyn about his other secret. It had felt good confessing his interest in the Grail to Bethany; perhaps telling Gwyn would feel the same way.

"Bethany Davis tells me you have seen the Nanteos Cup. I never told you this, but I actually have a . . . well, a fascination with Grail lore."

"Do you believe the Nanteos Cup is the Holy Grail?" asked Gwyn.

"No," said Arthur. "It dates from the fourteenth century, I think, but—"

"Well, then," interrupted Gwyn, "I guess it's good I never mentioned it to you. My experience with that cup is a deep and intimate part of my faith. It has nothing to do with science or experts on antiquarian artifacts. It's the reason I became a priest, and I don't need you scoffing at it."

Arthur knew better than to continue this line of conversation. As much as he loved debating with Gwyn, he could tell from her tone that this was not a topic for discussion. They walked for a minute or two in tense silence before he spoke again.

"Power restored, I see," he said.

"Much more than power has been restored, Arthur," said Gwyn. Arthur could tell by her tone that the awkwardness of the moment had passed—that both had silently agreed that neither needed to justify either faith or a lack thereof. "I should have rung you, but things were a bit hectic, as you can imagine. There's a little gift for you and Oscar in the library—for all of us really. One of the electricians was prowling around in the gallery above the north aisle following some ancient piece of wiring and he stumbled upon a wooden crate."

Arthur felt a quiver of excitement, and for just a moment he thought she would say, "The Holy Grail was boxed, labeled, and sitting in the rafters of the cathedral." But the Grail, it seemed, was a topic best avoided this morning.

"Let me guess," he said. "The bones of St. Ewolda."

"Nothing quite that dramatic," said Gwyn. "It was full of vellum book covers."

"The covers that were torn off the manuscripts during the Blitz?" said Arthur.

"Oscar thinks a lot of things were stored up there during the repairs after the war and that crate got left behind."

If there was ever a double-edged sword, thought Arthur, this was it. With the covers restored, the manuscripts would be much more attractive to Sotheby's, and therefore more likely to disappear forever from the cathedral library. On the other hand, this was the restoration, for now at least, of a part of Barchester's history.

"So I suppose now the idea of an auction is even more enticing to the chapter," said Arthur.

"That brings me to the other news," said Gwyn. "The chapter may have to decide about selling the manuscripts sooner than we thought. We've actually had an offer."

"You've had an offer? For which one?"

"For the whole collection. Quite a generous offer when compared to the estimates given by Mr. Mangum."

"And what is the source of this generous offer?"

"It comes from the gentleman who is financing the digitization project," said Gwyn. "An American named Jesse Johnson. Apparently, he heard the cathedral is in financial straits and he thought this would be a way he could help out."

This wasn't the plan, thought Arthur, feeling a rage boiling up inside of him. Bethany wasn't supposed to *sell* the manuscripts; she was just supposed to get Jesse Johnson in a generous mood. How the hell could she do this? Make him be in love with her one moment and infuriate him the next. Because of that woman, the Barchester manuscripts would probably end up in some gaudy mansion in America and he would be left with a glowing screen on which to read the ancient books that he had touched and smelled and stroked and loved for so many years. He was trying to imagine how he could even face her again, when a spasm of guilt shot through him. It wasn't her fault, he realized—it was his. He had suggested she ask Jesse Johnson to give financial aid to the cathedral. And surely she hadn't suggested he buy the manuscripts—he just wanted something in exchange for his twenty million dollars. Bethany had done Arthur a favor and the result had been disastrous. Arthur had never imagined that guilt and relief could be so intertwined. Bethany was restored in his esteem, but Arthur may have destroyed the very thing he so wanted to protect. And then he had another terrifying thought—what if Jesse Johnson really *was* looking for the Holy Grail? Maybe he had seen the Gladwyn portrait and the marginalia in the digitized version of the Barchester Breviary and suspected that the manuscripts held clues about the Grail. If Jesse Johnson, or one of his minions, found the Grail and spirited it out of Barchester, Arthur would never forgive himself

"Surely . . . ," he said, "surely the chapter isn't considering selling the manuscripts to America?"

"It's a *very* generous offer, Arthur. In fact, it's almost the exact amount needed to repair the north transept and build the Lady Chapel." Of course it was the exact amount, thought Arthur. He himself had as much as told the exact amount to that evangelical grave robber.

"And it has to be all of them?" said Arthur. "Even the breviary and the Gospel of John?"

"He said he wanted to keep the collection together. It's all or none."

"You know," said Arthur, "I've been thinking a lot lately about how we might make the library relevant again, give it a real purpose. I mean, what is our library anyway? Is it just a place to store old books, to try to preserve our history? Is it some old-fashioned forgotten room like the privy in the anteroom of the chapter house? Or can it be something more? Can it be an opportunity for outreach and education and the creation of new knowledge and ideas? And can it be any of that without the manuscripts? I think the library has real potential, but if you rip its heart out, it may never come back to life."

"It's not something I want to do," said Gwyn, "but most of the canons feel that given the choice between a library that is rarely used and the cathedral itself, the path is clear."

"So that's it, then," said Arthur. "They're going."

"It's not decided," said Gwyn. "He made the offer last night and gave us four days to respond. The chapter is holding a special meeting on Friday morning to make a decision."

"So, I've got until Friday to come up with ten million pounds?"

"Suppose we talk about something else," said Gwyn, slipping her hand through Arthur's arm as they approached a muddy section of the path. "Bethany was looking lovely at the funeral, don't you think?"

"Suppose we talk about something else," said Arthur.

As soon as Arthur could extricate himself from work, he did. With a little help from Miss Stanhope, he managed to send an e-mail to the members of the Advisory Committee for the Library canceling their meeting that afternoon. Whether Bethany was in the cathedral library or not, whether he was shockingly, inappropriately in love with her or not, he wanted to see those covers, and he especially wanted to see the cover of the ciphered manuscript. Maybe it held a clue that would help him break the code. If the lost Book of Ewolda was headed to America, Arthur would at least like to know what it said before it disappeared forever. As he sat on the bus back into town, imagining Jesse Johnson crating up his treasures and hauling them away from Barchester, another horrible thought occurred to him. If Jesse Johnson owned the manuscripts *and* he owned the company that digitized them, he would only have to lock his door and flick a switch on his computer and not just the manuscripts but the texts within would become inaccessible. Arthur was certainly not prepared to trust an American billionaire who claimed he was going to make the manuscripts available online for free.

If Arthur was afraid that Bethany would want to talk about what had happened at the funeral, if he thought that she could not help but sense how he truly felt for her, he needn't have worried. She was at her usual post, positioning a manuscript onto her stand for photographing. She wore a pair of glasses with dark blue frames that contrasted perfectly with her blond hair.

"Give me ten seconds, Arthur," she said. Completely businesslike, he thought, not a hint of intimacy. Good.

On the largest table in the center of the library were four neat stacks of book covers. They were a bit sooty, but other than that seemed no worse for their circuitous route back to the library. Someone had sorted them by size and Arthur picked up a few to examine them. Most still had a metal clasp pressed into the top right corner. It would be an interesting puzzle to match the covers with their manuscripts. He wondered if he would be part of that effort or if the books would be in America by then.

"I guess you heard," said Bethany, turning to him.

"I didn't know you wore glasses," said Arthur.

"Jesus, Arthur, is that the most important thing here?"

"And your language is getting awfully saucy for the daughter of a preacher."

"You're avoiding the subject as usual, Arthur." Here it came, he thought. Here came the conversation he was dreading—here came the talk about how it was very sweet that Arthur thought he was in love with someone fourteen years younger and grossly mismatched, but Bethany would prefer that they just be friends. But that was not the only subject, it turned out, that Arthur was avoiding.

"Listen, I am so sorry about the whole Jesse Johnson thing," said Bethany. "It never occurred to me he would do anything like that. I just told him the cathedral needed some money for repairs and the next thing I know he's trying to empty the library. I don't even know why he wants the manuscripts, to be honest. I mean, I've been sending the images to the home office like I'm supposed to, but there's nothing in here that would really fit in his Bible museum. A couple of old Gospel manuscripts, maybe, but why offer to buy the whole collection? I suppose he thinks he's being nice."

"Did you say you've been sending *all* the images to him?" said Arthur.

"Actually I don't send them. When I save them they go straight to the cloud and then he can look at what's been digitized."

"Does that include the coded manuscript?" said Arthur.

"God, I never thought about that," said Bethany. "I was just thinking of copying the coded pages so we could return the manuscript to the precentor. But everything I photograph is automatically uploaded, so yeah, he could have seen those pages."

"Maybe that's why he's so eager to get his hands on the library."

"You think he's deciphered the manuscript? You think it's something about the Grail?"

"I doubt he's cracked the code," said Arthur. "But maybe be believes he can, or that he can hire somebody who can. And he probably thinks that a coded manuscript must be hiding a pretty interesting secret."

"We all think that, don't we?" said Bethany.

"Yes," said Arthur. "We do."

"Oh, my God, I almost forgot the good news. Gwyn told you about the covers, right?"

"This morning."

"I thought I'd try to organize them a little bit and see if I could find one that might match the coded manuscript. Of course since we gave the book back to the precentor, it was a little tricky, but once I sorted out the ones that are the right size, it was easy to tell which one it was, and you're going to love the reason why."

"Why?"

Bethany crossed to the table with the piles of covers, picked one up, and held it behind her back. She had a bizarre smile on her face that Arthur couldn't interpret.

"What is it?" he asked.

"Something that's going to make you forget about Jesse Johnson for at least five minutes."

"Then let me see."

"I will, but first—yes, I wear glasses. I usually wear contacts, but of course you would only know that if you had ever gazed deep into my eyes." Arthur felt a cold sweat breaking out on his neck. "And yes, Daddy would not approve of some of my language, or of my going to a foreign country, hanging out in an Anglican cathedral—which sounds much too Roman Catholic for his taste—drinking wine, or basically being an independent woman. So my colorful language is the least of the ways in which I have disappointed my father."

"Will you please show me what's behind your back?"

"You brought these subjects up, Arthur. Now here's what I have to offer to the conversation. I believe the coded manuscript *is* the lost Book of Ewolda, I believe it has something in it about the Holy Grail, and I believe this is the front cover." She passed to Arthur the front board of a book, covered in vellum. It looked unremarkable to him. Yes, it was about the right size to fit the coded manuscript, but aside from some late medieval or perhaps Renaissance grime, it bore no markings.

"Turn it over," said Bethany, walking around the table to stand at his side.

Arthur flipped over the cover and stopped breathing. Ever since his grandfather had told him about the Holy Grail and its connection to Barchester he had dreamed of finding something like this. He only wished the old man were still alive to share this moment.

"Incredible, isn't it?"

Arthur felt his legs turn to jelly and he slid into a chair and laid the cover gently on the table. "No words," he said. "I have no words."

On the inside front cover of the coded manuscript was a sketch taking up nearly the entire height of the parchment on which it had been drawn. It was not an illumination—there were no colors, no gilding—and the ink had faded over the centuries so that one had to look closely to make out the details, but several things were immediately obvious without the use of the magnifying glass Bethany handed to Arthur.

The sketch showed a robed woman, standing beside a stream of water. She held two roses in her hand, and a halo hovered over her head. Underneath her feet, in simple lettering, was the word *EWOLDA*. This would have been enough to convince Arthur that the manuscript was in fact the lost Book of Ewolda, that he had found the missing chapters of Barchester's history, but what stood on a table next to the martyred founder made uncovering the story of an obscure Saxon saint pale into insignificance. To the right of Ewolda on a small table was a cup, and not just any cup but a chalice nearly identical to the one that appeared in both the 1888 portrait of Bishop Gladwyn by John Collier and the 1917 illustration by Arthur Rackham in *The Romance of King Arthur*.

"That's the damn Holy Grail," said Bethany, tapping her finger on the image.

"This is what Gladwyn was talking about," said Arthur excitedly.

"Gladwyn? When?"

"In those notebooks you tried to buy."

"Were they his Grail notes?"

"Mostly, no. Most of them were just notes on chapter meetings and ideas for renovations. But there is a page of notes on having his portrait made by Collier and he writes, 'copy image of Grail from MS.' I looked and looked and couldn't find any such image, but here it is."

"And Gladwyn says it's the Grail, too!" said Bethany. "Now we just have to decipher that code and find out where the hell it is."

Arthur felt a surge of love for Bethany that was as powerful as it was unexpected. He wanted to jump up and embrace her and never let go, except perhaps for meals and to crack a centuries-old code and find the Holy Grail. But he restrained himself, and said, in as calm a voice as he could manage, "I have an idea about the code."

"Not yet," said Bethany. "We should all be here."

Thirty minutes later, David and Oscar had joined them, and stood staring at the drawing of Ewolda.

"Are you telling me," said David, "that this manuscript has something to do with the Holy Grail?"

There was no way for Arthur to keep this particular secret any longer, with a medieval sketch of the Grail lying on the table, but, for now, he did not say anything about his grandfather's charge to him or his long-standing search for connections between Barchester and the Grail.

"Yes," said Arthur. "Bethany and I think there is some sort of connection between . . ." He did not want to state his belief in the reality of the Grail too directly. "Between the story of Ewolda and the legends of the Grail."

"Too bad we can't crack the code," said Oscar.

"Arthur had an idea about that," said Bethany.

"I was talking to a maths lecturer about ciphers," said Arthur, "and he said something about Enigma that got me thinking. He said it was like a polyalphabetic substitution cipher in which the key word and the order of the alphabet changed with every character. So I thought, what if it *is* a substitution cipher, but the reason we can't crack it with frequency analysis is because the key word keeps changing. But then why would the same three letters—*U*, *Q*, and *D*—continue to be the most frequent throughout the document?"

"That's the puzzle, isn't it?" said Oscar.

"That and, if you're right, finding a constantly changing stream of key words," said David.

"Unless," said Arthur, "you could solve both those problems with one solution."

"What do you mean?" said Bethany. She alone seemed excited about Arthur's little presentation; the others had distinctly skeptical tones in their voices.

"It hit me after Evensong when I was looking at the service bulletin," said Arthur, "and I saw that we had heard Psalm Twenty-three."

"The Lord is my shepherd," said Bethany.

"Exactly. Except in the bulletin, they give the psalm, and all the Bible verses, in Roman numerals. So it didn't say Psalm Twenty-three, it said Psalm X, X, I, I, I. So what if U, Q, and D aren't letters at all. What if they are numbers and each number gives the location of the next key word?"

"But how do you know what numbers they represent?" said David.

"*Unus, quinque, decem*," said Oscar.

"One, five, ten," said Arthur. "The first three Roman numerals. Those three letters are scattered throughout the cipher text, but if you look closely, you'll see that about every four to eight 'words,' if that's what we can call those groupings of nine letters, there appears a grouping in which those three letters dominate—between two and six letters of the nine are either U, Q, or D."

"So each could be a number between one and thirty-nine rendered in Roman numerals, since forty introduces the letter L to the mix," said Oscar.

"Except I think each is a *pair* of numbers. So this string of letters," Arthur pointed to a string about halfway down the first page of cipher text reading *ACHDKUQMI*, "can be read as ten and four. The D is X and the UQ is IV. If every string that hides numbers hides a *pair* of numbers in Roman numeral format, then the longest any one number can be is five digits, because there are never more than six of U, Q, D in a single string. That eliminates four of the numbers between one and thirty-nine. Looking at the rest, and knowing that no combination of numbers can exceed six digits, there are . . ."

"Five hundred eighty-three," said Oscar.

"Damn, you are good at maths," said Arthur. "There are five hundred and eighty-three possible combinations of numbers."

"Meaning, presumably," said David, "that there are five hundred and eighty-three possible key words."

"But what are they?" asked Bethany.

"You solved that problem," said Arthur, winking at her, "when you found that sixteenth-century inventory of the manuscripts. A key word is usually taken from another document. The combinations of numbers probably indicate a location in another manuscript—it could be a page number and line number; or a line number and word number . . ."

"Or a manuscript number and leaf number," said Bethany. "We know from the right-hand set of numbers on the inventory that whoever prepared it liked to use leaf numbers instead of page numbers."

"You've figured it out, haven't you?" said Arthur.

"I don't get it," said David. "What am I missing?"

"This manuscript was almost certainly made at the time of the Reformation, to protect whatever secrets are encoded here from the king's commissioners. A couple of weeks ago, Bethany found another document that was made at the same time."

"An inventory of all the manuscripts in St. Ewolda's library," said Bethany. "It's dated October 28, 1539."

"Tell them the best part," said Arthur.

"Each item is numbered with Roman numerals," said Bethany.

"The numbers are out of sequence," said Arthur, picturing the left-hand column of numbers on the inventory that Bethany had not understood. "And written in a different hand than the inventory. I think one person prepared the list and then whoever encrypted the manuscript added the numbers."

"Of course," said Bethany excitedly. "The inventory is the key to the code. It's perfect—there are thirty-five manuscripts and for Roman numerals written in five digits or fewer and not including *L*, there are thirty-five possible numbers."

"So you think the number pairs in the cipher text refer to the manuscripts?" said David.

"Exactly," said Arthur. "Probably the first number is the manuscript number and the second is the leaf number, with the key word being the first word at the beginning of the leaf. Or it could be the last word. I haven't actually tried it yet, but it all makes sense and it explains all those pesky combinations of U, Q, and D."

"Do we still have all the manuscripts from this 1539 inventory?" said Oscar.

"Aye, there's the rub," said Arthur. "Bethany checked it against the library and we're missing sixteen of the thirty-five titles—they were probably stolen by the king's commissioners during the Reformation."

"Still," said Oscar, "if you could decipher over half the text, that would be better than nothing."

"So let's get to it," said David.

For the first hour or so they worked as a team. David and Bethany looked up possible key words in the relevant manuscripts—copying out the first and last words on every leaf up to thirty-nine. Arthur and Oscar worked on decoding the Roman numerals. Over each string of letters that contained combinations of U, Q, and D, they wrote the corresponding number pair. Within an hour they had amassed enough key words and extracted enough number pairs to start to work. While Bethany and David continued to record key words, Oscar and Arthur began to apply the rules of a simple substitution alphabet cipher to the word strings for which they had corresponding key words. Arthur had been sure his idea had been right. It made such perfect sense, but as he and Oscar worked their way through key word after key word, they still came up with nothing but gibberish. Occasionally a word or two would leap out at them, but that might have been simple statistics—a monkeys-typing-*Hamlet* sort of thing. Bethany and David eventually exhausted the manuscripts in the library that corresponded with the ones on the inventory. Bethany, paranoid about working on her own computer because she feared Jesse Johnson was watching every keystroke, borrowed David's laptop and delved into some sort of research. At seven, David went off to a dinner date.

"It's not working," said Oscar after David had left. "We've tried almost fifty key words. There must be some other trick to it."

"The chapter has to decide whether to accept Jesse Johnson's offer in less than"— Arthur looked at his watch—"seventy-two hours. I think there is something in here that will make that offer superfluous, and I'm not giving up until I find it."

"You know, Arthur," said Bethany, closing the laptop and looking across at the two men, "Einstein said insanity is doing the same thing over and over and expecting different results."

"Einstein never said that," said Arthur.

"Well, I just did," she said. "Oscar, would you like to go get some dinner?"

"You're just going to give up?" said Arthur.

"No," said Oscar. "We're going to eat food. And if either one of us thinks of a new approach, we'll be back to try it."

"I can't eat," said Arthur, staring at the meaningless letters swimming on the page in front of him.

"You can," said Bethany. "You *choose* not to."

"You go on," said Arthur. "I just . . . I have to keep trying."

"Don't drive yourself crazy, old man," said Bethany, and she gave him a quick peck on the cheek. Arthur felt a surge of excitement as her lips brushed his skin, but he immediately suppressed it. This is no time for love, he thought—especially hopeless love. If he was going to engage in something hopeless, it was going to be code breaking. He deciphered the next Roman numeral, found the corresponding key word, and set to work turning one group of meaningless letters into another.

Wednesday had been a lost day of deciphering, since Arthur, Oscar, David, and Bethany had all had a full day of work. Arthur had returned to the library after the special Evensong for the feast of the Venerable Bede and spent a few frustrating hours attacking the coded manuscript. Now he stood in the early morning light listening to approaching footsteps on the stairs.

"Did you stay up all night again?" said Bethany, stepping into the library.

"Actually, I fell asleep on the sofa in the anteroom. It just seems like

I'm . . . I mean, we're so close. I keep getting words here and there, but never enough to string together a sentence."

"You need to get out of here for a little while," said Bethany.

"Did I miss Morning Prayer?"

"It's five a.m."

"Good Lord, I had no idea it was so early. What are you doing here?"

"I couldn't sleep, so I thought I'd take a walk. Come with me. Show me where this whole thing started."

"It all started right here," said Arthur. "The cathedral is built on the site of the original monastery, you know that."

"Yes, but we think the manuscript was written at St. Ewolda's Priory. You said you would show me the ruins."

"A walk by the river at five in the morning?"

"It's light," said Bethany. "What's the matter, are you too old for a four-mile hike at dawn?"

"Leaving aside the question of what I am too old for," said Arthur, for whom the question of his age cut a little close to the bone, given his recent revelations about being in love with a twenty-six-year-old, "I very much like the idea of tromping out to the old monastic ruins."

The sunrise had set the sky ablaze with color and though the morning air still bore a chill, Arthur found it bracing. To be not thinking of code breaking, not thinking of anything really, was a tremendous relief. They had walked on the riverside path nearly half the distance to the ruins when Bethany slipped on a patch of damp grass and grabbed Arthur's arm for support. As soon as he felt her hand, his empty mind flooded. Love, he thought, was a most inconvenient emotion.

"I haven't asked in some time," said Arthur, "but how are you getting on with the digitizing? Getting near the end, I should imagine."

"Are you that eager to see me go?"

Arthur could not respond that he both wanted her to leave as soon as possible and to stay forever. "Just curious. Just making conversation on a lovely morning."

"As it happens, I am getting near the end," said Bethany. "To be honest, I hate to think of leaving here. As much as I wanted to meet you, I never thought I'd end up on a real Grail quest. I thought I would spend my time here holed up in the library alone and maybe going off on weekends to see tourist sites by myself—but I've made so many friends. David and Oscar and Gwyn, and even dear Edward at the nursing home. I visit him twice a week, you know. I'm sure he's sitting in his window now, looking out at this glorious morning."

"And those are all your friends in Barchester?"

"Yes, Arthur," said Bethany in a teasing voice. "You're just someone that I enjoy working with and arguing with and solving mysteries with and drinking tea with and going to Evensong with—but that hardly makes us friends."

They walked on in silence for a few minutes, Bethany with her hand still slipped through Arthur's arm, until they rounded a bend and saw the ruins laid out before them in a closely mown field.

"There's some talk of putting up a fence and charging admission," said Arthur, "but we don't really have enough visitors here to make it worth the trouble."

"It's beautiful," said Bethany. "Glastonbury was so swarmed with tourists that it was hard to feel any connection to its legends. But this, in the morning light, so peaceful and abandoned—this feels like the ruins of Camelot."

Before them stood a collection of gray stone walls, some crumbled to no more than a foot above the ground, others tall enough to cast long shadows in the morning sun. In the center of the complex, they could clearly discern the remains of the monastic church. The south side and the chancel had completely collapsed, but parts of the nave walls remained high enough that their Norman barrel-arched window openings were still intact. The remains of the west wall stood perhaps twenty feet high, and at one end a circular stone staircase disappeared into the thick masonry.

"Shall we go up?" said Arthur.

"Is it safe?"

"The wall has been here for almost a thousand years. It will collapse someday, but probably not today."

"That's reassuring," said Bethany. "You go first."

For the most part, the stairs were illuminated by sunlight from either above or below, though for a few steps halfway up they felt their way in darkness. After a short climb, they emerged into bright sunlight on the top of what was left of the west wall. A small iron railing kept them safe from tumbling over the edge and confined them to a small space at the north side of the wall. From this vantage point they could see the entire complex mapped out on the ground below them—the cruciform shape of the church, the adjacent square of the cloister, and the outlines of dormitories and kitchens.

"Somewhere down there, five hundred years ago, a monk wrote our coded manuscript," said Arthur.

"Is that really what you want to talk about?"

Arthur felt his pulse quicken. "Isn't that why you wanted to come here? To see where it all started?"

"I know the British are good at avoiding unpleasant subjects," said Bethany. "What I don't understand is why you think this subject is unpleasant."

"What subject is that?"

"Oh God, Arthur—the subject of us. I don't see why you should be breaking out in a sweat and . . . and trembling. It's just me. You should know by now you can tell me anything."

"And what is it you want me to tell you?" said Arthur. He knew that escape was hopeless, that he would have to face the crux of this conversation within a sentence or two, but his instincts still told him to play dumb and maybe it would all just go away. And then he thought, Why should he want it to go away? Why should he want her to go away? He was trembling with fear, yes, but he was trembling with excitement, too. He was alone on a parapet with the woman he loved, her face aglow, the flecks of gold in her blue eyes like . . . like . . . God, for an English lecturer he was rubbish at metaphors. But why not? Why not tell her that he loved her? This, of course, was the voice of impulsive Arthur, the Arthur driven by emotion and . . . and foolishness. This was Bertie Wooster talking. It didn't take more than a few seconds for Jeeves to chime in. Why not? Because she is far too young for you to consider; she has seen far too little of the world to be grounded with Arthur Prescott; she stands in opposition to the very principles to which you have dedicated your life (this was exaggerating the point a bit, Bertie thought); she is argumentative and rude; she is a firm believer in things (God, for instance) in which you are a firm unbeliever. And then there is that ever so annoying wisp of hair, which even now is dancing around in front of her face in the breeze. There are, in short, irreconcilable differences. The match is hopeless, sir, said Jeeves, and thus to make a confession of love would only inflict further unnecessary injury upon your own heart and, in all probability, embarrassment upon Miss Davis.

"Earth to Arthur," said Bethany, laying a hand on his arm and shaking him out of his reverie. "Charmed as I am by your tendency to zone out, I don't really want to stand up here all morning. So why don't you just go ahead and say it."

"Say what?" said Arthur. Said Jeeves.

"Say how you really feel about me."

"What do you mean . . . I mean, why would I—"

"Arthur, you may think that your British stiff upper lip keeps you from showing any emotions, but you're actually pretty easy to read."

"I'm not sure that I—"

"Besides, a guy doesn't take a girl for a walk in the countryside and then to a romantic old ruin, and then to the top of a crumbling wall, unless he has something pretty important to say." She laid a hand gently on his cheek, her fingertips barely grazing his skin, and he just couldn't do it. He couldn't hide it any longer. He didn't care about Jeeves. Screw Jeeves.

"I realize this is grossly inappropriate," said Arthur, "and I beg you not to give it a second thought and to fly back to America and forget this entire conversation, but as you seem especially eager to know, the fact is I am . . . I am rather . . . I'm afraid I'm in love with you." Arthur had expected a surge of panic as he uttered these words, but he felt instead relief. He had held this terrifying, wonderful secret so tightly that releasing it seemed to release him. She could reject him now. Everything would be fine. He would have an ache in his heart for the rest of his life, but that put him in very good company, literarily speaking. For the first time in weeks, maybe years, Arthur felt giddy.

"I thought so," said Bethany, patting his cheek and giving him a little smile of triumph.

"So," said Arthur, taking her hand and giving it a little squeeze before letting go, "as you seemed to want to know, I mentioned it, but now you must finish up your work and go back to America and forget all about it. No need to discuss it further."

"No need to discuss it further?" said Bethany, grabbing Arthur's hand back. "For God's sake, Arthur, stop being such a milquetoast. You bring a girl up here, you tell her you love her, the next thing is not, 'no need to discuss it further'; the next thing is this." She put her free hand around his neck, pulled him to her, and a second later Arthur was as confused, and as elated, as he had ever been. Bethany Davis was kissing him. Not a soft peck on the cheek or even a quick dry kiss on the lips but wet lips and tilted heads and bodies pulled close together and tongues darting and eyes closed and so dizzy he thought they might both tumble off the wall and he didn't care.

After the longest, loveliest minute of Arthur's life, Bethany let him go and they fell apart and stood for a few seconds, breathing heavily and staring at each other, and he could tell that she desperately wanted to do exactly what he wanted to do and so they both burst out laughing. Arthur had no idea why. There was absolutely nothing funny about this situation, but somehow the release of laughter made them comrades even more than that amazing kiss had done.

"That was very kind of you," said Arthur when the laughter had run its course.

"Very kind of me? Goddammit, Arthur, you still don't get it, do you?" She stood on tiptoe and gave him another kiss—this one so quick it was over before he even realized it had started. "I love you, too."

"You what?" said Arthur, stumbling back against the railing, all of his fear surging back.

"I love you, Arthur Prescott." There was not a hint of irony or fear in her voice. If anything, she sounded happy. How could that be?

"You love me?"

"Yep."

"Bollocks," said Arthur.

"Oh, Arthur, you're so romantic. You should write greeting cards."

"It's just," said Arthur, reaching out and taking her hand again, feeling calmed by the mere touch of her skin, "what . . . what the hell are we going to do?"

"It's not that complicated," said Bethany. "We're going to climb back down the steps, and we're going to walk back to Barchester holding hands, not caring if anyone sees us, and at that one bend in the river, where the path goes under the branches of the willow tree, we're going to stop and kiss some more and then we're going to go about our day. And maybe we'll meet for dinner."

"But what about . . ."

"That's all we're going to worry about right now, Arthur," she said, squeezing his hand hard. "Promise me."

Arthur stood in silence looking at her, still trying to comprehend what had happened but unable to think of anything except what would happen under the willow tree.

"Promise me, Arthur," she said. "For today, we think only of today."

"I promise," said Arthur.

The dew was almost gone from the grass when they reached solid ground once again. They walked in silence for a few minutes, holding hands comfortably, Arthur doing his best not to let his mind wander past today, or even past the next few minutes. And they did stop under the willow tree and kiss, and it was wonderful, and Arthur employed every ounce of his mental strength to banish all thought of the future and simply live in that glorious moment.

When they rounded the last bend in the path and saw the cathedral towering in front of them, Arthur instinctively dropped Bethany's hand.

"Fair enough," said Bethany, stepping slightly to the side so that they walked a full three feet apart. "We'll keep it a secret for now."

Even if we keep it a secret for always, thought Arthur, I will be happy. Even if we only have a few lovely days of being in love and you go home and find some nice American man your own age and forget all about me, I will remember you always and take this walk every year on the morning of the Feast of Corpus Christi.

He had not spoken any of these thoughts, yet Bethany seemed somehow to hear him. She turned to him as they walked and asked, "What's the Feast of Corpus Christi? I saw it on the calendar for today."

"Well," said Arthur, happy to have something to talk about other than love, "Corpus Christi is Latin for Body of Christ. It's a feast that celebrates the Eucharist, and in the Anglican Church the doctrine of the Real Presence of Christ's body and blood in the bread and wine."

"Yeah, we don't celebrate that in the Jubilee Christian Fellowship Church," said Bethany. "Sounds far too Catholic for my dad. He hardly even uses the word *Christ*. To him it's always Jesus, like they're on a first-name basis or something. But I don't suppose he would want to celebrate the Feast of Corpus Jesus either. Not that they would ever call it that. I mean they couldn't have, because there was no *J* in classical Latin, right? Anyhow, it's Communion tonight instead of Evensong. Does that mean I won't see you there?"

"Wait a minute," said Arthur, pulling her to a stop. "What did you just say?"

"I said it's Communion tonight."

"No, before that?"

"I said my dad would never celebrate . . ."

"You said there is no letter *J* in the classical Latin alphabet. Bethany, you're brilliant." Arthur threw his arms around her and held her tightly for just a second longer than would have been appropriate for friends.

"Uhm . . . thank you?" said Bethany.

"The classical Latin alphabet has twenty-three letters; we've been trying to crack the code with the modern alphabet of twenty-six. That's why it's not working."

"And that's why you did get some words once in a while," said Bethany. "Because the alphabets are the same up to the letter *H*."

"So any word that's spelled with just the first eight letters of the alphabet would decode, but words that use letters that come after *H* would just translate as gibberish."

"Arthur, you look sick," said Bethany.

"I do?" said Arthur. "I feel . . ." Arthur didn't even have the words to describe how he felt—he was in love, she loved him back, and he may have just solved a five-hundred-year-old mystery, decoded the lost Book of Ewolda, and found the resting place of the Holy Grail. "I feel fantastic," he said, grinning.

"No," said Bethany, "I mean, I think you need to cancel your classes. You can't go to work today; you're too sick."

"Oh, I see," said Arthur. "Perhaps you're right."

Bethany pressed her palm against his forehead. "Yes, you're definitely running a fever."

They stood looking at each other for a moment, then turned and ran for the library.

XIII

THE GREAT EAST WINDOW

*Like most of the stained glass in the cathedral, the large
window over the high altar, a Tree of Jesse, was installed
in the nineteenth century. A traveler's diary from 1612 describes the medieval window as depicting scenes from the
cathedral's history, but when the window was smashed by
Parliamentary troops during the Civil War, that history
was lost.*

May 17, 1644, Barchester Cathedral

Laurence Rainolds knew the siege of Barchester would not last
long. The bishop had already been arrested on the road to London,
charged at Oliver Cromwell's instructions with "unedifying and
offensive ceremony and chanting." The Parliamentary troops had
arrived at the bridge over the River Esk a short time ago, and despite valiant efforts by a small garrison of Royalists, it was clear
that the Roundheads would soon overrun the city. Laurence had
heard what had happened at other cathedrals when the Roundheads arrived—memorials destroyed, altars overturned, furnishings smashed. In Winchester, Cromwell's troops had pulled down
the mortuary chests that contained the remains of early Saxon
kings and used the bones to smash the stained glass windows.
Their acts of sacrilege seemed to know no bounds. And within the
hour they might well be marauding through the aisles and chapels
of Barchester Cathedral.

Barchester's greatest treasures were unassuming, but Laurence was their Guardian and he was not prepared to take chances. With the cries of battle ringing in his ears, he rushed from the streets into the cathedral close and up the stairs to the library. Bishop Atwater's library was a masterpiece, thought Laurence as he arrived breathless at the top of the stairs. Gleaming spines of leather and vellum covered the sixty-foot length of the east wall, while individual cases stood perpendicular to the west wall. High windows let in enough light on bright days to read easily. Today was not bright. Not just storm clouds but the smoke of battle hung over the city. But Laurence did not need light. He did not need to read; he only needed to remove a single volume from the library. He wished he could take everything, that he could protect the accumulated knowledge that sat on these shelves from the . . . the damned Roundheads who threatened his beloved cathedral. But he had a job and he must accomplish it quickly.

He was halfway across the room when he stopped short. How could he have been so foolish? He could not remove the manuscript he was charged with protecting without the key. Bishop Atwater's chained bookcase protected the ancient manuscripts well—but Laurence did not have the key, and the conditions of his guardianship forbade him from telling Canon Wickart, who *did* have the key, why he needed to remove a single manuscript from the library.

Laurence stood in the center of the library for a moment, considering his options. He might be able to tear the cover off the manuscript, but surely that should be a last resort. Damaging a treasure with which he had been entrusted was hardly performing the role of Guardian. He could try to steal the key from Canon Wickart without the canons knowing, but Wickart kept the key on his person at all times. He saw no choice but to bring Wickart into his confidence, and that meant that a great load was about to be lifted from Laurence. When he was made Guardian, his predecessor had told him, "You will know when the time comes to pass the mantle on." Canon Wickart was twenty years younger than Laurence; it was time for a new Guardian.

Laurence found the canon in the treasury, helping the dean to fill a sack with plate.

"They are nearly upon us," said the dean. "I will flee the city. If you are able, meet at the ruins of St. Ewolda's and we will travel together, perhaps to France."

Laurence could not believe they were abandoning the cathedral. Even when the king's commissioners had come during the Reformation and thrown down the shrine of Ewolda, many church officials remained at Barchester. But there was no question of remaining now, and there was a very real question about whether the Church of England had any hope of survival. Presbyterianism was the preference of Cromwell, and lately Cromwell seemed to be getting everything he wanted.

"Might I have a word before you go, Canon Wickart," said Laurence.

"Quickly," said the canon, as the dean left the room with the plate that might pay for safe passage out of England.

"There is a manuscript in the chained library that I must take with me."

"I am as fond of books as you are," said Canon Wickart, "but there is no time to empty the library, and books will only slow us down in our flight."

"I do not wish to empty the library," said Laurence, who hated to think of the invaders touching a single volume in the collection. "I need only a single book from the chained library. Come with haste. I will explain to you as we go."

Laurence had no time for details, but he told Wickart that the book he needed held great secrets and was closely associated with a treasure that Wickart must now guard. As they removed the volume from the chained library they heard shouts in the cloister. The Roundheads had arrived. As they ran down the stairs, Laurence described to Canon Wickart the place outside the city where he had hidden the treasure.

"The manuscript and the treasure," said Laurence, passing the book to his fellow canon, "are of greater value than all our cathedral. You must guard them and you must appoint their next Guardian when the time is right. The rest I will explain when we meet again."

The two men stumbled into the cloister. A Roundhead stood just a few feet away, and Laurence pushed Wickart into the shadows and toward the archway at the southeast corner.

"Fleeing with treasures, are you?" shouted a soldier, waving a pike toward the two canons and moving in their direction.

"Fly," said Laurence into Wickart's ear. And the canon did. "I can show you the treasures of the cathedral," said Laurence, stepping between the Roundhead and the exit.

"We can find treasures on our own," said the Roundhead. "Now step aside, old man."

"I shall not step aside," said Laurence. He hoped once Wickart was clear of the cathedral precincts he would have no more trouble from the Roundheads, and there was no quicker way out of the precincts than through the cloister. In another minute, Wickart would be in the water meadows, making his way upstream toward the old monastic ruins in the deepening dusk. The Guardian would be safe.

"Do you see who I am, old man?" said the Roundhead. "I am master of this cathedral now, not you. You and your obscene chanting and your gaudy vestments and your popish ceremonies—you are past now. So step aside before I introduce you to my pike."

He needed to stand his ground a little longer to keep Wickart safe, so Laurence did something he knew would draw both the attention and the ire of this invader. He began to chant the Nunc Dimittis:

> Lord, now lettest thou thy servant depart in peace: according to thy word.
> For mine eyes have seen thy salvation,
> Which thou hast prepared before the face of all thy people;
> To be a light for to lighten the Gentiles: and to be the glory of thy people Israel.

Laurence got no further; he did not chant the Gloria Patri. The pike threw him against the wall of the cloister and tore into his flesh. He collapsed onto the paving stones and felt his blood pouring out. The Roundhead stepped into the center of the cloister and wiped his pike on the grass, then turned and walked back toward the cathedral. But Wickart and his precious cargo had escaped.

As he lay in the quiet of the cloister, Laurence thought he had picked the perfect canticle to chant—the Song of Simeon, an old man ready for death. Though he could not speak as the life ebbed out of him, in his mind he repeated the words. Just as the darkness was about to cover him, his peace was rent by a horrible thought: Canon Wickart might be safe, but he had no idea what he was protecting. The secret of Barchester's greatest treasure was about to die in a corner of the cloister. And it did.

May 26, 2016

FEAST OF CORPUS CHRISTI

"Even if this works," said Arthur as he placed the first page of the coded manuscript in the center of the table and pulled out several sheets of blank paper, "we still have the problem of the missing manuscripts. We only have about half the possible key words."

"Don't worry about that right now," said Bethany. "Just use the key words we do have and see if it works. And by the way, how does it work?"

Arthur pulled out the list of numbered possible key words Bethany and David had made. Next to each combination of numbers they had written two words—the first word on the leaf referenced by the number combination and the last word on that same leaf.

"OK, let's see," said Arthur, running his finger across the coded manuscript. "Here—this is the first numerical combination for which we have the key. He pointed to a string of letters reading *ADUUFHDDR. DUU* means XII and *DD* means XX. The rest of the letters are just trash, I think. So we look for manuscript number twelve and on leaf twenty we see our two possible key words. *Corpus* is the first word on the leaf, and *Domine* is the last word."

"Try *Corpus*," said Bethany. "We were just talking about it."

"Right, so if *Corpus* is the key word, we create the cipher alphabet by writing the key word, then beginning the alphabet and leaving out any letters we have already used. Like this." Arthur wrote out a series of letters on the blank paper.

CORPUSABDEFGHIJKLMNQTVWXYZ

"But I thought you said we were using the twenty-three-letter Latin alphabet," said Bethany.

"That's the alphabet we're translating *into*," said Arthur. "But if you look at the cipher text, you'll see that those missing letters *do* turn up. See, there's a *J*, and there's a *W* down here. So now we write the shorter Latin alphabet under the cipher alphabet like this." Arthur wrote another string of letters under the first, so that the two alphabets aligned with each other.

CORPUSABDEFGHIJKLMNQTVWXYZ
ABCDEFGHIKLMNOPQRSTVXYZ

"Now," said Arthur, "the very first string of cipher text contains embedded Roman numerals, so I think the key unlocks the section of text that follows, not the one that precedes it. So here, where we found the combination twelve and twenty, we see three strings of cipher text before the next string with embedded numerals." Arthur copied three strings onto the paper:

JLUMCURQF CMQJLCHIQ UGBCULUFD

"Now we find the cipher letter in the top alphabet, and change it to the corresponding letter in the lower alphabet." Arthur quickly wrote a second series of letters under the first. "Hours of failure has made me pretty good at this part," he said. The next strings of letters read:

PERSAECUL ASUPRANOV EMHAERELI

"And does that mean anything?" asked Bethany.

Arthur stared at the letters for a moment and then gave a loud "Ha!"

"It does mean something," he nearly shouted. "See, in the middle there is the word *supra* and it starts out with *per*, so . . ." Arthur drew five vertical lines between pairs of letters and then read aloud: *per saecula supra novem hae reli.* That last word is a fragment—the rest must be in the next bit of cipher—but if we guess that it's *reliquiae* it reads something like: 'This holy relic for more than nine centuries.'"

"It works," said Bethany, breathless.

"It works," Arthur repeated, turning toward her. The two sat there for a moment, grinning like schoolchildren. Arthur desperately wanted to kiss her again. Apparently this desire was evident in his expression.

"No more snogging," said Bethany. "We have work to do."

"Do they call it snogging in America?" said Arthur.

"No," said Bethany, "but I'm learning all the important parts of English culture."

"If only we weren't missing half the manuscripts," said Arthur.

"Not exactly half," said Bethany.

"What do you mean, not exactly?"

"Yesterday, after David and I finished with the manuscripts in the library and you were being so stubborn about decoding the wrong way, I went online and accessed the database that I've been uploading all my images to."

"But why do we need the images when we have the manuscripts right here?"

"We don't have *all* the manuscripts, Arthur. You just pointed that out. But I'm not the only one who's been uploading images to this database. You see, this part is going to make you a little more enthusiastic about digitization and bookless libraries. I managed to find eleven of the missing manuscripts."

"You . . . you found them?" said Arthur.

"Digital images of them," said Bethany. "You may not find yourself emotionally connected to the past through a digital image, but you can sure as hell use it to find a key word."

"Yes, but without libraries to protect and care for those manuscripts for hundreds of years, your digital search wouldn't have done much good."

"And without the ability to locate those manuscripts, no one could have ever broken the whole code. So it took both ancient and modern technology," said Bethany. "Pretty cool, isn't it?"

"Yes," said Arthur, "it actually is. Where did you find them?"

"Some in libraries at Oxford and Cambridge, like you thought," said Bethany. "One in the British Library, a couple in other cathedral libraries. Some of the digital versions I found in our database, others I found elsewhere. And I can tell they're the right ones because of that column of numbers and words on the inventory. That list was pretty clever. It gives me exactly what I need to identify the manuscripts."

"Whoever enciphered the manuscript must have had some idea that the books needed to decode it were in danger of being scattered."

"I'm still working on tracking down the last five manuscripts," said Bethany, "but I can go ahead and copy out the key words from the ones I have. Since we know now that it's the first word on the page it won't take long."

"Bethany, you're fantastic."

"Thanks for noticing. Now get to work."

And he did.

"I might have found another one," said Bethany an hour later. "It's in America, at a university rare-book library. It hasn't been digitized, but I bet I can get the librarian to check that it matches the description and send me the key words. It's just the time difference. I'll have to wait hours before they open."

"That's great," said Arthur, "but I thought you were going to copy out the key words from the ones you did find for me. I'm deciphering like mad over here, but all I have are fragments."

"OK, OK, Mr. Grumpypants. An hour ago you thought I was fantastic."

"You are, you are. You are amazing, and wonderful, and easily distracted by the search for missing manuscripts."

"Here is your list of key words," said Bethany. She handed him the list and peered over his shoulder. "So, nothing with meaning yet?"

"I have a lot of the sort of language you'd expect to find in a religious manuscript. Phrases like *most sacred, divine power of miracles, great flock of Jesus Christ,* but nothing specific to either Ewolda or the Grail. Not yet, anyway."

"Maybe these will help," said Bethany. "Do you want me to work on some of them? I think I understand the principle."

"Don't you need to look for the last four manuscripts?"

"I've got some feelers out. You'll hear a ping when I get an e-mail." She pulled a sheet of cipher across the table, sat down opposite Arthur, and set to work. "My Latin's not too good, so you'll need to do the actual translation, but I can at least do some deciphering."

The early afternoon shadow of the spire was just edging into the cloister when Bethany gave a gasp.

"What is it?" said Arthur.

"I can't read the Latin, but I think this says Evolda."

"That's it," said Arthur, jumping up from his seat and racing around the table. "I knew it had to be. It's the lost Book of Ewolda."

"Hey, not so fast," said Bethany as Arthur tried to pull her sheet of deciphered text away from her. "Let's just calmly put together your text and my text from this first page and see what we have."

"Calmly?" said Arthur.

"Calmly."

"Bethany, I have been looking for Ewolda's story for years and this manuscript not only contains that, it might contain something about the Holy Grail, which I have been searching for since childhood. And I am here in my favorite place on earth surrounded by the wisdom of centuries, working opposite the most beautiful creature I've ever seen, on the verge of finally solving these mysteries, and you want me to proceed calmly?"

"You really think I'm beautiful?"

"That's your takeaway?"

"Yes," she said, taking his hand and kissing it softly. "That's my take-away. Now, let's put all this Latin together and see what we have."

With all but a few strings of cipher text decoded, Arthur was able, for the most part, to fill in the blanks on the first page with reasonable guesses. He dictated his translation of the Latin to Bethany one phrase at a time and then, his heart pounding in his chest, he asked her to read it back to him.

> *There follows a true and accurate transcription of the life of Saint Ewolda, from the most holy manuscript dictated by her beloved brother and held sacred by the foundation which, following her departure to the Lord, was dedicated to her honor. For more than nine centuries this holy relic has told of our blessed Saint and how the waters of her sacred spring have been a source of divine power. Many are the miracles that have proceeded from the saint and her spring, and as our blessed Ewolda showed in her life God's love for women, so have her relics, through the divine power of miracles, healed those women who have drunk of her water and blessed with children those who have come before her barren.*

"What does it mean, 'her sacred spring'?" asked Bethany.

"I've no idea," said Arthur.

"Does all that talk of healing waters remind you of something? The Nanteos Cup perhaps? The Holy Grail?"

"It's tantalizingly close," said Arthur. "But for now it should be enough that this is, without a doubt, the Book of Ewolda."

"Do you really think there could be something in here that will . . . I don't know, save the cathedral somehow?"

"The resting site of the Holy Grail would probably attract some Heritage Lottery money," said Arthur. "Maybe an ancient sacred spring would too, who knows. But whatever happens, you helped me find this book. And you and I are going to be the first people in five hundred years to read this story."

Arthur pulled out the next sheet of cipher and picked up his pen, but

Bethany crossed over to him and took his hand. "Stop for a minute," she said. "You need to breathe in this moment. Come here." She pulled him up and led him to the window looking out into the cloister. "She walked there. Ewolda stood right there on that spot, and now she's going to speak to us."

They stood for several minutes holding hands, staring out the window at the vibrant green grass of the cloister and the spreading branches of the yew tree. Arthur felt no less excited than he had a few minutes earlier, but he did feel more peaceful. And this time Arthur pulled Bethany to him and kissed her deeply, and for a moment Ewolda and the library and the cathedral and the cloister and the incredible odds against saving the manuscripts or spending his life with Bethany all disappeared and there was only the girl in his arms. They almost didn't hear David's footsteps on the stairs. He nearly caught them.

"We've cracked it," said Arthur as David entered the room.

"Then what the hell are you doing standing by the window," said David. "Let's decipher this damn thing."

By midafternoon, Bethany had reduced the number of missing manuscripts to two, and David and Arthur had filled in most of the gaps in what was becoming an increasingly comprehensible translation of the lost Book of Ewolda.

"Listen to this," said Arthur. "*Ewolda's body fell to the ground, and where her blood had spilled there instantly sprang forth a font of clear, fresh water.* That must be why she's always depicted with water—the boss in the cloister ceiling, the drawing on the cover of the manuscript, even the marginal illustration in the Barchester Breviary. She's not spending a penny; she's standing in a stream of water."

"That must be the sacred spring," said Bethany.

"There are pages and pages about miracles at the spring and tomb," said David, "but I think the actual story of Ewolda's life is pretty short. It starts after the little prologue and it seems to end here." He pointed to a spot about halfway down the ninth page of cipher text.

"It makes sense," said Arthur. "First you tell the story of the saint's life, then you enumerate all the miracles that happened at the tomb, or shrine, or sacred spring. And at this point we're only missing a few bits."

"Including the end of her life story," said David, indicating a string of undeciphered text on that same ninth page. "We haven't got the key words for that yet."

"We're about three sentences away from having Ewolda's whole life story," said Arthur excitedly, "and it syncs perfectly with all the known depictions of her."

"Listen," said Bethany, her hand covering her cell phone. "I can't stop for the Corpus Christi service. I'm on hold with the Newberry Library in Chicago. I might have found the last manuscript."

"I thought we were still missing two," said David.

"I found the other one in Edinburgh," said Bethany. "I've got a graduate student copying out the key words. Should have them in an hour or so."

"She's a wonder," said David to Arthur, who blushed deeply but did not otherwise respond.

"You go on to the service without me," said Bethany. "I can't sit still when we're this close."

"This close to what?" said Oscar, appearing at the library door.

"To deciphering the lost Book of Ewolda," said Arthur.

"You did it?" said Oscar, dropping his bag and rushing across the room.

"Arthur did it," said David. "He cracked the bloody code."

"With a lot of help from Bethany," said Arthur, leaning back in his chair for the first time in hours and stretching his stiff back.

"And what does this lost book describe?" said Oscar. "Some great secret that will convince our leaders to leave the library unmolested?"

"It tells a great story," said Arthur. "A story no one has read since at least the Reformation and we are almost finished bringing it back to life."

"And not only that," said Bethany, "but there is . . . Oh, sorry. Yes, hello, is this Mr. Thomasen? My name is Bethany Davis." She strode off to the far end of the library to conduct her phone call, leaving the three men huddled around the mostly completed story of Ewolda.

"To be honest," said Arthur quietly, "I'm a little disappointed. After Bethany found the cover, I was hoping Ewolda's story would contain some new piece of lore about the Holy Grail." He had thought for sure, given his grandfather's belief, that the Book of Ewolda would finally lead back to the Grail.

"You don't need the Holy Grail," said David. "This is a great story. You've got love and rebellion and sacrifice and a juicy decapitation thrown in for good measure. You've got the last piece of your puzzle, Arthur. You'll have to rewrite your guidebook a bit, but what a story. And you can use the drawing as well."

"It's not a great enough story to cause the general public, or the Heritage Lottery, to come running to the rescue of the cathedral library," said Arthur.

"Maybe at least they won't sell this one," said David. "History of the founder and all that."

"They wouldn't have sold it anyway," said Arthur. "It's not in the library, remember. It's safe in the precentor's house."

"Yes, and why is that?" said David. "Did you ever stop to think why the precentor is hiding this particular manuscript?"

"Does it matter?" said Arthur. "I mean yes, I'm thrilled to have uncovered Ewolda's story and to be able to put her in her rightful place among Saxon saints, but as far as the library is concerned, I'm afraid we haven't changed anything."

"The chapter is due to vote on the Jesse Johnson offer tomorrow morning," said Oscar. "There would have to be something pretty earthshaking in the two or three sentences we've yet to decipher to change anything before then."

"We are the Barchester Bibliophiles," said Arthur. "If we can't keep the city's most valuable books here in Barchester, we're not really living up to our names."

"Got it!" cried Bethany from the end of the room. "I've found the last one and I should have the key words in a few hours." Arthur nodded at Bethany and the other two remained silent.

"Don't all thank me at once."

"It's brilliant," said Oscar unenthusiastically. "Really impressive work, Bethany."

"OK, what's going on?" said Bethany. "You guys look like a bunch of junior high boys who just got put in detention. Do you not realize that I just got the last of the key words?"

"We were just commiserating over the fact that, fascinating as this story is, it's not really going to do much to help the cathedral," said Oscar.

"Or save the library," said Arthur.

"Seriously? You really don't get it, do you?"

"Get what?" said Arthur. "You don't think Heritage Lottery is suddenly going to start pouring money into Barchester because we discovered the story of a saint nobody cares about."

"Oh, Arthur, I always knew I'd be visiting you at an old folks' home, I just never knew it would be next week. It's sad when the mind goes."

"Then mine's gone, too," said David, "because I have no idea what you're getting at."

"Come on," said Bethany. "A sacred healing spring over a thousand years old, the unmolested tomb of a Saxon saint—that's a Heritage Lottery wet dream."

"Yes, but we don't actually have those things," said Arthur. "We have a story about those things."

"You need to learn how to believe, Arthur," said Bethany gently. "And you need to learn how to pay attention. What was the first clue in this whole crazy adventure?"

"Bishop Gladwyn's portrait?"

"No, the first clue we found *together*."

"The . . . the . . . newspaper article?" He could not imagine what a news story about the Nazi bombing could have to do with a sacred spring and an ancient tomb.

"Exactly," said Bethany. "A newspaper article from the *Barsetshire Chronicle*, February 8, 1941."

"You have a good memory," said Arthur.

"And you clearly don't. I should have seen the clue in that article the moment I read it, but it took me until now to figure it out."

"Figure what out?" said Oscar.

Bethany stood over the three men silently for a moment, then burst out laughing. "You guys are like those three little monkeys with their eyes and ears and mouths covered. Arthur, do you have a copy of the article?"

"Uhm, at home, I think."

"Never mind," said Bethany, sitting down at the table and tapping away on David's laptop. After a few seconds, she began to read. *"The Dean this morning said he feared that efforts to extinguish the fire in the Lady Chapel would lead to the flooding of the main cathedral, but this did not come to pass."*

"Oh, my God," said Arthur, reaching out and grabbing Bethany's hand. "What would we do without you?"

"You should listen very closely to what you just said," said Bethany, giving his hand a squeeze and looking him right in the eyes.

"What?" roared David. "What the goddamned hell are you two talking about?"

"This is a cathedral," said Arthur. "Kindly refrain from using the Lord's name in vain."

"All right," said David, smiling. "What in the name of fuck-all shit are you talking about?"

"Much better," said Bethany.

"When the south transept of York Minster caught fire in 1980," said Arthur, "large sections of the cathedral avoided serious water damage, because the water used to put out the fire flowed out of the crypt through a Roman drainage system that had been there almost two thousand years."

"And when they put out the fire in Barchester in 1941, the water disappeared, too," said Bethany. "So where did it go?"

"And why would there be a drainage system under the Lady Chapel?" said Arthur.

"The only reason I can think of," said Bethany, still holding Arthur's hand, "is that the Lady Chapel, which, by the way, if you read Arthur's guidebook you will know housed the shrine of Ewolda, was built *over* her sacred spring."

"And the manuscript says that Ewolda was entombed *beside* the spring," said Arthur.

"In Winchester there was a hole in the shrine of St. Swithun," said Bethany.

"The holy hole," said Arthur.

"Where pilgrims could crawl in and be closer to the actual bones of the saint," said Bethany.

"And the account we have of Ewolda's medieval shrine describes the same sort of passage," said Arthur. "But what if that holy hole took pilgrims *above* the tomb of Ewolda. What if, when the shrine breakers came, they didn't destroy the actual tomb because they didn't realize it was right below them?"

"And right next to the sacred spring," said Bethany.

"The same spring whose drainage system took away all the water from the fire hoses in 1941."

After this torrent of explanation, Arthur and Bethany fell silent, still staring into each other's eyes.

"You're kidding me," said David. "You think a . . . what, a twelve- or thirteen-hundred-year-old spring with healing powers is sitting under the ruins of the Lady Chapel and nobody has known about it since the Reformation? And you think the tomb of Ewolda is sitting there beside it?"

"The tomb is conjecture," said Arthur. "The spring has to be there."

"Otherwise where did that water go?" said Bethany.

"Who the hell knows where it went?" said David. "Down the bloody toilet. Don't you think if there was a spring under the cathedral someone would have found it in the past millennium?"

"Actually," said Oscar, "I've wondered for a long time about the crypt. A crypt should be cruciform, like the church above it, but the crypt at Barchester is shaped like a *T*. There's no arm at the top."

"Or maybe there is," said Arthur. "Maybe there is an arm that's been sealed up. If they walled it off during the Reformation, to keep the king's commissioners from finding the spring and the tomb, that would explain why they encoded the manuscript at the same time."

"So we're going to do what?" said David. "Spend the rest of the afternoon sneaking into the crypt of a cathedral with a dodgy north transept and knocking down walls hoping to find some mystical birdbath before the whole damn building comes down on our heads?"

"No," said Arthur. "That would be a foolish way to spend the rest of the afternoon."

"Absolutely," said Oscar. "Extremely foolish."

"Are you serious?" said Bethany.

"We're very serious," said Arthur. "We'll wait until after Compline."

David folded his arms across his chest as the other three glared at him.

"Come on, old friend," said Oscar. "It's no worse than robbing the precentor."

"In for a penny, in for a pound," said Arthur.

"Oh, fine," said David. "But when they arrest us you can count on me to testify for the prosecution."

"It's hours until Compline," said Bethany. "What do we do in the meantime?"

"In the meantime," said Oscar, "we go to the Corpus Christi Mass. We listen to the lovely music and we act like nothing out of the ordinary is going on."

"Why are we keeping everything secret?" asked Bethany, finally dropping Arthur's hand.

"Because," said Arthur, "if there is one thing the precentor made clear at his party it's that he wants to sell those manuscripts."

"And if he finds out what we're up to," said David, "you can be sure he'll find a way to stop it. I don't trust that salmon-headed twit any further than I can throw him."

"I'm not leaving anything sitting out here," said Arthur, pulling together the piles of ciphered and deciphered text. "As long as we're being paranoid we may as well do it properly." He stowed the papers in Oscar's desk drawer, locked it, and pocketed the key.

"There's just one more thing that I don't understand," said David, smiling archly.

"What's that?" said Arthur.

"What the hell is going on between you and Bethany?"

"Oh, he's just in love with me, that's all," said Bethany.

XIV

THE CRYPT

There is little of interest in the crypt of Barchester Cathedral. The construction, though early Norman, is undistinguished, and there are no tombs or monuments. There is no evidence that the crypt was ever used for worship—it seems to exist solely for engineering purposes. The east end of the cathedral, built closer to the river, sits on somewhat softer ground than the west end, and the substructure of the crypt transfers the weight of the building to a firm gravel bed.

A.D. 560, St. Ewolda's Monastery

Wigbert seemed even weaker than before, thought Martin, as he entered the abbot's room. It was as if, now that he had dictated the story of his sister's life to Martin, his work on earth was done and he was beginning his transition to his heavenly reward.

"Read me the manuscript," said Wigbert. "The portion that tells of my sister's life. I should like to hear it one final time."

"As you wish, Reverend Abbot," said Martin. And he began.

In the twelfth year of the rule of King Acwald of Barsyt, Ewolda was given by God to His people. She was born of King Acwald and his Queen Ceolwen in the same hour as her brother, Wigbert. In that moment the darkness of the room was illuminated and those who witnessed this miracle, not yet being followers of the one true God, believed this light to come from her beauty, though we know now that an angel of the Lord sat vigil over her birth and ascended into heaven in shafts of light to bring word to our most holy Father. This was the first true miracle of St. Ewolda.

As Ewolda grew so her beauty did also, and in her twelfth year, there began a procession of suitors to the court of Barsyt, for stories of the princess had spread throughout the land. To all such suitors both King Acwald and the princess herself gave rebuff, until there came, in the sixteenth year of her life, Prince Hungstan of the Kingdom of Waldburgh. Waldburgh was a kingdom of some wealth, and King Acwald saw the wisdom of the match, and so Ewolda was betrothed to Hungstan and King Acwald agreed that the marriage would take place in one year's time.

After the departure of Hungstan, there came another leader who had heard of the beauty and purity of Ewolda, and this man came not to pursue her hand for himself, but rather to bring to her the most holy Gospel of Christ in the hope that Ewolda would dedicate her life to our Lord, and maintain her chastity in his honor. This visitor was a great leader in battle, but he was also a Christian and had learned of Christ in the hidden places of Britain, where the light of the Gospel still burned after the fall of Rome. Many hours did this king, for so he was called, spend each day with Ewolda, teaching her the good news of Christ, and after seven days, Ewolda declared her wish to be baptized. The king who had taught her traveled with a priest, and in the waters of the River Esk was Ewolda baptized and made one with Christ. After the baptism of Ewolda, the visitor remained for seven more days, teaching her the ways of Christ, and then he did depart, leaving Ewolda with the promise of his return and the blessing of Almighty God.

All this passed without the knowledge of King Acwald, who had been away at the court of Cearl of Mercia when the visitor came. On the king's return, Ewolda told her father of her new faith and tried all such ways as she knew to convince the king of the truth of the Gospel. But when she claimed her chastity for Christ and said that she would not marry Hungstan, her father flew into a rage and locked Ewolda away in a cell. There she prayed from dawn to dusk each day, and committed herself further to Christ, vowing to found a monastery on the site of her imprisonment.

Now it came to pass that Hungstan returned, and Ewolda was released from her cell and forced to marry him, but she said unto him that she would not allow him his marriage rights, for her body belonged to Christ alone and she would remain chaste. Hungstan grew wild with anger and vowed that he would claim his rights on the third night hence. Ewolda was locked again in her cell, but was surprised to find there her brother, Wigbert, who had entered the world so soon after her. Now, Wigbert had been abroad and had returned on the day of the wedding, and so he asked his sister why she was condemned to this cell. And when Ewolda confessed her faith to Wigbert, he was greatly moved and vowed to be baptized himself and to stand by his sister and aid her in the great work of Christ and in founding a monastery.

When the third night arrived, Hungstan came to claim his rights, but Ewolda cried from within the cell that she would die before giving up her virtue to him. Then there emerged from the cell a figure in the robe of a woman and a voice cried, "To Christ alone I give my life." Hungstan threw the figure upon the ground and demanded his rights, but the cry came back "No." And again Hungstan made this demand, and again the figure responded "No." And a third and final time, Hungstan demanded his rights, and the figure cried, "My life before my virtue." Then Hungstan raised his sword and was just about to rain his blow upon the figure when Ewolda ran from the darkness of the cell. For it was her brother, Wigbert, who lay beneath the sword, ready to sacrifice his life in the name of Christ and for the honor of his sister. But Ewolda could not accept so generous a gift, and as the blow fell she threw her body between the sword and Wigbert, and Hungstan hewed off her head. Ewolda's body fell to the ground, and where her blood spilled there instantly sprang forth a font of clear, fresh water. When Hungstan beheld this miracle he fell on his knees and begged forgiveness of Wigbert, who wept by his sister's body.

On the site of that holy and sacred spring did Wigbert found the monastery of St. Ewolda and there he did baptize Hungstan and King Acwald and Queen Ceolwen. Ewolda was entombed beside the spring and from that day forth the waters of Ewolda's spring had miraculous powers, and many were the sick and lame who traveled to that spot and were healed by the miracle of Ewolda's sacrifice.

"But who was the man who taught your sister?" said Martin. "Surely you must name the blessed man who brought the light of Christ to this place."

"I shall name him," said Wigbert. "But only I shall name him." And Wigbert, though by no means a scribe of Martin's skill, added a few words of his own to the manuscript that Martin had prepared.

"May I read what you have written?" said Martin.

"I believe," said Wigbert, "it is time you returned to France."

May 26, 2016

FEAST OF AUGUSTINE, FIRST ARCHBISHOP OF CANTERBURY

"During the reign of Cearl of Mercia," said Arthur in amazement. "That's early sixth century. A hundred and fifty years before we thought St. Ewolda's was founded. This makes Barchester possibly the earliest continuously operating Christian foundation in England." They had finished decoding all but the last few lines of Ewolda's biography and Arthur had just read the translation aloud.

"I wish we knew who the man was," said David, "the one who converted her to Christianity."

"I suppose he's one of those characters lost in the mists of time," said Arthur.

"The service is about to begin," said Oscar.

They made their way toward the cathedral, and as Bethany was about to enter the south transept from the cloister, Arthur pulled gently on her arm and she turned back while David and Oscar disappeared into the cathedral.

"I don't usually go to Communion services," he said.

"You came to Evelyn's Funeral Mass," said Bethany.

"That was different."

"You know, Arthur, you can decide to believe. That's all it takes some-times is a decision. You decided to believe in the Grail; you can decide to believe in God."

"You're so confident, aren't you?" said Arthur. "It amazes me how you just don't have any doubt."

"Oh, God, Arthur, is that what you think? That believing means not having any doubt? Of course I have doubt. Every time I turn on the news and see man's inhumanity to man I have doubts about God; every time I read some scholarly article about the 'legendary' King Arthur I have doubts about the Grail; and God knows every time I stop to think about who you are and who I am and how different we are, I have serious doubts about love. But doubt is what makes belief and love gritty and dirty and complicated and worthwhile and life-changing."

"I wish I could have your faith. I wish I weren't so weighed down by reason."

"Faith doesn't replace reason, Arthur," said Bethany. "Faith begins where reason leaves off."

"I think you may be the wisest person I know."

"You're welcome at that Communion rail with doubt, Arthur—just not with cynicism. And if there's one thing I've learned about you these last few weeks, it's that you may be a bit gruff on the outside, but you're no cynic. Now, the prelude is starting, and if I don't have the service and the music and my belief and my doubt to distract me for the next hour, I'm going to go batshit crazy waiting to get into that crypt." She took his hand and added, "And I'd really like to be sitting in there with the man I love."

Arthur swallowed hard and followed her into the cathedral.

When the time came to take Communion, Bethany nudged Arthur and whispered, "Try believing, Arthur, it's not so horrible."

The men of the choir were chanting the "Ecce Panis Angelorum," a hymn written by Thomas Aquinas for Corpus Christi. Though this Roman Catholic piece was not traditionally part of the Anglican service, the precentor, Arthur knew, was always pleased to have an opportunity for a little Anglo-Catholicism. The music felt more ancient than any sound Arthur could imagine, yet he knew it dated only from the eleventh century. Ewolda's monastery had already been five hundred years old when this Gregorian chant was written. He knelt at the altar rail, a sense, both comforting and terrifying, of the incomprehensible span of history enveloping him. How many thousands had knelt in this spot over the centuries and believed as they received Communion? What was the trickle of his doubt against that flood of faith? Even as Bethany, kneeling beside him, raised her hands to receive the Host, he was not sure what he would do. Yes, he doubted the nature of the Eucharist, but he also respected it. He was deeply moved by what it meant to those around him. As the dean stepped in front of Arthur, he looked up at her in the white vestments of this festival day that commemorated the very rite being performed. Gwyn smiled at him and waited silently, unmoving. Slowly Arthur raised his open palms toward her, but he simply could not force them into the proper attitude. His hands, almost of their own volition, it seemed, crossed over his chest, and he bowed his head as Gwyn made the sign of the cross in front of him, whispering, "May God the Father, Son, and Holy Spirit bless you and keep you." Maybe next time, Arthur thought. Maybe by then God would forgive him his doubts. As he walked back toward the pew, he felt Bethany's hand slip into his and there was one thing about which he suddenly had no doubt.

"I'm proud of you, Arthur," she whispered as they slid back into the pew. And then, like her, Arthur knelt and prayed.

Only Arthur attended Compline. They thought it would look suspicious if all four of them suddenly showed up for a service they were not in the habit of attending, so Oscar, David, and Bethany agreed to meet Arthur in the south transept at ten o'clock, leaving plenty of time for the precentor, who was leading Compline that night, to make himself scarce. They had gone their separate ways for dinner. David had a date he didn't want to

cancel. Arthur dined at home alone. Bethany, eager to ring back her contacts to check on the progress in obtaining the last group of key words,
didn't eat at all. Oscar actually had an appointment for dinner with the
dean to advise her on tomorrow's vote about selling the manuscripts.

"Are you going to tell her what we've found out?" Bethany had asked.

"Not yet," said Arthur. "Don't tell her yet. If we find what we're hoping
to find tonight, we can go and roust her out of bed, but I . . . I'm too fond
of Gwyn to get her hopes up." Arthur had been embarrassed to admit his
affection for Gwyn in front of Bethany, but she had squeezed his hand
and kissed his cheek as if his capability for fondness made him that
much more lovable.

At Compline, Arthur had scrupulously avoided eye contact with the
precentor. He felt as if his body glowed with conspiracy. How the precentor could be alone with him, for they were the only two in attendance, and not see guilt and treachery oozing from his every pore
Arthur did not know, especially when the precentor spoke the words,
"Vouchsafe, O Lord, to keep us this night without sin," to which Arthur
responded, "O Lord, have mercy upon us."

"A very pleasant evening to you, Arthur," said the precentor, shaking
Arthur's hand when the service had ended.

"And to you, sir," said Arthur.

"May I leave you to extinguish the lights?"

"Absolutely, sir," said Arthur. He often remained behind in the chapel
for a few minutes after Compline, so there was nothing unusual in this
exchange, yet still Arthur felt the precentor was testing him. He sat for as
long as he could bear after the sound of the precentor's footsteps had
died away, then finally looked at his watch. Nine forty. Twenty minutes
to go. He knelt and repeated the simple prayer he had whispered after
returning to the pew from the altar rail earlier that evening.

> *Lord, may our actions tonight preserve and protect this holy place
> and all its treasures.*

At five till ten, he blew out all but one of the candles, taking the last
one with him to light the way to the south transept. Before leaving the

chapel, he reached behind the altar and retrieved a book of matches kept there for lighting candles. Who knew what ancient wind might blow on his candle before the night was over.

Ten minutes later, the four conspirators stood next to a small wooden-and-iron door in a corner of the retrochoir, behind the main altar. They carried what looked like a fairly useless set of tools. Arthur had a Swiss Army knife, Oscar a garden trowel, and David a long bread knife, which he now pulled out of his coat.

"What the hell is that for?" asked Oscar. "Do you think the crypt is made of wholemeal?"

"I don't know," said David. "We agreed to bring tools, and I don't have any tools, so I brought this. Besides, you look like you're off to plant tulips."

"Enough, you two," said Bethany. "If we're going to do this, let's do it."

"I've never been down there," said David as Oscar pulled the door slowly open. A loud creak, magnified by the stones around them, seemed to push them away from the entrance, as if history itself were trying to repel them.

"Oscar and I went down about a year ago," said Arthur, shivering as a blast of cold air came through the open door. "When I was working on the guidebook." The crypt was not open to tourists, and as they descended the uneven stone steps, it was easy to understand why.

Oscar went first with a torch. David followed, then Bethany, who was using her cell phone to help light the way, and finally Arthur, who still held the candle he had taken after Compline. The dark seemed to swallow the three lights. The crypt smelled dank and the floor, when they reached it, felt slick underfoot. They found themselves in a low space, the ceiling of which was supported by squat Norman arches. Moisture glistened on the walls, which were black with the filth of centuries.

"One arm of the crypt runs west directly under the quire aisle to the central tower," said Oscar, "and then at the east end, where we are, the other arm extends in a cross almost the entire width of the chancel under the east wall. So the center of this wall, where the two sections intersect, should be directly under the great east window."

"And directly opposite anything underneath the Lady Chapel," said Arthur.

"Exactly," said Oscar.

"Well, let's go," said David.

Oscar led the way as they ducked under one arch after another. Arthur reckoned the distance couldn't be more than twenty yards, but it seemed to take forever until they passed into an even colder patch of air and realized they had reached the intersection. In three directions, the arches disappeared into blackness. Bethany slipped her fingers around Arthur's. "This is creeping me out," she whispered. "Are there . . . graves and stuff down here?"

"No marked ones," said Arthur.

"So what are we looking for?" said David, stepping up to the wall.

"Anything that looks like it was added later," said Oscar. They stood in a line for a moment, staring at the wall, which looked only ancient, wet, and filthy.

"Why do you suppose it's so wet down here?" said Oscar.

"Obviously because there is a sacred spring on the other side of this wall," said Bethany.

"Ever seen the crypt at Winchester?" said Arthur. "That place literally has a lake in it."

"Is this wall plastered?" said David. "I don't see obvious joints between stones, but it's so damp and dirty that I can't tell if there's some kind of finishing on it."

"It would be strange for a crypt, but not unheard of," said Arthur.

"But how do we . . . ," began Oscar.

"Oh, give me the trowel, Oscar," said Bethany in an exasperated tone. "If it's plaster and it's this wet, we won't be doing any harm scraping the stuff off." She handed her phone to David, took the trowel from Oscar, and scraped it loudly across the wall. Even though the cathedral was empty and they were hidden away in the crypt, they had been whispering, and the noise of metal on stone seemed deafening—as if the space hadn't heard a sound that loud for centuries, and was rolling it around out of curiosity. Three scrapes later, Bethany turned back to the men. "I'm surprised this stuff was even staying on the wall. It's like mush it's so wet."

Oscar pointed his torch over her shoulder and they saw three wide gouges about a quarter of an inch deep in the wall. The sodden plaster was easily coming off the surface. Twenty minutes later, with the aid of both trowel and bread knife, they had cleared the entire space within the central arch, and a pile of slick, wet plaster lay on the floor.

"Looks like there *are* graves down here," said David, pointing to a stone near the bottom of the deplastered wall. "There's lettering."

"Hang on," said Arthur, pulling out his knife. He knelt down in front of the wall, feeling the wet from the plaster soaking into the knees of his pants. With the long blade of the knife, he scraped out the residue from two lines of letters on the stone David had pointed to. "That's odd," he said.

"What is it?" asked Bethany, peering over his shoulder. "What's it say?"

"It's Latin," said Arthur. "It translates, 'Sacred to the Memory.'"

"That's not so odd," said David. "A fairly standard sentiment on grave markers, I'd say."

"Yes," said Arthur, "but it's written upside down."

"This is it," said Oscar excitedly. "This is a new wall. Or at least newer than the rest of the crypt. And it was put up in a hurry."

"What makes you say that?" said Bethany.

"Look," said Oscar. "Let's say you are a monk here at Barchester and you get wind of the dissolution of the monasteries. You hear that the king's commissioners are destroying all the shrines and desecrating the tombs of the saints. The most sacred thing in your cathedral is a spring, and you don't particularly want the commissioners tossing the rubble from Ewolda's shrine into this holy water. But you have an advantage over other cathedrals. Your sacred spring is not right behind the altar and covered with jewels like a typical shrine. It's in the crypt. And if you build a wall quickly, and slap some plaster on it, you can hide it. So, if I am this monk and I want to build a wall, I grab whatever building materials are at hand, including old gravestones, and I don't worry about whether I stick them in right side up or upside down."

"So you think this wall was built in the 1530s?" said David.

"Think about it," said Arthur. "The inventory and the coded manuscript were both prepared then. Barchester was one of the last monasteries to be dissolved. They had time."

"But weren't the inventory and the manuscript from St. Ewolda's up the river?" said Bethany.

"Yes, but the monks of the two monasteries must have known each other. And they shared an interest in protecting Ewolda. There must have been a concerted effort to hide her relics and her story from the commissioners."

"So what do we do now?" said David. "Just come back in the morning with a little plastic explosive and blast our way through?"

"If this wall was built hastily and it's not actually supporting anything, it shouldn't be that hard to take down," said Oscar.

"And we're going to do that?" asked David. "We're simply going to disassemble a five-hundred-year-old wall that's part of a scheduled building. Isn't that some sort of crime?"

"No," said Arthur, taking the trowel from Bethany and stepping toward the wall. "I'm going to hear a strange rumbling sound from the crypt as I'm leaving after Compline. I'm going to ring Oscar and we're going to discover that a poorly built wall has collapsed due to moisture damage."

"Arthur, you don't have a cell phone," said David.

"OK, I'll say I went and fetched Oscar," said Arthur, wedging the trowel into the thin space between two stones at the top of the wall. "These stones are loose. If we can pry one or two out, it will be easy to remove the rest."

"If it's a wall that's not really attached to anything," said David, "why don't we just shove it over?"

"Because," said Bethany, "we don't want the sacred spring filled up with rubble any more than the medieval monks did."

"Let me see that bread knife," said Oscar.

"The bread knife you made fun of?" said David.

"Oh, don't be a baby," said Oscar. "The mortar may be as damp as the plaster was, especially if the wall was never really made properly. A nice long bread knife might be just the thing to completely detach one of the stones."

Twenty minutes later, Oscar and Arthur had loosened or removed the mortar from three stones at the top of the wall, but the spaces between the stones were still too narrow to allow them to be pulled forward.

"How are we going to get these things out of here?" said Oscar.

"The frustrating thing is," said Arthur, "that once we get the first stone out, we'll be able to reach through and drag the rest forward without much trouble."

"So," said David, stepping forward and making a show of rolling up his shirtsleeves, "we don't push the whole wall over, but we do push one block through to the other side. There's not much chance a single stone, especially if you pick a small one, will damage your alleged spring."

"What do you reckon?" said Oscar to Arthur.

"Do it," said Bethany.

"We could come back down with an archaeological crew," said Oscar.

"The chapter is voting at nine a.m.," said Bethany. "Are there a lot of archaeologists in Barchester who work nights, do you think? Do it!" She shouted these last two words not with anger but with excitement and as they still echoed in the gloomy chamber, David gave a strong shove to the smallest of the stones on which Oscar and Arthur had been working. It slid backward an inch or more.

"Again," said Bethany, stepping forward until she stood right at David's shoulder.

He shoved again and the stone moved another couple of inches.

"Again," said Oscar, Arthur, and Bethany in chorus.

David gave the stone a final shove and it slid from its place into the darkness beyond. The floor shook as the stone thudded to the ground on the other side of the wall. For a moment they all stood in silence, until Arthur realized it wasn't silence.

"Do you hear that?" he whispered.

They held their collective breath and the sound was quite clear, tinkling in the dark chamber beyond the wall.

"Water," said Bethany. "Running water."

"Running water," said Arthur. "The sacred spring."

"Holy mother of God," said David. "I thought this whole thing was just . . ."

"It's real," whispered Bethany reverently, once again slipping her hand into Arthur's.

"It sounds real, anyway," said Arthur. "But we still have a lot of stones to move before we can get in there and take a look."

Removing stones, even poorly mortared stones, from a wall in which they had sat for half a millennium was not as easy as they had hoped, and it was nearly two hours later when, filthy and wet, their hands scraped and bleeding, they finally stood in front of a hole big enough to climb through. The sound of running water now echoed clearly throughout the crypt, but their efforts to peer into the blackness on the other side of the wall had revealed little.

"You go first," said Oscar to Arthur, handing him the torch. "This is your quest most of all."

"OK," said Arthur, "but not with this." He handed the torch back to Oscar and picked up his candle from the floor. It had blown out soon after they started working on the wall, but Arthur withdrew the matches from his pocket and relit it. "If no one has been in there since 1539, I think candlelight is appropriate."

Bethany held the candle for Arthur as he climbed through the hole they had opened in the wall, then handed it through to him. "Be careful," she whispered.

Arthur turned and looked into the darkness. He took a step. And then another. Still he could see nothing ahead but blackness. He was not in a wide continuation of the main east-west arm of the crypt, he realized, as he stopped and held the candle first to one side and then the other, but in a passage about eight feet across with a roof slightly lower than the one in the main crypt. Yet the sound of water became louder as he slowly moved east, and after a few more tentative steps he felt the air suddenly change. It felt purer, and he took a deep breath. Moving the candle around, he saw he had emerged into a large chamber. The ceiling was no longer visible by the light of his candle, nor were the walls. The antepassage, he realized, was the reason they couldn't see anything by peering through the wall.

He shuffled slowly ahead, until his toe caught the edge of something solid. Stooping to investigate, he saw, in the flickering light of the candle, a circular stone wall about two feet high and four feet across. When he leaned over the edge, he felt a refreshing coolness, nothing like the stale dank of the rest of the crypt. He lowered his candle farther, and looked into a pool of water so clear and still he could see every smudge of dirt on his face where it reflected on the surface. From the sound of running water, he knew that this was a spring and not a well, that water was draining away somewhere, but the surface remained like glass. Arthur suddenly realized he was both filthy and thirsty, yet he felt this water was not for satisfying ordinary needs. This, he knew as he sat on the wall surrounding it, was the sacred spring of Ewolda. Even if the story of its bursting forth on the site of her martyrdom was no more than a myth, it was the most ancient part of Barchester's history. And whether or not Arthur believed in its healing powers, according to the manuscript many over the centuries had, and their faith was not to be taken lightly.

Arthur sat staring into the water's depths for several minutes. He thought of the faith of Ewolda, of those who had come to her spring, and those who had used such ingenuity to protect it. He thought about what Bethany had said to him earlier that evening, what seemed like days ago. Was it really that simple? Could he just decide to believe in God?

He might have remained there all night, pondering faith, watching as the candlelight flickered in the glassy water. He didn't know how long he had sat mesmerized by that sight when he felt a hand on his shoulder.

"We were calling you," said Bethany gently. "We got worried."

"It's real," he said, not raising his eyes to her, but relaxing at the soft touch of her hand. The sound of Oscar and David emerging into the chamber barely registered on Arthur's consciousness. It was incredible, this sense of peace he was drawing from seemingly ordinary water. Perhaps he was tired, perhaps he was relieved, but he wasn't sitting here thinking of saving manuscripts or rewriting history books, or even of finding the Grail; he was thinking only of faith and love, of God and Ewolda, of his grandfather and the joy he would have felt in this spot, and of Bethany—until he felt another hand on his other shoulder, this one shaking him hard enough to bring the world of four trespassers in an ancient chamber back into focus.

"Uhm, Arthur," said David, "can I rouse you from your meditation long enough to point out that a fifteen-hundred-year-old sacred spring is not the only thing down here that is going to loosen those Heritage Lottery purse strings. Travel a little farther east, my good man."

Bethany took his hand and helped him stand, for Arthur's legs felt not quite of this world. They took a few steps past the spring to where Oscar and David now stood at either end of a stone sarcophagus. It bore no decoration, no fine jewels that would identify it as a saintly shrine. The tomb was not crafted from alabaster or Purbeck marble but from slabs of plain Barsetshire limestone. Arthur passed David and stood at the west side of the tomb as if at an altar. He noticed, as he ran his hand across the rough surface of the stone, that the spring chamber, as he now thought of it, did not have the dank and filth of the outer crypt. Perhaps because the water in here moved, it seemed to keep the air fresh and the stones, but for a layer of dust, clean. Arthur, still holding his candle, leaned over the tomb and gently blew the dust from its surface. There, incised into the stone in large, simple letters, was a single word— EVOLDA.

XV

THE CLOSE

In the fifteenth century, Barchester Cathedral close was said to be one of the most beautiful neighborhoods in the kingdom. The Civil War, however, wrought havoc. Trees were cut down for firewood, houses destroyed, windows used for target practice. Many of the homes and other buildings in the close were razed after the Restoration, and over the next two centuries a hodgepodge of domestic buildings grew up in the close. In the nineteenth century, Bishop Gladwyn undertook a major rebuilding effort, restoring the medieval layout of St. Martin's Close with a set of buildings designed by George Gilbert Scott.

July 14, 1660, Barchester

Gregory Wickart once again found himself as Canon Wickart. After sixteen years of Cromwell's protectorate, during which Anglican clergy had been hounded from their cathedrals, the Stuarts had returned to power, the monarchy had returned to England, the Church of England had returned to the land, and Canon Wickart had returned to Barchester. The memories of those dark days when the Parliamentarians had invaded the cathedral still haunted him. The clergy had been turned out of all the cathedrals in the realm, but Cromwell had been especially harsh in places like Barchester, which had gladly adopted Archbishop Laud's High Church ways of worship. Though the archbishop was already in prison awaiting execution when Barchester fell, Cromwell was ruthless in tearing the cathedral clergy from their homes, destroying their belongings, including books and vestments, and stripping the cathedral of anything that hinted at ritualism.

Gregory had waited a few weeks after the Restoration, not wanting to take a chance that the new status quo would be temporary, but with a month and a half passed since King Charles's coronation in May, it now felt safe to return. What he saw in the close as he passed through the gates grieved him greatly. The two rows of medieval houses that had faced each other across St. Martin's Close, houses reserved for the use of the vicars choral and the canons, lay mostly in ruins. Inside the cathedral, windows had been smashed, the altar overturned, and much of the woodwork from the quire stalls and altar rail had been carted off as firewood. There had been, Gregory heard, a plan to pull down the cathedral altogether, and only the objections of the mayor and burgesses had convinced Cromwell that this was an unwise course of action.

The library, Gregory discovered on mounting the steps to that magnificent room, was in disarray. It had been used to house troops— men who had thought nothing of burning books for warmth or putting their pages to even more unsavory purposes. When the troops had left, the room had been abandoned. Broken windows had let in wind and rain and many of the remaining books were damaged beyond repair. The collection of nearly four thousand printed books, largely built by Bishop Atwater, had been reduced to a few hundred. Thankfully, the manuscripts that had been chained in place by Bishop Atwater, being far from any broken windows, remained more or less unscathed. The archival records of the cathedral had been sent to a central registry in London, but Gregory understood they would soon be returned to Barchester. He hoped they would return intact.

Slowly, over the next few years, the cathedral came back to life. The new bishop was a man of independent wealth, and he personally paid for many of the repairs. Gregory oversaw the restoration of the library. He carefully removed all the books, disposing of those that were damaged beyond use and storing the rest in the Lady Chapel while the library was cleaned and the windows replaced. The treasure with which he had been entrusted so many years ago remained hidden for now outside the cathedral precincts, and the coded manuscript he had taken into his care he placed in the Lady Chapel with the other books. It seemed as safe a place as any.

When the time came to return the books to the library, Gregory mourned the wide empty spaces on the shelves. But this library had been built before and it could be built again. As it had before, it would depend on the donations of bishops, clergy, and benefactors, but Gregory knew that eventually the shelves would be filled.

On the morning of Pentecost 1665, the archbishop of Canterbury, Gilbert Sheldon, was to rededicate the restored cathedral. Gregory had looked forward to giving the archbishop a personal tour of the library, hoping His Grace might be moved to donate a few volumes. The cathedral dean had already given much of his own collection, as had a prominent merchant in the city, and the library looked a bit less barren than it had even a few months ago.

Earlier in the week, Gregory had been part of an entourage that had traveled to London to accompany the archbishop from his home at Lambeth Palace to Barchester. As he lay in bed while the early morning light filtered through the window, he realized what a mistake that journey had been. He shivered with chills, and his forehead sweated with fever, but that was not the least of his worries. Under his left arm, and on the side of his neck, were two painful, swollen lumps. Gregory knew he had been infected with the plague that was even then running rampant through London. He knew that no member of the cathedral clergy would come to his bedside. The risk of infection was too great. Gregory did not fear death. He had, he believed, served God on earth and looked forward to doing the same in heaven when the Lord saw fit to call him. However, he did fear a lapse in the guardianship. Though he had never understood exactly what he was guarding or why he was guarding it, he knew from the desperate tone of Laurence's voice all those years ago that the coded manuscript and its associated treasure must be protected. Gregory had made many sacrifices in his years of exile to serve as Guardian, but now he faced the reality of a speedy death and the necessity of appointing a successor. If no clergy came to his room—and he already felt too weak to stand and walk—could a layman serve as Guardian? Laurence's instructions had been hasty to say the least.

"Still abed, Father Wickart?" came a voice on the stair. "I thought you was to breakfast at the bishop's palace this morning."

"I am ill," said Gregory in a weak voice. "You had best stay away, Margret."

Margret was the housemaid, the cook, and the laundress all in one. Most mornings she made breakfast for Gregory, which he ate on his return from Morning Prayer.

"Indeed I won't," said Margret, appearing at the door of the bedroom. "Oh, me, you look like death himself. Shall I fetch the doctor?"

"The doctor, like everyone else of status in Barchester," said Gregory, "is breakfasting with the archbishop. Besides, there is nothing a doctor can do for me now."

"Some broth, then," said Margret. "Or some water, at least."

"You are kind, Margret, but there is nothing you can do either." Or was there, thought Gregory. Was it possible to pass the mantle of guardianship not to a clergyman, not even to a layman, but to a laywoman?

"There must be something, sir. I cannot stand here and do nothing to help . . ." Gregory looked up and saw that Margret was now weeping. "To help a man who's been so kind to me," she said.

She was a good woman, an honest woman, thought Gregory. And there could be no doubt that she cared for and respected him deeply. She had always done anything he asked without question and she had accomplished every task with integrity and efficiency. She feared God, said her prayers every night, and attended services every Sunday. And Laurence had stipulated no rules about who should be Guardian. Gregory thought that Margret would perform the task nobly.

"Actually, my dear Margret," he said, "there is something you can do."

A few hours later, Margret Barlow, a spinster who could neither read nor write, and who had no means of accessing the places where the objects of her guardianship resided, nonetheless became the first layperson to serve as Guardian. As Gregory predicted, she discharged her duties efficiently and effectively. Her guardianship lasted less than a day. She remained with Gregory through his last hours, carefully keeping her distance, save for changing the cold compress on his forehead that offered some slight relief. When the end came, night had fallen on Barchester, the archbishop had departed, and all the clergy of the cathedral, no doubt surfeited on the feasts of the day, had retired to their lodgings.

The next morning, Margret attended Morning Prayer in the Lady Chapel. Following the service, as instructed by Canon Wickart, she approached Canon Hammond and asked if she might have a word in private. The canon expressed his opinion that this was an unusual request and that he had a meeting with the dean in a quarter of an hour to discuss a matter of importance, but Margret assured the canon that this, too, was a matter of great importance and that she would impose on the good canon for only a few minutes. And so, in a quiet corner of the retrochoir, Margret Barlow's twelve hours of guardianship came to an end.

Two weeks later, Margret became Canon Hammond's housekeeper, and though she saw him every day for the rest of his life—a span of more than twenty years—she never again spoke to him of the manuscript or of the treasure. Even in his final days, when Margret knew he must have passed the guardianship to another, she did not speak of it, nor did he. After the canon's death, Margret left Barchester and went to live with her nephew in Somerset. There she often entertained the family with stories of life at Barchester Cathedral, but the secret of her hours as Guardian she took to her grave.

May 27, 2016

FIRST FRIDAY AFTER TRINITY

"Arthur?" said Bethany gently. "Arthur, what does it say?"

Arthur couldn't form the word. They had found Ewolda. Because of her, Barchester existed, the cathedral existed, the library existed. She was the reason for all the best parts of his life. Without her, he would never have met Bethany. And he still believed, though he would share that belief only with Bethany, that Ewolda might one day lead him to the Holy Grail. He stood transfixed, feeling that he should mutter some words of thanks to this woman who, fifteen hundred years ago, had sacrificed her life for a religion she hadn't even known about a few months earlier. But he couldn't speak. He couldn't move, not even to wipe the tears from his eyes.

"Are you all right?" asked David, laying a hand on Arthur's shoulder. Bethany stepped next to him on the other side and took hold of his arm.

"Amazing," said Oscar, joining the others in front of the tomb. They stood there for several minutes, the four of them. Arthur slowly emerged from his trance and began to wonder what the others were thinking. Bethany, he imagined, was saying a prayer. David perhaps was gauging how much longer he needed to stand there before he could go take a hot shower and start telling women he had uncovered an ancient secret. Oscar would understand better than any of them that this tomb and this spring certainly meant a huge grant from Heritage Lottery and an influx of tourist dollars into Barchester. Not only would the library be saved, there would be money to repair the manuscripts and the north transept and anything else that needed repairing. Gwyn might even get her glass-and-steel Lady Chapel. It was the thought of Gwyn that finally brought words to Arthur's lips.

"We should tell the dean."

"It's one o'clock in the morning," said David.

"No, Arthur's right," said Oscar. "She needs to know now. The whole chapter will need to see this before they meet tomorrow morning."

"We'd better get going," said David, dropping his hand from Arthur's shoulder and turning toward the pile of rubble they had created.

"Oscar," said Arthur, "will you tell her?"

"Certainly," said Oscar, "if that's what you want. I mean, it really should be you; you're the one who's been looking for Ewolda all these years, and you're Gwyn's . . . her friend. But if you want me to . . ."

"I'll see her in the morning," said Arthur. "You and David should tell her."

Arthur stepped back from the tomb without taking his eyes from the word on the stone. He turned and saw, in the dim light of the candle and the fading torch, the three people in the world whom he cared for most. A part of him wanted to draw all of them to him in an embrace, but even hidden away from society in an ancient burial chamber, this seem distinctly undignified. Instead he smiled at each of them in turn, trying to express with his eyes what he could not express in words.

"Do you mind if I take a minute?" said Arthur. "I mean, a minute alone?"

"Of course not," said Bethany. "Take as long as you need. David and Oscar will go to talk to Gwyn, and I'll wait for you in the main crypt."

"Wait for me in the Epiphany Chapel," said Arthur.

"Are you sure?" said Bethany. "Your candle is burning pretty low."

"I won't be long."

Bethany leaned forward and kissed Arthur lightly on the cheek. This had none of the passion of this morning's kisses, but Arthur felt such warmth and tenderness that he had a sudden vision of what a life with Bethany might be like—a life with passion, to be sure, but more important, a life where the lightest kiss, the gentlest touch, the merest glance could communicate concern and affection and, above all, connection at the deepest level of their beings. When the vision had passed, he was alone in the burial chamber.

Almost without thinking, Arthur lowered himself to his knees in front of Ewolda's tomb. He was not used to praying. The prayers he read as part of the daily cathedral services were printed in the Book of Common Prayer and, to Arthur, served as markers of the rhythm of his days and aids to reflection, but he never really saw them as communications with the divine, and he certainly never entertained the notion of praying to a specific saint. Now he knelt at the tomb of Ewolda and simply responded to the impulse he felt. He spoke aloud and the chamber swallowed up his words.

"I don't understand how you did it," said Arthur, "or why you did it. I've been going to this cathedral all my adult life, and I still can't muster the courage to take that leap of faith and simply believe. And I have so much pushing me in that direction—people I know and respect and love, the very stones that surround me. And you . . . you had a wandering . . . what, a wandering military leader who just said, excuse me, but here's a nice new religion. And you believed. You believed so deeply that you gave up your life. I can't imagine caring about something so much that I would give up . . ." And then of course, he thought of Bethany. Maybe Arthur didn't believe in God—not yet anyway, but he did at least believe in love. So he said the words he had really wanted to say all along. "Thank you."

Arthur felt exhausted and emotionally wrung out as he climbed the stairs back to the cathedral, yet he knew he wouldn't be able to fall asleep if he went home. His candle was almost too short to hold without burning his fingers on hot wax, so he walked briskly to the Epiphany Chapel, where he found Bethany, kneeling in prayer. She had lit the candles on the altar, and Arthur stood silently watching her for several minutes until she eased herself back onto the pew and looked up at him.

"How about a drink?" said Bethany.

"I'm not sure I can face a pub at this hour," said Arthur.

"Oscar has an open bottle of wine in the library anteroom," said Bethany. "Left over from his last BBs meeting."

"That sounds nice," said Arthur, taking her hand as she rose.

"Besides, I know the library is where you want to be right now," said Bethany, blowing out the candles and turning on the light on her phone. She took his hand and they walked quietly back through the cathedral, into the cloister, stopping at the lavatory to wash off the grime of the crypt, and then climbing the stairs to the library. There was so much to say that Arthur found it easier to say nothing. Once Bethany had poured them each a generous glass of wine, she respected Arthur's need to simply sit in silence, absorbing the reality of what had happened. Well, she respected it for about ten minutes, but then she couldn't contain herself.

"A pretty amazing evening," said Bethany, "even if there was no Grail." They sat on opposite sides of Oscar's desk. Arthur withdrew the ciphered text and its translation from the desk drawer and set the papers between them.

"I still wonder why she's shown with the Grail in that picture," said Arthur.

"It seems like all the rest of the Grail lore."

"How do you mean?"

"Almost every literary reference to the Grail dates from centuries after the stories are alleged to have happened. Here we have a manuscript with no mention of the Grail and a drawing, from almost a thousand years *after* Ewolda's story, that shows the Grail. Maybe it was wishful thinking on some late medieval monk's part."

"My grandfather believed in the Grail," said Arthur. "And I thought you were the one who said you can decide to believe."

"You can," said Bethany. "I'm not saying I don't believe in the Grail; I'm just saying we might not find it in Barchester."

"What is the Grail, for you?" said Arthur.

"I suppose it's a physical connection to the story of my faith," said Bethany. "I don't *need* it to support that faith, I can believe in Christ without the Grail. I'm not sure that's true for everyone. Some people are just wired to need proof. Maybe you're that way, Arthur. I suspect Jesse Johnson, my boss, is that way. I think if you got him drunk he would tell you that the reason he is spending millions of dollars searching for biblical artifacts is that he can't quite believe without them."

"Sad, in a way."

"Well, it's—" began Bethany when she was interrupted by a blip from her phone. "Hold on a sec. That's it, these are the last of the key words from Chicago. I got the Edinburgh ones earlier this evening."

"Might as well finish up that last section," said Arthur. "I think the chances of my getting sleep tonight are minimal." He pulled out the page of the ciphered manuscript that included the end of Ewolda's story. The last few lines were as yet undeciphered, as their key words all came from the manuscripts that Bethany had tracked down that evening. Bethany quickly looked up the key words, and within a half hour they had, together, decoded the passage into Latin.

"What does it say?" said Bethany. "Does that last word mean what I think it means?"

Arthur found it hard to breathe. He knew he needed to read the passage in English to Bethany, but his lips did not seem to work. Coming to the end of a journey, he thought, was a funny thing. You never knew when the end might come or how it might affect you. He thought the journey had ended at Ewolda's tomb, but there had been another bend in the road, leading to an even more astonishing ending. He realized that, like Bethany, he didn't need every question answered. Nonetheless, the answers that lay before him—answers that would make Barchester a place of pilgrimage for millions and secure the future of the cathedral— took his breath away.

"Arthur?" said Bethany. "Are you there, Arthur, it's me, Bethany."

"Sorry," said Arthur, finding his voice at last. "It's just . . . well, let me read it to you." He picked up the Latin transcription and scanned it once more, wanting to make his English translation as accurate as possible. Then he read.

> *Some years after Ewolda's death, an old man in a dark cloak came to that place where she had fallen and with him he carried an ancient and holy cup, which he called a grael. He begged of Wigbert, who was by then the abbot of that place, permission to drink from the holy waters and he dipped the cup into the spring. When he had drunk he threw off his cloak and his skin glowed dazzling gold and he revealed himself as that same man who had brought the Gospel to Ewolda. And the man's name was Arthur.*

"King Arthur?" said Bethany. "King Arthur converted Ewolda to Christianity?"

"And King Arthur drank from Ewolda's spring with a holy cup."

"The Holy Grail."

"Do you know what this means?" said Arthur. "This is a completely unknown reference to King Arthur and the Holy Grail. And even if this manuscript is from the sixteenth century, the story it tells predates every other record of Arthur." Arthur felt almost disconnected from his own body as he read the words over and over. His grandfather had been right. There was a connection between Barchester and the Grail, and they had found it.

"It seems so . . . so real."

"The skin glowing gold is a bit much."

"Compared to ladies in lakes handing out swords it's pretty tame," said Bethany.

"It's not a medieval romance."

"No," said Bethany.

"It's a Saxon . . . well, something between a myth and a historical account."

"But closer to the latter. After all, we know the spring and the tomb are there. Name one other Arthurian story that has that kind of physical evidence."

"We've done more than save the library," said Arthur. "We've made Barchester a major pilgrimage site. Even if the true Grail is only a myth, even if it's real but it only visited Barchester briefly fifteen hundred years ago, the cup on the manuscript cover is meant to be the Holy Grail. And so is the cup in the medieval roof carving in the cloister."

"And the cup in Bishop Gladwyn's painting. I guess the chapter will want to get that back from the hotel."

"People will come to see the Barchester Grail images," said Arthur. "And they will come to read this paragraph, even if it is in code."

"You're going to need to rewrite the guidebook," said Bethany with a smile.

"With pleasure."

"And do it fast."

"I'm sure the dean will want that," said Arthur.

"I want it," said Bethany.

"What do you mean?"

"I mean I'm finished," said Bethany. "I'm done with the job. The manuscripts are digitized and I'm going back to America."

Arthur felt as if the breath had been knocked out of him. "When?"

"In a few days," said Bethany. "I'm starting a new job."

"In a few days? When were you going to tell me this?"

"You knew this day was coming, Arthur. Now, do you want to hear about my job?"

No, I don't, thought Arthur, but he smiled weakly and said, "Of course."

"I'm going to be curator of digital assets at the library of Ridgefield University."

"Never heard of it," said Arthur sourly.

"I'm surprised you haven't. They have a great collection of rare books. Some nice medieval manuscripts, too."

"Do I even want to know what digital assets are?" said Arthur. "I don't, actually. I really don't. I don't even want to know that you're going. I mean, fine, I never expected that this . . . this relationship would go anywhere, and I didn't think you would stay here forever, but only a few more days? I mean, we only just . . . you know. And then there's the manuscript and the tomb and the spring and King Arthur and the Holy Grail. The excitement is only just starting. How can you walk away from all that?"

"Jesus, Arthur, you sound like me. No wonder I drive you crazy. I know the manuscript and the tomb and all the rest of it will be in good hands. And this . . . us . . . it doesn't have to end with me walking away."

"What do you mean?" asked Arthur. The reality of her departure, which had hit him like a punch to the gut at first, now settled weightily on his shoulders and the exhaustion that adrenaline had kept at bay for the past several hours seemed to overwhelm him.

"Here," said Bethany, handing him an envelope.

"What's this?"

"It's a job offer from Ridgefield. They want an Englishman in their English department, and I convinced them that the man who found the lost Book of Ewolda would be just the fellow. I'm sure the King Arthur bit will only make them that much more excited."

"You got me a job?"

"A job offer."

"In America?"

"All you have to do is believe, Arthur," she said, bending over and kissing him on the cheek.

XVI

THE EPIPHANY CHAPEL

With its High Victorian décor, the Epiphany Chapel is one of the most beautiful spots in the cathedral. In the floor in front of the altar is the simple tomb of Bishop Gladwyn, who restored parts of the cathedral in the latter part of the nineteenth century. The stained glass window by Edward Burne-Jones depicts the moment that the Magi recognize Christ as divine—bestowing gifts upon him. Gladwyn thought this a perfect metaphor for his vision for the cathedral, and often prayed alone in this chapel.

September 3, 1888, Barchester Cathedral Library

Bishop Gladwyn sat in the library of Barchester Cathedral. When he had become bishop the shelves surrounding him had been perhaps two-thirds full, and he had made it one of his goals to fill them during his tenure. There was, thought Gladwyn, more reason than ever for the cathedral to maintain a wide collection of books on all subjects. Since the reforms at Oxford and Cambridge in the last century, university students no longer limited their studies to divinity, mathematics, and classics. Now young men—and if some people had their way, God forbid, young women—studied every topic under the sun, and the bishop felt that while the primary purpose of the cathedral library was to preserve the foundation's history and support the needs of its clergy, it should also be open to anyone in Barchester seeking knowledge. He had made great progress in building up the collection, and planned to leave most of his own books to the cathedral—completing the resurrection of the Bishop Atwater Library—a library that, as he well knew, held not just books but secrets.

In front of him lay an open volume containing a drawing that seemed to depict St. Ewolda and the Holy Grail. He knew that, as Guardian, it was his duty to protect and hide this manuscript, not call attention to it. But the idea of hiding anything in Barchester seemed ridiculous. Nobody came to Barchester, least of all treasure seekers. Besides, he wasn't really sure if what he was guarding was even a treasure. Did it make any sense to feel completely bound by a promise made to a dying old man who claimed the tradition of the guardianship had been handed down for centuries? What if he had been hallucinating or in the throes of dementia? Gladwyn believed Barchester was connected to a treasure, but he believed the treasure's story had been corrupted over the years, leaving him guarding a worthless artifact and leaving Barchester's connection to that greatest of relics, the Holy Grail, obscured in the fog of history.

Gladwyn had suspected a connection between Barchester and the Grail long before he became bishop, even before he took on the mantle of guardianship from the dean, Mr. Arabin. He had just read *Morte d'Arthur* when he decided one day to climb the cathedral tower, and he discovered a pair of stone lions. He knew those lions from Malory, and knew also that no other cathedral in Britain boasted such a pair. When, as a young man, he had been called upon, as an enthusiast of the cathedral's history, to give a tour to the poet laureate Alfred, Lord Tennyson, he had shared his excitement about the Grail with the author. Tennyson, after all, had written *Idylls of the King*. The poet had expressed especial fascination with the yew tree in the cloisters and the carvings in St. Dunstan's Chapel, and Gladwyn had not been entirely surprised to see these details in Tennyson's poem about the Holy Grail, published several months later. And then, after becoming a canon, Gladwyn had been called to the deathbed of the dean and entrusted with a strange responsibility and a vague secret, and his guardianship had led him to this manuscript and its ancient drawing that just might be the Holy Grail.

Since his elevation to bishop of Barchester in 1872, Gladwyn had pursued a single goal—the return of Barchester to its medieval glory. He pursued this goal in spite of not being absolutely sure there had *been* a medieval glory. There were few records in the library from before the Reformation—much of the archive having been lost during the Commonwealth. But Gladwyn had found hints in a number of documents that Barchester had enjoyed a modest pilgrim trade around the shrine of St. Ewolda. If any detailed records of the shrine's appearance had survived, he would have considered rebuilding it. Gladwyn was, after all, among the highest of churchmen. As an undergraduate at Oxford in the early 1840s he had heard John Henry Newman preach, and had been immediately attracted to the ritual forms of worship espoused by the Oxford Movement. Now he wanted to transform a Barchester Cathedral made stark and barren by reformers and puritans into the thing of glory he hoped it once was.

With a major bequest from his friend Mrs. Martha Thorne, heiress to the Ointment of Lebanon fortune, he had employed a host of artists and architects to assist in this transformation. Edward Burne-Jones designed a stained glass window and William Morris, a tapestry reredos for the Epiphany Chapel—and this modest space in the north transept immediately became the bishop's favorite spot in the cathedral. George Gilbert Scott brought his Victorian Gothic sensibilities to the job of rebuilding the precincts. He restored the medieval layout of St. Martin's Close. Beautiful Gothic cottages sprang up on either side for the canons, and at the far end, Scott erected an imposing Gothic deanery built with three colors of brick, a pair of circular towers, and a forest of finials.

When Gladwyn had become bishop, it had been the custom of the chapter to hold their meetings in the dining room of the bishop's palace, as the medieval chapter house was considered too uncomfortable to be practical. Gladwyn would have none of this, however, and insisted that the meetings be moved to their proper place. At first the chapter resisted, but once the bishop was able to install a dean who was as much of a medievalist as he was, the chapter returned to the thirteenth-century octagonal room off the cloister. By way of a peace offering, the bishop paid for Gilbert Scott to design a set of Gothic chairs—the backs of which reproduced the design in the tracery of the windows in the chapter house itself. With the addition of embroidered cushions, these proved substantially more comfortable than the original stone seats set into the walls, and so the members of the chapter were placated.

Bishop Gladwyn felt that the chapter house lacked only some decoration above the seat that was reserved for his own eminence. A lover of art, he had first seen the works of the Pre-Raphaelites at exhibits at the Royal Academy in London in the 1850s. Now he looked to one of their followers, known in particular for his medieval-style portraits, to paint him into posterity. After all, he had done so much to restore the cathedral and its precincts that he deserved some lasting memorial, and who knew where the canons, many of whom still resented that he was both High Church and high-handed, would choose to stash him when he had the misfortune to pass from the world. If he were destined for a simple tomb in the cloister, rather than the elaborate memorial in the retrochoir he deserved, he would at least hang his portrait in the chapter house to remind those who came after of what he had done.

"My Lord," came a breathless voice from behind Gladwyn, "I do hope you do not plan to pose for me here in this library. The light is rather murky."

"Ah, Mr. Collier," said Gladwyn, crossing to greet the painter. "So good to see you again. I trust your wife is well."

"Quite well, sir."

"No, you may paint me in the chapter house, where the portrait will hang. I think you'll find the light excellent."

"Very well, My Lord," said Collier, "but why then send for me to scale the steps to this dim-lit place?"

"For this," said the bishop, turning the chained Ewolda manuscript so that Collier could see the illustration.

"What's this, then," said Collier. "The Holy Grail?"

"Perhaps," said the bishop. "Whatever it is, it has been a part of Barchester's history for centuries. Do you suppose you could paint me holding this cup?"

"Absolutely," said Collier. "I see the image forming before me. It could be magnificent."

"It must be magnificent," said the bishop. He pulled out a key that hung on a chain around his neck and unfastened a lock at one end of the bookshelf to which the Ewolda manuscript was chained. He drew back the iron rod and removed the chain, freeing the manuscript from the bookcase. Sliding the rod back into place, he refastened the lock and handed the book to Collier.

"It feels ancient," said Collier.

"Not as ancient as some," said the bishop. "The volume dates, I believe, from around the time of the Reformation, though I suspect the story it contains is far older."

"And may I read the story?" asked Collier. "Like yourself I am fascinated with the medieval period."

"I'm afraid you won't have much luck reading this manuscript," said the bishop, laughing. "Now, this must never leave the cathedral precincts and each day when you are finished painting, I will lock it back into its place."

"Very well, My Lord. Will you show me to the chapter house?"

"Indeed," said Gladwyn.

A month later, the painting was complete, Collier paid, and the manuscript locked back in place. Bishop Gladwyn had barely waited for the paint to dry before having the portrait mounted in an elaborately carved oak frame and hung on the east wall of the chapter house, above the largest of the stone seats. For the next ten years, he rarely missed a chapter meeting and a chance to sit under the portrait of himself holding the Holy Grail.

May 27, 2016

FIRST FRIDAY AFTER TRINITY

At four, Arthur finally gave up trying to sleep, dressed, and returned to the library. After walking Bethany back to her lodgings, he had lain awake trying to process her offer, but another thought kept intruding on his mental arguments about the disadvantages of moving to America. As much as he wanted to focus on Bethany, he couldn't get those extra characters in the cipher out of his mind. Each cipher string contained nine characters, but the strings that contained the hidden numbers never had more than six characters defining those numbers. That left a minimum of three extra characters in each of those strings—many hundreds of characters throughout the manuscript. He had assumed these were so-called garbage letters, not related to the cipher in any way. They certainly did not translate using the key words. But Arthur had started to believe things lately, and he believed that the cipher was perfect, that no character was wasted. So what purpose did those garbage characters serve?

The sky was just beginning to lighten as Arthur made his way toward the cathedral. He wondered if the dawn about to break would begin a day that would be marked in the history of Barchester. How soon would the spring and the tomb become public knowledge? And would this be the day he changed the course of his own life, or would he come to his senses, drive Bethany to Heathrow, and kiss her good-bye?

Back in the library, Arthur settled in at his favorite table. He needed the intimacy of that smaller space, not the wide trestle table on which the group had deciphered the manuscript. He carefully copied out all of the "garbage characters," half convinced that the spirit of Ewolda would allow him to see some pattern in them once they had been extracted from the rest of the manuscript. What further secret could this manuscript possibly possess? And what did he know about the manuscript, the key words, and the inventory that he had not used in deciphering the story of Ewolda?

He read over the Latin version of the story again, but it seemed nothing more than the remarkable account they had all taken it to be. He picked up the inventory that Bethany had discovered, and examined it closely under the light of his reading lamp. Sometimes, with parchment documents, one could detect where writing had been scraped off the surface, but this document seemed unusually neat and clean. The only thing that marred it slightly was a small crease down the left side, where it had been pressed into the gutter of the mathematical manuscript in which Bethany had discovered it. Arthur gave a start.

"Mother of God, Fibonacci," he said aloud. That had to be it. Bethany had found the inventory in a section of the manuscript by Fibonacci—and there were no coincidences. The code must somehow be based on the Fibonacci sequence. He spent nearly an hour trying to apply the sequence to the key words they had collected, but to no avail. He was just beginning to think this was another dead end when, almost on a whim, he decided to count the number of words in the Latin transcription of Ewolda's biography. There were exactly 1,597.

The Fibonacci sequence is a series of numbers created by adding the two previous numbers in the sequence. Thus the sequence begins 1, 1, 2, 3, 5, 8. The seventeenth number in the sequence is 1597. What if the key words for the garbage characters were within the deciphered manuscript itself? What if all Arthur had to do was circle the words in the manuscript that corresponded to the numbers in the Fibonacci sequence—the first word, second word, third word, fifth word, and so on—and simply rotate through the key words, using a new word for each string of garbage characters? It couldn't possibly be that simple. But it was. And the beauty of the code was that, unless one knew the inventory had been stored in a manuscript by Fibonacci, it would be virtually impossible to break.

The morning sun flooded the room by the time Arthur had decoded the message hidden in the extra characters. He glanced at his watch and saw that it was after eight. At nine the chapter would be meeting.

He carefully took all his papers off the table. He didn't think he would ever be able to work in this spot again. He pulled his chair back and looked at this unassuming bit of furniture with fresh eyes. The greatest treasure, he thought, had been under his nose the whole time. He gently ran his fingers across those words carved in the wood by some long-forgotten monk—*Mensa Christi.* The Table of Christ.

He stepped away, picked up his translation of the Latin, and read again the unbelievable words.

> *Here written in the first month of the archbishopric of Ethelhard is a true and real account of that most sacred of relics, the Mensa Christi. In his youth at Nazareth, our Lord, with his father Joseph, did fashion this table, for he was raised as a carpenter and would build the kingdom of God on earth. Those who knew Christ and that disciple who loved him brought the table from Nazareth to Jerusalem and here it rested in the upper room of a home near the city. On this table did our Lord bless the bread and wine on the night he was betrayed. After the Crucifixion of our Savior, Joseph of Arimathea did take the Mensa and the cup upon it—our Lord's cup. It came to pass that Joseph gave the Mensa and the cup to Aristobulus, who had been charged by Jesus to take the Gospel to the island of the Britons. Aristobulus, arriving in Briton, became the bishop of that land and built a church near the hill of Glastonbury, making the Mensa his altar. This same church, the Vetusta Ecclesia, did Paulinus protect and here the Mensa remained, its secret protected by the holy brothers. Those who knew the true nature of the Mensa did call it in secret the Grael or Platter of our Lord. Now we hear of brutal attacks by savages from the north, and the Mensa and its secret are to be borne to a remote and undistinguished house at a place called Barchester.*
>
> *To this account, which is a true transcription of the history brought to us by the monks of Glastonbury in the year of our Lord 793, I, James, of the Priory of St. Ewolda, do add the following honest history of the Mensa—that it did come to Barchester and there remained until the foundation of St. Ewolda was moved from that place. The Mensa then removed to the new foundation, always under the protection of a Guardian, each in his own generation the sole protector of the Mensa's secret. From generation to generation was the mantle passed. Now the king's commissioners approach. The Mensa will once again be moved to Barchester, and I prepare this account in cipher and pray to our Savior that as I pass the secrets to the next Guardian they may be kept safe from*

the evil that is to befall us. Written this twelfth day of October in the year of our Lord 1539.

"You can't tell her," said a voice from behind him. Arthur turned and saw the precentor standing just inside the doorway. "You probably shouldn't even tell me."

"You?" said Arthur.

"Until a few minutes ago, I was the Guardian," said the precentor. "But I never knew what the manuscript said or what the Mensa really was. I only knew it was my duty to guard them."

"But how do you know . . ."

"Of course I knew that you and your friends borrowed the manuscript. I was the Guardian, after all. You don't really think you could take the manuscript right out from under my nose without my knowing about it. But I thought, what's the harm. It was only when I realized that the images had been sent to that American billionaire that I began to worry. I could imagine your keeping a secret, but I couldn't imagine his doing it. And then this morning Gwyn rang to tell me the news. She even read me your translation and, thank God, there was nothing there about the Mensa. So I knew the real secret was safe. But judging from the way you were looking at the table, and the expression on your face as you were reading just now, I'd guess you somehow figured out the secret of the Mensa and why it needs guarding."

"What do you mean, up until a few minutes ago you were the Guardian?" said Arthur.

"You decoded the manuscript, Arthur. Only you know what the Mensa really means. That makes you the Guardian. And if that's not enough, there's the fact that I've been doing this for thirty-five years, and I'd like to retire to Majorca. So I'm *making* you the Guardian."

"But this is . . ."

"Don't tell me," said the precentor. "It's your secret now, and the only person you should ever tell is whomever you choose to be the next Guardian."

"You were the Guardian for thirty-five years, and you didn't know what you were guarding?"

"Some things we do on faith, Arthur. No matter what it says in that manuscript, the Mensa may be nothing more than an old table, but for over a thousand years the Guardians have had faith, and so have I."

Arthur thought about this unbroken chain of faith. He realized, looking at the Mensa, that he was not like Jesse Johnson; he did not need evidence to believe, but being a part of a guardianship that reached through the faith of more than a millennium might just allow him to make the leap.

"Is that why you were always . . ."

"An ass? Yes, that's part of it, I suppose. I always had my eye on you. After all, Arthur, it was your grandfather who passed the guardianship to me. He was a good man and a good friend, and when he made me Guardian, I promised to at least consider you as my successor."

"My grandfather was Guardian of the Mensa?" said Arthur.

"And of the manuscript," said the precentor. Of course it made perfect sense. When he read his grandson the Arthur stories, when he swore him to secrecy on the subject of the Holy Grail, Arthur's grandfather had been preparing him to be the Guardian and testing his worthiness. Even though his grandfather, and probably every Guardian since the Reformation, couldn't read the manuscript, he'd had his suspicions, and he had, without betraying the secrets of the Guardian, nudged Arthur toward the discovery he had finally made.

"From the day you arrived at the cathedral library and chose the Mensa as your favorite spot," said the precentor, "I knew you would either be trouble or you would be the next Guardian—possibly both."

"And what does it mean, exactly," said Arthur, "being the Guardian?"

"It means whatever secrets you know, you protect. It means that keeping the Mensa and the manuscript safe until you can pass them on to the next generation is your first priority. It means no foreign travel or long absences from Barchester."

"And what about . . ." Arthur couldn't believe what he was about to ask, but the precentor seemed one step ahead of him.

"Love?" he said. "I was in love once, and I had to choose. It's hard to be married when you're handcuffed to a cathedral and you can't tell your wife why. So I chose to sacrifice myself for what I truly believed was a higher calling. I think about her sometimes and wonder if I chose well, but I've lived with my choice, and that's enough."

"So you're asking me to give up on . . . on life and on happiness."

"Not at all," said the precentor. "There are advantages, too. You are now a part of a chain of Guardians that reaches back to the earliest days of Christianity on this island. You will spend untold hours in this most glorious room in the kingdom, surrounded by the wisdom of the ages. You will possess knowledge that no one else on earth will possess, and that knowledge will change you and strengthen you and connect you to so much that is past and is yet to come. And unlike me, you know the full secret of the Mensa. I can only guess that your life as Guardian will be richer even than mine."

Arthur could picture it, and in many ways the vision the precentor painted was the fulfillment of his lifelong dream. To be Guardian of the Grail, even if the grail was not exactly what he had expected, to keep secrets that had been hidden for over a thousand years, and to pass those secrets on to the next Guardian when the time came—the little boy who had learned of the Grail at his grandfather's knee could imagine nothing better.

"But why should the true nature of the Mensa have to be a secret?" said Arthur. "Maybe the time is right for the world to know."

"The cathedral is in desperate need of money and there is a billionaire American buying up Christian artifacts for a museum. The time has never been less right."

"And if I am the Guardian, it will be part of my duty to appoint a successor?"

"Exactly," said the precentor. "You may, for all I know, be the first layperson to guard the Mensa. Your grandfather told me the names of several previous Guardians. One of them moved that portrait of Bishop Gladwyn out of the chapter house."

"Because it showed the Holy Grail?"

"Gladwyn was a Guardian," said the precentor, "but he wanted to glorify medieval Barchester. I suspect he's the one that had legs put onto the Mensa and installed it in the library. And he certainly used the drawing of the Grail from the manuscript in his portrait—a drawing I never knew of until today, by the way. A little dangerous, if you ask me. That painting doesn't just show the Grail, you know, it shows the Mensa. Mallory called it a silver table. Collier copied that from the drawing as well. I imagine that's the real reason the portrait got banished. You never know what choices you will be called upon to make as Guardian."

"And what if I say no?"

"If you say no, then you go on with your life. You chase after the girl; you live happily ever after."

"And the Mensa?" said Arthur.

"For the first time in over a thousand years, the Mensa will be moved from Barchester. I will need to hide it from you and I will find another protector."

"So you're saying that a hiding place that survived Vikings, and Normans, and reformers, and civil war, and Nazi bombs might not survive me?"

"Dangers come from unexpected places, Arthur."

"Can I ask you one more question? Do you believe in the Holy Grail?"

"It's no longer about what I believe," he said. "What do you believe?"

Arthur wasn't quite ready to answer that question, but he looked back at the Mensa and felt an almost physical pull toward it and its history.

"Well," said the precentor, "I've got a chapter meeting in a few minutes, and then I have to tell the dean of my intention to retire." He took a few steps toward Arthur and held out his hand. "By the way, you can call me Edmund."

"Thank you, Edmund," said Arthur, shaking his hand firmly, and for the first time that he could remember, the precentor smiled at him.

XVII

THE LADY CHAPEL

Dedicated in 2020, the Lady Chapel is the first significant new construction in the cathedral since the Reformation. The award-winning design merges the ancient and modern, giving the visitor a true connection with the cathedral's deep roots in Saxon history and its grand reach into the future. At the dedication service for the chapel, the archbishop of Canterbury called it "unique among worship spaces in Britain."

October 12, 2020

FEAST DAY OF ST. EWOLDA

Arthur knelt at the altar rail and accepted the Communion wafer from Gwyn. He hoped that even in her unwavering focus while celebrating the Eucharist, she would be able to enjoy the triumph of this moment. Behind her stood the archbishop of Canterbury, the first to visit Barchester in three hundred and fifty years, here for this dedication of the new Lady Chapel. Because the chapel held only about fifty people, the bulk of the service, attended by hundreds, had taken place in the nave, but the congregation streamed through the new chapel to take Communion.

The building of the Lady Chapel was just part of a larger works project at Barchester that had included a major archaeological dig around the tomb and spring of St. Ewolda, repairs to the north transept, the restoration of the cathedral's collection of manuscripts, and the hiring of a librarian, all financed by a grant from Heritage Lottery.

Arthur's favorite room in the world was rarely as peaceful as it had been in years past, but he had no complaints. The previous day in the library, Oscar had brought a school group on a visit to look at the musical notation in the Barchester Breviary, a lecturer from the university had met with his class on medieval history, the new full-time librarian had checked out books to a dozen readers, and Arthur himself had delivered a lunchtime talk on the history of the collection. He was pleased to see Edward Alford, the onetime choirboy who was now a frequent visitor to the library, in the audience. That same day, and every day, hundreds of visitors climbed the stairs to see not just the beauty of the room and its books, but the new glass-fronted display that had drawn tens of thousands of people to Barchester since its installation.

The case included a coded manuscript, the only surviving record of the earliest reference to a possibly real, possibly mythical figure named King Arthur and a cup called the Holy Grail. Next to the mysterious manuscript were an English translation and the detached cover of the ancient volume, illustrated with a picture of the Grail. As Arthur had predicted, people flooded to Barchester to see the now famous Grail images. But they also came to see Ewolda's tomb and spring. It had taken her nearly fifteen hundred years, but she had finally succeeded in making Barchester a significant place of pilgrimage.

The Lady Chapel was exactly as Gwyn had dreamed it, thought Arthur, as he rose from the rail. Constructed almost completely of glass, it seemed both a part of the ancient building to its west, and yet fully immersed in the beautiful gardens that surrounded its other three sides. The dedication service took place on a Saturday afternoon, but the previous evening, Arthur and about a dozen others had attended the first service held in the chapel—Compline. The full moon had been the only light necessary, though two candles burned on the altar. Arthur, who had attended Compline hundreds if not thousands of times, could not remember a more moving service.

The crown jewel of the chapel might have gone unnoticed in the bright light of the afternoon sun but had been astonishingly evident the night before. The floor between the front pews and the altar rail, a space about ten feet deep and some twenty feet wide, was made of a thick, scratch-resistant glass. Below, beautifully but subtly lit, one could clearly see the tomb of Ewolda and the shimmering waters of the spring that flowed by her side. Arthur considered the entire space a triumphant unification of past and present. He stood for a moment at the edge of that window in the floor, looking down on what only he and two other people on earth understood was the *second* greatest wonder of Barchester Cathedral. Tourists and pilgrims would flock to Barchester to see the manuscript and the tomb and the spring. The sick, who believed, would sip the waters in hopes of healing. But none would know the secret of the *Mensa Christi*, and even Arthur did not know where the table now rested. He nodded to Gwyn, who smiled at him and returned to distributing Communion. He had chosen well, Arthur thought. Gwyn had made an excellent Guardian.

Arthur leaned down and picked up little Oscar. The two-year-old was on his hands and knees, peering through the glass.

"Your mother's waiting for us," said Arthur. "And Gwyneth will be waking up soon."

He turned to see Bethany standing in the entryway to the chapel, her hair glowing in the sun, the baby asleep on her shoulder. She smiled at him and Arthur's heart flooded with joy.

Yes, he thought, he had chosen very well indeed.

AUTHOR'S NOTE

Although the city and cathedral of Barchester are fictional, they are not my own invention, and I am indebted to Anthony Trollope for providing me with the setting for this novel as well as of the description of the church at Plumstead Episcopi on page 164.

With the exception of *Spring Heat*; *Petunia and Pricilla*; *Harding's Church Music* and *The Almshouse*, which are inventions of Trollope; Arthur Prescott's own *A History of Plumstead Episcopi*; *Black's Picturesque Guide to Barchester*; and *Lives of Twelve Christian Men*, all the published books named in the text, their descriptions, illustrations, excerpts, and bibliographical details are real, though I have inserted biographical details of fictional characters into some of these real books. *Lives of Twelve Christian Men* is based on the book *Lives of Twelve Good Men* by John William Burgon, but that book was published in 1888 before the death of Bishop Gladwyn, so it could not contain his fictional biography. The Winchester Manuscript is real; the manuscripts in the Barchester Cathedral Library are entirely fictional, though similar to real manuscripts in cathedral libraries throughout Britain.

The text of the letter from a monk of Lindisfarne on pages 40–41 is taken, in part, from an account by Symeon of Durham of the first Viking attack on Lindisfarne. The description of the altar screen on page 139 is paraphrased from a memorial in Winchester Cathedral. Oliver Cromwell's accusation of "unedifying and offensive ceremony and chanting" was made against the clergy of Ely Cathedral and the damage done by the Parliamentarians to Barchester was typical of that done to many real cathedrals throughout the realm. The Nanteos Cup and its history are real, as is the article about it in *Ladies' Home Journal* (John Cottrell, "My Search for the Holy Grail," April 1971).

All the music sung in the cathedral is real, and I commend it to my readers.

St. Ewolda is entirely fictional, and although Bede's *Martyrologium* is a real book, it makes no mention of my invented saint. Many of the characters in the historic sections were real people, including Beaduwulf, Hereferth, and Dunstan of Glastonbury; the architect and designer George Gilbert Scott; Thomas Cromwell; Thomas Malory; Arthur Rackham; Archbishop of Canterbury Gilbert Sheldon; and John Collier. As for an early British King named Arthur, I leave it to the reader to decide whether he existed or not.

ACKNOWLEDGMENTS

Richard Mackenzie took me to my first medieval cathedral in 1980 and to him I will always be grateful. I am indebted to all those over the years who have welcomed me into English cathedral communities in particular canons Peter Brett, Thomas Christie, John Darlington, and Nigel Stock, and retired dean Alan Webster. Canon Jeremy Haselock, precentor of Norwich Cathedral, has been a good friend, a consummate host, and an invaluable resource.

The staff of Worcester Cathedral Library, and in particular Deirdre Mckeown, not only showed me a wealth of materials that inspired some of the books at Barchester but also gave me the chance to soak up the atmosphere of a cathedral library.

My knowledge and love of English church music is due to many choir directors over the years but particularly to Kristin Farmer and Christin Barnhardt. My love and knowledge of liturgy has been nurtured by Reverend Faulton Hodge and Reverend Steve Rice. Stephanie Lovett provided both Latin translations and careful proofreading. Anna Worrall's direction and advice have served me well, as has that of everyone else at the Gernert Company.

Kathryn Court offered sage guidance before a single word of this novel was written and with Sarah Stein has made up the best editorial team an author could ask for, constantly pushing me, seeing potential where I had missed it, and making sure that this novel was much better than I could have made it on my own. Thanks also to the rest of the great staff at Penguin—the creation of a novel is an act of teamwork, and I am fortunate to work with professionals who value my opinions and make that teamwork a true pleasure.

Without the support of my family, I could never have written this or any book. Thanks to Jimmy and Jordan for your love and encouragement. Janice has been not only a careful reader and thoughtful critic, but also the woman who makes me smile, makes me laugh, and teaches me daily how to love. Thank you for sharing the adventure.